Three Doses of Murder

The Aliki Pateas Mystery Series, Book 2

Three Doses of Murder

The Aliki Pateas Mystery Series, Book 2

Anne Azel

P.D. Publishing, Inc.
Clayton, North Carolina

ISBN-13: 978-1-933720-38-8
ISBN-10: 1-933720-38-7

9 8 7 6 5 4 3 2 1

Cover art by B.L. Magill
Cover design by Barb Coles
Edited by Day Petersen/Medora MacDougall

Published by:

P.D. Publishing, Inc.
P.O. Box 70
Clayton, NC 27528

http://www.pdpublishing.com

Acknowledgements:

My thanks to Inga for her excellent support and guidance over many years of story writing.

Special thanks to B.L. Magill for taking the time to create original works of art for all my book covers.

Dedication

To Anne and Jenny

Dead Duck

A few months later, the Pateas and Williams families found themselves together again. Aliki had invited them, on her father's behalf, to visit the Pateas ranch in Alberta. Baba wanted to meet Robbie and introduce her to her half brothers. It had taken some doing to organize everyone's schedule and to work out logistics but at last they were on their way.

Janet Williams sighed and then smiled when Dawn Freeman reached over and poked her in the ribs. They exchanged a knowing look as they settled back to wait for their Toronto plane to go through its landing pattern for the airport in Edmonton, Alberta. Across from them sat their partners, the famous actress and director, Robbie Williams, and her half-sister and forensic anthropologist, Dr. Aliki "Alberta" Pateas. These two women did not look relaxed. They looked stiff and stormy.

It had been difficult in the extreme to get the two stubborn women to come to an agreement about the flight, and it had resulted in some irritation of an already sore subject. The root of the problem was money. Dr. Aliki Pateas had been seconded from the RCMP to the Toronto forensic labs and earned a good middle class income. Her partner, Dawn Freeman, had written the best-seller, *Growing Up Free,* and had followed it up with the award-winning suspense thriller, *The Fire Clown*, for which she had also sold the movie rights. Her talent and the money her uncle had left her had made her a very wealthy woman. And Janet and Robbie Williams were worth millions. In short, three out of the four could afford first-class seats; Aliki hadn't felt that she could. It was awkward in the extreme.

"You two sit in first class, and Dawn and I will fly economy," Aliki had insisted.

"Oh, great! Just what I need is for the press to find out I fly first class while my sister sits in the back. No way!"

Aliki shrugged. "Then buy economy seats."

"I can't," Robbie had mumbled, looking awkward.

"Why not?" Aliki crossed her arms over her chest, looking stubborn.

"Because I'm an actor, and it would cause a small riot," growled Robbie, not liking at all that she had to admit that her fans were a problem. "I have to travel as a VIP."

Enjoying her sister squirming, Aliki teased with a smile, "Ooh, aren't we something special!"

Partly in fun and partly in annoyance, Robbie threatened, "I'm going to bop you."

Janet had intervened, recognizing her T-Rob's famous temper rising to the surface. "I think I see a solution here. Aliki is being very sensible. She has responsibilities to Dawn and Mac and can't be throwing her money around on unnecessary expenses. On the other hand, Robbie, you are being sensible, too; you can't just step out into the public. You need to go through VIP clear-

ance, and you need to have security. Seeing as Aliki is a trained RCMP officer, she can be your bodyguard, and we can solve the logistics problem and get you protection at the same time. Aliki, you can pay for your and Dawn's tickets, and Robbie's office will upgrade them to first class so that you can be near her to provide security."

The two sisters stared at each other grumpily, neither one willing to be the first to agree to this proposal. "That's a great idea." Dawn got up and went over to wrap an arm around her stubborn partner. "Isn't it, Aliki?" She rubbed her lover's back to ease some of the tension.

"Robbie?" Janet's voice held a hint of a warning, as did the look she gave her wife.

Robbie sighed in defeat. Her half-sister she was willing to take on, but not her wife. If Janet wanted it, Janet got it. "Yeah, it would make it easier to have Aliki as my security. Then we wouldn't be stuck with some Rambo type standing outside our bedroom door."

"I can live with that, if you trust me to do the job," Aliki agreed, throwing in her own towel to please Dawn.

"Good, then it's settled," Janet said lightly, ignoring the fact that it would have taken a chainsaw to cut the tension in Aliki's living room.

That had been a month ago, and the truce was holding up under great strain.

Nor was that Janet's only worry. Behind her she could hear the quiet murmurs of her stepdaughter, Ryan, and Dawn's adopted daughter, Mac. The young teens had not seen each other for several months, and they had a lot to catch up on. Sooner or later, Janet was going to have to tell Robbie that there was something up.

While Robbie was away on business, the Bartlett School for the Gifted had called to tell Janet that Ryan had been cutting classes on a regular basis and Lou down at the garage had casually mentioned that Ryan was filling up the car twice a week now. Where was Ryan going? At first, Janet had been annoyed more than angry and had meant to have Robbie talk to Ryan as soon as she returned from her business trip to Britain. But just before they left, Janet had found out from Eiffel, who worked at Bartlett's only bank, that Ryan had withdrawn five thousand dollars from her account.

Eiffel had wondered innocently whether Ryan was going south for March Break, like so many teens did in their last years of high school. Janet had answered vaguely, pretending to be preoccupied with her banking statement. What the hell was Ryan up to? She needed to talk to Robbie, but now was not a good time. Robbie had been delayed with last-minute filming issues in Britain, and she had just made it back in time to get organized for the flight out west. At long last, Robbie was going to meet the father that she and Aliki shared. It was not a good time to burden T-Rob with a mystery involving her daughter. She was hyper enough already. Moreover, Robbie wasn't always a rational thinker when it came to Ryan. It would be better to find a few minutes while they were out west and talk to Robbie first before they approached Ryan.

A tug on Janet's sleeve got her attention, and she looked down into the face of her other daughter, who would be celebrating her fourth birthday during their visit. "Mommy, are we landed yet?"

"No, sweetheart, but we will be soon."

"I got to go," Reb announced loudly.

Janet looked up at the flight attendant. "There's time, if you are quick," the man responded with a smile before being asked.

"I'll take her." Robbie unfastened her seatbelt and got up to release Reb from hers.

Janet smiled at the beautiful woman who was her wife and soulmate. "Thanks, hon."

Robbie gave her a wink and then focused on Reb's biological emergency. "Come on, Reb. You have to be quick because the plane can't land until everyone is in their seat."

Reb followed the tall actress down the aisle to the head, at the back of the first-class section.

"I go by myself," the determined child said when Robbie unlatched the door for her.

"Okay, kid. But it doesn't flush like the one at home."

"I know. It a plane."

Reb stepped into the small washroom, and Robbie closed the door and leaned against it to keep it shut.

In a few minutes, Robbie heard the toilet flush, and a little while later it flushed again. "Reb?"

"I finished now, Obbie," came a voice with a giggle.

Robbie opened the door to look down on her beaming daughter. "Obbie, the toilet goes VOOM!"

Robbie laughed. "Yeah, the water is sucked out under pressure, Reb. It's because the air pressure in the plane varies as we go up and down. Pressure is what makes the water run down the pipes. What is that smell?"

Reb stepped out and waited for her Obbie to close the door once again. "I try the purfoom. It was by the sink."

Robbie sniffed. "I think you picked the aftershave lotion. Next time, use a spot behind each ear, not half the bottle in your hair. You didn't drink any, did you?"

"No. Mommy said I can't eat or drink anything without asking," Reb said matter-of-factly as they made their way back down the aisle.

"Good. That stuff would really make you sick. Kid, you reek! I'm glad you're sitting by your mommy," teased Robbie, as she fastened her little daughter into her seat again. "She tried out the aftershave," Robbie explained when she saw her wife's nose wrinkle.

"'Olives'!" muttered Janet, smiling down at her daughter.

"The toilet has a vacuum 'cause it don't have pressure, so it goes VOOM," Reb explained.

While Robbie was close, Janet took the opportunity to whisper in her ear, "Talk to your sister. The two of you look like you're on the way to the executioner, not to your brother's wedding and to visit your father."

Robbie pulled a face, then smiled into Janet's beautiful deep green eyes. They had been married over two years, but being close to Janet still took Robbie's breath away. The director reluctantly returned to her own seat and buckled in to listen to the landing instructions.

Robbie considered how she could open up a conversation with her half-sister. On her way out west for her half-brother's wedding and to meet her biological father for the first time, she felt a mixture of excitement, curiosity, and downright fear at the prospect. What if her father didn't like her? Aliki had been pretty good about the discovery, but what about the two half-brothers that she was yet to meet?

Robbie searched for something to say. It wasn't easy making small talk. Funny, she never found it hard to talk to Janet, but then her wife was someone very special. "I'm sorry about this," she found herself saying with some embarrassment.

"About what?" Aliki asked, looking up in surprise.

"About putting the family through all this. Sometimes I feel like someone who has some horribly contagious disease and must be isolated from the rest of humanity."

Serious, intelligent eyes looked at her thoughtfully. "It's okay. I was a bit difficult about it, too. I'm sorry. I guess my ego was feeling threatened, and I wasn't thinking that traveling could put you in harm's way. Dawn and I talked, and we're okay about the flying arrangement now."

"Before I married I didn't care about the potential dangers; I practically courted trouble. Most fans are really nice people, but there is always that dangerous fringe. I worry about my family all the time. It was my celebrity that resulted in our kids being kidnapped. Reb's gotten over it quickly, but Ryan still gets nightmares now and again. Not that she'd ever admit it," Robbie said sadly. Aliki remained quiet, allowing Robbie to go on in her own faltering way.

Robbie shifted in her seat. "Reb wears her emotions up front. You know when she is happy or sad. It's written all over her face. If she's upset, she howls and gets it out of her system. For a young kid, she's really comfortable in her skin." Her long fingers nervously moved back and forth across the control panel on the arm of the chair.

It had been Dawn who had pointed out to Aliki that Robbie had nervous hand movements when she was upset. There was more her sister had to share. Aliki smiled and nodded, waiting for Robbie to go on.

"Ryan holds everything in and stews about it. That's my fault for not being there for her. She has always had to take care of herself. Something is bothering her right now. I don't know...maybe because I've been away a lot. She's got something on her mind, and she's not sharing."

Aliki shrugged, not sure what to say to relieve her sister's anxiety. "It could be nothing, Robbie. Maybe she has a boyfriend and is daydreaming about him."

"Ha! Wait until Mac goes out on her first date. I was a basket case when some guy picked Ryan up to go to the community centre dance. It was the longest four hours of my life."

Aliki laughed, and Robbie smiled and blushed. "You wait. You won't be laughing for long," she warned.

Aliki considered this revelation. "I imagine I'll be a little overprotective. I've seen firsthand what happens to nice girls who fall into bad situations," Aliki murmured sadly.

Seeing the sorrow in her sister's eyes, Robbie wisely didn't ask questions. Aliki's career as a forensic anthropologist brought her into contact with violent death on a regular basis. What would it be like to live with the memories of what she had seen?

"Tell me more about my family," Robbie said, changing the subject.

Aliki smiled. Robbie had often asked the same question since her discovery that Nick Pateas, Aliki's father, was her own biological father as well. "Dad is really excited about meeting you. Everyone calls him Baba. It is a Greek word for dad. He's very outgoing and social and is well liked and respected in the community. He's strict, though, kind of old fashioned. I would never have told him about my orientation. It's probably one of the reasons that I didn't go home for many years."

"What changed?" Robbie asked, smiling her thanks at the flight attendant who had just brought them an assortment of sweets in preparation for the change in pressure while landing. The guy had the look of a star-struck fan. Robbie had worried all during the flight that he might say something in front of her sister that Aliki would tease her about later.

"Janet impacted my life for one thing. She encouraged me to go home and deal with some of the ghosts of my childhood. When I got there...well, Baba had already worked it out for himself. He was good about it. He doesn't like it, but he was accepting of me. I think part of it was that I fell in love with Dawn. Baba had sort of adopted Dawn and Mac before I ever got there."

"They met when Dawn's uncle and her brother were killed, right?" asked Robbie, as she sucked on a sweet.

"After the plane crash, Dawn and Mac were left stranded up at the Freeman cabin. They'd have starved up there if Dawn hadn't walked the two of them out. How she did it, I'll never know. That's really wild country, but Dawn grew up in the Canadian bush and she really knows her stuff. She made her way to the ranch. They were half starved and exhausted. Baba took them in, and Dawn sort of became his housekeeper."

"He must miss Dawn and Mac."

"Yeah, a lot, but since Ari got engaged, Baba has Ari's fiancée, Joan, in his life. Since their wedding date was originally over a year ago, Joan has been around a while for Baba to spoil."

Robbie nodded. She knew that Aliki had had three brothers. Yirgos, the oldest, had committed suicide after his Salish mistress had died. MacKenzie, the child that Aliki and Dawn now raised as their own, was the child of that union.

There were also the twins, Ari and Nick, Aliki's younger brothers, whom she had raised with Baba after the untimely death of their mother.

Robbie's hands moved nervously over the arm of her seat as she fretted about how her natural father and half-brothers would react to her.

Being famous had more disadvantages than advantages. Her family would undoubtedly have heard all the media gossip about her life. Even if they had not known before, once word got out she was visiting, people would go out of their way to spread the stories.

Robbie leaned back and considered what they might know. They would have heard about her arrest and trial for the murder of Philip Williams and how Aliki and Janet had proved her innocent. The world knew that. It had been sensational front-page news, as had been the revelation of her gay marriage to Janet.

They had probably heard about her wild years, too – the parties, the substance abuse, the lovers... Robbie cringed with embarrassment. She wished she could have those years back to relive better. Aliki had said her father was conservative. How would he feel about a daughter like her?

The Air Canada plane soared cross the nation. Two thousand kilometres had separated her from her natural father. Two thousand kilometres and a lifetime.

Ryan and Mac sat with their heads close together, whispering softly. "I think you should just tell them," Mac stated. "You are going to have to sooner or later."

"No way! Mom would have a bird. She has my life all planned out for me. I'm going to be a scientist like Aunt Bethy. Once I get better, then I'll tell her."

"Do you want to be a scientist? I don't think Aunt Robbie would make you be anything you didn't want to be. She's nice and really funny."

Ryan pondered the question, chewing on her lower lip in thought. "I don't know. I like a lot of things. I like maths and computer programming, and I like film. I was thinking that I would like to work for a company like Sound and Magic someday. But now, well...I'm hooked. I mean, it feels great, Mac. I can't describe the high I get...what I see in my head and feel in my heart. The world just disappears. I...it's hard to explain."

Mac looked at her cousin with worry in her eyes. "You'll find a way that is good for you, Ryan. I know you will."

As their plane taxied into its berth, Aliki clipped on her identification tag. Immediately, her sister reached for it and read: Inspector Aliki Alberta Pateas, Forensic Division, Royal Canadian Mounted Police, No. 7205. Robbie smiled, with that look in her eye that meant the wheels were turning behind the startling blue eyes that had made her famous.

"It had better not show up in one of your movies," sighed Aliki. It was a Williams' family joke that anything that happened in the family was likely to be worked into a scene of a script. Robbie was genius out of control. The two families gathered their belongings and prepared to leave.

Although Janet had suggested that Aliki be Robbie's bodyguard as a compromise to a very tricky situation, she had known that Aliki would take the assignment seriously. That was evident at the terminal in Edmonton. Two RCMP constables met them at the plane and escorted them through the back halls of the airport to a waiting van with tinted windows. Aliki got her family safely inside and then supervised the loading of the luggage. Once everything was seen to, she thanked her fellow officers and slid into the driver's seat.

"How far is Swan Hills, Aliki?" Janet asked.

"We'll be a few hours getting there and then another hour to reach the ranch. It will be long after dark before we arrive. The ranch is back of beyond," Aliki added with a sigh. As a youth she had yearned to escape the isolation of the ranch and the responsibility of helping fill her late mother's role in maintaining the home and raising her twin brothers. Now she had to admit it wasn't bad going home, but the old bias still remained.

Dawn, on the other hand, loved the wilds of Alberta. "Wait until you see the countryside, Janet, you'll love it. I'll take you to meet MacKenzie's Salish family."

"Cool." Ryan smiled, unconsciously mimicking her mother's mannerisms. "Mac has taught me some Salish words."

Robbie said nothing. She hadn't been so nervous since her first time on stage. In some ways, the situations weren't that much different. She swallowed hard and felt Janet's warm, reassuring hand slip into her own. Robbie smiled at the woman beside her and held onto the hand tightly. Janet always understood and was there for her.

"You're wearing a path in the rug," Ari laughed, as he watched his father check out the window yet again.

"My family is coming home. I want to be at the door to greet them. I want to make Robbie welcome in her father's home. Everything is ready, no? Can you think of anything I forgot?" Baba asked as he paced across the room once more.

Joan laughed. "We have enough groceries in to last the winter, and the house is spotless. Try not to worry. Robbie will feel as welcome as I have."

"Nick should be here," Baba fretted, looking out the window again.

"He should," grumbled Ari in agreement, then he softened his criticism. "He'll be back tomorrow."

Baba shrugged, making it clear that this was not good enough in his eyes.

Aliki cursed, brought the van to a stop, and then reversed back to the driveway that she had missed. "I said 'Put up a sign.' Does he? No. Everyone knows where the road to the ranch is, he says. The damn thing is impossible to find in the dark." She turned down an overgrown lane, and they bounced slowly along, the headlights bleaching the darkness to reveal an island of trees and lane ahead of them.

"Complaining about this road is Aliki's favourite pastime while she is here," Dawn laughed, as she held on as best she could to the rocking van.

"Well, really, they have more money now than they know what to do with. Why don't they put in a decent road?" her partner grumbled as she manoeuvred the van through the ruts.

"Baba likes the road the way it is. It gives the ranch privacy," Dawn explained to the bouncing figures in the back.

Robbie snorted. "It must be a northern thing. Janet won't let me put a decent road in to the lodge either."

They rounded a corner and pulled into a clearing, floodlit by the warm glow of light from the windows of a massive log home. "Aliki, it's beautiful," exclaimed Janet.

Aliki looked at her family home objectively. "It is almost impossible to find cedar logs of this size today," she concluded matter-of-factly. Then the door opened, and Baba was on the porch.

Dawn and Mac were out of the van immediately and in Baba's arms. He gave each of them a bear hug, tears in his eyes. Then he turned to greet his daughter. Aliki smiled, and Baba pulled her into a hug, whispering Greek words of endearment into her ear as he had done when she was a child.

"Tecanes, Baba. It is good to be home. Hi, Ari, tecanes," Aliki called over Baba's shoulder.

Then she pulled free from her father's embrace and turned to the Williams family that now stood in a group nearby. Aliki put her hand on Robbie's shoulder and pushed her nervous sister forward. "Baba, this is your daughter, Robbie Williams."

Robbie opened her mouth to give a greeting, but words failed her. She looked into the face of a man whose eyes were the colour of a tropical ocean. A handsome man, who wore his age with dignity. She could see herself reflected in his features. Tears pricked at her eyes.

"Robbie, tecanes, Robbie," Baba said softly and wrapped his long lost daughter into a tight hug. They stood there for a long time, holding on to each other as they came to terms with the bond that tied their lives together.

Aliki looked at Dawn and smiled. Dawn's eyes sparkled with happiness. Robbie was home, accepted into the growing Pateas family, and all was well.

At last, Baba pulled away. "So you introduce me to your family, Robbie," Baba said, smiling and turning to the remaining three, who stood awkwardly nearby.

Robbie beamed, filled with pride at her family. "Baba," the word seemed strange on her lips, "this is my wife, Janet, and our daughters, Ryan and Rebecca, whom we call Reb."

"Welcome! Tecanes!" Baba said and laughed, hugging each in turn. He turned to shoot a look at Aliki, partly seriously and partly in fun. "You see this, Aliki, my Robbie is married. This is good."

Everyone laughed, and Aliki rolled her eyes and shook her head while Dawn blushed deeply. Aliki quickly changed the subject. "This is Ari and his fiancée, Joan." The couple came down the porch stairs and hugged and greeted the new members of their family. "Where's Nick?" Aliki asked.

Ari and Baba exchanged looks. "He had a meeting tonight. He will be here tomorrow," Baba stated, a slight edge to his voice, then the voice softened. "Come, come into your family home. We have much to say to one another."

The first evening passed quickly in a buzz of family stories. Robbie sat on the couch, Janet beside her, holding her hand, and Baba to her other side, his arm over the back of the couch enfolding her into the family. Robbie had feared that the evening would be awkward, but she soon realized that Ari, Joan, and Baba were far more comfortable socially than she or her half-sister Aliki. They kept up a lively, teasing conversation with Dawn and Mac and drew in the new members of the family whenever they could.

It was late at night when Robbie carried her sleeping younger daughter upstairs and Janet herded a tired Ryan off to bed. Exhausted, the two women stripped and slipped into the shower together. They stood there wrapped in each other's arms, letting the emotion of the day drain from them. Janet kissed her partner tenderly and dried her as she would a small child before leading the emotionally exhausted woman to their bed.

"How are you doing, love?" Janet asked, snuggling close.

It didn't matter how many times Robbie found herself close to Janet, each time sent a flood of desire through her. Janet was so sexy and so in tune with her soul. Their love was something special and rare. Robbie held on tight. "I gotta tell you – that was one tough day to get through. Baba and Ari are great. They really made us welcome. I think it's going to be okay. They're different from Aliki, not so prickly."

A laugh blurted from Janet's lips, and Robbie looked down at her lover. "What?"

"You and Aliki just *have* to compete. You can't help yourselves. Aliki isn't a bit prickly; you two just egg each other on."

Robbie blushed. "Well, maybe a little bit," she conceded with a smile that transitioned to a hard look of need. "You excite me," Robbie growled softly, pulling her wife closer. Their lips feathered over each other, the kisses gradually growing longer, deeper, and more earnest. Robbie's hard, lean body slipped over Janet's sensuous form, and Janet spread herself wide to the unspoken demand. The feeling of Janet beneath her sent a wave of excitement through Robbie that settled deep in her being. Her lips played with Janet's nipple, and her hand slipped between her partner's legs.

"Yes," Janet groaned and nibbled hungrily at her lover's shoulder.

Their love was hot, needy, and explosive. Exhausted from the day and the rush of sexual pleasure, they fell asleep in each other's arms.

It was quite early the next morning when Nick pulled up in his pickup truck. He knew his father was not pleased with him for going to a church meeting in Edmonton last night instead of being home to meet his new sister and her family, and he didn't want to push it. Having recently renewed his faith in God and the Church, he knew that he was right to put his Bible study class first, but he also knew that the Lord commanded that one "Honour thy father and thy mother: that thy days may be long upon the land which the Lord thy God giveth thee."

He knew that his family had faith in God, but he hoped that they would reaffirm their belief as he had. Then there was his sister Aliki, his half-sister Robbie, Dawn and Janet. He felt it was his duty to show them that their gay lifestyle was a sin and help them to find strength to fight their affliction so that they too could be saved. He had prayed about it, and during the night he had realized that he should talk to Dawn. He felt that this revelation was God showing him the way.

Blowing out a deep breath, he stepped into the house and followed the laughter to the kitchen where his extended family sat around the large table over the remains of breakfast.

"Hi, everyone," Nick called cheerfully. "God bless," he whispered as he gave Aliki a hug and then hugged Dawn and Mac.

Aliki raised an eyebrow, and Baba leaned over and whispered, "He's got religion now, he tells me. I thought I had already given him a religion, but he says not."

Aliki shook her head and smiled knowingly. She knew her brother — he was inclined to get caught up in things but never took the time to really understand what he was involved in. "Robbie, Janet, Ryan, Reb, this is Nick. Nick, our sister Robbie, our sister-in-law Janet, and our nieces, Ryan and Reb."

Nick greeted each new member of the family pleasantly enough, but the dynamics of the room had shifted with his arrival and the conversation became stilted. In the end, Dawn and Aliki offered to clean up so that Baba could drive Robbie, Janet, and his three grandchildren around the ranch. Ari and Nick excused themselves and headed off to their own jobs — Nick to work in the barns with the hired help and Ari to work in the ranch office. Joan had come by earlier, but had to leave for her job as a head nurse in the Swan Hills hospital and had missed out on the family breakfast.

Dawn was taking a bucket of peelings out to the compost heap when she was grabbed from behind and lifted off the ground. "There you are! I've missed you so much, Dawn." Nick laughed as he twirled her around and then carefully deposited her back on her feet.

"Nick, you big oaf," Dawn chastised with a laugh. "You scared me half to death!"

Her chiding did not in any way dent Nick's enthusiasm. "That's what comes from living in the East in one of those big cities. There are so many weirdos that you get to jumping at shadows." Nick picked up the bucket from where it had spilt on the ground and dumped the remains into the compost heap.

Dawn folded her arms and looked at him, shaking her head in disbelief. "You are just full of it, Nicklaus Pateas! And I'll have you know that Toronto is a safe city, and your sister lives in a beautiful area. You should come out and visit sometime."

Nick's eyes widened in shock. "To a city in the East? No way!"

"So, how are things, Nick? You and Sally setting a date any time soon?" Dawn was surprised to see anger flash across Nick's normally happy face.

"We broke up. She was stepping out with someone else. I caught her with him at a community dance," Nick explained gruffly.

"Oh, Nick, I am so sorry. Are you okay?" She took his arm and walked with him back toward the barn.

"Yeah. I'm best without her," he mumbled, looking miserable. Then his face softened, and he brightened noticeably. "But it helped me to find the Lord again. I learned that the Lord's looking after me."

Dawn's smile was forced. She had been raised by an uncle who saw the hand of God in the beauty of the wild land around them, but she had never really had anything to do with organized religion and she wasn't comfortable with it. "I'm glad your faith has supported you," she responded neutrally.

Nick stopped and looked down at Dawn. "I'd like to take you to some of our meetings and services, Dawn. I...I'm worried about your and Aliki's lifestyle, and I'd like to help you see that there are alternatives."

Dawn sighed with annoyance and rolled her eyes. "Nick, don't go there. Let's have an agreement that I'll respect your beliefs and you will respect mine."

"But, Dawn, yours are not based on faith! They are based on...on..." Nick fumbled for a word.

"Love?" Dawn suggested, raising an eyebrow and enjoying the sight of the red rising in Nick's face.

"I don't think so," he responded pompously. "I don't think that's possible. I blame myself. I should have insisted on taking you to that dance two years ago instead of stepping aside and letting Aliki court you." Nick looked miserable. "I had lost touch with my faith and thought I was being broadminded about the issue. I realize now I was wrong."

Dawn snorted. "If you had tried to kiss me that night, Nick, Aliki would have kicked your butt all over the ranch. I think your ideas are all wet, and I am not the least bit interested in your religious views or going to any meetings. Nick, I am gay, Aliki is gay; we are very happy together and very much in love. If that sticks in your craw then feel free to ignore us, but please don't try to force your views on me." Dawn took the bucket from Nick's hand and turned and left before she really lost her temper.

Nick watched with sad eyes as Dawn marched off toward the house.

Robbie leaned on the rail beside Baba holding onto a squirmy Reb as they watched Janet, Ryan, and Mac laughing as they tried to get a halter on a young heifer. It felt wonderful and weird at the same time to be standing by the man who was her father. She felt...connected. She had never felt that way with Phillip Williams.

"I help!" Reb demanded, trying to slip from the rail into the corral.

"Not this time, slugger." Robbie gave her little daughter a kiss on the head. "You are too small to chase cows yet."

Baba patted Reb's head. "They are good girls," Baba said with pride in his voice.

"Yeah, they are," Robbie agreed boastfully. "They've had to face some pretty rough and scary moments in their lives, and they acted intelligently and with remarkable courage."

Baba nodded but said nothing. Instead, he reached out and wrapped his coarse, work-worn hand around Robbie's long, slender fingers. "You and Janet, my Aliki and Dawn, you are wonderful people." He shrugged. "It is not the life I would have wanted for you, but I can see that you are happy and my grandchildren are healthy and happy, too. This makes me happy."

Robbie looked into blue eyes so like hers. "Your acceptance of us means a lot."

"What is to accept? You are people like everyone else. Now I know you are good people. That is all that matters. Here, I'll hold my little Rebel. You go help these three and try not to get kicked," Baba added, taking a willing Reb into his arms and watching with sparkling eyes as Robbie climbed nimbly over the wood fence, eager to get in on the fun.

They returned from their tour laughing and very dirty and went up to wash for lunch. As they listened to the happy chatter of the returning party, Aliki stirred the soup and Dawn sliced thick pieces of fresh bread. "I think they have really taken to Baba and the ranch," Dawn said, smiling.

Aliki considered as she tasted the turkey and vegetable soup that she had made that morning. "Yeah, things are going really well. I'm glad." She offered a taste to Dawn.

"Mmmm, you are such a good cook; that soup is great. Glad you're my lover," Dawn teased, stretching up on her tiptoes to give Aliki a kiss.

"Ah, so I won your heart with my culinary skills, did I?" Aliki pulled Dawn in for a hug.

"Well, that and the fact that you're great in bed," Dawn responded cheekily, patting Aliki's backside.

"Keep that up and no one will be getting lunch," growled the tall woman as she kissed Dawn fiercely. Her face took on a worried look as she met Dawn's eyes. "You okay? You were kind of quiet this morning. Has something upset you?"

"I'm fine," Dawn evaded, not wanting to get into the conversation that she'd had earlier with Nick. Aliki could become very aggressive if she felt that either Dawn or Mac had been upset by someone. Dawn wanted this holiday to go smoothly for the Williamses, and she knew that Nick meant well, even though his views didn't jibe with hers.

The next few days were spent getting to know each other and catching up on family news. Nick's arrival and sulky attitude did little to curtail the laughing and fun. Baba made sure that his new daughter and family felt that they had come home.

It was the morning of the fourth day that Baba came into the living room and found Robbie staring out the window. "Good morning, Robbie. I do not like the look of worry on your face. You tell Baba what is on your mind," the old man said, moving to stand next to his daughter.

Robbie smiled. She felt like she had known Baba all her life. In just a few days, she had become far closer to him than she had ever been to Phil Williams, the man she had thought was her father. "Ryan," she stated. "She's up to something."

Baba laughed. "She is a teenager. Of course she is up to something."

"Yeah, but your grandchild has a way of getting into big trouble." Robbie frowned. "It's not that she is a bad kid, it's just that...well, she's an 'olive'." Robbie blushed.

Baba looked at his daughter in confusion. "What do you say?"

Robbie leaned on the windowsill and folded her arms. "That's what Janet calls us. She thinks we are like olives: we take some getting used to, but with time you get to love us."

Baba laughed. "So, my new daughter and family are olives, eh? A very good thing, an olive." He smiled.

Robbie couldn't help but smile back. Baba had a way that put one at ease. He had been so accepting of her family that it had really been easy. Ari and his fiancée had been good, too. She wasn't sure about Nick. He was friendly enough, but his sincerity seemed forced and a bit artificial. "I didn't do very well by Ryan," Robbie admitted, looking at the floor as a blush crept up her face. "I have a lot of regrets about my conduct in my early years. I thought I was doing Ryan a favour by not letting her know who her mother was, but I wasn't. Everything the kid is, she did on her own. We get on okay, you know, but well...she can be close. She's used to doing it on her own and...and I don't think she will ever completely trust me."

Baba looked out the window and nodded sadly. "We do the best we can with what we know at the time. I was not fair to Aliki. I think that she was like her mother just because she was a girl. I think she would enjoy being in charge of the house and helping raise the boys. I plan that she will marry a local boy and stay on the ranch. I never see that my daughter wanted more. We make mistakes, Robbie. Then we do our best to learn and make things better."

Robbie nodded, still looking worried. "You go talk to my grandchild. You go make it better," Baba ordered, giving Robbie a nudge.

Robbie smiled, gave her father a quick hug, and went to find Ryan. Baba watched her go with a look of sorrow in his eyes. Had he known that she was his child, perhaps a lot of pain could have been avoided.

"Hi, kid." Robbie leaned against the fence rail. Ryan and Dawn had been helping Nick with the chores, and Ryan was in the process of putting pitchforks of hay into the corral manger.

"Hey, Mom. Aunt Dawn said she would take us all riding into the hills this afternoon, can we?"

"Sure, that sounds like fun. Just don't embarrass me by knocking over a mountain or anything," Robbie teased.

"Mom!" Ryan flicked some hay in her mother's direction. Robbie shifted quickly, and the wad of hay sailed over her shoulder. Ryan smiled. Her mother had the most incredible reflexes. She was powerful, yet so very graceful in her movements. She really was something else to have as a mother.

"Ahhh, I noticed that you go out each morning with your knapsack." Robbie's long fingers ran nervously over the grain of the split rail fence.

Ryan hesitated only a second. "Yeah, I like to go for a quiet walk in the morning. You know, commune with nature...aah...do a little studying... read...you know."

Robbie looked deep into Ryan's eyes. The kid wasn't lying, but she wasn't telling the truth, either, and that made her very sad. She nodded. "I'll leave you to your work then." Robbie gave a weak smile. "You'll want to get the chores done so that you are ready for the ride."

Ryan watched her mom walk away. *She knows some thing's up,* Ryan realized, *but she is not going to push, at least not yet*. Ryan bit her lip. *Maybe Mac is right. Maybe I should just tell my mom the truth. But how would T-Rob react? I'll wait a bit yet. At least until I'm better.*

In the barn, another scene was playing out. Aliki had offered to help Nick, as one of the hired men was sick. Nick smiled, stopping to lean on his pitchfork.

"It's good to have you back here, Aliki. I was glad to see that you and Dawn had not gotten engaged after all."

Aliki hesitated, then straightened from the manger that she had been scooping chop into. "We *are* engaged," she corrected in a tight voice.

Nick looked surprised and upset. "She's not wearing a ring," he argued.

"I haven't given one to her yet," Aliki agreed, "but we are engaged."

Nick sighed, put down his pitchfork, and came over to place his hand on his sister's arm. "Aliki, this isn't right. I know you have these...feelings, but giving in to these unnatural temptations will only lead you, Dawn, and Mac into a tragic future. If you care about them, I mean really care, then you will pray for the strength to return to a heterosexual lifestyle."

"Don't go down this path, Nick," Aliki warned, her voice rough with emotion and her blue eyes dark and stormy.

"Sis, I have to. I care about you. Don't you see what you're doing is a sin? It states quite clearly in the Bible that homosexuality is an abomination in the eyes of God."

Irritated, Aliki shook off Nick's hand. "As always, Nick, you have seen the damn tree and missed the forest. I know what the Old Testament says. I also know that it approves of slavery, revenge, and taking more than one wife. I don't hear you speaking up for those things," she growled, her anger at Nick's bias and narrow-mindedness growing by the minute. "You know what you are? You're a religious bigot. Oh sure, you can quote all the standard verses and think yourself all high and mighty, but you know dick-all about the history and philosophy of your faith. You believe, not in order to find enlightenment and understanding, but to save your ass while having the fun of condemning all those that don't think like you. You're the sort that gives true believers a bad name."

Nick bristled with indignation. "I know what I believe. Faith is trusting in the Bible and that its word is truth. I will not be tempted away from my faith by an unbeliever."

Aliki shook her head and turned back to her job. "Believe what you want, but keep it to yourself. I promise you, if you upset Dawn or Mac with this crap, I'll knock your block off."

"There, you see!" Nick exclaimed in disgust.

Aliki sighed in frustration, as she scooped out more of the pulverized field corn called chop from the sack that she had filled at the silo. "See what?"

"Threatening me with physical violence, as if you were a man. It's not natural, Aliki. You are not a guy, you're a girl, and you need to act like one."

Aliki gritted her teeth but said nothing. Rather than ending the conversation, her silence seemed to encourage Nick to press his point. "Besides, I have already talked to Dawn about this whole situation and—"

"YOU WHAT!" Aliki roared, dropping the bag and scoop and stepping around the manger to face her brother.

Nick straightened. "Aliki, I will always be very grateful to you for replacing the mother I never knew, but I am not a child anymore. I am a grown man, and you are my sister. You can't intimidate or boss me around anymore. I have talked to Dawn about her living in sin with you, and I mean to continue to seek—"

The blow to Nick's backside came so quickly that he didn't even see Aliki's foot leave the ground.

"So I am only a woman and can't intimidate you anymore, huh? Well, let's see just how well your sick concept of God will protect you. Come on, you good-clean-living asshole. Show me!" Aliki taunted, her body quivering with anger.

Nick rushed at her. Aliki's hand shot out, and her brother staggered and rolled as a stinging shot through his ear. "What's the matter, Nick? You're the one with balls, come on," Aliki hissed.

Again Nick charged blindly. This time, Aliki hooked him behind the knee and sent him to the ground heavily.

"Aliki!" came a roar from behind her. "Enough!"

Breathing hard and white with emotion, Aliki stood stock still as her father passed her to kneel by her brother.

"Are you all right, Nick?" the old man asked in concern.

"Yeah, yeah," Nick mumbled, red with embarrassment as he staggered to his feet with his father's help.

"Are you hurt?" Baba fretted, looking at the knee that Nick was clearly favouring.

"Only in his male ego," drawled Aliki. "If I had wanted to break bones or rupture organs, I could have. I didn't."

"You be quiet, Aliki," Baba ordered in frustration. "If you can walk on that knee, then you go up to the house and you have one of the men drive you to the doctor's. You hear?"

"Baba..." Nick began, looking defiant.

"Go," Baba ordered softly, giving his son's shoulder a squeeze. Nick swallowed his objection and with a nod, he limped past Aliki and out of the barn.

Baba looked at his daughter. This was a side of her he had never seen before. She radiated controlled strength. "Why you beat up on Nick, Aliki?"

Aliki swallowed, trying to tamp her emotions down. She felt like an elastic band stretched to its limit and ready to snap. In a tight voice, she tried to explain. "He can call me any name in the book – I've heard them all – but I will not allow him to preach his bigotry and upset my family." Her voice quivered with emotion.

Baba looked into his daughter's eye and saw for the first time the deep pain of being gay in an unaccepting world. He walked over and wrapped his arms around her. For a minute, she felt rigid and resisting in his arms, then the walls fell and she leaned against him and sobbed uncontrollably. Baba rocked her gently in his arms as he had done when she was a little child and let her cry. She had every reason to.

Baba was not happy, although he tried not to show it. He was disappointed with Nick's attitude, and he was annoyed with Aliki for hurting her brother. Nick had phoned from the doctor's office to say that he had a badly bruised knee and was planning on taking the rest of the day off and staying in town. Now they were two men short on the ranch. So when Aliki got the call from the RCMP station in Swan Hills just at lunchtime, he frowned. "It is for you, Aliki," said Baba, not pleased that the call had come just as they had all sat down to lunch, especially since the call had come from the police. Good people had no business with the police was Baba's view, and he found it difficult to accept that his daughter was a police officer.

Sergeant Nicholson's voice came over the wire. "Inspector Pateas?"

"Hi, Brad," she responded. "What can I do for you?"

The voice on the other end of the line brightened and relaxed a bit. "Hi, Aliki. Listen, I got some bones here I'd like you to have a look at. They're not human or anything, but, well, the whole thing is kind of weird, and I'd like your opinion before I decide whether or not to send them on to the crime lab in Edmonton. Any chance of you coming into town today?"

Aliki frowned. She had wanted to go riding with the group, but something in Brad's uneasiness made her feel she should take a look. She glanced over at Dawn. Their eyes met, and Dawn nodded ever so slightly. Having been reassured by her lover that it would be okay, she responded, "Yeah, I could look at the bones this afternoon. I'll be there around two."

"That's great." Nicholson sighed in relief. "Aaah, is it true that Robbie Williams is up at the ranch?"

Aliki kept her face deadpan. She was damned if she was going to let her sister know what Nicholson was asking. "Yeah, that's right."

"Aaah, I mean, is there any chance of getting an autograph?" he asked sheepishly.

"Sure, this afternoon; leave it to me," Aliki stated confidently and hung up. If she knew her sister, getting the autograph was going to be a simple as taking candy from a baby.

She took her seat, aware of the silence around her and deliberately ignoring it. The silence lasted all of five seconds.

"What bones?" demanded Robbie.

"Police business," Aliki responded, baiting her sister.

Baba sighed. "Always police business."

Robbie was fairly squirming with excitement. "I want to come, too."

"You're not a cop," Aliki taunted, helping herself to a slice of bread.

Janet looked at Dawn, her eyes shining with amusement, and Dawn tried not to laugh.

"I played the part of a detective once," Robbie whined.

Aliki laughed as she leaned back in her chair. "Oh, well, that makes all the difference."

"I can come?" Robbie asked, surprised at how readily her usually stubborn sister had given in.

"Sure, to the station, but you are not getting anywhere near the evidence," Aliki warned.

"Cool." Robbie smiled, planning already how she was going to do just that. Then her expression changed, and she looked around the table, gauging reactions until her eyes finally settled on Janet's face. "Is it okay?" she asked, remembering belatedly that she was going riding into the hills with the family.

"You go and don't get in Aliki's way," Janet said, her eyes sparkling with laughter.

"Now," said Baba firmly, "we eat, we talk, but we don't talk about police and bones at the table."

Dawn slipped the cord of her whistle over her head. It was a good weapon to use if a bear crossed their path. Failing that, she had a rifle tucked into its sheath on her saddle. Grizzlies were extremely territorial and at two thousand pounds and eight feet tall, there was very little chance of escape if they attacked. The chances of meeting one this close to civilization, however, were slight.

She planned to take Janet and the girls down into the meadows and then along the river basin up into the foothills. She smiled, recalling how she and Aliki had found love up in the hills only a few summers ago.

"Aah, it's none of my business, but I happened to notice you and Nick having a few words this morning. Is everything okay?" Janet asked as she tucked sandwiches into a saddlebag.

"No, it's not," Dawn growled. "Nick has been trying to show me the errors of my ways. He has been at me every chance he gets. He tried again today, and he pushed it too far. He said that being gay is a sin and that God would forgive me if I prayed. He offered to introduce me to some nice men who could show me a better and healthier lifestyle."

Janet looked pained and shocked. "Asshole."

"Yeah. I told him that the error was on his part and that Jesus never preached in favour of fanaticism or against homosexuality. I told him to keep his views to himself because I found them offensive and ignorant. I made it pretty clear that I'd had enough. Then he made the mistake of taking the subject up with Aliki."

"Good for you." Janet smiled. "So that's why Nick was limping."

Dawn sighed. "Yeah. Aliki was furious with him. I was pretty hot today, too, but after I calmed down I felt bad. I don't want to cause trouble in the family."

Janet shrugged and gave Dawn a hug. "You didn't. He started it, and hopefully he will take your advice because I don't think Aliki would forgive Nick if she knew he was continuing to harass you."

Dawn leaned on the counter and shrugged. "Some days I believe that; other days I'm not sure. Aliki proposed to me months ago, but do you see a ring on my finger? Have we set a date? It's like the proposal was good enough for her." Dawn ran her fingers through her hair. "Honestly, Janet, I don't know what to do."

"Have you talked to her about it?" Janet asked, as she tied the saddlebag closed.

"Once or twice. I get stonewalled. She doesn't want to talk about it. It's the money issue, I think. I don't know. Maybe she just doesn't feel a commitment is necessary." Dawn sighed.

Janet nodded but said nothing. She knew better than to get involved, but maybe she could get Robbie to give her stubborn sister a good swift kick. "Here come the kids with the horses. Are you ready?"

Dawn straightened and smiled immediately. "Sure am. Let's go."

Part 2

Dawn fastened the saddlebag to the back of Janet's saddle while Janet watched Ryan and Mac mount their quarter horses. Then Janet lifted the excited Reb up in front of Mac. Mac and Dawn were by far the best riders, so they were going to take turns riding double with Reb. The two adults then swung up into their own western saddles and led the way out the gate and down the road.

"Hold on to the leather horn of the saddle, Reb," Mac explained, "and squeeze in with your knees."

"I drive a horse, Ryan!" the little girl squealed with delight. "I like horses."

"Way to go, kid. You're a regular cowgirl." Ryan laughed as she struggled to get comfortable in her own saddle. She had taken English riding at several of her earlier boarding schools but wasn't used to the big western saddles.

"Don't post like you would with a horse trained for English riding, Ryan," Dawn directed.

"Lean back in the saddle and loosen your reins and give the horse her head. Western horses are trained to pick a path through rough terrain, so they are not used to a tight rein," Mac added.

Ryan did as she was told and found that the saddle was very comfortable when she wasn't trying to post. Also, once she loosened the reins, her horse stopped fighting the bit, shook its head in relief, and plodded happily along the trail.

They cut through a small bush in a single file, ducking under branches and emerging in a wide meadow of tall grass and flowers. Dawn led them down to the river's edge, and then they turned upstream and followed the bank of the meandering river. As they went, she told them the story of how she and Aliki had come face to face with a grizzly.

"Weren't you scared?" Ryan asked in awe.

"Mom knows the Swan Hills better than anyone," Mac bragged. "She can take care of herself."

Dawn smiled at her daughter. "We were lucky. Grizzlies are very territorial and aggressive. Aliki was prepared to take it on with a knife, and she'd have got herself killed trying to save me. Fortunately, I had this." Dawn pulled on the cord around her neck and showed them her metal whistle. "I'm just in the habit of carrying it. I blew it really sharply, and it scared the bear away. It must have wandered down from the high country in search of food. Being out of its normal territory, it was less aggressive and more skittish. It sure gave us a fright, though," Dawn admitted and then pointed. "Look over there, girls. Mule deer."

On the other side of the river, they could see three reddish deer about three and a half feet in height looking at them as they rode by. The deer chewed slowly, grinding their lower jaws back and forth like cartoon characters. Their long ears were up and alert, however, and their short, black-tipped tails swished in annoyance.

"They like to graze on grasses and herbs, so this flood plain is ideal for them. It is unusual to see them at this time of day. You mostly see them in the early morning or evening," Dawn explained. "We have white-tailed deer, too, like you have back east. But they are browsers, not grazers, so you find them closer to the woods. They like twigs, shrubs, acorns, and the like. Usually all you see is the warning flash of their white tails before they disappear deeper into the bush."

Mac smiled with pride at Ryan as if to say, *See, I told you so. My mom knows everything.* Ryan winked back to show her agreement.

"Aunt Dawn? Does Santa Clause have mule deer or white-tailed?" Reb asked seriously.

Dawn smiled. "Neither, hon, he has reindeer. They come from Finland and Russia in Europe."

Reb thought about this information carefully. "Obbie was in Ourope, but she made a movie. She didn't see no reindeer."

"She didn't see any reindeer, Reb," Janet corrected.

"See this weed. It's in the Angelica family, a type of parsley. That's probably what brought the mule deer out to munch. You can tell it by the purple colour of the stem. This is one of the few places in Alberta that you find it," Dawn concluded.

Ryan looked around nervously. "Aahh, Aunt Dawn, is that grizzly still around?"

"No. Baba called the forest rangers, and they set a trap for it. It was tranquilized, put in a sling, and lifted by helicopter to a safe zone," the writer explained. "We try not to kill them unless they are known to have attacked farm animals or people."

They set a steady pace, moving higher through the beautiful mountain valley. Mac was now in deep conversation with her mom and Reb about the legend of Swan Hills, so Janet fell back so that her horse was side by side with Ryan's.

She had been waiting for an opportunity to talk to Ryan, and this seemed like a good moment.

"Ryan, I've been worried. I know you're up to something and have been for some time now. You need your privacy, of course, and I do trust you, however, the school phoned to say you have been cutting classes and by accident I learned that you have taken quite a bit of money from your emergency account. It puts me in an awkward position. I feel I have to talk to your mom about what I know, but I wanted to talk to you first."

Ryan sighed and rolled her eyes. "You're too late. Mom has already been asking me questions. Look, Aunt Janet, I will tell you, I promise, but not yet...just not yet."

Janet's eyes widened in surprise. She hadn't realized that Robbie had noticed that something was up with Ryan. It was not like Robbie not to talk to her about it, but then, they'd had very little time since Robbie got back from

England. "Ryan, your mom is a wonderful person, and she loves you very much, but patience is not her strong point. She is under a lot of stress at the moment. Her movie will be released this month, and she's here meeting her father for the first time. Don't add to her stress levels, okay, or you are likely to be facing T-Rob. I don't want to see the two of you getting your feelings hurt. Those sorts of wounds take a long time to heal."

Ryan nodded seriously. "Okay. I hear what you're saying."

"Look, just ahead of us," called Dawn. "A herd of elk."

Janet and Ryan rode up to join the others and watched as a herd of some twenty animals waded across the river to the opposite side. They were large, rusty coloured with yellowish rumps. Some had large racks of antlers. "We'll wait until they've all crossed and settled down again before moving on. Elk don't like humans to get too close. Many a tourist to the West has learned that the hard way." Dawn shook her head. "When a 152 centimetre tall animal weighing in at four hundred and ten kilograms,with an antler spread as wide as he is tall, gives you a butt to the backside, it is going to hurt!"

They waited patiently, the last huge male with a magnificent rack taking his time before he crossed to join the others. Dawn tutored the children while their horses grazed. "See, Reb, that blue-grey bird is a Belted Kingfisher. See his bushy crest and how he can hover over the water looking for his dinner."

"He look for fish," Reb explained knowingly.

"Yes, and crayfish, small frogs, salamanders, and things like that. Oh, look! Do you see the big, yellow and black butterfly? It's a beautiful Tiger Swallowtail. Can you see how its hind wings have long tails like some swallows? If you look closely, you'll see it has a lovely band of blue on each of its hind wings, too. I imagine they are feeding on wild cherries this time of year."

"Look over there." Ryan pointed. "There are lots of smaller yellow butterflies."

It was Janet who responded. "They're Clouded Sulphurs. They like moist places, and they usually are seen in swarms. You find them out east, too."

"Okay, the elk have moved off. I know a nice outcrop just around the bend where we can stop to picnic, then we'd better head back. I'll take you inland a bit, and if we're lucky, we might see a moose." Dawn put her horse in motion, and the party set off again.

"Okay, give me one of your forensic shirts," Robbie demanded, flopping down on the bed in Aliki's room.

Aliki raised an eyebrow. "I don't think so."

"You let Ryan wear them," the actress sulked, "and I'm your sister and partner in crime."

"When did that happen?" Aliki asked as she sorted through her luggage.

"Hey, we've worked two cases together. Two is a pattern," Robbie insisted stubbornly.

Aliki rolled her eyes and pulled out two black t-shirts with white lettering on them. She had many such shirts, each with one of her own definitions of forensics stenciled on it. "I only brought two." She laid them out on the bed. "Which one do you want to wear?"

Robbie looked from one to the other, laughing. One read: "Forensics: The Straight and the Marrow". The other said: "Forensics: We Operate on a Skeleton Staff".

"I want to be the skeleton staff," Robbie decided gleefully. She whipped off her shirt to pull the black t-shirt on while Aliki slipped into the other. Robbie smiled. "Hey, we look like twins."

Aliki took out a navy blue baseball hat with RCMP stamped in big gold letters across the front. "Now we don't," she said, settling it on her head. "Let's go."

"Can I wear the hat?" Robbie asked, bouncing happily along beside her sister.

"No."

"Can I drive the van, then?"

"I begin to understand why Janet complains that you see Bartlett as your personal playground," the scientist muttered, handing over the keys.

"Hey, I'm on holiday!" Robbie protested as she slid into the driver's seat.

Playing the radio loudly, they drove into town going much faster than they would have if they'd had their families with them. Robbie pulled up in front of the RCMP station, surprised to see that the parking lot was nearly full. "Busy day," she said, getting out. Aliki smiled but said nothing. As they walked in and all eyes turned to the famous Robbie Williams, the office fell silent.

"Hi, everyone," Aliki said into the quiet. "Let me introduce you to my sister, Robbie Williams. You wanted autographs, and Robbie said she would come down and sign a few for you while I see to business." Robbie's stage face slammed into place immediately, but the eyes she turned on Aliki shot daggers. Aliki laughed. "Looks like the station staff called some of their family and friends."

"How nice," Robbie responded through stiff lips, as Aliki walked over to Sergeant Brad Nicholson. Released from Aliki's protective custody, a small crowd of well-wishers formed around Robbie while Aliki and Brad disappeared into the back room.

Brad got out a shallow box with a lid, the kind used to store forensic evidence. He placed it on the table and stepped out of the way to allow Aliki to have a look. The scientist lifted the lid and set it aside, then looked with interest at the mix of bones, charred feathers, and sinew inside. She sighed; it was a hell of a mess.

She slipped on rubber gloves and took out a magnifying glass and then sat down to sort, examine, and classify. Birds were not Aliki's area of speciality, and she was careful not to do any damage in case a professional in the field was called in. Counting beaks, she realized that at least half a dozen ducks had been killed. The repeated cracking and grinding marks found on the small bones of the upper vertebrae indicated to Aliki that the ducks had most likely been strangled. The weathering and pattern of decomposition was interesting, too.

A little over an hour later, she looked up. "Did you take photos?"

Brad smiled, pleased that he'd had the foresight to do so even though there was really no reason.

"Yeah, I took black and whites and colour. They turned out pretty well, too." He got a brown envelope out of a nearby file cabinet and handed it to Aliki. She took out the snapshots and spent a long while looking at them.

"It certainly bears some looking into, Brad. Yeah, I think you should send it on to Edmonton, although to be truthful, I don't suppose there will be a follow-up. It covers you, though. Can you give me directions to the site? If I have time, I think I'd like to go out there and have a look around."

Robbie signed another piece of RCMP stationery with "To Helen, with fondest regards, Robbie Williams," and handed it over to the giggling woman on the other side of the counter.

"I think word's gotten out," laughed the duty corporal as he ripped open another packet of paper.

"There you go. Don't forget now, a new movie will be out in a few weeks." Robbie forced a smile for the fan even though her jaws were starting to ache, then turned to the police officer. "At this rate there won't be a piece of paper left in the station. You want me to tell them to get their own?"

The corporal shook his head. "Nah, it's community good will. It can't hurt having a celebrity seen supporting the police."

The smile Robbie gave him didn't quite reach her eyes. She had been jailed for weeks on a charge of murder because of the police and she still harboured resentment, despite the fact that her sister was a cop.

Suddenly, Aliki was there beside her. *The woman walks like a cat*, Robbie thought grumpily.

"Thanks, folks. Robbie has really enjoyed having this opportunity to mix with some of her Swan Hills fans. If you see her around town, please allow her to enjoy her stay here by providing her with some space," Aliki announced to those still in the office. Then she whispered into Robbie's ear, "Come on, I have the van out back."

Robbie nodded and quickly signed her name a dozen times on a single sheet of paper so that waiting fans would not be too disappointed. She then followed Aliki through the back room and out the back door, where Brad waited with the van.

"Thanks, Sergeant." Aliki slid into the driver's seat as Robbie hurried to get in the passenger side before anyone spotted her. "I'll be in touch." Nicholson nodded and waved as the two women drove off.

For a while there was silence while Robbie nursed her sore hand and sulked, then the actor-director shook her head and looked at her sister. "I have suspected for some time that your sense of humour ran toward the macabre; I was right. You set me up."

Aliki chuckled. "You had it coming. Besides you walked into it with your eyes open. I didn't invite you; you begged to come along."

Robbie gave her sister a playful swat. "This means war, you know." Aliki's eyes sparkled with delight as she glanced over at her sister, but she said nothing. "So, tell me what you learned," Robbie asked.

"Later, when the others are back," Aliki promised.

"Jerk," Robbie grumbled.

"Hey, I'm your sister."

"Jerky sister," Robbie amended and, swift as lightning, she swept the RCMP cap off Aliki's head and placed it on her own.

Mac and Ryan were ass-end up along the riverbank, helping Reb catch a frog. Having just finished tidying up the picnic remains, Janet and Dawn sat on the rock outcropping. Their conversation was punctuated with outbursts of laughter.

"So, can you imagine? I reach my hand into the fridge for a plate of meatloaf without looking and deposit someone's chopped off hand on the kitchen table! When I finally could speak to the woman rationally again, I immediately sent her out for a fridge to put in the garage to keep her homework in. Honest to God, most partners just bring home a briefcase!" The two women broke out in renewed laughter.

"So what bugs you the most about Robbie?"

"Her feet," Janet answered immediately. "No matter how many times I tell her to take her shoes off at the door, I am always finding a muddy trail of sneaker prints through the house. And when she and Ryan bring the Bartlett Volunteer Fire Department home after they've been out on a call, I could plant potatoes on my kitchen floor after they've left. Of course, the nice thing about having Robbie in the fire department is that she needs lots of extra showers." Janet smirked, wiggling her eyebrows comically.

Dawn pondered. "I wonder if they look alike naked."

"Hmmm, Robbie has this cute little mole on her abdomen," Janet shared.

Dawn shook her head. "Nope, no mole on Aliki, but you know what she does have?"

"What?" She could see by Dawn's excitement that she was about to reveal some good information.

"You have to promise not to tell a soul."

Janet grinned. "Okay."

"She has a really small red maple leaf tattooed on her left hip," Dawn whispered

Janet's eyes widened. "Aliki-sobersides-Pateas has a tattoo!" Dawn nodded. "Well, still waters *do* run deep!"

"Mommy, we caught a frog! Can I keep it?" Reb's called excitedly from down by the river.

Janet rolled her eyes, and the two women got up. "No, sweetheart. You have to leave the frog here so that it can find its way home. But tonight I'll give you your crayons and some paper, and you can draw me a really nice picture of your frog."

It was very late in the evening. Ari and Joan had said good night and Ari had left to drive Joan home. The kids had been put to bed, Baba and Nick had gone out to the barns to do their nightly check, and the four women finally had a chance to talk about Aliki's consult.

"You mean someone offed a duck?" Robbie laughed incredulously.

Aliki smiled tolerantly. "It appears so. Hard to tell."

"What do you think, Aliki?" Dawn sat beside her partner.

"I'm not sure what I think. Counting beaks, there were at least seven ducks killed and burnt. Looking at the weathering and drying of the bone, I suspect that they were killed one at a time over...perhaps a year or so. Strange."

Janet paled and looked distressed. "They were dead, weren't they? I mean, this wasn't some really sick mind—"

"The damage to the bones of the vertebrae would indicate to me that they most likely had their necks wrung, then they were soaked in something and torched. The feathers and skin burnt off, and the remaining tissue was left to rot or be gnawed at by scavengers."

"It wasn't someone's barbecue pit?" Dawn suggested.

Aliki considered. "I don't think so. It was more of a sacrifice. Would the Salish do anything like this?"

"Gifts of food are left to appease the spirits, but they are tokens, nor do they burn their offerings," Dawn supplied.

"What about when the native people burn sweetgrass or tobacco?" Robbie asked. "The legends Janet tells are always full of stories about burning sweetgrass or smoking tobacco."

"True," Janet agreed. "But it is not the same thing. The sweetgrass is used in a manner similar to incense in the Catholic Church, and the tobacco is part of establishing a link, either politically or spiritually. It is not sacrifice in the sense that one would find it in the Old Testament."

Dawn shifted on the couch so that she could see Aliki better. "Do you think there is someone who is practising some strange religion of their own creation?"

Aliki shook her head. "We have many religions in Canada. This might be as simple as a ritual that we are not familiar with that has been brought to the area by an immigrant. If that is the case, it will be a matter of tracking down the perpetrator and asking the SPCA to check to make sure that these are domesticated birds and that they have not been tortured. We don't want duck hunting going on out of season or in some illegal manner. It could also be just a lone crackpot who is very misguided, in which case it will probably end up in the hands of social services."

"What if it's more than that?" Robbie asked. "Magic or voodoo or something."

Aliki shrugged. "Citizens have the right to practise their faith any way they wish, as long as no law is broken. If the ducks are domesticated, bought legally, and killed humanely and if no one has been threatened by the action, then it is not the business of the police."

"But you don't think so, do you?" Robbie persisted.

Aliki weighed her words carefully. "I think it bears some looking into."

Robbie beamed. "When do we start?"

"*We* do not start," Aliki stated emphatically. "First, you are not an officer of the law, and second, this is a local police matter and not our business."

"You were called in to help with the case. And I'm your sister and right-hand support system."

"I was called in to ID bones, *not* to get involved in this case, and you are not so much a support system as you are a pain the butt." Aliki snorted, rolling her eyes in feigned frustration.

Robbie folded her arms. "Be difficult, Ms. I've-got-a-badge-and-you-don't. Just don't expect me to bail you out when you find yourself among the ducks on some weirdo's altar."

Aliki waited until she heard Dawn's shower running, then she slipped the small black velvet case from a side pocket of her suitcase. She opened it up to look at the beautiful diamond engagement ring. She had been putting money aside for it all year; she had started before she came out West over a year ago. In spite of her not seeing Dawn and wondering if they weren't meant to be together, she continued to grow her nest egg for a ring. It had cost her a small fortune, but it would be worth it. It was important to her to give Dawn a ring that expressed her love and that didn't look shabby next to the rock that Robbie had given Janet. Not that Dawn would care, she wouldn't, but Aliki needed to feel that Dawn was not being short-changed by marrying her.

Aliki picked it up from the jewellers before they left on this trip and didn't want to leave it behind. Sometime during the holiday she would give it to Dawn. That thought sent an icy chill through her. Not that she didn't love Dawn and Mac. Hell, they had lived together for nearly a year. It was just the responsibility of thinking of some romantic way to make the moment special for her partner. Aliki knew she wasn't very good at that sort of thing. She was going to have to think of something soon.

She put the ring away and went to knock on the bathroom door.

"Need help drying off?" she asked, opening the door to see the naked form of her lover standing in a swirl of mist. As her eyes traveled slowly over the inviting curves, a raw need rushed to her loins.

Dawn smiled and walked toward her, hesitating only to slip Aliki's black housecoat from her shoulders. Flesh met flesh, and a shudder of desire coursed through them both. Aliki picked Dawn up in her arms, gasping as the smaller woman ran her fingers wickedly over Aliki's nipples. The kiss that followed was long and deep as Aliki carried Dawn to their bed.

The next morning, Robbie watched from the window as Ryan stepped from the woods, looked around to see if anyone was watching, and then, clutching her small knapsack to her, bolted for the house. Enveloped in worry, she didn't hear Janet approach until she felt arms around her.

"What's up, lover? You look deep in thought."

"I'm worried about Ryan. There's something on her mind, and she keeps disappearing into the woods," Robbie muttered.

"I've been worried, too." Janet moved around to look into her partner's face. "What have you noticed?"

"She's been distant since I got back from England, and since we've been here, she has gotten up early each morning and disappeared into the woods with a knapsack. At first I didn't think I should interfere, but I'm getting worried. Do you think I should follow her and see what's up? I don't want to be an interfering mother but...well...Ryan has a way of getting in trouble."

Janet smiled softly and pulled Robbie over to sit on the edge of the bed with her. "She is an olive off the same tree, that's for sure."

Robbie smiled at the old family joke. Robbie's fiery and moody personality made her very difficult to get to know and to deal with at times.

"I need to talk to you about Ryan, but first I need you to promise that you won't overreact."

The colour drained from Robbie's face, and in one startling movement she was on her feet. "What the hell is going on?"

Janet raised an eyebrow in warning. "Probably nothing, but if you charge in with that attitude there will be a problem. Now sit down, and let's talk through this."

Robbie bit her lip and then sheepishly sat down beside her wife. Only Janet could stand up to her and get away with it. Robbie trusted Janet completely.

"You're right, there is something going on, and it has been for about six months now," Janet said. Robbie's expression changed to one of shock and apprehension.

"Ryan has been leaving school early and driving somewhere. I don't know where she's going, but it uses up an extra tank of gas each week. Lou down at the garage mentioned it to me."

"Shit." Robbie's stomach tied itself into knots. Maybe Aliki had been right, maybe Ryan did have a secret boyfriend...lover... The word sent a shiver down Robbie's spine. Ryan was just a kid.

"There is something else, too." Janet took Robbie's hand. "She withdrew five thousand dollars from the emergency account you set up for her."

Robbie's features convulsed with anger, and she surged to her feet, dragging Janet with her as the smaller woman held on for dear life.

"What!" Robbie snapped. "She knows very well that is supposed to be emergency money for her in case something goes wrong and she needs to take some action if you and I are not around."

"Hold it." Janet's voice was calm, but it held a note of warning. "Ryan is a good kid, and I'm sure there is a logical explanation for what is going on in her life. She just doesn't want to share it."

"We're her parents, and she is just a little kid," Robbie growled.

"She's a teenager and a very insecure one at times. We need to talk to her, but we need to do it in a way that is going to provide positive guidance, not prompt resentment."

"I won't yell; I'll just chain her to my wrist until she confesses," Robbie suggested with irritated humour.

Janet laughed. "I was thinking more that we tell her what we know and ask her to be open with us."

"A frontal attack." Robbie smiled, regaining some of her typical good nature. "I'm all for that."

Janet stood fast as the impulsive director made for the door. "Let's set the ground rules first. No yelling."

"No yelling," Robbie agreed.

"No overreacting in any way," Janet clarified.

Robbie considered. "Does that mean that locking her in her bedroom closet until she is thirty-five is out?"

"Yes." Janet snorted, loving her partner and understanding that Robbie's silly humour covered a really deep love and concern for their daughter.

"Okay, but I am reserving the right for a dawn execution if necessary."

They found Ryan in her room. The teen looked up guiltily as she quickly stuffed papers into her suitcase.

"Hi, kid. Listen, your parents here need some reassurance," Robbie joked. "Can we come in?"

Ryan forced a laugh. "Whatever it is, I didn't do it, and I wasn't there."

Robbie folded her arms and looked at her daughter from under arched eyebrows. Ryan had her mother's features, strong, classic lines, but strangely her colouring was more like Janet's, even though they were not related by blood. The blond hair and green eyes had come from her father.

Looking at her daughter, Robbie recalled the hellish time a few years earlier when a lab accident had almost taken her daughter's life. Sitting by her child's unconscious form, Robbie had realized how much they had both missed by her keeping her identity a secret from her daughter. The thought of that terrible time fed Robbie's insecurity, and to Ryan and Janet's surprise, instead of making some witty retort, she suddenly dropped the cocky attitude, stepped forward, and wrapped her daughter in her arms. "You mean the world to me," she whispered into her daughter's thick curls.

"Hey, Mom, it's okay, honest," Ryan stammered, hugging her mother tightly.

She wished, not for the first time, that people could know how special her mom really was. It had not been easy at first. She had harboured a lot of resentment against the mother who had paid to have her raised instead of raising her herself. Now she knew that Robbie had only been trying to protect her. That's what made her problem so difficult. The last person in the world she wanted to disappoint was her mother.

"Your other mom and I have heard things, seen things. We haven't been spying, Ryan, but you know what small towns are like, especially Bartlett. We know you have been leaving school early and driving somewhere a few times a week. We know you took five thousand out of your emergency fund, and we know that you take a knapsack and disappear early in the mornings, even here. We're worried because we don't know what's going on and how to protect you. A...and I guess we're a little hurt that whatever you're up to, you don't feel comfortable sharing it with us."

Way to go, Robbie! Janet thought. Her partner, for all her insecurities and often unorthodox methods, was a really good mother.

Robbie felt her daughter stiffen in her arms and pull back, and she reluctantly let her go. Ryan paced around the room, obviously considering what to do next. Janet pulled Robbie's hand and indicated that they should sit down. It was a less threatening position, and yet it sent the message that they meant to stay until they had gotten some answers.

Ryan stopped and looked at them. She licked her lips and swallowed hard. She opened her mouth to speak, closed it, and then went to her suitcase, from which she withdrew a violin case. With reverence, she placed it on the bed and opened it to take out a worn instrument. "I spent the money on this. I'm sorry, Mom, I know that is not what the money is for, but it came on the market, and it is a really good instrument for the price. I...I've been taking lessons."

She saw Janet's eyes fill with understanding and compassion. Her mother's eyes widened with surprise and confusion.

"So you're taking music lessons. That's cool. Why didn't you just tell us?" Robbie grumbled.

Ryan looked down at the instrument. It was plain and worn, a warm honey colour. She carefully packed it away again, giving herself time to brace herself before telling the rest to her mother. "It's not just a matter of learning to play an instrument, Mom. I love it. I...I might want to make it my career."

There was silence in the room. Ryan looked at the floor, not wanting to look at the disappointment in her mom's eyes. Janet stole a sideways look at her partner, who had stiffened beside her. She could see Robbie's jaw working with emotion.

Finally, she managed, "I see. Well, okay, I guess you need to explore this avenue, like you want to learn about film. Okay, it's good to be diversified. Ahh, you are not thinking of dropping out of school or anything, are you?"

"No, Mom. But I might take a degree in music," Ryan stated bravely.

"Oh," Robbie said weakly. "From whom are you taking lessons?"

"Mr. Scott, the music teacher, recommended a retired musician from the Toronto Symphony, Alex Fielding. He used to play first violin." Ryan beamed. "Alex said that if I practice, I'll be far better than he ever was."

"I guess you'd better practice, then." Robbie smiled weakly. "Are you past the cat-squeak stage?"

"Mom! Of course, geez." Ryan was relieved that things were going so well.

"In that case, you'd better practise in the house and not out in the bush. You could traumatize the squirrels and get us in trouble with the forest rangers."

Robbie stood, and Janet followed her partner's lead. She knew the signs. Robbie was *very* upset.

Ryan was so relieved that things had gone well that she had missed the signs at first. She hugged both her moms with feeling "You two are the greatest!"

Robbie hugged her child closely, mumbling the appropriate words and walked out of the room.

Ryan looked at her adopted mom in surprise. "She's really pissed, isn't she?" the teen asked in worry.

Janet gave Ryan's hand a squeeze. "More shocked. Give her time; she'll be fine with it. You know that she will be your biggest fan. Ahh, you can play that thing, huh?" Janet smiled, knowing that Ryan was brilliant at most things she took on. Robbie didn't fully appreciate just how bright her daughter was.

"Yeah, I'm getting pretty good." Ryan blushed. That was not a statement she would feel comfortable making to many people, but her second mom had a way about her that made Ryan feel safe.

Janet found Robbie in the garden. "How are you doing, hon?"

"First, she wanted to go into film, now it's the damn fiddle." Robbie paced in agitation. "What's wrong with science?"

"A career in science is what *you* wanted for your life, Robbie. It might not be what Ryan wants. You just have to accept that."

For a second, Janet hesitated and then proceeded with caution. "Do you remember when you first brought Ryan home and I went over her CAT test results with you?"

"Of course I do. That's why I'm so worried about her future. She is bright, and she should be using that intelligence, not playing the damn fiddle."

Janet sat down on a rustic wooden bench and patted the spot beside her. Reluctantly, Robbie joined her. "First, let's not call it a damn fiddle. Ryan wants to play the violin, and music is a very difficult and exacting profession that requires skill, intelligence, and passion. In your more reasonable moments, you are well aware of that." Janet gave Robbie a playful nudge with her shoulder. She was relieved to see the blush rise in Robbie's face. She was going to be reasonable.

"I don't think you realize just how bright Ryan is. She is not going to be satisfied with one focus in her life, Robbie. I think you'll find that she will jump from one interest to another, achieving success in many of them before she finds her life's passion. You need to support her in that process of discovery and not make her feel guilty."

"I was good about it," Robbie protested.

"You were wonderful about it," Janet agreed, leaning over to give her lover a kiss on the cheek. "Keep it up, okay? Ryan needs you. You might not be aware of this, but Ryan adores you and wants so very much to please you."

Robbie sighed. "This raising a kid is really hard. Neither Ryan nor Reb will ever have to worry about money, but I want them to have careers and feel like they have purpose and direction in their lives."

"I know, darling, but don't push too hard. The Williams name is very difficult to live up to."

Robbie snorted. "It seems she doesn't have to. Neither Ryan nor I are real Williamses."

"Does that bother you?" Janet asked, looking at her partner with concern.

"I don't know....it's hard. I didn't respect my father. I hated him after I found out what he'd done to Elizabeth and Billy. It's just, I don't know...your identity, I guess. It's hard to readjust after all these years."

"Baba is pretty special, isn't he?" Janet said carefully, trying to help her partner toward a comfort level with her biological relatives.

"Yeah, he is. I like my brothers, too. Ari and Joan have really made us welcome, and Nick is all right."

"It will be good for our children to have these family ties. They need a bit of so-called normalcy in their lives."

"Yeah." Robbie smiled, but there was more concern than happiness reflected in those marvellous blue eyes.

Ari walked along the river in the early morning light, Aliki at his side. "Nick is really into this stuff, Aliki. Baba thinks it's good. You know he is of the old school that believes religion can only be a positive influence in a person's life. I think that can be so, but Nick was a pretty good guy to start with. Baba and you brought us up to know right from wrong and to be tolerant of others. I don't like the way he has started to draw lines in the sand. He...ah...he's made a few comments about trying to help you and Dawn see a better way," he finished awkwardly.

Serious eyes the colour of glacial ice snapped up and flared with anger. "He's already tried to make me see the errors of my ways. Unfortunately for him, he also admitted to preaching to Dawn. We got into a fight, and I bruised some of his muscles for him. I hope that teaches him to keep his views to himself."

Ari laughed. "So that's how he got the bruises. He should have known better than to take you on. He told me he'd run into some trouble in the barn. I guess he did. I doubt your reminder will make him stop, though, Aliki. He's seen the light, and it appears that he is beyond reason." Ari sighed in annoyance.

"Shit."

"It's worse than that. He wants to divide up our business interests because he wants to give twenty percent of everything to his church. Says that they need the money to do good, and he has far more than he will ever need. Up to now, we've just taken a salary from the business like everyone else in the company, and the rest has been turned back into development, investment, and diversification. I'm not going to argue that he hasn't a right to half of everything; I just don't want him to do something he'll regret later."

Aliki listened moodily, kicking a stone with her foot as she walked. "You tried talking to him?"

Ari snorted. "You know Nick; he's got the Pateas stubbornness. I'm delaying. I'm putting up as many roadblocks as I can to the legalities, hoping he'll come to his senses."

She shook her head. "How did he get caught up in this group to start with?"

"Nick was thinking pretty seriously about marrying Sally. This spring, they were supposed to go out to the dance at the Lions' Hall. Sally said she couldn't go, that she had made other plans. Anyway, Nick decided to go stag and walked in to find her dancing with some cowboy from Fox Creek way. The shit hit the fan, and our brother got religion."

"Oh, boy! I thought he and Sally were an item. I can see why he was shook up."

"I guess it was all a misunderstanding, but you know Nick when he gets his back up. He can be impossible. He was embarrassed in front of everyone, and he's really pissed."

"What do you know about the Reformed Western Church?"

"Seems okay. They're one of the groups that broke from the United Church of Canada when they decided that homosexuals could be ministers." Ari stopped and stared off into the distance as he considered. "They aren't some radical fringe or anything, just conservative and traditional in their outlook, like most Protestant churches. Joan and I have gone a few times with Nick. It's just your regular service. They have quite a dynamic minister, Paul Jarvis. He seems an all right sort of guy. Plays on the Old Timers hockey team. Has degrees in anthropology and world religions. He's popular in town, and the congregation is growing."

Looking at the ground, Aliki frowned. "I'll try not to let Nick get to me, but if he makes comments in front of Dawn or Mac there is going to be hell to pay. I won't tolerate my family being upset."

"I told him to keep his views to himself, but you know Nick; fools rush in where angels fear to tread."

Aliki snorted. "He is a great guy, but as Baba says, he hasn't got the sense that God gave a billy goat."

His laugh trailing behind him, Ari headed over to the ranch office while Aliki doubled back to the ranch house. Baba had taken the Williams family and Mac out to his favourite fishing hole, and that left Dawn and Aliki free for a few hours.

She trotted up the steps of the house and was greeted with a big kiss. "Hey, slugger, guess what? We have a few hours to ourselves."

Aliki held Dawn tightly in her arms. "Mmmm, nice. You want to do something?"

"What?" Dawn murmured, dropping soft kisses on her lover's throat.

"You want to hike up and see the duck sacrifice site while Baba is keeping Robbie out of my hair?" Aliki asked excitedly.

Dawn snorted and then laughed, giving her confused partner a playful push. "Pateas, you have to be the last of the great romantics."

Aliki blushed deeply as she realized what she had done. "I...er...I mean..."

"It's okay, sweetheart, I understand where thousands wouldn't. You need to see this site, and now is a good time. Give me five minutes to grab a few things, and we'll be on our way."

Aliki looked flustered but relieved and bent to place a gentle kiss on Dawn's lips. "Thanks," she said with sincerity.

Dawn gave her a slap on the backside. "This isn't over. You owe me," Dawn warned, and Aliki blushed and smiled like a lovesick goof.

They drove as far as they could and then hiked in to the site. There wasn't much to see. A table of rock formed a small lookout over a hanging valley. It was a pretty spot but certainly not sinister. They found a rocky ledge where the birds had been burnt. There were no other signs, symbols, or marks that would indicate what had gone on there. The vegetation around had been badly trampled, however, indicating that a goodly crowd of people came frequently to the site.

"How was the site found?" Dawn asked, looking out over the valley below.

"A geologist came across it while doing a mineral survey. He thought that there might have been some illegal hunting going on so he reported it." She glanced around disinterestedly, then hesitated and sniffed the air, moving about the clearing and brushing back the vegetation. She sniffed again.

Dawn was suddenly alert. "What is it, Aliki? What do you smell?"

"Death," Aliki muttered. She pushed through some underbrush to see a decomposed hand sticking out of the earth where some animal had been digging.

Part 3

The RCMP detachment in Swan Hills consisted of Sergeant Brad Nicholson and two constables. Nicholson was glad to be able to turn the responsibility of the crime scene over to Inspector Pateas. Aliki, on the other hand, was not glad.

She waited with the remains until Dawn could drive into town and bring Nicholson back out. At Aliki's request, Nicholson called for the crime scene team to be sent out from Edmonton. It was a long wait. After sending Dawn back to the ranch, Aliki helped Nicholson seal off the area.

It was well into the afternoon by the time the Edmonton team arrived and well into the night before the decomposed body was fully excavated from its shallow grave and bagged for shipping to the forensic labs in Edmonton.

"Well?" Andy Chen asked as he leaned on a squad car and lit a cigarette. The police floodlights highlighted his tired face.

Aliki raised an eyebrow. "That's your job."

Chen snorted. He had known Pateas for a number of years. In Canada, homicide specialists were a small group and their members clannish. "That body is more skeleton than tissue, and I'm standing with the best bone specialist around. Cut me some slack here, Pateas."

Not wanting to get involved in this case if she could avoid it, Aliki shrugged. She was there for her brother's wedding and hopefully to get up enough nerve to give Dawn an engagement ring. The last thing she needed was to get involved in a murder case. "I observed what you observed. The deceased is most likely female. A guess would put her in her late twenties, early thirties. Cause of death was most likely strangulation, seeing that the cord is still around her neck. She was a dyed blonde, most likely Caucasian, and on the taller side for a woman."

Chen looked at her sourly. "Well, I did figure out the body was probably female. I need you to come to Edmonton and examine the bones after they are cleaned up. Will you?"

Aliki sighed. She had been afraid of that. "The chief coroner would have to approve. I'd be working out of district," Aliki observed, making a last ditch attempt to stay out of the case.

"I'll get their approval. Give me a number where I can reach you, and I'll be in touch." Chen smiled. "You live around here, huh?"

"I was raised on a ranch nearby. My home is in the East now," Aliki stated firmly as she punched the ranch number into the palmtop that Chen handed her.

"Rotten luck. No one should have to live in the East," Chen observed, finishing his cigarette and dropping the butt to grind under his shoe.

Aliki shook her head at the regional loyalty that was so much a part of the Canadian mentality. She said her goodbyes, and Nicholson gave her a ride back to the ranch. To Aliki's annoyance, he had no trouble at all finding the Pateas driveway.

"It's hard to find this damn driveway in the dark," she complained.

Nicholson shrugged. "Not that I come up here all that much, but I've never had a problem. Everyone knows it's there."

It was four in the morning when Aliki crept into the bedroom. "Hi, sweetheart," Dawn whispered. "You okay?"

"Yeah, just tired. Wait 'til I have a good shower, and then I'll give you a morning kiss." The smell of death always seemed to cling to her long after she had left a scene. Aliki knew it was mostly a psychological response, but she didn't like to touch her family until she'd had a long scrub under a hot shower.

Some time later, just as the pink of dawn began to tint the sky, she slipped under the covers beside her lover.

"Long night, huh?" Dawn observed, holding her partner and kissing Aliki's temple.

"Yeah, I'm going to have to go down to Edmonton in a few days and have a look at the remains," Aliki groused.

"I figured that." Dawn smiled. "Do you have any—"

"Aliki? Dawn? You up?" came Robbie's excited whisper from outside the door.

"Not for long. Go away," Aliki responded, rolling her eyes.

The door opened, and Robbie trotted in, curling up on the end of their bed. "Okay, tell me all about it," Aliki's sister demanded.

Dawn laughed, and Aliki blushed. "Robbie, I am in bed...with Dawn... Do you mind!"

"No, I don't mind," came the cheeky response.

"I'm sorry. I was asleep, and she escaped," Janet declared, as she hurried into the room doing up her housecoat.

Robbie smiled. "Hey, you're just in time. Aliki is going to tell us all about it."

"Hi, Mom. Hi, Aunt Aliki. Ryan and I heard your voices, so we thought we'd come and find out what happened," Mac explained as she and Ryan came trotting in.

"Are we sleeping in a bus station here?" Aliki asked, thumping back against the pillow in exasperation.

"Okay, everyone is here. Tell us all about it," Robbie demanded impatiently.

"It's a police investigation and confidential information," Aliki protested.

Robbie looked around the group of eager faces. "We won't tell," she promised, making room for Janet to curl up beside her.

The recounting of the events took some time, and eventually they all ended up downstairs, discussing possible theories over an early morning breakfast.

"Does Sergeant Nicholson have any open missing persons cases?" Mac asked, by now being quite familiar with the process that the police went through when a body was found.

"Three," Aliki said. "A middle-aged man, who probably left his wife and ran off with a waitress half his age. A seventeen-year-old, who ran away from home, and a twenty-eight-year-old secretary who didn't meet her boyfriend after work like she was supposed to."

"It could be her," mused Robbie.

"Maybe, maybe not." Aliki warmed to her topic. "Bones are quite varied and can be misleading. I would need to do a close examination and point check to verify my initial conclusions. And then there is no guarantee that these remains are those of the missing woman. The victim could have been murdered anywhere and simply buried out where we found her."

"Then it is a murder, Aunt Aliki?" Ryan asked, helping herself to another piece of toast.

"Hmmm, I think so. That's a hard call. There's a cord around her neck so she probably died by strangulation. It could be a suicide or foreplay that went terribly wrong. She surely didn't bury herself," Aliki mused sleepily, rubbing her face.

"Freaky," Ryan commented.

"I think Aliki needs some sleep, now," Dawn observed. "Come on, you," she said, giving her partner's shoulder a gentle shake.

Janet was immediately supportive. "Good idea." Then she turned to the others. "And you lot can help me clean up this mess."

Baba sat at the kitchen table scowling as Aliki worked at preparing lunch. Janet and Dawn had taken the girls to town, and Robbie and Reb were over at the ranch office using their Internet hook-up. "I don't like it, Aliki. You have no right bringing murder to the ranch, especially when your brother is getting married. How does that look? We will not seem respectable."

Aliki gave her father a hard look. "I had nothing to do with the killing, and there is nothing wrong with police work," she stated firmly.

Baba sulked and waggled his hand to indicate he felt there were two sides to that argument. Then he went off on a new tangent. "When are you going to marry Dawn? It is not right, you living with her. What will my Mac think? You set a bad example."

Aliki put down the pan with a little more force than she had intended and turned to look at her father. "We are engaged; we will get married when we are ready," she snapped.

Her father was not a man to be put off if he had something on his mind. "What you wait for?"

Aliki sighed and looked around to make sure no one was near before answering. "I needed to give her a nice ring. She deserves the best. I had to save," she confessed awkwardly.

Baba looked surprised. "Dawn, she wants a big ring like Janet's?"

Aliki blushed. "No. I...I just...I'm the only one without a lot of money. I don't want her to regret that she made a commitment to me."

He snorted in disgust and picked up his extra big coffee mug and had a sip. Aliki made the best coffee, and he had missed it. "This, I do not think would happen. Dawn is not like that. Besides, you are an important person, even if you do work for the police," the older man insisted. "You are a good catch."

Undeniably pleased with her father's approval, she was laughing as she went back to preparing lunch.

"While we're in town, I think we should make a visit to Reverend Jarvis," Dawn suggested as she watched her daughter leaving the restaurant with Ryan in tow. Having done the stores and had lunch out with their moms, the two girls were now heading off on their own to see some of the sights in town. "We won't be meeting up with the girls for another few hours."

"Won't Aliki be annoyed if we interfere?" Janet asked because she felt she had to. In reality, she was quite excited about going to see Jarvis.

"Yeah, but she's getting used to it." Dawn laughed. "Besides, we have a chance of getting away with it. If Aliki or Robbie tried to find out anything, they would be in a sad amount of trouble."

Janet nodded. Neither of their partners was known for her subtlety of speech. "But why just Jarvis?"

Dawn considered. "The other three congregations in town have older leaders who have been there for years. Jarvis is the new boy on the block. Also, he is younger. He is more likely to hear from the teenagers what's going on. It is a good starting place."

The two women paid the bill and headed out. They walked up the street and found the small manse where Reverend Paul Jarvis lived next to the Reformed Western Church. "I had a little talk with Nick about his church and the minister the other day. It seems that Jarvis has never preached against homosexuality in his services, but of course, there are those more militant members of the congregation that see it as the foremost reason for their break with the United Church of Canada," Dawn related.

"Jarvis chose to make that break, too, and head the Reformed Western Church. That rather indicates that he holds the same views," Janet pointed out.

Dawn cocked her head as she considered. "Maybe, maybe not. According to Nick, Paul Jarvis is in his late thirties and has never married. It could be that he is waiting for someone special to share the responsibility of his calling, or it could be that he is firmly in the closet."

Janet sighed in disgust. "Some of the worst gay bashers are those who can't admit that they have the same orientation."

"How do you think we should handle this?" Dawn whispered as they started up the walk.

"Honesty. Follow my lead," Janet said as she knocked on the door.

A face appeared from around the side of the house. "Oh, hello there. I'm back here in the garden, tying up some fencing with a bit of cord. It's part of my endless battle against Benjamin Bunny and his ravenous friends." The good-looking man came around the edge of the house, jamming some twine into his pocket and pulling off his work gloves. "I'm Paul Jarvis. How can I help you?"

"Hi Paul, I'm Janet Williams, and this is Dawn Freeman," Janet explained with a smile. "We just wondered if we could have a word with you about Ari Pateas' wedding?"

"Ari and Joan? I thought they were members of the Anglican Church, like Georgeos. They have been out to a few services with Nick, though. Come on around back. I put in a nice little patio out there last fall, and the plants have taken well. You're in luck, Mrs. Farley has sent over a plate of her famous chocolate chip cookies. I'll get the coffee on." He led them around to white wicker chairs on a flagstone patio in the shade of an enormous old cedar tree.

"We don't want to intrude if you have work to do," Dawn demurred.

"Nonsense. I was just wishing for an excuse to take a break and have coffee and cookies, and the good Lord has provided." Jarvis laughed. "Make yourself at home, and I'll be right back."

Dawn looked around. The garden was lovely, and the view beyond of the Swan Hills was wonderful. Over to one side was a splendid vegetable garden that was in the process of being fenced in with chicken wire. "He's really put a lot of work into this place. When the McDonalds were here, the backyard was just patchy grass and baby toys."

"He seems really nice," Janet said, leaning back in the comfy chair with a sigh.

"Well, if we get Violet Farley's chocolate cookies out of the deal, it won't be a wasted trip. They are the best."

A few minutes later, Jarvis returned with a tray holding three mugs of coffee, milk and sugar, and a large plate of cookies.

"Dig in, ladies, and then tell me what I can do for you." Jarvis took a mug from the table, picked out a cookie, and settled himself in a garden chair.

"Paul, you might have heard about my marriage to Robbie Williams," Janet opened.

If Jarvis was uncomfortable with the subject, he gave no indication. Instead, he laughed. "I think the world heard about the marriage. It really made front page news."

Janet smiled wearily. "There are disadvantages to marrying the woman who is the number one box office star," she said with a sigh. "What you might not know is that Dawn here is engaged to Robbie's half-sister, Aliki Pateas."

"Yes, Nick has talked to me about his sister and Dawn." His concern was apparent in his voice.

"He has also talked to us," Janet said, putting down her coffee mug, "and we have taken some offence."

Jarvis sighed. "Oh, dear. I am well aware of Nick's views. I have to tell you, ladies, that although I am not as militant about it, his views are not much different than mine. I am sorry, however, if he has spoilt this important family reunion by expressing his disapproval. He is...aah...enthusiastic about his faith at the moment, which is good, but he hasn't yet learned that condemnation does not bring people to a knowledge of the faith."

"We wonder, then, where he got his intolerance, because he certainly wasn't raised to be a bigot," Dawn persisted, perhaps more sharply than she should have.

He frowned. "There are members of the congregation that take a pretty hard line. You have to remember that we are a breakaway church, and the rift caused some very deep feelings. I know that Nick has been working out at our retreat and that he mixes with members who are very firm in their faith. Would you like me to talk to Nick?"

Dawn looked Jarvis straight in the eye. "That depends on what you're going to say to him."

The minister put his mug down carefully on the tray and then looked at each of his visitors. "I cannot and will not approve of your lifestyle, but I also do not believe that it is my right to judge you. That is the prerogative of God. If either of you wish to seek counseling, I would be glad to help you come to a better understanding of God's plan, but I am not here to find fault nor to condemn, and I am disappointed in the attitude that Nick has taken. I can talk to him about this."

"Thank you, we'd appreciate that." Janet stood up.

"Where is your retreat?" Dawn asked, as she stood along with Jarvis.

"Up on Pine Ridge, the Myrdals' old hunting camp. Do you know it?"

"Yes. I knew the family. They were of Icelandic descent. My uncle used to buy lumber from their mill sometimes. I've been to their hunt camp once or twice. Where are they now?"

"I heard that their daughter married a schoolteacher in Calgary, and they decided to sell out and retire down there," he responded conversationally as he walked them around to the front of the house.

"What did you think?" Janet asked afterwards as they walked down the street to meet the girls at the library.

"I think he is either quite an honest and reasonable Christian or one hell of a good actor." Dawn looked thoughtfully off into the distance.

"Yeah, I'm not sure that got us anywhere," Janet confessed. "I'd like to know whether Paul Jarvis is what he seems, or if we just got stonewalled."

"We'd better go for stamps, then," Dawn concluded, picking up the pace. "Rita Sage is better than the *Who's Who* — far more detailed and always up to date on the latest gossip."

Trusting Dawn's judgment, Janet followed along. They crossed the street and went down a block before entering the red brick post office.

"Here you go, Ted, a postcard from your sister in Florida. It's about time she wrote; she's been down there nearly a month. Says the weather is fine but Jerry still has that cold," Rita announced, handing over the postcard. "And I see you got your water bill. Open it up here, Ted, and let me see what you were charged. My bill is up nearly seven dollars, and as I said to Mabel, I haven't used any more water than I did last month, so what am I paying for?"

"There's been a hike in the water prices, I reckon," Ted suggested, tearing open his bill and dutifully handing it over to Rita.

"Nope, they gotta announce that after they get it approved by the government, so I'd know. Well, your bill looks about right. I'm going to have to get after them. I think they made a mistake."

"Could be. I'll see ya around," Ted said, taking his opened bill and previously read postcard and heading for the door.

Dawn smiled as she stepped up to the counter. "Hi, Rita."

"Dawn! Well, you're a sight for sore eyes! I read your books. Oh, I wish I had them here for you to sign," Rita rambled. "I hear Robbie Williams and her...aah...partner are up at the ranch. I missed out on getting her autograph, too. She was over at the police station the other day, but I was working."

Seeing her opening, Dawn quickly inserted, "If you bring the books in, the next time I'm in town I'll pop in and sign them. Rita, this is Janet Williams, Robbie's wife."

"Oh. Bless me!" Rita laughed. "And me speaking of the devil. Nice to meet you, Janet." She leaned over as far as her immense bulk would allow and asked in a stage whisper, "Does she really have a tattoo of a red dragon on her breast, like in the movie?"

Janet kept a straight face. "I can honestly say, from intense personal research, that Robbie Williams does not have a tattoo anywhere on her body." She also knew how to ingratiate herself with the postmaster. "I will see that she comes in and gives you an autograph, and you can verify that with her."

Rita roared with laughter. "Well, aren't you the one! Thanks. I'm here each day except weekends. Wait 'til I tell the girls down at the hair-dressing parlour! Dawn, how are Ari's wedding plans coming along?"

"Fine, Rita. We were just talking to Paul Jarvis. He seems like a nice chap. Good looking, too. I'm surprised that he isn't married."

"Well, there are some in town that certainly would agree with you. Now Stella Picaski did her best to catch him last year, but he wouldn't have nothing of it. Not that I could blame him. Stella is nice enough to look at, but she don't have an ounce of common sense." Again Rita leaned forward and whispered loudly enough to be heard for several blocks. "She was a bit of a tramp when she lived down in Calgary with that Billy Picaski."

"Isn't she the one whose boyfriend reported that she'd disappeared?" Dawn asked, trying to sound only mildly interested.

"Jed Casse. That's right. He still insists that something happened to her. He don't want to admit she was just usin' him, because his mother warned him 'bout her. Stella always was a bit wild. Mind you, she settled down a bit once she took to the religion, but that didn't stop her from putting the moves on Reverend Jarvis. Knew each other, they did, down in Calgary. Plain as the nose on your face what she was up to. I'm not surprised that Jed Casse couldn't see it. He's a nice boy is Jed, but a bit of a slow thinker. Good with his hands, though. He can fix anything."

"Well, people are funny. I don't think Stella had any family around here, did she?" Dawn asked.

"Sure she did. Vince Dandurand is her brother. That's why she moved back up to Swan Hills after she divorced that no good Billy. Why she ever got involved with that man, I'll never know. Them Picaskis all drank hard and turned mean. Nice enough when they're sober, mind."

"Could I have a pack of stamps, please, Rita?" Dawn didn't want it to seem as if she was interrogating the postmaster. Not that Rita seemed to mind at all. To her, the collection and distribution of gossip was as much a part of her job as handing out the mail.

"Here you go, hon. The price has gone up again. That's $5.80 for the pack of ten. Now if you ask me, it should be Vince Dandurand that should be after the police to find her, him being her brother and all holier-than-thou because he's an elder in that new church. It's his responsibility, eh? Blood's thicker than water, isn't it? Doesn't seem to give a fig that his sister's not been seen. Still I shouldn't be saying that. He's a good friend of your Nick's, he is, so there must be some good in him. To be fair, Ivy Marintette said she saw Stella getting into a car with Billy Picaski that night. Drunk, she was, according to Ivy. But Ivy's been a few bricks short of a full load all her life, so there's no tellin' if that's true."

"Well, thanks for the stamps, Rita. Please remember to bring your books in, and I'll bring Robbie in to give you a personal autograph," Dawn promised.

"Well, that would be something! Nice meeting you, Janet. You hold onto that one now. And watch that Peter Lanzlow. He was all over Robbie like a rash in that movie *Firebrand.*"

Janet laughed. "Nice meeting you, too, Rita, and thanks for the advice."

Janet shook her head as they left the post and hurried up the street to meet their daughters.

"Whew! That woman can talk!"

"She sure can," Dawn agreed, "but I think now we have some information to share with Aliki."

It was several days later that Aliki made the trip to Edmonton. The resident pathologist had examined the remains, and samples had been sent out to various labs, then the bones had gone through the process of being cleaned for Aliki's examination.

Aliki picked up her ID card with Andy Chen and met Dr. Ben Bernstein in the forensic lab.

"Dr. Pateas, nice to see you again. We met at the California Conference two years ago. Your paper on the effects of frost on bone was most helpful." Bernstein used one hand for handshakes while the other pushed his thick glasses back up his nose.

"Dr. Bernstein, good to see you again. I see you are chairing this year's symposium on recovery techniques. I hope to be in Chicago for the conference."

Chen moved restlessly at Aliki's side. He didn't want to stand there while two colleagues talked shop. Bernstein took the hint.

"Come this way. I had the bones laid out for you this morning. I'll show you where everything is and then leave you to your work."

After Bernstein had showed them around the lab, Aliki slipped into a lab coat, snapped a plastic safety shield down over her face, and pulled on a pair of latex gloves. The protective gear, in this case, was more to meet lab safety regulations than out of any fear of contamination. The cleaned bones had been carefully laid out in anatomical order on a metal table. Aliki nodded her appreciation at the good lab procedure.

"How long are you going to be?" Chen asked, sticking his hands in his pockets and looking at the bones with disinterest.

"I'll need at least the morning."

Chen sighed.

"I'll be back later then, after lunch." He hated coming in there. The place reeked of death with an overlay of disinfectant. The detective was eager to get out of the labs and have a smoke; he quickly departed before she could object.

Aliki pulled up a stool, picked up a tape measure, and started to calculate height. The lengths of the femur, tibia, and fibula bones indicated that the victim was 167 to 175 cm in height. The estimation was done using a formulae based on charts derived from some five thousand cadavers from American military casualties from the Korean War and World War II.

The examination of the teeth showed that the third molars were fully erupted, yet still firmly imbedded in the alveoli; that put the victim most likely in her twenties. This was confirmed by examining the skull. Aliki observed that the epiphyseal union was complete and yet there were no degenerative signs of old age.

She next turned her attention to the hipbones. The lateral flare of the iliac blades and the wide sacrum confirmed the indicators that Aliki had noted in the skull bones. The victim was female.

Next the scientist checked to see if the woman had ever given birth. She did not find the telltale dorsal pits near the symphyseal border of the pubi. It was unlikely that the woman had ever had a child.

Next came the very exacting examination of each bone, one by one, to establish time of death and possible cause. The hyoid bone, the U-shaped bone that formed the supporting structure of the larynx, was shattered. The cracked ends were still attached by the stylo-hyoid ligaments to the styloid process of the temporal. That sort of break was in keeping with a strangulation.

She found no other indications of violence. The damage to the bone made by gnawing animals seemed to have mostly occurred after weathering. This indicated that the body had been buried in the late fall, had frozen before there had been much deterioration, and had lain there all winter before the scavenger bugs and animals started their work in the decomposition process.

She had just started typing up her findings when Chen returned.

"What have you got?"

Aliki clicked on Save and then turned and leaned back in her chair to look at the detective. "The victim is a woman, between the ages of twenty and thirty, although my guess would be late twenties. It is unlikely that she has had children. She was somewhere between 167 and 175 centemetres in height, and suffered from lower back pain due to some worn discs. Probable cause of death was strangulation by hanging. There are no other signs of violence. If it wasn't for the fact that she was found in a shallow grave, my guess would be that the strangulation was a result of suicide or possible dangerous foreplay. She should be easy to ID from her dental records. There is a crown and several fillings. One other thing – the weathering would indicate that she was buried in the late fall."

"Yeah, the bug department agrees," Chen said, referring to the recovery and classification the entomologist unit would have done. "They didn't find first-generation larva, or something, so they figured the frost must have come right after she was buried."

"Do you have Stella Picaski's dental records?" Aliki asked, working her shoulders to get the kinks out. Leaning over examining tables for hours on end had taken its toll on her back.

"Yup, got them right here." Chen handed over a manila envelope. "They just came."

She carried the packet to the table, folded back the sheet so that only the skull was exposed, and propped the diagrams of Picaski's dental arch up on the sheet-covered pelvic girdle.

She slipped on gloves, picked up a dental pick, and started to make her entries of the dental arches of the deceased on a blank forensic record diagram. Half an hour's work proved conclusively that the skeletal remains were those of Stella Picaski.

"Looks like you've got a place to start in your investigation." Aliki handed the results to Chen.

"Start, nothing, we'll be making an arrest this afternoon. That coat she was lying on...it had the owner's name written on the clothing tag: the Reverend Paul Jarvis. Seems Stella had a thing for him. He was probably jealous of her other boyfriend." Chen sighed and shrugged.

Aliki frowned. "Andy, I wouldn't move too quickly on this one. I'm not convinced she was murdered."

"Why?" he asked sharply.

"Nothing I can put my figure on...it's just that you get to know after you have seen a lot of cases. This one lacks the violence, that's all."

Chen snorted. "And after she was sure she was dead, she dug a hole for herself, laid out her lover's coat as a bed, lay down, and pulled the dirt over. Don't think so, Aliki. This one's murder one. I'll hold off on laying a murder charge, but I am sure as hell going to hold Jarvis for questioning."

Hours later, after a long drive back to the ranch from Edmonton, Aliki crawled into bed beside Dawn. "You must be tired, love," Dawn whispered, snuggling close.

"Mmmm, not now. You feel so good. Have I told you yet today that I love you?" Aliki murmured as she kissed and nuzzled Dawn's ear.

Dawn kissed Aliki, allowing the kiss to lengthen and demonstrate her mounting passion. "How did it go in Edmonton?" she asked softly, knowing her lover always needed time to unwind after she had worked a case. Sometimes, Dawn would rather not know what her lover had seen and done, but she knew that talking about it helped Aliki to work through it.

"We got a positive ID. It's Stella all right. Strangled, most likely with the red cord that was around her neck." Aliki sighed, lying still in her partner's arms, then went on hesitantly. "The coat she was lying on belongs to the Reverend Jarvis. He is being taken in for questioning. Seems Stella was pretty open about her attraction to him."

"You aren't comfortable with that, are you?" Dawn asked, sensing her lover's unease.

"I think it is premature. It's nothing I can put my finger on; I'm just not convinced this was a violent crime. But she sure didn't bury herself, that's another consideration. Killers don't waste time with shallow graves. They usually find a hollow, dig it out a bit, drop in the body, and cover it up with the surrounding debris. This wasn't a deep grave, only enough to cover the body, but the body was laying out full length with her arms at her sides, and the grave had been lined with Jarvis' coat and her face covered with his scarf. It was...a burial of compassion, not violence. I just don't get it."

Dawn recognized the signs. Dr. Bates, Aliki's supervisor and friend had put it best. "Aliki," he would say, "is ten percent scientist, and ninety percent cop." Aliki bristled at the mere mention of her being anything but a forensic anthropologist, but in truth, she couldn't help becoming intrigued by police cases. "So what are you going to do?"

"Right now, I'm going to forget all about this case and make love to the beautiful woman beside me." Aliki's teasing kisses moved from the soft, scented warmth of Dawn's throat to the hard tips of her nipples, while one hand slid down to feel her lover's wet excitement. "Have you any idea how much I love you, need you?"

The smaller woman shivered with anticipation. "I love and need you, too," she murmured. Their lovemaking was tender, a physical work of art created by two souls bonded physically, emotionally, and spiritually. Later they slept safely in each other's arms, each trusting the other to guard her soul.

"Freaky, the minister did it!" Robbie exclaimed as the four women walked along the riverbank the next day.

"I don't believe it," Dawn stated unequivocally. "He's not the type. What do you think, Janet?"

"I think it's possible, but unlikely. If he did it, he is one very cool customer. He was perfectly relaxed with us and politely honest about his views. No, I can't see him killing in passion. Now, if he felt threatened or something...I don't know."

"What about this weird cult that Nick is involved in? Isn't that Jarvis' baby?" Robbie argued. "It's always the quiet, nice guy down the street who is the axe murderer."

Aliki snorted and shook her head. "Only in the movies. Am I ever glad you're not a judge. You'd be crying, 'Kill them all!' Nick is not in a cult. He is just taking a pretty hard line in his religious views. Sadly, a lot of people do.

As for the retreat, churches often have camps like that. It's not out of the ordinary."

"I think we should go up there and check it out. What about those ducks? Now that is pretty far out stuff," Robbie countered.

"She's got a point there, Aliki," Dawn admitted.

"Yeah, the ducks don't make sense." Aliki picked up a stone and sent it skipping six times across the water. Robbie picked up a stone immediately and sent it flying: one, two, three, four, plop. Aliki smirked.

Janet rolled her eyes, and Dawn giggled. "I think Janet and I should go and talk to Nick again and see if he will introduce us to his friend, Vince Dandurand."

"And it wouldn't hurt if you two did go up to the retreat and look around," Dawn added as she bent, picked out a nice flat stone, and sent it skipping eight times across the water. "It's all in the wrist, ladies." Aliki smiled proudly as Dawn and Robbie laughed.

"We are *not* investigating a murder here. I have done my bit, and now it is up to the local police."

There was a moment's silence while the other three women looked at Aliki in disbelief. She blushed, realizing that the others knew that now she had been called in on the case she would be unable to let it rest until the mystery had been solved.

Robbie smirked, crossing her arms and looking at her sister. "So when do we go?"

"Ari is taking the girls for a helicopter ride out to the oil fields this afternoon, so this would be a good day to go. The wedding is in just a couple of days, so we don't want to leave it too late and disrupt any plans," the scientist reasoned.

"Aliki, do you even know the trail to take to Pine Ridge?" Dawn asked.

"Hey, I grew up here," the taller woman protested, not liking Dawn questioning her ability in front of Robbie, who never missed an opportunity to tease.

"You be careful, Olive, and do what Aliki tells you," Janet warned her partner with an affectionate poke.

The actress' face transformed into a look of pure despair as she pretended to cry on Janet's shoulder. "Our kid wants to play the fiddle for a living. What does it matter? Life is meaningless!"

The other three applauded. Janet gave her partner a quick hug as she laughed. "Just for that bit of bad acting, I am not going to buy you a ticket to see Ryan play at the Royal Thompson Hall someday."

After lunch, having waved goodbye to their three girls as they took off in the helicopter with their uncle, the women went their separate ways. Aliki and Robbie packed knapsacks to hike up to the church camp on Pine Ridge, and Janet and Dawn went to saddle two horses to ride out to the north forty where Nick was working, helping some of the hands fix fencing.

"I've got a bad feeling about this," Dawn admitted to Janet as they trotted their horses down the dirt road.

"What? About talking to Nick?" Janet asked, enjoying the opportunity to be out riding again.

"No, about Aliki's ability to find the camp." Dawn sighed. "I did go over the directions with her, but she had that glazed look she gets when she has no idea what I'm talking about. She is a wonderful woman with many talents, but a sense of direction is not one of them. Aliki thinks in terms of road signs, not the third tree on the left."

Janet laughed. "I thought she got a medal for single-handedly catching a criminal in the Canadian Arctic."

"That's true, but I suspect they were both lost and just ran into each other." Dawn snorted. "Aliki can't find her way across the park without asking directions."

"Well, if they're not back by dark, we'll start to worry."

The two women on horseback soon came to the spot where the men were replacing some rotting fence posts. "Hi, Nick," Dawn called. "We were out for a ride and thought we'd pass by and say hello."

Nick looked back down the trail and then smiled broadly when he realized that Aliki and Robbie were not along. "Hi, ladies. Good to see you. Bring the horses over here to graze a bit, and we'll sit in the shade of the oak and take a break. I'm glad of the excuse to leave these young guys to finish this job," he said with a laugh.

They settled down in the meadow and for a few moments just enjoyed the blue sky and the chirping of the field birds.

"Nick, I won't lie to you. We came here deliberately without our partners to ask you more about your church. Janet and I talked to Reverend Jarvis the other day, and we thought he was a really decent man. We don't think he is a killer."

Nick's face clouded over, and he looked close to tears. "This is awful. I have prayed about it. I understand that God is testing our faith, but the Reformed Western Church was just starting to grow and Paul is such a great guy. Some of us are going to visit him again tonight."

"You saw him after he was questioned?" Janet asked.

"Yeah. Vince and I went over as soon as we heard. Paul is pretty shook up. Naturally, he wasn't about to reveal any confidences that he has been told in Christian fellowship, but he sort of told us that he'd had to let Stella know that their friendship was based on the love of God and not anything more." Nick blushed. "He said he knew nothing about Stella's death, and he had no idea how Stella got his jacket and scarf. He told the police that he hadn't worn them since last fall."

"Vince is very active in the Reformed Western Church, isn't he?" Dawn asked casually.

"Oh, yeah. He really knows his Bible. Some members of the congregation don't like him much because he's always going on about saving the environment and that doesn't always sit well with people working in oil and lumber. He's smart, though. He really knows his stuff."

"Well, I'm all for anything we can do to save the environment," said Janet with a smile as she picked a grass blade and nibbled on the end. "What are some of the things he's told you, Nick?"

"Well, like did you know that the Antarctic ice cap is melting far quicker than scientists had originally predicted? Places like Bangladesh, The Netherlands, and even New York City are in grave danger of massive flooding in the next few years." Nick's voice was excited, and he sat up straighter.

Dawn was surprised. "What?"

Nick nodded. "It's true. I checked his information. It was all available on the 'net after the big international environmental conference in Europe. A lot of coastal plains will completely disappear by the year 2010. That's going to displace 200 million people. And at the same time, the oceans are impacting negatively on the prevailing winds. The deserts are growing, and by 2025 three billion people will have to leave areas where there is a chronic water shortage. It's hard to believe that the end is not near. That's why it is so important to me that my family reaffirm their faith in Jesus," Nick explained earnestly.

"How come people don't know about this," Dawn asked. "Did you know, Janet?"

Janet nodded sadly. "Yes, I was aware of the effects of global warming, but I hadn't realized how close we are to the crisis. Like many, I have unfortunately stopped listening to the warnings and am far more interested in the economy than our long-term future. I have heard, however, that some scientists think that the ice caps might not be so much thinning as they are moving further apart." Janet turned to Nick. "I'd really like to speak to Vince. Where can we find him?" She got up and then offered her hand to Dawn to pull her to her feet.

Nick jumped up and dusted off his backside. "He's been up on Pine Ridge at the church retreat for a few weeks. He came down last night, and he said he'd be back tonight as well. He's taking his holiday time up there in order to help out doing some repairs. He's good with a hammer. And...well, you know...he's got some funny ways."

"Funny ways?" Dawn echoed.

"Yeah, you'd understand, Dawn. He's got some Indian blood, and he sorta feels he can help the environment by doing rituals and stuff, you know." Nick blushed, nervously shifting from one foot to the other.

"I don't understand," Dawn answered stubbornly. "What sort of rituals?"

Nick flushed an even brighter red. "Well, you know, we have sunrise prayers, and we plant trees and pray outside, you know," he answered vaguely, waving his hand to indicate it wasn't important.

"How about sacrifices? Do you ever make sacrifices?" Janet asked point blank.

Nick looked very uncomfortable. "Not me. Reverend Jarvis doesn't believe that the practices of the Old Testament are applicable today, but some have their own way of seeing things. You know, some see God more universally, sort of like Mother Nature."

The two women looked at Nick in confusion. He either knew a lot more than he was saying, or he had no clear idea what was going on up on Pine Ridge. Knowing Nick as she did, Dawn suspected the latter. Nick wasn't dumb by any means, but he tended to accept things at face value.

"Well, thanks for your time, Nick. We'd better not keep you from your work any longer." Dawn smiled and gave Nick a sisterly hug.

"But I was hoping to talk to you a little more about your faith and trying to get you back on the Lord's path," Nick said, disappointed.

Dawn looked at him with concern. "Nick, I am gay. Aliki is gay, and so are Janet and Robbie. We don't see that as a sin. God made us what we are, just as he made you. We do not accept the scant references in the Old Testament that Christian fanatics pull out to justify their bigotry any more than we accept human sacrifice, selling children into slavery, marrying more than one wife, or seeking revenge for a wrong — all things that are referred to as okay in the Old Testament. You are welcome to your faith, faith is a positive element in life, but blind bigotry is not. I will not tolerate my family, friends, or myself being judged and found wanting by a nasty, narrow religious view that I cannot and will not accept." Dawn's tone left no doubt of her certainty. "Let it drop, Nick, before your views tear the family apart."

The two women mounted their horses and rode away, leaving Nick with a lot to think over. Dawn sighed. "Nick's facts on the environment were really scary. It makes you wonder why the President of the United States refused to sign the international fresh air bill."

"For the same reason, they have never been able to bring in gun control laws; the will of the people does not rule, lobby groups do. Just like the new hydrogen engines will never get off the drawing boards until the oil runs out. The oil companies will see to that," Janet responded bitterly. "And by the sound of things, that will be too late."

They were silent as they fretted over the future that their children might have to face, then Dawn gave herself a mental shake. There was no use worrying about decisions that at the moment she had no control over. Once she was back in Toronto, she meant to get more actively involved in trying to push for environmental controls. "What do you think about heading up to Pine Ridge?" she suggested as they headed down the path.

Janet's interest was caught by the prospect of visiting the church camp and meeting Vince Dandurand, but still she hesitated. "We wouldn't have time, would we?"

"We'd have lots of time if we cut through the swamps and head up Pine Ridge itself on one of the deer trails. That cuts a good four kilometres off the hike," Dawn said with a smile. "I just didn't send Aliki and Robbie that way because they would have been sure to get lost and sink into the muskeg."

"Let's go, then," Janet agreed with a grin.

Dawn led the way across the meadow, and they forded the river to the area of swamp beyond. Carefully, she picked a safe way for the horses to travel through the tall grasses and bullrushes. Janet could see how Aliki and Robbie would have had to make a big loop around on higher ground and then cut down to Pine Ridge. Her hero was going to be pretty tired by the time they returned this afternoon. Maybe they would meet up, and then they could ride double back to the ranch.

A little over an hour later, they galloped their horses up the last embankment of birch trees and trotted along the ridge's backbone until they arrived at the church camp. It wasn't much, really – a small meeting hall with walls half of board and batten and half of screen. At one end was a large, rough fireplace and at the other, a blackboard. "Jesus Saves" was written on it in pink chalk outlined with blue. There were also half a dozen log cabins and what looked like a small cookhouse. Some distance away was a row of outhouses.

It's like being the marshal riding down the main street of a ghost town, Janet thought.

They tied their horses to a pole at the front porch of the cookhouse, dismounted, and looked around. No sign of a horse or the three-wheel all-terrain vehicles that were sometimes used to bring cargo into the camp.

"The doors are all locked, and the fireplaces don't look like they have been lit in a while," Janet reported to Dawn, who had been looking at the grounds and checking out the outhouses. "Someone has been here, though, because there is a new patch on the roof over there, and someone has put a new latch and padlock on cabin number three. Otherwise, everything seems in order. I don't see any evidence of a nature cult or sacrifices."

Dawn nodded. "I don't think anyone has been staying here since last fall, but someone has been working up here. It seems funny that Vince would make that trek in and out every day when he could just bunk up here. Aliki and Robbie haven't been here, either. No one has used the outhouses in a while, and there are no fresh footprints. In this damp soil, they should be quite clear. The only footprints I saw are a man's, and they weren't made today, maybe yesterday or the day before. The edges are starting to crumble."

Janet looked around, her green eyes serious. "Maybe he doesn't like staying up here all by himself, and of course with Jarvis being in so much trouble, he might feel he needs to stay in town. Do you think Aliki and Robbie are lost?"

"Probably. Do you want to take the long path around and see if we can find them? It might get us back late, but I'm sure that Baba will enjoy cooking for the girls." Dawn laughed. "The big old guy can't miss an opportunity to show off for his grandchildren."

Janet considered. She knew that Reb would take it in her stride, and Mac would know that her mother was safe in the bush, but Ryan would fret until they returned. Still, she'd fret more if they returned without Aliki and Robbie. Baba knew they had talked about going up to Pine Ridge so he would not be concerned. Heading back by the longer route seemed like a good plan. "Let's go."

Aliki and Robbie had hiked up the river meadow earlier that day, but they had traveled due west up the valley and into the deep firs of the Swan Hills. Then they had turned northwest and made their way along a series of trails that crossed and re-crossed over the undulating ridges of the pristine wilderness. By noon, they had climbed to the top of a high ridge and had turned west again, following along its back in search of the church retreat.

"Uh oh," Aliki said as the two hikers came out onto a rocky point that had a clear view of the surrounding area.

"Uh oh, what?" Robbie shifted her shoulders to settle her knapsack more comfortably on her back.

Aliki pointed to a ridge off in the distance. "We should be over there. I must have taken a wrong turn."

"Oh, shit."

"We've probably come five or so kilometres out of our way." Aliki sighed.

"Double shit," Robbie added, taking out her water bottle.

"I think we're lost."

"And swimming in the cesspool," Robbie concluded. "We should have sent Dawn and Janet out here. They know what they're doing in the back bush."

"Nah, they'll be better at getting Nick to talk. We aren't any good at that." Aliki frowned as she looked around for a possible trail to the distant ridge.

Robbie snorted. "So what are we good for?"

"Getting ourselves into damn messes," Aliki muttered in frustration.

"I was afraid of that."

Part 4

Dawn and Janet carefully followed the trail back down from the church camp, using the path that Aliki and Robbie should have taken. They were nearly down to the meadow when Dawn reined up and jumped from her horse.

"Footprints?" Janet asked hopefully as she tried to get more comfortable in the saddle. She was beginning to get worried that their partners might have gotten themselves good and lost. She loved her partner's free spirit and full-speed ahead attitude, but it had caused a lot of emotional anguish for her. Being married to an "olive", however fun, took its toll.

"No, it's a trail bar wrapper like the kind that they took with them." Dawn shook her head. "It must have fallen from one of their pockets because neither one of them would litter. I can't believe it! The first split in the trail and Aliki took the wrong path."

"Those third trees on the left can be tricky." Janet chuckled. "Where do you think they are?"

"Up on Sugarloaf Hill. It's pretty rocky. We can't ride the horses up there, and it will be well after dark by the time we rescue them and make our way back." Dawn surveyed the sky. "At least there should be good moonlight tonight."

Janet looked up the trail, a frown on her face. Dawn would find them faster without her and the horses, and there were the girls to consider. Ryan and Reb would worry. She hated to turn back and leave her partner out there lost, but it was the best thing to do, however hard. "Well, this is your territory. If it would help, I'll take the horses back to the ranch and let them know what's up," Janet offered. "I'm worried about Ryan. She frets when she thinks any of us are in trouble."

Dawn considered the offer. "Yeah, that's a good idea. I can move much quicker then, if you don't mind." She handed over the reins of her horse.

"Just make sure you bring my olive home safe and sound," Janet said, smiling bravely to cover her uneasiness.

Dawn returned the smile, understanding that Janet was torn between her responsibilities to the children and to her partner. She transferred what water and snacks they had into one saddlebag and draped it over her shoulder, then she slipped the rifle from its saddle sheath. "We'll see you later tonight," she promised and set off up the Sugarloaf trail.

Janet watched her until she disappeared over a ridge, and then, leading Dawn's horse behind her own, she rode down toward the meadow.

Dawn climbed steadily, moving at a quick and sure pace. Despite her concern for her lost partner and friend, she was enjoying being alone in the wild, northern terrain. No matter how long she lived in Toronto, the Canadian Northwest would always be her home. The land spoke to her. She could hear the message of the Ancient Ones in the thunder of their wings.

Robbie stopped and yelled to Aliki who was up ahead on the trail, "Hey, stop; I got to get some of the mud off my boot treads. I feel like I'm lifting half of Alberta with every step." She stepped off the narrow deer trail to wipe her boots in some thick underbrush. "Did we have to cross that swamp?"

Aliki walked back and stood watching her sister, a lazy grin on her face. *This was just too good to be true.*

"What?" Robbie asked, seeing the look.

"Having a rough day?" Aliki enquired conversationally, feeling both sorry for her sister and yet wickedly amused.

"I've had better." Robbie muttered, "Why?"

Aliki chuckled. "It just got worse. That's poison ivy you're standing in."

"Oh, shit!" Robbie looked down at the sea of broad green leaves surrounding her feet and bare legs. "How bad does it get?" she asked, gingerly tip-toeing out to the path again. *Just what I needed. Why do these things always happen to me?*

"Red rash, open weeping sores. Itches like hell. It can last weeks." Aliki felt a little guilty for finding amusement in Robbie's predicament.

"God damn," Robbie muttered. Janet was going to kill her with the wedding only a day away.

Aliki's eyes twinkled with amusement. "Worst part is — it spreads really easily, so there goes your sex life."

"Oh, that's it!" Robbie snapped in frustration, looking up to heaven in mock despair. "Take me now, Lord! My kid wants to play the fiddle, I'm lost in the back bush knee deep in poison ivy, and now I have no sex life."

A cough ended the exchange and brought them about to see a wiry, middle-aged man standing in the path, a shotgun resting across his arm. "Er, didn't mean to overhear a private exchange," he muttered, looking red and flustered.

"It wasn't private." Aliki smirked. "My sister was announcing to the world in general. Aah, I don't suppose you would know if there is a shortcut over to Pine Ridge from here."

"Sure would. You're the Pateas girl, aren't you? And this must be Robbie Williams," the man opined, looking at Robbie with interest.

"Yeah, that's Robbie, the other Pateas girl," Aliki added, much to Robbie's surprise and quiet comfort. Aliki could be all right when she wasn't being so competitive.

The man nodded. "I'm Vince Dandurand. I'm glad I got this opportunity to thank you, Miss Pateas, for finding and identifying my sister. I can't say we was close, but I feel better knowin' what happened to her and seein' that she gets a decent burial."

"That's Inspector Pateas," Robbie corrected, returning the favour. "Or better still, it's Aliki and Robbie."

Vince Dandurand grinned sheepishly and shuffled his feet. "Sure. I'm Vince," he repeated, in case they'd forgotten. "Aaah, I'll show you the path. Leads right to the church camp. I got me a hunt cabin about a kilometre and a half away on Sugarloaf that I can reach by road. I put in a trail so that I can take my all-terrain across to the church camp. It makes gettin' supplies in there a lot easier," he explained as he pointed the way they were to go.

"I don't stay much at the camp on account that it often gets used by the Young People. I aren't used to a lot of teens around." Vince walked up the trail with the two sisters following. "I've just been out buildin' my blind down in the swamp, gettin' ready for duck season. It starts September first. Had to carry everythin' there. The darn all-terrain is in for repair again, and I can't pick it up until tonight."

Robbie looked at Aliki pointedly. Aliki rolled her eyes. "I was able to find your sister because the police found some duck bones up on Swan Hill peak," Aliki said conversationally.

Vince stopped dead and turned. "They did, did they? Why were they snooping around there?"

Aliki kept a smile on her face and her voice casual. "Weren't. Some geologist reported it. He figured that there might have been some out-of-season hunting going on."

Vince snorted. "Aren't true. I bought those ducks down at Perkin's Poultry Farm. Some of the concerned church members and me meet up there now and again to get in touch with the good Lord's land. You tell your police friends there is nothin' of interest for them there. I got no quarrel with the police, but I don't want them up there with their guns. It's a holy place for us."

"That's where your sister was found," Aliki said. "You have any idea why?"

Vince looked visibly upset. "Wasn't proper, buryin' her up there. Wasn't proper at all." For a second, Aliki felt bad that she had brought up his sister's death, but then he continued. "That there is a sacred place, and it was defiled with the likes of her buried there."

Robbie moved forward, anger radiating. "I don't think it was her choice," she drawled sarcastically. "The poor woman was murdered, after all."

Vince looked annoyed. "I aren't saying it was right, but she lived a poor life, and I'm not surprised it ended violently. It's no secret that she worked the streets down in Calgary supportin' that no-good Billy Picaski. Got religion from Jarvis and came home to start a new life, she said, but I'm a thinkin' she was just interested in the Reverend. Made a fool of herself over him, she did. I told the police so, too. She was like that — got obsessed and went off without thinkin'."

The three climbed a steep rock ridge in silence. At the top, while they stopped to catch their breath, Aliki tried for more information. "I heard you visited Paul after he was questioned by the police. Does that mean you don't think he was responsible for her death?"

Vince looked shocked. "Of course he didn't do it! Why would he do an evil thing like that? If anyone in town felt like killing her, it would have been me. She brought shame on us all. But I didn't do it. The Good Book says to forgive, and I did my best to be civil to her. Don't see how it did much good, though, with the Reverend bein' in trouble and all. He'll get off once they find that Picaski. It's gotta be him, I figure."

"When did you last see Stella?" Aliki asked, holding back a branch so it wouldn't snap into Robbie's face.

"You ask a lotta questions." Jarvis stopped and looked into Aliki's face. "I told you – it had nothin' to do with me."

Aliki didn't move a muscle. "I'm a cop, and I'm involved in the investigation. I need to know where she was and what she was doing before she met her murderer."

Jarvis thought about that one for a while and then nodded. "Okay. Don't want it said I didn't co-operate. It's enough those old women in the Bible study group are chewing that it never would have happened if I'd taken more interest in Stella. It wasn't my responsibility, was it? She was all grown up. She never worried about the shame she brought on us, did she?"

"So when did you last see her?" Aliki repeated stubbornly.

"The night she disappeared. She flagged me down on Main Street and asked for a lift. She'd just come from Bible meeting at the church. Said it was too cold to walk. I gave her a lift to her boyfriend's place and then circled back to clean the church and get it ready for Sunday service." Vince added, "The police reckon she never got inside, on account of she was wearing the same things I saw her dressed in when her body was found."

"What about Jed, the guy Stella had been dating? What do you know about him?" Aliki asked as she trudged along behind her suspect.

Vince snorted. "Nice enough, but he wasn't standing in the line when they were handin' out brains, that's for sure. Stella was usin' him. She needed a place to stay, didn't she? She couldn't afford an apartment on what she got on welfare." Vince turned and pointed. "That there is the path you need to take. It's a bit rough on account of I am the only one that uses it, but it will get you where you want to go."

"What about the dead ducks?" Robbie asked, stubbornly keeping to the point.

Vince looked uneasy, and a deep red wash of anger spread up his neck. "Forty thousand acres of forests are cut down each year. There hasn't been any real fresh air produced on earth since the late 1960s. The air you just breathed in has been through four to five sets of lungs before you. Our world is dyin', and there ain't nothin' we can do about it. Sure, we gotta get back to some of the basic truths that the Good Book tells us. But more than that, we gotta love this land and pay homage to Mother Nature. Nothin' wrong with that. I know Reverend Jarvis don't like it, but I figure the likes of Abraham and Moses ought to know. A sacrifice sends a message to the land that you care. We aren't doin' nothin' wrong up there. It's our business, and I don't need others meddlin' in it. I gotta go."

Vince nodded, then started up the path in long, angry strides. He stopped, turned, and took a few steps back toward them. "The police said she was strangled, that was all. Was that true?" he asked, for the first time looking genuinely upset for his sister.

"There were only bones, Mr. Dandurand. We could not say for sure what happened the night she died. I can tell you that there was no evidence of violence other than the burgundy string around her neck that was used as a garrotte." Aliki was interested in how Dandurand would take this information. Vince looked surprised, then nodded unhappily, and turned and left.

Robbie leaned on a tree trunk, watching him go. "I think Jarvis has his work cut out for him. Some of his flock seem to be missing a few skeins of wool."

"He does seem to have some pretty confused views." Aliki sighed. "I really need to talk to Nick. He has got to see that he is getting confusing messages. Jarvis has traditional, conservative Christian views, while Vince Dandurand seems to be running some sort of strange nature worship cult out here around the church camp."

"Are we going on there?" Robbie asked, becoming aware that her left calf was starting to itch annoyingly. She used her right leg to scratch it.

"You're going to regret doing that," Aliki warned with a smile. "Nope, it's getting late. I think we would be better to make our way back the way we came instead of going on."

The itching was worse from having scratched, and Robbie lifted her leg and scratched furiously with her fingers. "Do you know the way back?"

"Sure," Aliki said. "Sort of. We'll be okay. Come on...and stop scratching!"

The two women headed back down the trail at a steady pace, Aliki anxious to get down to the meadows before evening came on. She didn't want to be lost in the forest at night, and she wasn't really sure which path they had taken. They had walked for about an hour when suddenly, there was Dawn, coming up the trail toward them. Aliki had never felt so relieved.

"Hi, my love. Hi, Robbie. Got lost, eh?" Dawn smiled, watching the blush climb up Aliki's face.

Though Robbie thought teasing Aliki was her right as her big sister, she was now quick to defend her sister. She knew that Aliki didn't like to disappoint her partner. "Actually, we just came from talking to Dandurand. You know, he has a cabin on Sugarloaf Hill. He is one strange guy." Robbie stood on one leg and rubbed the other against the rough bark of a tree.

Dawn raised an eyebrow at Robbie's own strange behaviour. "She went wading in a patch of poison ivy," Aliki explained with a smile.

Dawn shook her head. "Come on, you two. If we set a steady pace, we should be able to get back to the ranch just before dark. Janet went ahead with the horses so the girls wouldn't worry. Robbie, stop scratching. You're going to be a mess." Dawn took Aliki's hand and gave it a squeeze. She was greatly relieved to have found the missing women safe and sound.

"But they'll be all right, won't they?" Ryan asked fretfully, after hearing all the news from Janet.

"Sure, hon. They'll be fine." Janet smiled as she brought the teapot over to the kitchen table where the family was meeting. Truthfully, she was worried that Robbie and Aliki might have gotten themselves into trouble, but she knew she had to appear unconcerned in front of the girls.

"You no worry, little one. My Dawn could track a spider through a hurricane. Now, Aliki, that is another matter. Once I sent her to count the newborn calves and she couldn't find the herd. How could you not find eight hundred head of cattle?" Baba laughed, trying to ease Ryan's tension.

Reb, sitting on the telephone book for extra height, giggled. "Obbie in trouble again." She sighed dramatically. The tension eased a bit as they all laughed at her antics.

Janet sat for a minute looking into her tea, half listening to some tale Baba was telling about a skunk in the outhouse that had the girls in stitches. There was some elusive clue, a thread of an idea that was just out of reach. It had been bothering her all day.

"Girls, what do you say we take the van into town and get some gas?" Janet suggested, her worry making her restless. "Maybe by the time we get back, Dawn will have returned with the others."

"Okay, Aunt Janet." Mac leapt up to take the cups to the sink and to put away the rest of Aliki's home-baked cookies.

Reb was already climbing off her chair. "I go, too. I know the way," the small child boasted.

Ryan frowned. "Maybe I'll stay here and play chess with Baba. I'm trying to improve his game," she joked to hide her worry.

"Ah! You win one game, and now you think you are Bobby Fischer! Ha! I will not let you win tonight to teach you a lesson," scolded Baba good-naturedly, winking at Janet to let her know that he would keep an eye on the fretful Ryan.

Mac, Reb, and Janet headed out to the van. Mac waited until Reb had been fastened into her seat and they were underway before she asked excitedly, "So, what is our real reason for going into town? Are we going to interrogate someone? Ryan will be so bummed if we catch the murderer, and she isn't there."

Janet laughed. "Nothing so dramatic. But I thought it wouldn't hurt to go talk to Jed down at the garage."

"He was Stella's boyfriend, right? They lived together."

"That's right." Janet didn't want to go into any details with the young teen, especially with Reb listening in.

Mac, however, was used to discussions about crime and passion around the dinner table with Aliki, no matter how much her mom discouraged it. And then there was the fact that there were often boxes of bones around the place, and the things that her Aunt Aliki was liable to bring home and leave in the garage fridge were the stuff of horror movies. That train of thought reminded her of a funny story.

"Aliki brings human bones home all the time. Once, Mom put a partly decomposed hand on the table. She thought it was the leftovers." Mac giggled.

Janet shivered comically. "Yes, your mom told me. Honestly, between your Aunt Aliki and Aunt Robbie, anything is likely to happen."

"Rufus has lots of bones, too," Reb reminded them. She thought her dog's collection of bones was pretty impressive.

"He sure does," Janet agreed.

Mac smiled and then frowned in worry. "Ryan's worried about her mom," she said. "She worries a lot about things like that."

Janet nodded. "Ryan has some insecurities because she has only known her mom a few years. I'm sure that your mom has found our two strays by now and they are on their way back to the ranch."

"I don't remember my birth mom," Mac said quietly. "Just the night my dad died."

Janet reached out and took Mac's hand, well aware that the trauma of that night had resulted in Mac being unable to speak for years. Children often paid for the mistakes of adults. They rode the rest of the way in silence, Janet stroking Mac's hand.

Jed was just locking up the small variety store as Janet pulled up to the pumps, but he grudgingly unlocked the pump and filled the van's tank. "Been a slow night and I thought I'd close a mite early," Jed informed them in his slow speech pattern.

"Well, it's really nice of you to let us have some gas. How are you doing with all this police investigation? It must be hard on you, with you and Stella having been so close," Janet asked softly, concern in her voice.

Jed seemed surprised that anyone would worry about him. "I kept telling them something bad had happened, but no one listens to me. They should have listened," he finished angrily.

"Yes, they should have."

"Weren't right, her buried up there all winter long. They should have found her," he complained, having fixated on the issue. "I worried all winter."

"I'm so sorry." Janet was a bit uncomfortable with the intense emotion that Jed was displaying to someone he barely knew.

"There you go. That's your gas. I don't want to unlock the till, so you can pay me the next time you are in town. It was $45.00. I'm going to lock up now." Jed's eyes kept shifting over to where Mac and Reb stood looking at a trail bike in for repair and at the goods in the window of the small variety store.

Mac hadn't yet gotten anything for Reb's birthday. She had helped Reb down out of the van to see if there was anything in the store window that Reb would take an interest in.

"Sure, thanks, Jed. I...I hope everything works out all right now," Janet added awkwardly, but Jed had already turned and was locking up the pumps. "Come on, you two," she called, and the teen hurried back to the van with Reb running ahead of her.

Janet pulled back onto the street. "He's a bit of a strange one."

"He seemed in a hurry, didn't he?" Mac observed. "Nick says he drinks a lot."

By the time Dawn led the lost pair back, Robbie was miserable. "Damn county; they should give it back to the Indians. Ice, snow, mosquitoes, black fly, poison ivy, the country is not fit to live in. I'm moving to Hollywood," the actor-director bitched, scratching furiously at her arm.

"No country would willingly let you immigrate. You have the disposition of a miserable camel, and besides," Aliki smiled evilly, "you have a skin disease."

Before Robbie could snap off a reply, Baba and Ryan came out onto the porch. Ryan smiled with relief at the sight of her mom and leapt off the porch to greet them. Aliki wrapped her arm around the teen before she could touch her mom. "Don't get too close. Your mom has been swimming in poison ivy. It started as a small patch on her leg, but she has been working very hard at covering herself with it. I think we should make her wear a bell and call out 'Unclean' when she enters a room."

"Mom!" Ryan giggled. "How did you get into that stuff? One of the kids at school got into poison ivy, and she itched for weeks."

"Thanks, kid, that's reassuring," Robbie muttered, scratching her elbow.

Just then the van cleared the driveway and pulled up in front of the homestead. Dawn told Janet and Mac the whole story with a few asides from a smirking Aliki. With a shake of her head, Janet led her afflicted partner up to their room to apply some first aid while the others went to wash up and prepare dinner.

"I'm miserable." Robbie tried to stand still while Janet applied pink calamine lotion to the affected areas so the infection wouldn't spread.

"You've been scratching and spread the stuff," Janet accused.

Wriggling in discomfort, Robbie lied. "Only a little bit."

Janet snorted and stood on her tiptoes to give her lover a kiss. "You are going to be a mess for the wedding. Tomorrow, I'll take you into town to get a shot and a prescription at the doctor's. That will help. By the way, you are sleeping in the spare room."

"No!" Robbie whined pathetically as she stopped pulling on fresh clothes and looked at Janet in horror.

"'Afraid so, my silly olive. I'm not going to the wedding looking like a remake of *The Mummy*," Janet said firmly. Robbie sighed dramatically and sulked.

It was after dark when Baba came out of his den and made his way to the kitchen where Aliki and Janet were busy preparing a late dinner. "I can't find Nick," he announced in worry. "The boys, they tell me he made a phone call and then left them to finish the repairs on the fence. He said he was coming back to the ranch to clean up and then go into town. His horse is not in the barn. Nick, he never misses a meal, especially when his sister is cooking."

"Do Ari or Joan know where he is?" Janet asked as she prepared a salad.

"They drove up to Kinuso this morning to pick up Joan's granny to bring her back for the wedding. They won't be back until tomorrow," Baba reminded them.

"Oh, that's right. It's unusual, then, for Nick not to be around when Ari is away, isn't it? What do you think, Aliki?" Janet asked.

Aliki put down the paring knife and wiped her hands on a dishcloth. "It's not like Nick not to report in. It's Friday night, and he usually goes into town after dinner. But if he'd come back, his horse would be in the barn." Aliki looked out the window. "There will be plenty of moonlight tonight. I think Dawn and I had better take a ride out and look around. It's probably something simple, like he decided to check a few more fences and his horse threw a shoe," Aliki said in reassurance. "Don't wait dinner," she told Janet.

She found Dawn in the living room, playing Monopoly with Robbie and the girls. "You owe me two million," Robbie reminded Ryan.

"Hey, not fair, I let you stay on Boardwalk rent free because you gave me a loan," Ryan protested.

Dawn and Mac laughed at the antics of the mother and daughter who made the rules up as they went along.

"Dawn, Nick hasn't come back, and Baba is worried. I think we should saddle up a couple of horses and go see if we can find him," Aliki said bluntly. The laughter at the table stopped, and everyone looked at the serious woman.

"You worried?" Robbie asked. "Because we could all come."

Aliki shook her head. "No, then we'd have a bunch of people lost in the night. No, Dawn can track anyone. She'll find him; I'll just go along as her tail gunner. It's probably nothing; most likely his horse came up lame."

"I go, too," Baba stated from the doorway. Aliki nodded. "Okay, Baba." The three of them went to the barn and saddled up.

Baba and Aliki rode a little behind, staying out of Dawn's way. They had galloped a good distance up the trail and then slowed to a walk. Dawn now leaned over her horse's neck, using her flashlight to look for any signs Nick might have left on the muddy path. "He came up this trail, but he didn't come back this far."

Aliki looked at the hoof marks left on the trail by a half a dozen horses since yesterday. "How can you tell?"

"Nick's roan has a built-up horseshoe on its right front hoof. It needed it because of the wear to the hoof from barrel racing," Dawn muttered as she pulled up and leapt from her horse. Squatting down, she looked carefully at the ground, then she wandered off into the bush.

There was the rustle of leaves in the darkness, then a cry of terror. "Nick! Oh, God! No!"

Baba and Aliki swung off their horse and were charging after Dawn before her cries had faded into sobs. They found her kneeling beside Nick's still body, giving him mouth to mouth. For a second, Aliki thought that her brother's throat had been slit, then she realized that a thin cord had been pulled around his neck so tight that it had cut into his flesh. He would have been dead for sure had he not been wearing a neckerchief around his throat. The material had provided just enough protection that his laryngeal cavity had not been crushed.

Aliki moved around to the other side of Nick so as not to get in Dawn's way. Swallowing hard, Aliki pulled the embedded cord and scarf from around Nick's neck while Dawn continued CPR. Then she felt his neck through the warm blood to see what damage had been down. She could not feel any. The cord, thank God, had cut into the small area below the thyroid cartilage and above the cricoid cartilage.

"Aliki?" Baba asked, holding his son's hand.

She placed her fingers on her brother's pulse. It was weak but steady. Nick was one lucky boy. "I think he'll be okay. He hasn't been without oxygen, I don't think."

Suddenly Nick's hand came up, and he pushed Dawn away and gave a wheezing cough. Dawn sat back in relief, wiping blood off her hands onto her pants.

"Lie still, Nick. Looks like someone tried to bump you off." Nick nodded, tried to say something, and passed out again. "We need to get him out of here. Baba, can you ride back to the ranch and call an ambulance? He needs to be taken out on a backboard, just in case."

"I go," Baba stated, getting up awkwardly and moving toward the horses. "You no let him die, Aliki," he ordered and then swung into the saddle and was gone. The women took off their jackets and covered Nick. Aliki found his horse standing nearby and tied him up, then she and Dawn settled down for the long wait.

Aliki looked at the bloody piece of cord. It was a thin, tough, burgundy nylon. "The same line that was used to garrotte Stella," she muttered.

The cord rang a warning bell in Dawn's head, but she couldn't remember why. Then it came to her. "Aliki! Paul Jarvis was using this cord to tie up some chicken wire fencing around his vegetable patch. B...But wait, Paul couldn't have done this. He's in jail," she spluttered in confusion.

"No, he isn't. He was held for questioning and then released." Aliki growled in frustration. A cold chill ran down her back. Whoever it was, she was going to get the bastard that had done this to her brother.

An interminable hour later, Baba returned with help. The next hours were a blur of lights, forms, and hospital wards for the worried family. It was in the early hours of the morning when Aliki, Dawn, and Baba made their way back from the hospital to the ranch. Nick was in serious but stable condition and resting. Early tests indicated that he was responding to stimuli. When he was rested, additional tests would be conducted to make sure that there hadn't been any brain damage. Nick regained consciousness now and again during the long night, but slipped off each time without saying anything. In addition to being strangled, he had taken quite a blow to the back of the head.

Back at the ranch, they had barely gotten inside the door when Robbie and Janet came down the stairs, tying the sashes on their housecoats. "How is he?" Janet asked, hugging each of the three in turn.

"The doctor is optimistic that he will wake in the morning and be okay. They run tests tomorrow to make sure." Baba's voice cracked with emotion and fatigue.

"Come on, you three need a good cup of tea and some light sandwiches, and then it's off to bed with you," Janet instructed, taking Baba's arm and leading him into the kitchen.

Robbie kept her sister from following the others. "What do you think, Aliki?"

"I think he'll be okay. We can't know for sure until he fully wakes up. Someone really clobbered him," Aliki muttered, her anger showing.

The tea and sandwiches were consumed mostly in silence, and then the three exhausted people headed off for a shower and sleep.

"You going back to bed?" Janet asked Robbie, who was sitting moodily staring into her tea.

"No, I hate that spare room. It's too small, and the bed's lumpy. I can't sleep anyway. I itch." The truth was she missed having Janet beside her.

"Never mind, lover. We'll get you fixed up today, and in a week or so, you'll be a lot better." Janet smiled sympathetically, understanding what was really bothering her partner. "Robbie, I think I know something," she went on. "It's been bothering me all day, and tonight when Baba came back for help and said that Jarvis was released after questioning, it came to me. The day Dawn and I went to Jarvis' house, he was putting up chicken wire with thin red cord. I think it might be the same stuff that the killer has been using."

Robbie looked up sharply. "If it's him, that bastard is going away forever if I have anything to do about it. That's my kid brother!"

"I know, hon," Janet soothed, rubbing Robbie's hand that wasn't covered in bandages. "But we need more proof than that. We don't want to jump to conclusions."

Her jaw working with stress, Robbie nodded. Having been thrown in jail for a murder she didn't commit, she understood what Janet was saying.

The women filled in their time tidying up and preparing food that could be easily warmed up. With the wedding only a day away and Nick in the hospital, there would be little time to prepare meals. It was coming up on nine o'clock when a squad car pulled into the driveway.

Knowing that her partner was not at her best when she had to deal with the police, Janet went out to meet the RCMP officer. "Hi. I'm afraid most of the family is still in bed. We had a bit of a long night last night."

"Hi." Brad Nicholson smiled up at the cute woman. He placed one booted foot on the bottom step of the porch and looked with obvious approval at the beautiful homestead. "There've been some developments. I thought Aliki might want to hear."

Janet nodded. "Come in and have some coffee and toast. I'll get Robbie to get her sister." Janet stepped aside and held the door open.

Brad readily took Janet up on her offer. He'd been up since before dawn himself. "Hi, Robbie." Brad blushed, a little unnerved to find the famous actress in her silk housecoat. There sure as hell were a lot of beautiful women staying in this house. Then he noticed the bandages. "What the hell happened to you?"

"Poison ivy." Robbie sighed in annoyance.

"Robbie, the sergeant needs to see Aliki," Janet explained. "I'm just going to get him a cup of coffee."

Robbie nodded. "I'll get her." She headed up the stairs.

Brad watched her go with more than simple admiration in his eyes. Realizing that Janet had caught him staring, he blushed. "Ah...er..." he stammered.

Janet laughed. "It's all right, Sergeant. I think she's pretty hot, too." Brad went beet red and, still laughing, Janet preceded him into the kitchen.

A few minutes later, Aliki, Robbie, and Dawn came in and took seats around the kitchen table.

Brad swallowed his cookie with a sip of coffee and then got to the point. "Jed Casse is missing. From all accounts, he locked up early last night and just disappeared."

"Yes, he was locking up when the girls and I went to get gas last night around four," Janet said.

Aliki looked at the sergeant with annoyance. "Did you search his apartment and the garage?"

Nicholson readily reported all he knew. "Jed's mom reported him missing. She showed up to do the books at the garage variety store like she always does at the end of the month and couldn't get in. She doesn't have a key. Jed is the sole owner of the business; it was left to him when his dad passed away. His mom just does the paperwork. I'm waiting on a search warrant to get in and have a look around. I looked through the windows. He's not on the floor or anything, and things look in place." The officer stopped for another slurp of coffee, then continued. "The landlady let me into his rooms. It was hard to tell if he'd been there or not. I don't think he makes his bed or washes his dishes very often. There was no evidence of a break-in or ransacking, and no one could recall seeing him about. His truck is still at the garage, though."

Aliki frowned. "It's damn funny that Jed would go missing the same night Nick was attacked."

Brad almost spilt his coffee. "What? Nick was attacked? When the hell did this happen?"

Aliki recounted the sequence of events, ending with Dawn finding Nick in the dark and their long night in the Swan Hills emergency ward. "Shit," Brad muttered. "This is one hell of a mess. Did Jarvis try to kill them both, or did Jed attack Nick and then go on the run? And what about those crazies up there burning ducks? Or is none of this related?"

Janet and Dawn both started to talk at once, then stopped. "You go ahead, Dawn. I think we must have both twigged to the same clue last night," Janet said.

"I think so. Sergeant, Janet and I visited Paul Jarvis a few days ago, and he was putting up a chicken wire fence. He was using thin red cord to attach it to bamboo stakes. It was very like the cord that Aliki took from around Nick's neck last night."

"I think I need to go talk to the good Reverend Jarvis," Brad growled, chagrined that he had failed to notice this vital bit of evidence when he and Chen had picked Jarvis up for questioning.

"I'll come with you, if you don't mind," Aliki said, "but I think we should go see Nick first. If he saw his attacker, then we're on pretty solid ground in solving the girl's murder."

"Good point, Inspector." Brad was feeling tired and well out of his depth on this case. He was glad that murders were few and far between in his district. Now that there seemed to be enough evidence to try and convince a judge to charge Jarvis with murder, he didn't want the suspect getting away while they sat over coffee. Still, Pateas was a pretty big name in homicide investigation. If she said wait, he'd better.

The women went upstairs to change, and Janet got a sleepy Reb ready as well. Once they had left a message for the girls and Baba, they were ready to visit Nick at the hospital. They found him looking a lot better than the night before. He was still pale, but he was sitting up in bed and looking alert. Nicholson shook his hand, and each of the women gave him a hug and kiss. Reb gave him some slightly wilted flowers that she had picked on the way to the van.

"Hell, if I'd known this was a way to get kisses and flowers from beautiful women, I'd have gotten myself strangled years ago," Nick croaked, barely above a whisper.

Aliki gave her brother a playful swat. "Cut the bull, and tell us what you saw," she bossed, covering her relief. She remembered she'd already lost her oldest brother and didn't want to lose another. She never wanted to have to face anything like that again.

"I can't remember," he muttered. "I know I was going back to town to meet Vince Dandurand about something important. I remember that part because I phoned him on my cell phone. The next thing I remember was being in pain and you guys being there with the rescue personnel. I've been trying since early this morning to recall anything more, but it's a complete blank. The nurse said that can happen with a bad blow to the head," Nick justified to his sister nervously.

"Yeah, it often does, even without a blow to the head. Shock does strange things," Aliki allowed, taking Nick's hand in an uncustomary display of affection. "You scared the shit out of us, little brother."

The sergeant went to phone the station to see if the judge had signed the search warrant; the rest of them stayed. They were relieved to hear that Nick would be released later that day and would be able to stand up for his brother at the wedding the next day. When Nicholson returned, they said their good-byes so that Nick could rest.

As they left, Nick called his sister and her partner back. "Aliki, Dawn."

"Yeah?" She leaned closer to her brother in order to hear what he had to say.

"I was wrong. I'm sorry. I've thought about it a lot since last night. What you and Dawn have...it's good. I got all caught up in the condemning and not in the love and understanding. Can you two forgive me?"

Aliki smiled down at her brother and then tugged at a lock of his hair. "Of course we do. You can't help being cute but stupid," she teased, tucking in his sheets like she used to when he was a little boy. Dawn leaned down and kissed him on the forehead, and the two women left.

Once outside, Janet pulled a reluctant Robbie away from the group to go over to the clinic across the street to get some treatment for her poison ivy. "We could go with them," Robbie protested. "They might need our help."

Janet snorted. "As if. Let Aliki and the police do their job and don't interfere."

Reb looked up at her tall second mom. "You have to go to see the doctor, Obbie, like a good girl," she said seriously.

Robbie laughed, and the three of them headed over to the clinic.

Sergeant Nicholson stopped at the squad car and turned to face Aliki and Dawn; his expression was worried. Considering the relationship between Aliki and Dawn, he didn't know quite how to broach the new information he had received during his call to the station. "The warrant is not ready yet, but a bit of information about Paul Jarvis was sent up from Edmonton. Seem a few years ago he was caught with a male prostitute. He was charged, paid a fine, and was released." Much to Nicholson's relief, the inspector's response was case-oriented.

"That might be motive. He certainly spouts off as if he thinks homosexuality is a sin. If he is in the closet, he might have felt really pressured if Stella came on to him," she speculated.

"Or Stella found out about his arrest and was putting the screws to him," Dawn offered.

Aliki nodded. "Let's go talk to Reverend Jarvis."

Mac had slept deeply after the night's events, and when she woke she immediately went to find Ryan. "You awake?" Mac asked, poking her head into her cousin's room.

Ryan put down the sheet music that she had been memorizing. "Yeah, I didn't go back to bed. I snuck out to do some practising in the bush. When I got back, I found this note on the kitchen table." Ryan picked up the folded piece of paper and waved it at Mac in disgust. "They've gone and left us out of it again."

Mac took the letter and read it.

Hi, Kid of Mine,

Out scaring the squirrels again, huh? I saw you sneaking out. That Mountie showed up this morning. It seems the guy down at the garage (Jed Casse) has vanished. We're going over to the hospital to see how Nick is doing and find out what he knows. Then we're going to have a word with Jarvis. Janet and Dawn say he ties his veggies back with the same red cord that is preferred by the local murderer. Oh yeah, Janet's going to take me to the clinic to see if they have a bell I can wear. <bg> Let Baba and Mac know what's going on, okay? Don't get into any trouble.

Your itchy Mom

P.S. We have Reb.

"Red cord," Mac muttered, staring at the piece of paper.

"What's up?" Ryan asked as she carefully put her music into her case.

"Mould resistant cord for gardening. I saw it for sale in the variety store at the garage when Aunt Janet took Reb and me to get the gas and talk to Jed yesterday." Mac frowned in thought.

"So anyone could have that cord." Ryan sighed, closing her violin case with a snap.

"Yes, but...I'm not positive but I think the all-terrain vehicle I saw parked in the garage belongs to Vince Dandurand. Ryan, what if Jed Casse was upset because Vince didn't care that Stella was killed, so he killed Dandurand and then ran away?"

"Or maybe Jed killed Stella because she was having it off with Jarvis, and Vince found out and killed him in revenge! We'd better go do a little snooping down at the garage. Maybe our moms have got it all wrong in suspecting Jarvis; maybe the murderer is Vince or Jed." Sheer devilment sparkled in Ryan's eyes.

Mac's eyes narrowed. "Ryan, it says right here," she slapped the letter in her hand to emphasize her point, "that you are to stay out of trouble."

"Yeah, but she didn't mean it. She knows I can't stay out of trouble any more than she can. We are olives," Ryan announced, as if that justified everything. "I have my driver's license now, and I know where the keys to the truck are kept."

"What about Baba?" Mac asked practically.

Ryan was itching with excitement. "We'll add a postscript to the letter and leave it on the kitchen table again. Are you coming?"

"Of course, I am!" Mac smiled, and Ryan gave her a hug of appreciation before the two headed off downstairs.

They took the ranch pickup, Ryan driving carefully and responsibly, which was her way when handling machinery. She'd driven a truck before, but not one with an extended cab. They parked a half-block from the garage, not far from the historical trapper's cabin. From there, they cautiously advanced on the garage. "It's probably too late to mention this, but if Jed has vanished, how are we going to get inside the garage and what are we looking for once we're in there?" Mac asked.

"We'll get through the back window – there's always a back window in every movie – and then we'll find the body, let the murderer chase us around with a butcher knife for a couple of scenes – just for dramatic effect – and then subdue him with the karate blow that we've been keeping in reserve, before we call the cops," Ryan explained with a smile. She really didn't have a plan either, but being out snooping about seemed so much more fun than sitting at home waiting for their moms to return.

Mac laughed. "I think you've been watching too many of your mom's movies."

They cut down an alley and came up behind the garage. With a cocky smile, Ryan pointed to the small window at the back. Mac sighed and rolled her eyes. "Okay, so you got lucky," she muttered.

Ryan moved an empty oil drum over, balanced on its top, and pulled off the screen. She used the Swiss Army knife her mom had given her for Christmas to pry open the window. She looked in, discovered it was a storage area at the back of the garage, and slipped inside. "It's safe, come on," she whispered, but Mac was already working her way through the window and down onto the workbench, as Ryan had done.

Together, they moved over to the open doorway and looked cautiously inside. The two bays were empty and silent; the old-fashioned mechanic pits formed dark, rectangular eyes in the floor. A three-wheeled motorized vehicle sat parked in a corner. "That's Vince's all-terrain vehicle all right. Ari was telling me about it. It's Korean made," Mac whispered, then gasped as noise exploded around them. They both jumped in fear and then sighed nervously as they located a tin can with a few metal nuts inside that had crashed to the floor, the contents rattling and rolling across the oil-stained cement. The perpetrator, a spooked cat, gave a hiss, jumped from the counter, and tore past them to leap up on the workbench and out of the window. The girls waited a minute; nothing stirred.

Ryan gave a jerk of her head, trying to act braver than she felt, and the two of them entered the garage, fanning out and around the outer edge of the bays. Ryan looked searchingly at her friend. Mac shook her head – nothing. Ryan shrugged and turned to check behind a stack of tires. Mac moved cautiously to the edge of the pit closest to her – still nothing. She moved around to join Ryan by the second pit.

"Oh, Jesus Christ!" Ryan drew in a sharp breath of fear and heard Mac gasp in horror. There in the bottom of the pit was a man's body. His face was bright red and the tongue that hung from his mouth was swollen and black. He lay wedged in the corner, his stiff hands out in front of him, as if warding off some evil. The fingers were bent like claws in death.

"Who is he?" Ryan asked, her voice shaky.

"I don't know. It might be Jed. I...I...can't tell. I think I'm going to be sick."

Ryan went to take Mac's arm, missed, and tried again. "Come on, let's get out of here. We have to get Aunt Aliki," she said in a rush, pulling her wobbly friend along.

"Ryan, that was awful!" Mac moaned, as she climbed up on the workbench and crawled through the window. She could feel Ryan close behind her, hot and sweaty with fear.

"You're telling me," the teen muttered, gasping in deep breaths of fresh air once they were outside. "Come on, we have to get our moms. They must be at Jarvis'."

The pair ran down the street and climbed into the truck. Ryan tried to start the engine, failed, and had to try again. She pulled out into the street and drove toward the edge of town. When Ryan checked her rear view mirror, her heart almost stopped. They were not alone. Dark, angry eyes stared back at her from a face rough with stubble and etched with pain. "Just keep on goin'," the man hissed, "or I'll kill your friend."

Mac choked as the garrotte slipped around her throat and pulled tight. Ryan felt her world tilt and then forced herself to concentrate on her driving. They were in big trouble.

Aliki, Dawn, and Nicholson found Paul Jarvis in his garden, weeding on his hands and knees. He got up and took off his gardening gloves as the three approached.

"We need to ask you a few more questions, Reverend Jarvis," Sergeant Nicholson announced. Jarvis didn't respond. He nodded dully and indicated with a jerk of his head that they should sit down.

He looked tired and old, Aliki observed. Fear aged people overnight, and she could smell the fear on Jarvis. She sat on the edge of her garden chair and waited for Brad Nicholson to start the questioning.

Dawn took the chair furthest away. She knew she shouldn't really be there, and she wanted to keep a low profile and leave the investigation to Aliki and Nicholson.

"We need to know where you were last night, Reverend," the big police officer started, looking uncomfortable in the small garden chair.

"I was here, all night, but I can't prove it. Vince and Nick were supposed to come around, but they didn't show."

"Why didn't they?" Nicholson asked.

"I don't know." Jarvis did not look at them, but off in the distance. "I got a call from Vince that he and Nick were coming over. Apparently Nick wanted to talk over some things. They're worried about the effect that my being questioned in a murder case is going to have on the congregation."

Nicholson looked at Aliki, and with a nod, she took over. "Reverend Jarvis, we know about your arrest for picking up a male prostitute."

The eyes now made contact with Aliki's. They were filled first with pain and then tears. Paul Jarvis buried his face in his hands and sobbed. Nicholson squirmed uncomfortably. Aliki looked at him and shook her head. Dawn bit her lip and sat on her hands so that she wouldn't interfere. They waited.

Finally the tears slowed, and Jarvis wiped his face on his sleeve. "You don't know what it's like to be born with such an awful affliction. I denied it for years, and when I couldn't anymore, I turned to my faith to give me the strength not to sin," the minister sobbed. He swallowed hard and then went on. "I...I...it was only the once...I just needed...we were caught. It was awful."

"Did Stella know?" Aliki asked.

Jarvis looked at the ground. "Not at first. She kept coming on to me, and it was very awkward. Then, last fall, she went to Edmonton to sign her divorce papers. She must have talked to some of her old friends, because when she came back she knew all about it. She laughed at me, wanted money to keep quiet. God forgive me, I gave it to her." The tears started again, and Jarvis went on between raspy sobs. "Dear God, I was so relieved when she disappeared. I didn't care what had happened to her, I was just glad she was gone." The man broke down completely, and Nicholson shook his head in disgust.

Aliki's face showed no expression. "Did you kill her, Paul?"

The man looked up, tears staining his face. "No! No, I never killed her. Please, I wouldn't hurt anyone. I weakened just once and accepted sin into my life, and look, look what happened."

Aliki stood, and so did Nicholson and Dawn. She didn't think that Jarvis was involved, but he certainly was in no state to be left alone. "Reverend Jarvis, Sergeant Nicholson is going to take you down to the station so that you can make a statement. We're going to hold you for additional questioning. You need to make sure that you contact your lawyer."

Javis obediently stood, his head down and his shoulders still shaking with emotion. Nicholson took him by the elbow, and he went along quietly. Aliki watched him go with sympathetic eyes. She promised herself that she would keep his secret if she could. The poor man just couldn't accept being a homosexual.

"Reverend Jarvis," Dawn called. The broken man stopped, and the eyes that looked back at her were haunted with guilt and pain. "You are only going to be truly happy when you accept what God made you."

The minister shook his head, evidently unable to get beyond his own bigotry.

Holding Reb's hand as they came out of the clinic, Janet gave her lover a sideways look. "Stop pouting. You needed that shot. You'll see. It will take the itch away."

"It hurt," Robbie whined. "Did he have to give it to me in my backside? I think he just wanted to see my tush."

Janet laughed. "Have no fear, I was there guarding your rear-admiral. We need to go down to the drug store and get this prescription filled. What..." Janet stopped and stared, then grabbed Reb up into her arms and started running for their car. "That was Ryan and Dawn in the ranch pickup! There is someone in there with them."

Robbie leapt inside as Janet put the van in reverse and spun out of the driveway. "Are you sure it wasn't Baba?" she asked, doing up Reb's seatbelt and then her own and looking for the car phone.

"It wasn't Baba. They looked afraid," Janet said firmly.

"Don't let them see you're tailing them; I'll contact Aliki."

The phone vibrated in her pocket as Aliki walked down the street, discussing the case with Dawn. They planned to meet Robbie, Reb, and Janet at the clinic and catch them up on what was happening. "Wait a minute, love." Aliki pulled out her phone and flipped it open. "Pateas."

"This is Robbie. We're in the van following the ranch pickup truck. Ryan and Dawn are in the front seat, and according to Janet, who saw them when they passed by us, the kids looked scared and there is some wild-looking guy sitting in the back."

"Where are you?" Aliki asked, already looking around for transportation.

"On Main Street, but we're just turning east heading out to the highway." Robbie tried to sound calm, when all she wanted to do was scream.

"Keep them in sight, but don't get too close," Aliki ordered. She hung up and dialled the station. "Constable, it's Inspector Pateas. I am at the corner by the Legion. Come and pick me up immediately. Hurry!"

Aliki relayed the information to Dawn as they waited impatiently for the squad car to arrive. Aliki was opening the door before the car was at a full stop, and Dawn jumped in with Aliki right behind her. "Red flashers, no sirens unless someone is blocking your way. We're heading out to the highway. It looks like our daughter and niece are driving the ranch truck, being held against their will. There is an unidentified male in the back seat," Aliki explained crisply as she reached for the mic and sent in the call to be on the lookout for a truck that might be involved in a possible kidnapping.

While she was doing so, Dawn took the phone and called Robbie back. "Where are you?" she asked, nervously playing with the strap of her shoulder bag.

Robbie's voice came through clearly enough that Dawn could hear the strain. "We're a few cars back. The truck is maintaining a steady speed going south on the highway. It looks like they may be heading for Edmonton."

Dawn repeated the information to Aliki and the constable. The officer nodded and increased his speed. Aliki reported the information to central dispatch, who relayed it to all cars in the area. Dawn went back to the phone. "Robbie, we're just coming out on the highway now. We're in a squad with the flashers on, so we should be catching up soon. Stay on the line, okay?" Fear for Mac and Ryan gripped at her heart.

"Okay," came the nervous response.

"They all think I'm stupid," the man in the back seat grumbled. "They didn't think I knew. I did, though. I knew Stella was sleepin' with Jarvis. Suddenly she's got all sorts of new fancy stuff and said she bought them with her own money. She didn't get that much from her welfare check. He was givin' her gifts, I figured. I'm not as slow as everyone thinks I am. I had to kill her, didn't I? I didn't want to; I loved her. But a guy has to have some pride. The police were too dumb to even find the body," the man wheezed in a strained voice.

"I left her some place they ought to have found it, what with all them wackos up there burnin' sacrifices to the Swan gods. Poor Stella had to stay in that awful grave all winter long. Wasn't right; they shoulda found her. I meant her to be found. And they say I'm slow," he muttered angrily.

Mac struggled to breathe, trying to keep her fingers under the cord so it wouldn't bite into her neck. The man didn't seem to be aware of the cord tightening around her throat. She could see the worry on Ryan's face as she drove. Every now and again, Ryan would glance over at her to see if she was okay.

"Then that Nick know-it-all Pateas had to go pokin' into my business. He phoned me askin' questions. Him and Vince Dandurand worked it out, didn't they, because they knew the cord came from the store. They're so stupid. Shoulda known to keep outta my business. I had to kill them, too!" He stopped complaining long enough to cough up blood and spit it out on the floorboard of the truck.

"I took Vince's all-terrain and met Nick on the road back to the ranch, and then I came back to the garage to wait for Vince to come and pick up his all-terrain. I'm smarter than people think, ya know."

The man was babbling. Ryan realized there was something wrong with him.

"Stupid bastard Dandurand stabbed me. He shouldn't have had a knife! He stabbed me, and I passed out. Stabbed me in the gut, the bastard. I had to hide out 'cause I couldn't drive in this state." His words were becoming more slurred. The garrotte tightened as he fought to remain conscious. Mac gasped and choked.

"Let up on the cord! You're strangling her, you idiot!" Ryan roared, swatting at the man as she tried to drive with one hand and one eye on the road.

"Fuck you, bitch!" He let go of the garrotte and slammed his fist into the side of Ryan's head.

Ryan's sight dimmed, and she slumped forward. She vaguely heard Mac's panicky voice call "Ryan!" and then she heard no more.

Robbie and Janet watched in horror as the silver truck ahead of them down the road, swerved violently off the highway, ran sideways along the ditch in a cloud of dust, and then rolled over and over until it came to a stop in a field. Janet slammed on the brakes and pulled to the shoulder, as did others who had witnessed the accident. Robbie was out of the vehicle and running before Janet had even gotten the van into park.

She got to the truck and looked in through the broken window. Mac was conscious, but cut and banged up. She was cradling Ryan's head in her lap.

"He hit her in the head," she sobbed, realizing that because Ryan had suffered a serious head injury a few years earlier any blow there now could have grave complications.

Terror gripping her heart, Robbie paled. "Ryan," she called softly. "Ryan, hon." There was no response.

Awkwardly carrying their younger child over the uneven ground, Janet came up beside Robbie. She made sure she had Reb facing over her shoulder so that the small child couldn't see and then looked into the truck. Janet took in the situation at once, and her heart skipped a beat. Mac looked badly shook-up, and Ryan lay still and limp. In the back seat, she could see the bloody form of an unconscious Jed Casse. She moved away and put the frightened child down. "Stay beside me, Reb. Don't worry, Ryan and Mac are going to be okay."

She flipped the cell phone open. She forced herself to stay calm. "Dawn, the truck rolled. Mac's cut, and she's going to bruise, but she looks okay. Ryan is unconscious, and Jed Casse looks seriously injured." She wrapped one arm around Reb's shoulder, comforting the frightened child and keeping her close to her side.

There was a moment of shocked silence at the other end, then a voice tight with fear responded, "I'll have Aliki call for emergency assistance. Don't move them."

Robbie sat beside the hospital bed, holding her daughter's hand. Ryan had not yet regained consciousness. It was eerily like the time a few years back when she had been called to her daughter's bedside after a school lab explosion had put Ryan in a coma for three weeks. At least now she had Janet and Reb there with her; she wasn't facing this alone, like she had then.

Robbie looked over at her wife. Janet had fallen asleep with Reb in her arms. Sometime earlier, Baba and Ari had come to the hospital and picked up the others. Both Mac and Nick had been released, but Ryan was still unconscious. She had some swelling in the frontal lobe area of the brain in addition to the cuts and bruises, and the Williams family waited at her side.

Ryan's hand moved, and Robbie looked up to meet her daughter's eyes. "Is Mac okay?" Ryan whispered.

"Yeah, she's fine, Ryan," Robbie choked out. "How are you feeling? Can you see okay? Can you move everything?"

Ryan wriggled her fingers and toes. "I'm okay, just got a bad headache." The teen sighed with a weak grin. "Why is it always the head?"

Too upset to respond, Robbie shook her own head and then rested it on the sheet beside Ryan's hand.

"Hey, Mom, it's okay. I'm fine," Ryan protested awkwardly. Robbie's rare displays of vulnerability always surprised her and made her feel embarrassed.

Robbie kissed Ryan's hand and forced back the tears. "You have to stop scaring me like this, kid. I'm going to get grey hairs, and that would ruin my career."

Waking to the soft voices, Janet placed Reb's sleeping form on the seat and came over to stand by the bed. "How are you doing, sweetheart?" she asked in relief.

"I'm okay. I just got my bell rung again." She smiled and then frowned. "What happened to the bastard who was choking Mac?"

Janet looked at Robbie, and it was she who answered. "It was Jed Casse. He was dead on arrival. Bled to death from the knife wound. Mac has made a statement to the police, but you'll have to talk to Aliki, Sergeant Nicholson, and Detective Chen later on when you're feeling better."

"Okay." Ryan sighed, then she looked suddenly worried. "What about the wedding tomorrow?"

Robbie looked at her watch. "Today, actually. Nick and Mac have both been released. We'll see what the doctor has to say about you. If you're not released, maybe they would let us take you out on a leash for a few hours."

"Mom!" complained Ryan good-naturedly.

"Hey, is it me that is always getting into trouble?" questioned Robbie in response.

"Yes," Ryan and Janet said together, and the three of them laughed.

Ryan was released in time for the wedding, which went beautifully despite the fact that a number of the wedding party looked like the walking wounded. Nick wore a bandage around his neck, Mac and Ryan had a series of plasters to cover cuts and abrasions, and Robbie was still sporting bandages to cover the larger areas of poison ivy. The reception with friends and family afterwards was lively. Ryan was allowed to stay for a little while, but then Robbie and Janet took their daughters back to the house for an early night. This was partly out of concern for Ryan, who was looking pale and admitted to still having a bad headache, and partly so that people could relax. The presence of the famed Robbie Williams tended to make people gawk and act in a manner that they wouldn't normally.

After sending Ari and Joan off on their honeymoon in a blizzard of rice and well wishes late in the evening, everyone slept in the next day. It was as the family was sitting around finishing a late brunch that the helicopter landed in the paddock.

"What is this about?" Baba asked, looking with surprise out of the window. He was feeling rather put upon, his quiet life having been turned upside down in only a few weeks.

"That's for Dawn and me," Aliki informed the surprised group. "We're going up to Dawn's cabin for the day."

"We are? Oh, Aliki, what a nice thing to do." Dawn smiled her appreciation. Although she loved her new life, she did miss the beauty and peace of her cabin home in the alpine valley, kilometres from civilization.

Mac grinned knowingly. "Next week, when Ryan is better, Aliki said we can all go up there and do some fishing and hiking for a few days," she informed the others.

The two women got into the helicopter as Janet wrapped her arm around Robbie. "Wonder what that's all about?" the actor mused as they watched the helicopter lift into the sky. Janet laughed. "What?" asked Robbie in confusion, looking down into eyes that sparkled like emeralds.

Janet snorted, giving her partner a happy hug. "You are soooo lovable – and so clueless."

Aliki had everything planned. She had thought about it for a long time, her pragmatic mind struggling to be creative, and then had finally hit on what she thought was a really romantic moment. Doing this right was the most important thing that she had ever undertaken. She nervously licked her lips as Dawn unlocked the door to the old cabin and then stood blinking in surprise. The cabin was spotless; the smell of hot soup and warm bread filled the air, a CD of pan flutes played softly in the background, and a fire snapped in the fireplace.

"Wow! How did you arrange all this?" Dawn turned to give her lover a big hug. "Thank you, Aliki. You couldn't have done anything nicer."

Aliki smiled and swallowed nervously. "I need you to come over here and sit on the couch," she said. With a quizzical look, Dawn went over and curled up on the sofa.

Aliki went down on one knee. "Dawn, I love you and Mac very much and I want us to be a family." She took Dawn's hand. "I have already asked you to marry me, but now I want to make that commitment public and more official."

She reached into her pocket and took out a small box. From it, she withdrew a beautiful solitaire. Fumbling a bit, she slipped the diamond ring on her lover's finger. "My love, my life, now and always," she promised.

Dawn wrapped herself in Aliki's arms and held on tight as tears of joy rolled down her face. She had wanted this for so long, and Aliki had made the moment so very special.

Aliki held on to her lover tightly, relieved that she had managed to do it right and that Dawn now wore the ring that she had saved for so long. She knew that Dawn would have been just as happy with a simple gold band, but Aliki had a need to do things right. She never wanted this wonderful woman to ever have any regrets about becoming her wife.

Aliki kissed Dawn's ear and then her mouth. The kiss deepened, and Dawn pulled at Aliki's t-shirt.

"You, here, now," the woman moaned.

Aliki pulled her lover off the couch and down onto the rug beside the fire, and they quickly shrugged off their clothes to lie naked together.

"You mean the world to me," Aliki whispered, kissing Dawn's throat as her hand teased a hard nipple.

"Show me." Dawn leaned up to catch one of Aliki's nipples in her mouth.

The scientist growled with need, and bathed with the warm glow of firelight, Aliki showed the depths of her love. Far off, thunder roared — the sound of the legendary giant swans taking flight across the sky.

Kilometres away, Ryan waited as her mother took a seat beside Nick, Baba, and Janet. Ryan stepped forward, holding her violin nervously. "Aah, I'm going to play Antonio Vivaldi's *Concerto No. 1,* and Mac is going to turn the pages, and Reb is going to introduce me," she explained, and then went back to her music stand and settled the violin comfortably under her chin. "Go ahead, Reb," Ryan said to her little sister.

Reb stepped forward. "My big sister is going to play *Spring* from the *Four Seasons,*" she stated proudly.

Ryan fidgeted and adjusted her violin under her chin. Mac smiled at her encouragingly, and Ryan put the bow to the strings. Music floated out across the room, music that was filled with the joy and warmth of spring. It was light and lyrical and touched the souls of the listeners. When Ryan finished, there was stunned silence. Finally, Janet shook herself from her trance and clapped, and Nick and Baba joined in with a cheer or two. Robbie sat completely motionless and stared at Ryan.

"Mom?" Ryan prodded hesitantly.

Robbie got up and rushed from the room. Ryan's world crumbled. She desperately needed her mom's approval. Suddenly, her Aunt Janet was there beside her.

"Go talk to her, Ryan. She needs you," Janet whispered, giving her adopted daughter a hug and taking the violin from her hands.

Ryan found her mother standing in the kitchen, sobbing. Confused by her mom's reaction, she asked timidly, "Mom?"

Robbie turned and looked at her daughter with new eyes. She walked over and wrapped the teen in her arms and held on tightly. "That was some of the most beautiful music I have ever heard, Ryan. I am so proud of you. How the hell did I ever end up with a kid as special as you?"

"Just lucky, I guess," came the muffled laugh and reply as Ryan snuggled deep into her mom's arms, knowing that everything was going to be okay.

Outside, the distant thunder echoed across the Swan Hills.

Dead Right

The adventures of the summer had passed and the first colours of autumn were turning the trees red and gold. Aliki lay in bed reading a book while Dawn chatted on the phone with Robbie about the upcoming wedding ceremony. Aliki's relationship with her half-sister was stormy but close, and Robbie and her wife, Janet, were hosting the wedding ceremony in their northern Ontario home. Aliki was looking forward to publicly recognizing Dawn as her partner and legally adopting Dawn's daughter, Mac, as her own. At least, *most* of the time she was looking forward to the wedding ceremony. Sometimes it scared the hell out of her. With commitment came a raft of responsibilities, as she knew from having helped raise her brothers. Was she ready to take on that responsibility again? Did her profession, dealing so often with the criminal world, lend itself to a secure family life?

"Robbie wants to know what kind of flowers we want," Dawn said, turning to look at her partner.

"Living ones would be nice," Aliki drawled from behind her book.

Dawn pulled a face and listened to what Robbie had to say about Aliki's response. "Robbie said I should dump you and run off with the Avon Lady."

Aliki looked up from her book with steely eyes. "I think we should have sprays of white roses for the purity of our love and put them on a bed of colourful autumn leaves to reflect the depth and richness of our family. I have talked to Mac, and she would like navy blue ribbons on the bouquets with gold maple leaf medallions."

Dawn blinked. "You made that up just now."

"You will never know for sure, and Mac did express a few opinions over her cereal bowl the other morning." Aliki went back to her book.

Dawn gave her lover an affectionate swat and finished her conversation about the wedding plans. Putting the receiver down in its cradle, Dawn snuggled close to Aliki. "Robbie and Janet sure are going all out to make it a very special day for us." She sighed in contentment. "I don't think I could be happier."

Aliki put her book away and turned off the light, then moved to take Dawn into her arms, only to be interrupted by the shrill ringing of the phone beside her bed. Aliki's phones, one in the kitchen and one in the bedroom, were on a separate phone line. They were strictly for business. As a forensic anthropologist working out of the Toronto laboratories, Aliki could be called at any time, night or day, to respond to an investigation involving human remains.

"Pateas," she said abruptly, and then listened to the voice on the other end. "I'm on my way." Her mind racing over the equipment she needed to gather, Aliki slipped from their bed and started getting dressed, all thoughts of love crowded out by the disaster toward which she was traveling.

Dawn turned on a light. "What's going on?"

"Sorry, love, I'll be gone a few days, at least. There's a plane down."

A plane is down. The words sent a chill through Aliki. She had worked several crashes when she had been with Interpol. Those four words evoked scenes of such carnage that even the most violent of horror movies would not come close to an accurate portrayal. Unconsciously, she rubbed her hands together. It was her particular psychological reaction. They all had one. In the next few weeks, she would compulsively wash her hands over and over again until they were red and raw.

A plane is down. In this case a 747. It would mean six million separate parts produced in thirty-three different countries, one hundred kilometres of electrical wire, and three hundred tons of twisted aluminium and fittings spread over an area as vast as one thousand square kilometres.

A plane is down. It fell five kilometres breaking up as it plummeted. When it hit the ground, it would have been recorded first as earthquake action on nearby seismograms, approximately a 1.6 on the Richter Scale. Some of the large pieces, such as the engines or landing gear, would create craters six to seven metres deep.

That was the hardware of a crash. It was the collateral damage that left images that made sleep a thing to fear. A flight crew plus twenty-one first class passengers, seventy-seven business class, and three hundred and twenty-two economy passengers. They, too, would be scattered over a wide area in bits and pieces. A loss of over 3 000 litres of blood.

How did one explain that to anyone who had not been there? One couldn't; you simply say, in hushed tones, "A plane is down."

Aliki sat next to Dr. Bates in one of the aft jump seats of the helicopter. They didn't talk. There was nothing to discuss yet, and the noise of the engine made talking nearly impossible. She stared straight ahead at a green canvas harness that swung back and forth from a Velcro fastener on the grey fuselage, acutely aware of everything around her. Her senses seemed sharpened by the crisis. The air had an oily metallic smell with overlays of stale body sweat, canvas, and dust. The blades overhead caused a tremble throughout and a throbbing roar. The fabric of her jumpsuit was coarse and stiff under her fingertips. She took it in and tried to focus on the ride. *Let that be the lingering memory and not the images of the days ahead.*

It was still dark when they arrived at the site. Hunched, they ran from the 'copter like scavenger beetles. One of the crewmen followed with their bags, leaving them in the grass just beyond the range of the major turbulence, then running to climb back aboard. The craft was soon airborne again, leaving the two of them cowering in its turbulence.

When the dust settled, Bates moved off toward a cluster of police and emergency vehicles, their lights pulsing red into the night. He headed the forensic unit out of Toronto, and rank had its privilege. Aliki was left to tote the two gym bags in which their gear was kept. Nearby, the floodlights set up by the police and the fire department gave the area a surreal look.

"Who is in charge?" Bates asked as he reached the trailer with the makeshift cardboard sign that read "Command Centre – report in". He held up his identification card in the light of the doorway for the officer to read. "I'm Dr. Bates, and over there is Dr. Pateas. We'll be in charge of your forensic recovery unit."

"Captain Brian Oleskow, the Barrie attachment, sir," said the young officer who stood in the doorway. His attempt at bravado did not hide the nervous energy that he was doing his best to control.

"I know Oleskow, Dr. Bates," Aliki said, dropping the bags to the ground by the trailer door. "He took the course on handling a major disaster that I ran two years ago. He did well, asked a lot of intelligent questions. With the traffic heading out of the city each weekend for the cottage country, he's seen his share of major accidents out on the highway near here."

Bates nodded. "Good. Then we can hope all the proper procedures have been followed. Where can we find Captain Oleskow," Bates squinted at the man's name tag, "Officer Richmond?" Bates liked to call people by their name. Aliki never bothered.

"He's out on the site, sir. The people from the airline are here, and he wouldn't let them stay on site unsupervised. He said the site had to be left alone until the qualified personnel arrived. You have to sign the order of entry form before you can go on site, sir." The officer swayed back and forth in the doorway, anxious to do things right and afraid that he would make a mistake. He had only been on the force a few months. He'd seen one bad car accident, but this was different; this was going to be awful. He tried to look serious. A lot of people had probably died, but what he felt was a mounting sense of excitement, of being there when things happened. He didn't think he should be feeling like that, but he couldn't help himself.

Bates cleared his throat. "Officer Richmond, if you were to step aside, Dr. Pateas and I could come in and sign the entry form."

Richmond jumped as if he'd been poked. "Yes, sir."

Aliki smiled. Bates could be a bugger. He was having a bit of fun with the young officer. She was pleased that Captain Oleskow seemed to be doing things by the book. "Officer Richmond, do you know if Captain Oleskow has issued a press statement?"

Richmond unconsciously shifted his weight to the balls of his feet so he was almost as tall as the good-looking woman who stood in front of him. Her hair was dark and her face classically beautiful. She was in great shape, too, although he was doing his official best not to look. "Yes, Dr. Pateas, he issued a statement that the area is closed to all but rescue personnel and that all efforts are being made to search for and assist survivors." Pateas nodded her approval. Richmond frowned. He wondered if he should tell her that Oleskow had not yet let ambulance and firefighters out on the site. Better not, loyalty should remain with his commanding officer. Still, he wondered why the captain was not doing more to help the crash victims.

Bates had seen the look of concern and indecision on Richmond's face. He put his hand on the young officer's shoulder and gave it a reassuring squeeze. "Don't worry about it, son. Everything is being done that can be done for those people on board."

"Yes, sir," Richmond acknowledged, flushing bright red. He hadn't been aware that his feelings had shown so clearly.

"Now just step outside and toss in our bags. We need to change before heading out on the site."

The officer was quick to obey. He, like the others who had been standing around since they'd arrived an hour earlier, were unsure as to what was going on and why they had not been allowed on the site to help. Other than being ordered to make a list of all the people – police, ambulance personnel, and firefighters – who were standing by, he'd done nothing but wait.

He tried to keep out of the way as the two forensics people slipped into overalls and work boots and put on hard hats with miner lights, masks, safety glasses, and latex gloves that they then covered with thick leather work gloves. Each carried a plastic clipboard as they carefully climbed up a wooded ridge to the main area of impact on the other side. Richmond watched from the doorway for some time and then went back inside the trailer to continue to wait.

"Dr. Pateas, good to see you again," called Oleskow as he saw the two carefully making their way into the hollow. Relief was evident on his face. "This is Fire Chief Brenda Hardy. We've kept the site secure except for the initial survey and putting up the police tape. The airline people are here, though. They're over there, painting. They say the tail section is about a half kilometre to the northeast in some farmer's field. They've got people there, too, and I've got an officer on the scene. We have instructed the media to stay in a hanger by the local airport. I thought it would give them a good backdrop. We've got several helicopters flying over with searchlights, filming."

"Sounds like you have things in good shape," Aliki said, and Oleskow let go of some of the tension that had gathered in his neck and shoulders. There was going to be an enquiry, that was for sure, and he wanted his department to look good. "This is the head of the forensics unit, Dr. Thomas Bates."

Bates shook hands with Oleskow and Hardy. "Good to be working with you. Give us a few hours, and then you can let the recovery teams on site. Where is the temporary morgue set up?"

It was Hardy who answered. "We are using the old skating rink. It's about twelve kilometres from here. I have people there getting things set up according to the information provided in the emergency measures binder. My people are keeping the press out, too."

Bates smiled, pleased by how well things had been handled. So often, the area of a disaster was swamped by would-be rescuers trampling the evidence into the dirt. Or worse still, efficiency was lost because of departments questioning each other's authority. "Good. You two have done a splendid job. Captain Hardy, before we start moving bodies out, you could allow the press in for a tour of our temporary morgue to show that we are on top of things. Make sure, however, you do that after Captain Oleskow has made the second press statement confirming definitively that there has been a significant loss of life."

Oleskow nodded. "I'll get on that right now, if you want."

Bates nodded. "Yes, you'd better. The press will know by now that a morgue has been set up. It is better that we stay ahead of them by releasing the statement that many lives have been lost. Then give them the tour of the preparations at the rink. Someone is sure to ask how many are dead. For now, the answer is simply that search and rescue teams are at the crash area and all possible preparations are being made for any eventuality."

Hardy looked grim. "I'll let my people at the morgue know what to expect and what to answer. Dr. Bates, my crews and the ambulance attendants are getting pretty upset. They want to know why they are not out on the site helping."

"I'll go with you and have a little word with them before I go on site. Where are the families of the passengers being sent?"

Oleskow looked tired, but he sounded confident and clear-headed when he spoke. "We have counsellors and airline representatives standing by at a conference room in the Community Centre. I've also arranged with the larger motels in the area to hold their rooms for arriving family members."

Aliki couldn't suppress a smile of pride. Oleskow had done a superb job in less than an hour's time. Bates echoed her thoughts.

"Excellent, you have done a wonderful job here. Dr. Pateas, I suppose we should get on with ours. I'll go with Captain Hardy and do the first crew briefing. You go see what the airline chaps have come up with."

Aliki's face hardened into grim lines. "Yes, sir."

The airline emergency and recovery crew were often on the scene as quickly as the rescue personnel, if not sooner. As a matter of courtesy, they were always notified first when a plane dropped off the radar screen. Once they arrived on site, they would take aerial photographs, if possible, pinpointing the various areas of wreckage. Their next step was to paint out the logos of the company on any wreckage. Human memory was short. In a few years people would ask, "Do you remember that plane that went down?" They will have forgotten the name of the airline the plane belonged to. A photo lasted a much longer time, so removing the logos was an airline priority.

"Aliki! Good to see you. I don't think our paths have crossed since that conference in Paris. How are you doing?" asked a big, burly, large-nosed man who stood on the edge of an impact crater.

"Kyle Ragle, it has been a while," Aliki responded, and then she acknowledged the slight man with greying hair at Ragle's side. "Hi, Mo."

"How do you do, Aliki. Very good to be working with you again."

Mo Rashid and Kyle Ragle were like Mutt and Jeff: where one was, so was the other. They had worked together for the airline for years. Kyle was a widower, Aliki knew, with a married daughter. Mo was married, with three grown sons. Those that worked crash sites were a small, tightly knit group. Their experiences and realities were like no others; they were bonded by their memories.

Aliki looked down into the crater. "What have we got here?"

"Landing gear and about three metres of the port side of the fuselage directly behind the wing. We've got pieces scattered for bloody kilometres."

Aliki nodded and started down the yellow ladder that leaned on the side of the crater.

Mo called down to her, "You let us know if you find any of the crew." Aliki nodded her understanding. Crewmembers were the most vulnerable because they were rarely strapped in. During decompression, they could be sucked out of the plane, and often their remains were found kilometres from the impact site. Flight personnel were close, part of the airline family. Every effort would be made to find their colleagues' remains.

The smell of fresh paint, fuel, and burnt flesh grew stronger as she descended. She had already noted the charred bones sticking up in the wreckage. Her work had begun.

Bates was surrounded by a sullen crowd. "I know this is hard for you, and it is going to get harder. You have not been allowed on site because there are no survivors. There are never any survivors from such a crash. It just doesn't happen.

"Once my partner and I have done a sweep of the area, you will be allowed on the site. Please wear a pair of thick gloves and safety boots. There is a lot of sharp metal on site. When entering and exiting the site, you will please stay within the pathways that have been marked with yellow police tape. We do not want any evidence trampled. Do not remove any body parts until you have the okay from one of the forensic team.

"Lastly, watch where you are stepping. There is no hurry for these people now, but we would like to solve the riddle of their untimely deaths. That is the least we can do for them. Any questions?"

A truculent ambulance attendant crossed his arms over his chest and looked at Bates with contempt. "Seems to me there is always a chance of someone surviving. The radio said that we are looking for survivors. Why aren't we?"

"I repeat, there are none. You will realize that when you see the devastation for yourselves. We do not immediately release that information to the public. It would not be fair when family members are on the roads trying to get here or the airline has not yet been able to locate a next of kin. Gradually, over the next few days, we will remove their hope. Let's give them something to cling to until they can be helped through this terrible loss by trained emergency personnel. It is a white lie for a greater good. Please respect that and don't talk about it to the press, your families, or friends, not yet."

That said, Bates left Hardy to organize her people while he returned to the site. He and Aliki methodically searched for body pieces amongst the wreckage, in trees and undergrowth, or partly buried in the dirt. Some bodies were relatively intact. Two men sat side by side, in their seats still, their heads bent forward as if asleep. Only their legs were missing, and most of their clothing. The sudden pressure drop and air traveling at five hundred kilometres an hour had ripped and shredded fabric, leaving most of the victims nearly naked. Aliki made her notes and then used a marker on a strip of plastic to record the location of each body when found, along with the number on the arm of their seat. These two would be easily identified. Her plastic tags were clipped onto their ears, then a coloured plastic flag was stuck in the ground. They had three colours, each indicating the relative level of mutilation. Red indicated body parts only, yellow, a body almost intact, green, a body damaged but whole. The pattern these flags left would help investigators piece together the source of the fuselage's failure.

Mostly, though, there were just disjointed parts — an arm lying against a boulder, a foot with no toes buried in leaves, a torso still in a twisted seat, missing its head and limbs. Horror piled on horror. Gradually, more of their forensic colleagues arrived, working quietly among the twisted bits and pieces of metal, hunting through underbrush and leaves, and scanning tree branches. Each piece was carefully tagged and left for the ambulance attendants and firefighters to enshroud in a body bag and load on a stretcher to carry out to the makeshift morgue.

Pale dawn brightened to daylight, and the extent of the damage became more visible. As Ragle had observed, the carnage stretched for kilometres. The Army was going to have to be called in to mop up. They would walk shoulder to shoulder along the trail of debris, looking for even the smallest of pieces. There would be millions, some of them once human. Another group would walk across the land downwind of the crash, looking for light material that had been carried off by the wind. Clothes from luggage, papers, seat covers, all sorts of debris would be found, sometimes hundreds of kilometres away.

"Aliki," Bates called from some distance away, "we are meeting at the command trailer for lunch and a debriefing. Let's go."

She nodded and carefully picked her way to one of the now well-worn paths that would take her to the main pathway and off the site.

She pulled off her outer gloves and set them on a bush, then she removed her plastic gloves and used a disinfectant to wash her hands several times, rinsing them at a tank set up by the fire department. There was a strong smell of feces and vomit in the air — the scent of horror.

A local hardware store had provided lawn chairs, and they had been placed in a circle under a few trees. There was now quite a large group of forensic personnel assembled from various forensic teams and auxiliary personnel. They ate sandwiches that had been prepared for them by a local church auxiliary. Aliki's was peanut butter and jam. There was little talking. Faces were grim and strained with emotional and physical fatigue. Behind them, a never-ending stream of once hopeful workers brought the human remains out in plastic body bags.

Aliki sipped her coffee from a paper cup. Its warmth helped revive her. The coffee was black and very sweet. It had been donated in big plastic containers by the local coffee and doughnut shop. Tragedy brought out the finer qualities of humanity.

"I'm going to phone Dawn," she mumbled to her boss who sat at her side, sucking on his pipe absentmindedly. In the office, he was not allowed to light up; there in the open, no one objected.

Bates nodded. "The meeting will be at thirteen hundred."

Aliki moved down the dirt road a ways to get away from the noise of the rescue workers and find some privacy. She pulled out her cell phone and punched in Dawn's number. The phone was answered immediately. Not before, however, Aliki's sharp eyes had caught sight of a disembodied head, cracked in two and staring back at her from the shallow ditch. She turned her back on it.

"Aliki?"

"Hi."

Dawn knew by the strain in that one word that things were bad. Her voice was sympathetic. "How's it going, lover? It's been on TV. They showed pictures of a temporary morgue that's been set up. Are you there? They're now saying there has been a loss of life. Is it bad?"

Aliki skirted the question. "It's never good. I'm still at the site of the crash. I don't know when I'll be assigned to the morgue, but I suspect it will be soon. We have a good crew. Things are going okay. We have a debriefing in a few minutes."

Recognizing from the clipped account that Aliki was not able to talk more freely, Dawn curbed her curiosity. "That's good. I miss you, hon."

"I miss you, too. Sorry I had to leave you to finish all the arrangements."

"No, you are not," Dawn teased gently. "I know you have a tough job there and that you need to get back to work. Just feel my love, okay?"

"I do, sweetheart. My love to you and Mac. I'll phone...I don't know, tonight sometime," Aliki finished with a sigh of frustration.

"Okay. Take care of yourself. I love you. Bye, Aliki."

"Bye, Dawn."

A wretched loneliness engulfed Aliki as she snapped her phone shut and clipped it back on her belt. Moodily, she headed back to the command trailer, making a mental note to go and retrieve the head as soon as she was back in her safety gear.

Oleskow's family's holiday trailer with its frilly pink curtains was not going to be big enough to hold the team. Instead, Bates had taped chart paper to the back of the trailer and people had pulled their lawn chairs around.

With a marker, Bates drew a sketch of the debris field as nearly as they had identified it.

"The tail section is about a kilometer away in that corn field over there." He pointed behind him and then marked it on his sketch map. "I've been over there and had a look. Looks like the craft broke in half, with the greatest damage in flight occurring forward of the wing. There is also early evidence that the port side of the craft has heavier damage than the starboard side. Dr. Pateas, perhaps you could address some of the forensic patterns that are showing up."

Aliki referred to her notes. "What I am finding is that the passengers in first class and business class show injuries associated with violent decompression and impact injuries. Those amidship are badly burnt. Those economy passengers in the tail section have a high incidence of broken necks, the sort of injury associated with a wind sheer factor. That is in line with Dr. Bates' assumption that the tail section broke off in flight. As I am sure you are aware, this evidence is based on very little data. So far, we have only nineteen relatively intact bodies." Aliki looked up from her notes to make eye contact with her boss. She had said all she needed to say.

Bates reluctantly pulled his pipe from his mouth. "Mo, Kyle, what do you have to add?"

It was Mo who answered. "I would posit the supposition that an explosive fire occurred midship, breaking the plane into two sections. The aluminium we are finding certainly is ripped and torn in a manner that would indicate an explosion midship, port side. The debris field indicates that seconds after the explosion, the craft banked sharply to port, dropping a trail of debris. Then the craft appears to have broken in two. The bow continued in the initial bank, rolling a full three hundred and sixty degrees and nose-diving into the brush in front of us. The tail section might have rolled tail down and dropped at a much sharper angle. That is why we have a narrow, long debris field. The wind was blowing north by northwest at only six kilometres per hour, so that is favourable for our search. We probably have an area of around one hundred square kilometres to search for heavy remains and of course a much wider band for light debris."

Bates nodded and then shifted his gaze. "Captain Hardy?"

"I have eight teams on site. There were some areas smouldering, but we soon had those out. Fortunately, the heavy rain the other day worked in our favour. We hope to have all located human remains delivered to the morgue by late this afternoon. It might be advisable, Dr. Bates, for us to have a meeting with my personnel later today about procedures for the search and recovery of any remaining human remains."

"An excellent suggestion. I'll arrange that with you right after this meeting. Captain Oleskow, anything to add?"

"No, sir. My men are managing, and I have some extra personnel coming in from surrounding areas. So far, the biggest problem has been keeping gawkers and reporters away."

"Good. We will need extra security tonight. That is when the lowlifes will move in to try and loot the site. They'll be after small things mostly – jewellery, wallets, credit cards, passports, etc. Your people need to be a visible presence, patrolling the back roads downwind of the crash site particularly." Bates did not add that members of the rescue teams would also do their share of looting. There were some things that simply could not be controlled. It was easy, when checking a wallet for I.D., to justify to your conscience that the dead person no longer needed the money in the wallet or that the jewellery worn by someone would be covered by insurance so no one would be out of pocket.

"Yes, sir."

"If there is nothing else?" Bates looked around, "Very well, then, we have a job to do. Let's get on with it." The chairs rattled as the group moved off to their assignments. "Aliki?"

"Yes, sir?"

"I need you over at the morgue. You're in charge until I can get there. Take five others with you, the ones that have been on the site the longest." Aliki nodded and turned to leave. "Aliki, I'm sorry about this coming so close to your wedding. I'll get you out of here as soon as I can spare you."

Aliki blushed and smiled awkwardly. "Thanks, Dr. Bates."

Some time later, Aliki pulled into the parking lot of the old skating rink, the location of the temporary morgue. The parking lot was nearly filled by an emergency fire truck, several police cars, three media trailers, and an assortment of cars. As Aliki slid from one of the rented cars that the department had arranged for the forensic team and walked to the trunk to get out her gym bag of equipment, the restless crowd outside the main doors fell quiet. Those who had been crowded in the small car with her followed her to the door.

Bugs Strasser snorted. "Look out, Aliki, here they come."

Sure enough, a number of reporters were making a beeline for her. She tried to recall what their last statement to the media had been. She sensed, more than saw, her colleagues moving away from her. Heads down and faces grim, they moved as one toward the doors and disappeared inside. Aliki was stopped by a swarm of men and women barking questions at her as they held out their mics.

Aliki calmly but firmly pushed a microphone away from her face. "I have a statement to make, if I could have you quiet. Then I would be glad to answer three questions before I need to get on with my work."

The group settled down reluctantly while Aliki stood stone-faced, waiting. "Thank you. I have been at the crash site since very early this morning. Needless to say, with a crash of this magnitude, there has been a loss of life. The police, fire department, ambulance service, airline, and the forensic department are working closely to provide all the aid we can to those involved in this tragedy."

Aliki took a quick breath and plunged on before anyone could fire a question at her. "As of yet, no victims have been identified. We will be starting that process shortly. I will now answer three questions."

A tall blonde pushed her way forward. "Witnesses said they heard an explosion and saw a ball of flame streak out of the sky. Was terrorism responsible for this crash?"

Aliki weighed her words carefully. "That is out of my frame of expertise. I can only say that the airline has had their people on the site since shortly after the craft went down. It has been my experience that it will be months before any clear answers emerge as to why this crash occurred."

The man next to her pushed a mic in her face, and Aliki's eyes flashed with annoyance before she controlled her feelings. "We've heard rumours that survivors are being booked into nearby hotels. Is that true?"

"Hotels have been asked to hold rooms for arriving family members. I am not aware of any other activities."

A tall man at the back let his deep baritone roll over the heads of the others. "You've been on the site. You must know whether there are survivors and if so, how many."

Aliki shook her head, buying a little time. She had hoped to avoid that particular question. "Everyone has a job to do out there, and we are doing our jobs as quickly and as efficiently as we can with great consideration for the passengers who were on that flight and their families and loved ones. As a member of the forensics team, I am responsible for identification, and I need to be getting on with that task right now. Excuse me, please." Aliki moved forward, using her momentum and body against a resistant wall of reporters.

"Are there survivors? Has any terrorist group taken responsibility? How many dead? Have they found the black boxes? Was weather or pilot error a factor? When was the last time this plane was serviced?"

Aliki pushed on to the door.

An older couple waited there, looking pale and frightened.

"Our granddaughter? Please, she is only twelve."

Aliki's gut twisted. What if anything had happened to MacKenzie? Impulsively, she wrapped an arm around the couple and shepherded them through the doors with her. Out of sight and hearing of the media, she spoke to them. "You need to prepare yourself for the worst, just in case. You give me her name and a description, and I'll do my best to let you know as soon as I can. Do you have a place to stay?" The man nodded dully as he hugged his wife to him. "Good. Write down the hotel name, too, and your room number. Okay?"

"She was visiting us," the woman sobbed. "Our daughter and son-in-law live in Europe. We hadn't seen her since she was a baby."

Aliki nodded her understanding and pulled a notebook and pen from her pocket. "If you give me your name and where you are staying, I will contact you as soon as I know anything. Also, if you know of any distinguishing characteristics, such as a birthmark, or the clothing that she might have been wearing, it might help."

The man's voice shook. "My name is Sam, Sam Dillon. This is my wife Millie. We are staying at a friend's house in town, actually. Number Twenty-two Rose Street. I don't know about characteristics..." The man's voice faded as he struggled to recall anything that might help with the identification.

Millie spoke up. "She has a gold locket we gave her; it has pictures of us in it. She was wearing it when we put her on the plane." The woman fished around in her handbag and came up with a school picture. A dark-haired child caught between childhood and the teen years smiled happily from the photograph Aliki took from Millie's hand.

Aliki smiled her thanks. "Go on home, then. Wait there. It could be days, you understand, but I promise to let you know as soon as I find out anything."

Tears born of fear and hope trickled down the old woman's face. "Thank you. Thank you."

The man smiled weakly. "God bless you. Come on, Millie. Let's do as the lady says."

An hour later, Aliki stood beside an examining table. She wore a white plastic apron that was splattered in blood. Bugs was working at the next table, Olly and Neil nearby. Over on the far side of the room, Shez and Chen were working. Aliki was feeling around the nape of the neck of the man who lay on the table. His spine was broken between the number two and three cervical vertebrae. The sudden blast of winds traveling at speeds of five hundred kilometres per hour had literally lifted their heads from their necks. This passenger had been sitting near the stern of the plane. His body had been found in seat 30C. His name was Bill Casati, and he was thirty-two years old. This one had been an easy I.D.; others were going to be much harder. Wiping her hands with a paper towel, she filled out a request for x-rays that would verify her findings. Such evidence would be needed at the inquiry and any court cases that might ensue.

"Shit, look at this," muttered Chen Lai. "I just found a lower jaw of some guy right inside the chest cavity of this old lady. Talk about 'bite me'!"

Shez Ahmed looked up from his table. "A mandible? I had a middle-aged male just a while ago that was missing one. Let me have a look." Chen hosed the blood off the jaw while Shez stood by. "Yes, it could very well be part of him. I'll just take it, if you don't mind. After I finish with the one I am working on, I'll go see if it fits."

"Jesus Christ!" exclaimed Bugs, unzipping a body bag. "This one is a beauty!"

Olly walked over to have a look. "Oooh, how sweet it is. I sure hope she didn't die a virgin; that would be a hell of a crime. Look at those knockers."

Aliki frowned. Crude humour was ever-present in labs. You could try to control it, but you had to let a little slip by. It was one way of relieving the stress and horror and so had to be tolerated to some degree. Aliki opted for humour to get her message across. "Come on, guys, stop drooling on the customers; there's a lot of work to be done today."

Bugs blushed deeply. He always thought of Dr. Pateas as one of the guys, part of the team. Once he'd gotten over her knockout good looks and realized she was damn knowledgeable at her job, he just saw her as a good person to have on his team. Reminded now that she was a woman as well, he was embarrassed by his insensitive comments. "Sorry," he mumbled.

Olly scooted back to his own table and resumed his harmless banter. He was never silent for long; it was his way of handling stress.

"Hey, Shaz, this is your first big disaster, eh?"

"Yes, and I hope, my last," responded the quiet Jordanian.

Olly peeled back the flesh on a shoulder to see if the arm he held fit into the remaining bone of the glenohumeral joint. "Pateas and I have worked a number of plane crashes together. We were both in that line of work for a bit, weren't we, Aliki?"

Aliki was focused on examining a woman's teeth. "Yes."

Olly, satisfied that the arm belonged to his body, stuffed it into the body bag. "Hey, Pateas, you remember that one in South America? The plane went into a mountainside. All this shit got caught up in the canopy of the rain forest. It rained rotting body parts on us for days. You remember?"

"Vividly."

"And then there was the time that airliner went down into the ocean just off the coast. Aliki and I went down in a mini-sub to check it out. The whole fucking sea bottom was covered with white crabs feasting on the dead. I damn near threw up. That was a hell of a thing. Grossed me right out. I haven't been able to eat seafood since, and I used to love the stuff." And so it went on, each team member working late into the evening to piece together the remains and secure a clear identification.

Aliki came across the body of the Dillon's granddaughter just before they called a halt to their work. After she hosed the blood from the corpse, she concluded that the child wasn't in too bad shape, considering. All the parts were mostly intact, but her bones were shattered; she was totally flattened like she'd been rolled over by a steamroller. Skin bags, these were known as. She verified the I.D. using the photo and description that the grandparents had given her. The gold heart carrying the picture of her grandparents was still around her neck. Aliki gently unfastened it and washed it off before dropping it into a plastic bag. She recorded her findings on her clipboard and zipped up the body bag. It was time to call it a night. She had put in an eighteen-hour day.

The rink was now piled with remains — the unexamined along one side, while along the other two distinct rows were forming. One was for the identified and one for the examined but not identified. It was gruesome work.

After washing in the team change rooms, the forensic team piled into Aliki's rental and headed for the local Tim Horton's, a fast food chain specializing in doughnuts and coffee. They ordered subs, doughnuts, and coffee and commandeered the back corner tables. The talk was general. What were the Blue Jays chances this year? Should the Raptors basketball team have made that most recent trade? Would it rain tomorrow? They knew better than to talk of their work in public. There were already too many rumours circulating without their overheard conversations adding to the gossip brew.

Aliki sat back and sipped her coffee, letting the others talk. This was their decompression time, a way to unwind before heading back to lonely motel rooms. Aliki wanted to phone Dawn, but she knew it was important not to truncate this time for herself. Instead, she observed her colleagues with detached interest.

Olly Gertler, like her, had come out of a police force background and had taken a degree in medical forensics. They had first met while they were both assigned to Interpol. Some years later, Olly had left Germany and emigrated to Canada, ending up working in the same forensics lab as Aliki. He always reminded her of a Buergermeister — a German word for a mayor. Loud, friendly, and sociable, Olly was everyone's best friend. He was, Aliki knew, a widower with two grown sons.

Her eyes drifted to Shez Ahmend. A graduate of Amman University in Jordan, he was a medical doctor. Unable to practice in Ontario, he had drifted into forensic work to make a living. He was a young man and hoped to improve his English enough that he could write his medical exams soon. He was a quiet, gentle spoken individual, not comfortable at times with the open, easy ways of North American society. A lonely man, Aliki suspected, and perhaps homesick.

Chen Lai was talking to him, probably noting, too, his emotional isolation. Chen was a fourth-generation Canadian and hated being asked where she was from. She was new to the field, having grown up in North York, a satellite city of Toronto, and attended the University of Toronto. She was intelligent and ambitious and would probably go far.

Beside her was Neil Ross, nursing his coffee when he would have preferred to be steadily drinking his way into oblivion. He was close to retirement and grudgingly resigned to a life that had been mediocre. Divorced years ago, he spent most of his evenings watching Sports TV and drinking. His work was average, at best. Dr. Bates tried hard to keep him out of the courtroom if he could. Ross' lack of a grasp of details frequently lost the case for them. If he had been young, he would probably have been put on probation or let go, but since he was only a few years from retirement, he was being allowed to carry on with less and less responsibility coming his way. He knew it, resented it, but didn't care enough to make a greater effort.

Aliki's blue eyes shifted to Bugs Strasser, who was in an animated conversation with Olly about the Canadian Football League. The legend was that Bugs had gotten his nickname from eating a maggot on a bet while in graduate school. Whether true or not, Bugs was a larger-than-life character. When Bugs was around, people were always laughing. He was also an incurable practical jokester and had to be watched like a hawk. In the lab, however, he got the job done, and he was as cool as a cucumber in court.

They dumped the paper detritus from their trays into the receptacles, placed their trays on top, and filed out. Aliki looked at her watch. There was still time to see the child's grandparents before she phoned Dawn.

She dropped the others off at the motel and popped into the manager's office to get a sketch map of how to get to the address that the grandparents had given her. The modest bungalow was only a few kilometres away in a subdivision now made liveable by the growth of tall trees and the individual gardens that softened the look-a-like facades. Number Twenty-two had a rose garden and a garage door painted pink. Aliki parked the rented car and found the door opening for her before she had made it up the sidewalk.

"Good evening. I'm Dr. Pateas from the forensic labs. You asked me to let you know if I found your granddaughter." The old man nodded and stepped aside to let Aliki enter. She pulled the plastic lunch bag from her pocket. "Is this your granddaughter's?"

The old man took the bag and ran his thumb caressingly over the locket. Tears welled in his eyes, and he nodded. "I'm sorry," Aliki murmured. "Her remains have been identified, and we'll be able to release them to you in a few days."

Just then Millie came up the hall, wiping her hands on a tea towel and followed closely by a woman who looked worried. "I thought I heard someone. Oh, it's you. You've found Nicole? Where is she?"

Aliki nervously shifted her weight from one foot to the other. She hated these moments. "Her remains will not be released for a few days yet, but I thought you would want to know that we have identified her."

Millie looked annoyed. "What are you saying? Nicole is not dead. Where is she?" she demanded snappishly.

"Now, Millie," her husband soothed gently.

"No! I want my granddaughter! What have you done with her? I want her back immediately!" The old woman was in Aliki's face, frantic and aggressive.

Aliki stood her ground, responding quietly, "I am sorry, Mrs. Dillon; Nicole did not survive the crash. We have identified her remains and will release them to your family in the next few days."

It was then that the woman struck out, drumming her clenched fist on Aliki's face and shoulders. Aliki did not stop her. "You're an evil woman! You're lying! You kidnapped Nicole for your own! I want my granddaughter!"

Sam and the other woman recovered from their shock and rushed forward to intervene. While the woman wedged herself between Aliki and the frantic grandmother, the old man took his wife by the shoulders, pulling her away. "Millie, she's dead. What are you doing? We have to accept Nicole's loss."

As she turned and buried her face against her husband's shoulder, Millie seemed to shrink and age before Aliki's eyes. He held her close. "There, there, Millie. Don't take it out on the messenger. Dr. Pateas is just trying to do her job." He looked up at the tall woman standing there stoically. Blood from a scratch was trickling down her face. "I'm sorry."

Aliki nodded. "Will you be all right? Is there anyone you need to call?"

The old man patted his wife's back as if she were a baby. He looked at the other woman for guidance. "I'm Margaret Stevens. I belonged to the same church as Millie and Sam before retiring up here. I'll call their minister, and he can notify Nicole's parents. Don't worry, I'll be here for them."

Saddened, Aliki took her leave. There was no nice way to tell someone that they had lost someone they had loved to violence. A deep blanket of depression settled on her soul. How the hell had she ever gotten into such a shitty business?

She drove back to the hotel in a mood that was part anger and part depression, slamming the car door behind her after she got out. Thomas Bates was sitting in a metal rocker outside his door, fouling the air with his pipe smoke.

"Aliki, come and sit down," he called, indicating the seat beside him with the stem of his pipe.

The last thing she felt like was making pleasant conversation outside some cheap motel on a verandah that looked over the parking lot, but she gritted her teeth and went over. Scowling, she flopped down and hooked her long legs over the railing.

Bates sat puffing his pipe for a few minutes, letting the heat of anger bleed off his assistant before he spoke. "I observe, Dr. Pateas, that you are sporting a nasty-looking scratch and what appears to be the growing discolouration of a black eye. I conclude from this that once again you have been using your famous tact and diplomacy on individuals in the greater world."

Aliki laughed; she couldn't help herself. Bates was such a bugger. "I promised an older couple that I would notify them if I found their granddaughter. I went over to their house, and the old lady went ape-shit on me. Insisted her granddaughter was alive and that I'd kidnapped her. The old guy was okay about it, but it took him a few minutes to react and pull his wife off me."

Bates chuckled. "Well, I won't let it be known that the woman with a ninth dan in Karate got beat up by a little old lady."

Aliki gave him a sardonic look. "Thanks."

They sat again in silence, listening to the crickets and the steady traffic not far away on Highway 400. "This job stinks. I don't know why I continue to do it," she muttered.

Bates took his pipe from his mouth and studied it for a few seconds. "We, Aliki, are the last thread that binds society. When violence rips a community apart, leaving only death and pain in its wake, we quietly go about our business. We give the dead back their names, we provide closure for those that mourn, and most importantly, we endeavour to answer the question, 'Why?' Gradually, stitch by stitch, we mend the rips of our society, sewing them back together again. It is often horrific work and has very few rewards, except for that satisfaction of knowing that you cared for that lost soul long after others had walked away from the grave. And in the end, you saw justice done."

Tears rolled down Aliki's face, and she brushed them away with annoyance. Bates pretended he didn't notice. "Remember, Aliki, someone has to care." With a groan of weariness, he got to his feet. "We must be up early so I think I had better turn in. I assume you will be talking to that wonderful woman who has agreed to marry you?" Aliki nodded. "Say hello to Dawn and assure her that both you and I will be at her wedding in good time. I wouldn't miss seeing you tied down for the world."

Aliki watched him walk away with tired, dragging steps. He really was an amazing man, and Aliki was very fond of him. She got up and stretched and went inside to phone the woman she loved.

Dawn had not had a good day. She was worried about Aliki and whether the emergency would keep her away all week. She had gotten into a silly argument with Mac about the amount of time she spent on the Internet with her cousin Ryan; her publisher was pressing her about getting her next book completed; and Sally Slurp, Mac's cat, had clawed the back of Aliki's favourite chair.

By the end of the day, she was worn out running from one crisis to the next and organizing the last details of the wedding whenever she had a moment. At eleven o'clock, she slumped down into one of the living room chairs and massaged her throbbing temples. She had a blistering headache. A few minutes later, the phone rang.

"Hello."

"Hi. It's Aliki."

"Oh I'm glad you clarified that." Dawn smiled. "I thought it might be my spare lover, seeing as you are out of town."

Aliki snorted. "Funny. How is it going there?"

Dawn sighed and gave Aliki a list of troubles and annoyances that had plagued her all day. Her head aching and her body weary, it was hard not to sound whiney. "So, how is it going up there?"

Aliki, who had put the receiver down on the pillow and who had been lying with her eyes closed in a state of only half awake, started at the question and quickly picked up the phone. "Ah, well, okay," she muttered. How could she say anything more? There had been a tragic loss of life. It was a nice catch phrase that covered the horror of the mutilated and shattered bone and flesh. And disregarded the anger and anguish of the families.

"Is it bad?" Dawn probed impatiently.

Self pity suddenly descended on Aliki's shoulders. She was overtired and still upset about the incident with Millie Dillon. She hadn't phoned to hear all of Dawn's woes. She snapped back, "Yeah, it's bad. It's never good when people fall like stones from five kilometres up."

Dawn was in no mood to be understanding. "I was just trying to be supportive. You don't need to take my head off."

"Well, damn it, Dawn, I didn't phone to hear this crap."

For a second there was no response from the other end, then Dawn's voice came quietly and calmly. "I thought you'd want to know. Have you any idea how long you'll be up there?"

"No."

Dawn gritted her teeth. Aliki could be really exasperating when she got into one of these moods. It didn't happen very often, thank God, but the way she shut down and refused to share made it all very difficult. "Okay, well, phone me when you can. I love you."

"I love you, too. I'm sorry; I'm not very good company tonight. We've got over four hundred dead and I had to tell an old couple tonight that their only grandchild didn't survive. The old lady didn't take it very well. She blackened my eye, actually." Aliki got it all out in a rush, feeling awful about the way she had been acting and wanting to make it up.

"I'm sorry, lover. You didn't need that. I wish I could give you a hug. Would it help if I drove up there?"

Aliki shook her head. "No, I mean, yes, it would help, but I wouldn't get to see you. I'd be putting in eighteen-hour days and then I'd need to crash. Thanks for offering, though."

Dawn was disappointed, even though she knew Aliki was right. "Okay then, you try to get some sleep. I'll talk to you tomorrow. Good night, lover."

"Good night, Dawn." Aliki hung up, feeling stupid and lonely. She hadn't handled that well. With a sigh she went to shower and then to curl up in her narrow, lonely bed.

By seven the next morning, she'd picked her team up again. They breakfasted at a small diner where the pancakes and homemade sausage were particularly good. Well fortified against a long day, they returned to the makeshift morgue, slipped into their lab gear, and manned their respective tables.

Neil unzipped the body bag. "Uck! This one is ripe! I don't mind that they pee themselves in fright, but do they have to take a crap in their pants, too?"

Olly looked up with a smile. "Hell, I'd like to see you fall five kilometres out of the sky and not shit yourself."

And so the gruesome work went on. First, quickly identifying those bodies that were relatively intact or still strapped into broken seats. Later came the slow, grisly process of matching body parts and identifying the dead through dental records. Aliki got most of the severely burnt victims, bones being her area of expertise. She knew that despite her best efforts there would be human remains never identified, and once again a mass grave would be dug for the victims of violent death.

By the third day, all the forensic personnel were working full time at the temporary morgue. The Army was called in to do the large area sweeps looking for any remaining evidence. Bates was now in charge and Aliki — free from the responsibilities of collecting and maintaining documentation and ordering x-ray evidence, swabbing skin, organ, and fabric samples — could give her full attention to the identification of the dead.

By the end of the week, they were able to close down their makeshift facilities and move the investigation back to their main labs in Toronto. The public now knew the worst. The aircraft had been nearly full; there were 409 dead, no survivors. Bodies were slowly being released to families for burial. The processes of grieving and of assigning blame were well underway.

Aliki had mixed feelings about going home. On the one hand, she missed Dawn and Mac terribly. On the other, she didn't want to talk about what she had been through. She just needed to be left alone to come to terms with the enormity of the horror that she'd had to deal with. When at home, she read a lot in her den or worked on her reports at her desk.

She went to bed hours after Dawn to avoid intimacy. She didn't feel clean. The smell of death still clung to her and her hands were chapped from compulsively being washed. After the first few rejections, Dawn left her alone. She and Mac busied themselves with wedding plans and other activities, giving Aliki the space she needed. For that, Aliki was both grateful and embarrassed. She knew she was not being fair to her family, but emotionally she just needed to shut down.

On the following Tuesday, Dr. Bates was again into work early, trying to catch up on the backlog of other responsibilities that had been set aside because of the airline crash. He looked up through bushy white eyebrows to see Aliki standing at his door, white and shaken. He was on his feet in an instant and led his valued assistant and friend to a chair.

He asked no questions. Instead, he disappeared into his private washroom and came out with a paper cup of cold water and a cold damp cloth to put on the back of her neck. When he saw some of her colour returning, he sat on the edge of his desk and asked gently, "What is it Aliki?"

With a shaky hand, she took two plastic Baggies from her labcoat pocket. One contained an open envelope and the other, a page of a letter. Bates nodded his approval. However deeply shocked Aliki had been by this correspondence, she had shown her training by making sure any evidence would be preserved.

The message had been typed on a computer and printed on standard bond paper using a laser printer. The words were all in upper case and bold in twelve gauge font.

THE PLANE CRASH IS YOUR RESPONSIBILITY. THEY ARE ALL DEAD BECAUSE OF YOU, BITCH. THIS IS JUST THE FIRST OF THOSE THAT WILL SUFFER BECAUSE YOU PUT ME AWAY. YOU RUINED MY LIFE NOW I AM GOING TO RUIN YOURS. LIVE WITH THESE DEATHS AND SO MANY MORE ON YOUR CONSCIENCE. JIGSAW

Bates looked up and met blue eyes filled with pain and bewilderment. "It has to be a hoax, Aliki. Jigsaw died in the prison riots and fire several months ago. It is just someone trying to hurt you."

Aliki's voice was tight but controlled. "Who did the autopsy?"

Bates grimaced. "Neil Ross."

Aliki stared back, her face like stone; Bates knew what she was thinking. Ross had been assigned the case because it was a closed shop: prisoners had butchered each other in rage and frustration. The legal system would not be concerned about potentially shoddy forensic evidence. They would make recommendations to see the opportunity for such a situation did not happen again; the recommendations would be ignored because of lack of money and personnel; and the dead would soon be replaced with new inmates, equally dysfunctional and crowded together.

"I need an order of exhumation," Aliki said through tight lips. "I have to know for sure."

Part 2

Aliki had been even more withdrawn than usual that night. Dawn waited until their daughter was safely off to bed and then broached the subject with her moody lover. "Aliki, we need to talk, hon. The plane crash, I know, has been pretty traumatic for you. You've really withdrawn. If you feel you can't talk to me about what is going on inside you, maybe you should make an appointment to talk to one of the police counsellors. You are just not yourself."

Aliki put down the report she was reading and looked at Dawn, her eyes filled with annoyance and guilt. She didn't think she could handle one more strain in her life at the moment, and yet she knew she was not being fair to Dawn or Mac. "Something has come up in relation to the crash, something pretty serious. I...I can't talk about it. I'll be leaving very early tomorrow. A body is being exhumed for re-examination."

Dawn saw the pain in Aliki's eyes. Whatever her lover was holding in was no small matter. She went over and put her hands on Aliki's shoulders, rubbing out some of the tension before leaning forward to place a kiss on Aliki's brow. "Just remember, we are here for you. This Saturday we'll officially become family, but I don't need that ceremony to know in my heart that you are my partner, my soulmate, my reason."

Aliki swallowed and reached up to place her hand over Dawn's that rested on her shoulder. "Sometimes the past can come back to haunt you. I...I am really worried."

"Tell me about it."

With effort, Aliki tried to get out what they had seen and done at the crash site and then the horror of the letter. Dawn listened but said nothing until Aliki came to a jerky halt, then she wrapped her suffering lover close in her arms. "You can only do what you can for the victims, Aliki. You didn't cause their pain, although sometimes when people are in shock they may lash out at whomever is near. Nor are you responsible for the crash or the actions of this Jigsaw. Your life is not an extension of theirs. Tell me why this Jigsaw might have a grudge against you."

Aliki held on to Dawn tightly, needing her warmth and understanding. "It was one of my first cases when I was assigned to the forensic lab. Jigsaw, her real name is Marsha Higgins, killed her parents. She tortured and stabbed them to death because they wouldn't let her have the car for the evening. She doused them with gasoline and set the house on fire. Then she took the car and picked up some friends and went to a movie."

Dawn looked shocked. "Holy crow, that is one disturbed girl!"

Aliki nodded. "The police were fairly certain it was her, but they couldn't make her vary from her alibi, and they couldn't pinpoint the time of death close enough to be absolutely sure it was her. There were other deaths, women, where the MO was similar after that. The police could never get enough on Jigsaw to make anything stick, so she was still free as a bird.

"When I started working forensics, I was going back over cases that had not been closed. One was the murder of Jigsaw's parents. I noted that on the description sheet taken the first night of her questioning, it had been observed that she'd had a scratch on her arm from her dog. I went back and checked all the scrapings that were kept from under the fingernails of each parent. By using some pretty sophisticated enhancing techniques, I was able to prove that a minute amount of skin tissue found intact under one nail of the mother had come from Jigsaw's arm. It placed her at the scene, and we got the conviction."

"So she has it in for you?"

"She probably would, but she's supposed to be dead — stabbed and burnt in the prison riots a few months ago. Neil Ross did the autopsy."

Dawn sat on the edge of the desk. "You don't think Ross' lab work is all that good, do you? And you feel the prison stabbing and the burning of the body repeats a pattern. You think that Jigsaw is still alive. Is it her remains you want to exhume?"

Aliki nodded. "At the age of seventeen, Jigsaw got away with murder. And she probably killed others over a number of years before we were able to convict her of her parents' death. She is intelligent and deeply psychotic. A few years in prison would have given her a lot of time to plan and to pick up criminal knowledge. Yeah, I have a really bad feeling about this. Dear God, Dawn, what if she is alive and did blow up that aircraft to get back at me?"

Aliki's eyes were filled with horror and pain. Dawn wrapped her close. "Then she has committed a heinous crime, and I know you and the police will find her and bring her to justice. You are not responsible for her atrocities, Aliki, only for seeing that justice is done."

They went to bed then, Dawn snuggling close to try to warm the wounded soul of her lover and Aliki lying stiff and awake beside her well into the night, her mind playing over and over every minute of Jigsaw's trial and images of the crash site.

The scream of passengers' panic suddenly silenced by death woke Aliki with a start from the nightmare that had terrorized her dreams. Dawn was holding her, trying to calm her. Like a siren in the distance, the alarm clock wailed softly. Aliki reached out and shut it off.

"You okay, lover?"

Aliki wiped the sweat from her lip and nodded, then she gave Dawn a reassuring if shaky hug. "Nightmare. I'm okay. It's three thirty. I've gotta get up and get over to the gravesite. You go back to sleep."

Dawn dropped a kiss on Aliki's cheek. "Okay. When will I see you?"

"I don't know. It will depend on what I find. I'll do the identification as soon as the bones are delivered to the lab." Aliki returned the kiss and then slipped out of bed. "I'll phone, hopefully around noon."

Dawn nodded, sympathy and concern written on her face. "Just you remember you are getting married in a few days."

Aliki smiled, but the light didn't reach her troubled eyes. "I will."

She headed off to the bathroom to get ready, and Dawn lay brooding for a few minutes. If Jigsaw had brought that plane down, Aliki was not easily going to be able to live with that knowledge. How could she help her partner work through this horror?

Exhumations always happened at dawn, an old tradition from the turn of the century but one still practised in some places to avoid the attention of the public. A backhoe had been brought in to dig up the casket, and a flatbed truck stood by to carry the remains to the lab. Aliki watched as two men slid down into the grave and cleared away the excess soil from the plain coffin. It was still in relatively good condition, but then it had only been in the ground a few months. They got ropes around it, and it was hoisted slowly from the earth by the backhoe and lowered onto the truck. Caked dirt broke loose and trickled back to the ground, and the morning light reflected blood red off the wood.

Canvas was tied over the coffin, and the truck departed. The gravediggers covered the scar in the earth with wood and put up caution tape. Aliki signed the witness of exhuming form presented to her and then slipped into her Honda van for the drive down to the labs. There had been no tears, prayers, or concerned relatives, just a dirty job done quickly and efficiently. Jigsaw had left no one alive that cared.

Bates watched from the doorway as Aliki methodically worked on cleaning and measuring the grave remains. She had been at it most of the morning, obviously going out of her way to make sure that her findings were precise and accurate. She jotted one more thing on her lab sheet and then went to clean up. The lab technicians would see to the removal of the bones and the cleaning of the workspace.

A half hour later, Aliki appeared at Bates' office door looking grim and determined.

"Come in. Well, what have you found?"

Aliki nearly growled in frustration. "It's not her. Marsha Higgins had broken her right tibia as a young teen, and there is no evidence of such an injury. She also had her wisdom teeth removed. The female in there is missing one wisdom tooth, and the others have fully emerged. Height and bone structure are similar and probably age, but that's about as far as it goes. Neil never did a complete examination. He saw a burnt corpse with roughly the same characteristics and concluded it had to be Jigsaw."

Bates sighed, looking equally annoyed. "We need to know how this misidentification could have happened. Someone else must have been missing."

Aliki picked up a thick file folder from her lap and placed it on Bates' desk. "I think I might have an idea. After her conviction, Jigsaw stayed in the city jail waiting on lawyers' appeals and such. Then, a few months ago, she and another inmate up on prostitution charges were transferred to the main prison facility. The riot and fire occurred that night. It might be a lucky coincidence, but I think Jigsaw started both the riot and the fire so that she would have the opportunity to murder the woman she went up with and change places with her. She did her time for prostitution and walked away a month later."

Bates looked up in surprise. "Surely that wouldn't be possible."

"I think it was. Jigsaw is not only criminally insane, she is very smart. She could have pulled this off. And I think she had been planning an attempt right from the very beginning. Check the file; she had access to the records. She volunteered to work in the prison office to gain parole points. I think she switched the fingerprints and photos between her file and the other woman's as soon as she knew they would be going up together. It was an opportunity made in heaven for someone as devious and bold as Jigsaw." Aliki's facial muscles rippled with suppressed anger and the attempt at control.

"She would not have access to the data files, though," Bates reasoned.

"No, she would need a user passcode. But as long as no one compared the two, that wouldn't be a problem."

Bates leaned back in his chair. The leather squeaked and settled again. "We'll need to get the authorities to check. If Jigsaw did escape, the wheels have to be put in motion to get her on a Most Wanted list and back in the hands of the justice system."

Aliki snorted in frustration. "And how long will that take? And in the meantime, how many more people will she kill in my name? I can't wait that long...this is personal."

Bates looked up sharply. "We are not in the business of making things personal, Dr. Pateas," he reminded her coldly. "It is our job to be objective and mete out justice impartially. You did your job efficiently; now you have to let the justice system do its."

Aliki's eyes were the colour of blue ice. "I am not going to sit back and let Jigsaw kill again. She wants me to come after her, and I mean to do just that."

Bates slammed forward in his chair. "Damn it, Aliki. You have no proof that your crazy theory has any merit to it at all. This department will not support you on some wild goose chase. This is a police matter."

Aliki stood slowly. "No. Once that letter arrived, it was no longer a police matter. This is all about her and me."

Bates stood and made one last appeal to Aliki's common sense. "This could ruin your career. Damn it, Aliki, you're getting married on the weekend."

For a second she looked away from Bates, blinking back tears. "No, I'm not."

"What!"

"I can't, can't you see that? It would put Dawn and Mac in grave danger. It would be taunting Jigsaw. The wedding is off until I can find Jigsaw and put her away." Aliki used Bates' stunned silence to pick up the file. "I'll make copies of what I need and return the originals."

"I can't do anything to help you, Aliki, not officially," Bates warned. She nodded sadly and walked out.

A few hours later, Bates wandered into Aliki's office and sat down. His office was always an eclectic pile of files and specimens, seemingly randomly left balancing precariously on every surface. Aliki's office was rigidly neat, every bit of paper filed and every speck of dirt swept away. Not for the first time, Bates wondered how his assistant could work in such a sterile environment. The only concession to human weakness was a framed picture of her with Dawn and Mac, sitting on a large boulder by a northern lake. Bates knew that Aliki's half-sister, actor/director Robbie Williams, had taken the picture.

"I received a call from Personnel. They tell me you have applied for a leave of absence."

Aliki looked up from her computer screen where she had been methodically going through all of Jigsaw's documentation. "It seemed the best way. I don't want my actions to reflect badly on the lab."

Bates looked up sharply. "Dr. Pateas, let us establish this point right now – I do not approve at all of this undertaking, but if your mind is made up, I do expect you to conduct yourself within the parameters of the law and of your moral and ethical conscience. Is that understood?"

Aliki straightened. "Yes, sir." Intellectually she knew that Bates had no authority over her outside of the forensic lab, but her respect for him was so great that she couldn't stop herself from accepting his right to set the parameters of her investigation. In a way, it was a relief to have these emotional safeguards outlined. It set boundaries that would be hard for her to cross, even in the heat of the moment.

"Good. You will keep in touch. I have made arrangements. Here is a key to a locker at the Union train station downtown. In it you will find a cell phone that will be kept charged for you. There will also be a supply of money, should you need it, a spare weapon, and ammunition. Your new name is Alberta Freeman. Here are your driver's license and health card."

Aliki accepted the battered and worn documentation and looked at it with interest. How had Bates arranged all this in such a short time? She smiled to see the old devil had used Dawn's surname for her cover. He might be helping, but he was not about to let her forget that she had a family and responsibilities to look after. "Thanks."

Bates looked grim. "Naturally, this department knows nothing about this undercover assignment you have taken on."

"Naturally," Aliki agreed wryly.

Bates nodded. "You have been in the West and have recently moved to the East looking for work. You had a room in Calgary; the address is on your license. You worked for the Calgary Stampede Association in grounds care until you lost your job due to downsizing. Questions?"

Aliki shook her head. "Thanks, Dr. Bates. I owe you for this. I know you don't agree with what I'm doing, and I appreciate your support."

Bates stood with a noise that sounded much like a growl. "You do not have my support. I am just trying my best to protect a valuable member of my team from her own stubborn stupidity and to make sure that long suffering partner of yours might actually someday have a decent life with you." For a moment he hesitated. "Good luck," he said, and he was gone.

Aliki blinked as she felt the pain of Bates' disapproval deeply. What was she going to tell Dawn? How could she make her understand that doing this had to come before their wedding plans?

Lunch had come and gone and so had dinner, with no word from Aliki. Dawn went through the normal routines of the day, covering her growing anxiety as best she could. Things could not have gone well for Aliki today, or she would have phoned. The fact that she had not heard from her moody lover could only mean one thing: Aliki didn't have the nerve to talk to her and that could only spell bad news. She loved her dearly, but there was no denying that Aliki was an emotional coward.

It was well past eight when Aliki's van pulled into the driveway. Mac came bouncing down the stairs immediately. "Hi, Aliki. Where have you been? What's up?"

Aliki looked around for help, but Dawn's quiet, defensive manner did not seem to offer much hope. "Hey, let me get in. Why don't you go put a kettle on? I could sure do with a cup of tea."

"Okay," smiled Mac, who could see no wrong in her hero. She headed off up the hall, leaving Dawn standing watching Aliki from the living room doorway.

Aliki squirmed. "I should have phoned."

"Yes, you should have."

Aliki swallowed and blushed. "Sorry." This was going to be even harder than she imagined. "We need to talk."

"Okay." Dawn turned and walked into the living room. Typically, they snuggled up together on the couch; tonight Dawn chose the chair in a dark corner on the other side of the cold hearth.

Mac came trotting back up the hall. "I got the kettle on..." Something was not right; she could feel the tension between them like a physical barrier. "What's up?" she demanded, looking back and forth between her mother and Aliki.

Suddenly overcome by the enormity of the task ahead, Aliki sank into a chair. "Mac...Dawn, I..." She swallowed and proceeded. "I believe that a very disturbed woman that I helped convict a few years ago has escaped from the justice system. She sent a letter to me stating that she was responsible for the death of the passengers on that downed aircraft last week. She said this was just the first of the killings she means to do to get back at me for her imprisonment."

Filled with horror and confusion, Mac looked at her mom. She wasn't sure what this all meant, but it didn't sound good. Dawn held her arms open, and Mac went over and cuddled closely to her mom.

"Mac, Dawn, I can't in good conscience allow this woman to continue with her mad plan. I am also terribly afraid for you two. I believe this is a sick, twisted challenge, that she is taunting me to come after her, and I mean to do just that."

There, it was said. Now the rest tumbled out before she could lose her courage. "I need to delay the wedding. I don't know how long. It could be some time. Jigsaw will be living on the streets, and I am going to have to do the same to track her down. I'll be leaving tonight. I don't know when you will hear from me again."

For a beat of a heart, there was no response, then Dawn stood and walked over to pat Aliki on the shoulder. "You will need time to get ready. Mac and I will see to making the tea and putting together some sandwiches for you. Come on, Mac."

And that was it. They were gone. No tears, no questions, just quiet acceptance. The surprising reaction chilled Aliki to the bone.

In the kitchen, Mac was trying to work through the unexpected turn of events. "What am I going to tell my friends? They have just accepted that my parents are gay and are going to get married, and now I have to tell them it's all off."

Dawn gave her daughter a hug. "It is not off; it's delayed. Aliki doesn't have a nine-to-five job, Mac. We might not always understand her motivation, but we have to accept that she knows what she is doing and this is the only way. Aliki would never deliberately hurt us. She loves us. She feels that what she is doing has to be done in order to protect us and others."

The words sounded sincere and had the quality of truth about them. Dawn hoped they would help her daughter to accept this blow to their plans. For her own part, all she felt inside was a growing numbness.

Looking annoyed, Mac slapped egg salad on fresh slices of bread. "Her job is to find the evidence; the police should be the ones going after this woman. Why aren't they?"

Dawn shrugged. She thought it was a reasonable question, but out loud, her words were supportive. "Aliki is a skilled forensic scientist, but she is also an RCMP officer. You know she has used her police skills before to solve crimes. That's the way Aliki operates. Mac, over four hundred people died on that plane. That is very hard for Aliki to accept and just sit back and do nothing."

The sandwich got dumped on a plate roughly. "We could have the wedding first, and then she could take off."

Dawn shook her head. She didn't have an answer for her daughter. She didn't even have an answer for herself.

Upstairs things were not going any better. Aliki was on the phone with her sister.

"Are you fucking nuts?" Robbie snapped. "Everything is ready, damn it. What about your family? They're arriving in two days time. They're expecting a wedding, not a damn wake. And what about Dawn and Mac?"

Aliki had a hell of a headache. "We've talked. They understand."

Robbie was good and pissed with her half-sister. "Bullshit. Even I don't understand. This is not your job; you're just using this to chicken out again."

Aliki snapped. "Back off! You know better than that. I wouldn't be doing this if I thought there was a better way. Do you really think I'd walk out on everyone if I thought I had options? I don't. I know this is fucking hard on everyone; it's fucking hard on me, too. Just help me out here and get this wedding called off with as little attention as possible."

There was silence for a second at the other end. "Dawn has agreed to this?" asked a quiet, cold voice.

"Yes."

"Then Janet and I will see to getting everything cancelled. We'll be down in a day or two to pick up Dawn and Mac. If you think there is that much danger, then they'll be safer up here for the summer. Besides, they're going to need some family support."

Aliki felt the sting but didn't react. Her anger spent, she felt only numbness. She had made her decision, and there was no going back. "Thanks. Thanks for taking care of them, Robbie. Goodbye." She heard Robbie's uneven sigh as she fought with her emotions.

"We don't have to agree on this. Janet and I are here for Dawn and Mac, and I hope you know that we are here for you, too, if you need our help. Be careful."

"I will. Thanks. Bye."

For a few minutes, she stood by the phone, dealing with the rawness of her feelings. Then she gritted her teeth and headed back down the stairs to face her family.

It was a strained gathering. Subdued, they sat around the kitchen table and talked about how to proceed. Aliki related the bare essentials of her conversation with Robbie. Dawn nodded and promised to phone Aliki's father in the morning and tell him and her two brothers and Ari's wife not to fly out for the wedding after all. They talked about wedding gifts and what to do about them and made a list of guests that would need to be contacted. They talked about everything but what was really important – Aliki's decision to go after Jigsaw.

Mac was quiet. That was usually her way anyway. She knew her mother wanted her to support Aliki's decision so she was going to, but inside she felt betrayed by her hero. She felt angry, too, that her mother was being ditched at the altar. It wasn't right. She left as soon as she could and hid up in her bedroom, writing e-mails back and forth to her cousin Ryan, Robbie's daughter.

"Dawn, thanks for supporting me in this," Aliki said, once they were alone. "I know it is hard."

Dark, stormy eyes snapped up. "I don't support you on this. It is more than hard; it is embarrassing and degrading. But I don't want to hurt my daughter any more than she has been hurt by your actions. I won't dump my anger on her. I will not criticize your actions to anyone. Something like this is a family matter and far too sensitive a topic, for me at least, to want to discuss. Just don't count on me being here when you get back, Aliki. You have decided which path you feel you need to take, and I guess now I need to sit down and re-evaluate where I am going, too."

Aliki felt like she had been punched. "Dawn, I love you!"

Tears welled in the smaller woman's eyes, and she blinked them back with determination. She was not going to make a scene, no matter what. "I love you, too, Aliki. But love by itself is not enough; there has to be commitment. You have things to do to get ready. Go do them; I'll see to the dishes. I need to be alone for a bit."

Aliki nodded miserably and left.

There wasn't much to do. Jigsaw would make for the streets of Toronto. Having run away from home on any number of occasions, she knew the streets and how to survive. She would be out there waiting for Aliki on her own territory. Aliki would not have the element of surprise, but she might, thanks to Dr. Bates' help, be able to move onto the streets before Jigsaw realized she was there. Shedding an identity was not as easy as it seemed. Her face was known, and on the street there was a well-plugged-in grapevine. If she was spotted, everyone would know within days. She would need to be very cautious.

She went into the bathroom and cut away at her hair with a pair of scissors, combing her hair forward to create a deep bang and cutting the rest ragged and short. She used tweezers to drastically thin her eyebrows and popped in tinted lenses to change her eye colour from glacial blue to grey.

She chose a pair of her old black gardening jeans with the torn knees and ragged, discoloured cuffs, a scuffed pair of hiking boots, a black sleeveless t-shirt, and a worn black Levi jacket. Her Shinto knives slipped nicely down the side of her boots. Into an old knapsack, she tucked underwear, a change of shirt and jeans, toiletries, and her service revolver with two extra clips. She was ready.

She found Dawn in the living room, curled in a corner of the couch. How did she say goodbye to someone she loved but was walking out on? "I'm going now," she stated awkwardly, standing in the doorway.

Dawn got up and came over, wrapping her arms around her partner. Aliki dropped her bag and held Dawn close. "I'm sorry."

Dawn nodded. "You look a mess."

Aliki kissed Dawn's head. "I'll look worse soon. You and Mac be very careful. I...I love you."

Dawn gave her one last hug and then stepped back. "I love you, too. You come back safely."

Aliki nodded, picked up her bag, and fled the house. The whole situation was just too painful to prolong.

She walked down several blocks and caught a streetcar for the centre of the city. It was time to start building her street identity. Tonight she would stay at the bus station, making sure that the night crawlers saw her about. The assumption would be that she had gotten off the late bus in from the West and had no money or place to go.

The window of the bus reflected back a ghostly image of herself superimposed over the beating flashes of store windows as the streetcar bumped along. Already she looked streetworn and tough. In a few days, she would have left her old identity behind altogether to be someone else, someone hardened, calculating, and bent on evening a score.

Dawn lay awake well into the small hours of the morning, trying to come to terms with what had happened. She wasn't sure she could. Intellectually, she could rationalize Aliki's decision; emotionally, it was a totally different matter. The more she thought about the enormity of calling off the wedding and the embarrassment associated with it, the angrier she became.

Her heart was a cauldron of emotions. Confusion, anger, and fear for Aliki's safety churned around and around in her soul. Watching the grey light of a city dawn creep into the night sky, she set her jaw firmly. She could get through this. She had faced worse situations in her life. First, she would have to talk to Robbie and Janet about calling everything off. Then she needed to see to their own safety and pack to join Robbie and Janet at their home in the north of Ontario. Lastly, she needed to get on with her novel. There was no use keeping everything on hold. She needed to get on with her life — a life without Aliki.

Aliki spent the remainder of the night sitting in the downtown bus station. Then, cramped, hungry, and grimy with a layer of dust and diesel fuel, she headed out onto the streets. There was a small place she knew that the police used that would help her get deeper into her character. She walked the seven or eight blocks, stopping along the way for a coffee and bagel at a corner store.

Her destination was a small tattoo shop on a seedy back street. The owner was an East Indian woman who had a small apartment in the back of the store and rented the rooms above to students scraping by on next to nothing.

The place smelt of curry and bird droppings. Shazenna had two large parrots in a cage on the counter. She wore a lime green, flowered sundress that even in its fullness did not hide the many rolls of fat that formed Shazenna's being.

"Whadda ya want?"

"Hi to you, too, Shazenna," Aliki rumbled, coming to stand at the counter and absently holding up a piece of browned apple for one of the birds to peck at.

Shazenna smiled, leaning back on the counter and looking with interest at the tall woman. The smile did not reach her eyes. "Dr. Pateas. It's been a while. Whadda ya want that is going to fuck up my life?"

"I need to be on the streets, Shazenna. Seeing but not seen."

The old woman chuckled softly. "You ain't got a snowball's chance in hell. You stink of cop shop."

Aliki raised an eyebrow and leaned closer, speaking in a soft, steely voice. "Let's start with some henna tattoos that won't wear off for a while, then we'll talk about hair dye."

The old woman's smile faded. She couldn't afford not to have the police on her side. If the police decided they didn't like her, they could make life fucking miserable. She reached under the counter and pulled out a worn album. "Take your pick."

That afternoon, Aliki emerged from Shazenna's with dirt-brown hair and two henna tattoos. One was a chain of barbed wire around her upper left arm, the second was a skull with the words "fuck you" on a banner below it. She'd had that one put on the left side of her throat. People's eyes would be naturally drawn to the tattoo and away from her face. That was important. The last step in her new identity was a pair of tinted glasses.

Shazenna looked her over critically. "You're too fucking clean and walk with too much pride. Ya gotta slouch like a beaten dog. That's what them people are out there — either mad or beaten dogs. Sometimes both."

Aliki nodded. While Shazenna had worked on her, they'd had time to talk. The old woman had no time for crazies that blew up aircraft. Grudgingly, she had offered help and advice, even a bowl of well-stewed curry. She had no time for cops but believed strongly in revenge. "Don't wash or stand in the fucking rain and them'll last you through to the winter," the old woman advised as Aliki left.

Aliki headed back down to Younge Street and hung around until late at night. The summer streets were an exotic blend of pimps, hookers, nightclub yuppies, tourists, and street people. Aliki walked up and down the street doing the usual street shit. She rooted through dustbins, wrote on a scrap piece of cardboard that she was out of work, and begged change. All the while, her eyes scanned the crowds looking for that one familiar face that she knew she would never forget.

It was a matter of survival, slowly sinking into a lifestyle and identity that would be accepted on the streets. For now she was sleeping under some bushes in one of the city parks. The days were hot, and the nights cool. It was okay. She had to remain alert, and she knew in a few weeks that she'd need some place warmer, but for the time being it was okay. Each morning, she'd head into the train terminal and report to Bates, then phone Dawn on the cell phone that had been left in the locker. Then she'd wander the streets, slowly and methodically checking out the old haunts she knew Jigsaw was likely to frequent. At noon, she'd head over to the soup kitchen run by the Salvation Army and have a bowl of chicken soup and bread. Then it was back on the street again well into the night — waiting, watching, and listening.

There were rumours. Nothing definite, just some talk of a tough female bragging about bringing the airliner down. No one seemed to know her or where she might be. The description was vague, and the general feeling was that whoever she was, she was just another damn crazy with too big a mouth and too little brain. Aliki knew different. Jigsaw was playing with her. Leaving her crumbs to tantalize her but no clear trail to where she might be. She knew she needed to be careful. Jigsaw would be listening and watching, too. She would know if anyone was asking questions or taking too great an interest in the woman who was bragging about bringing the plane down. Aliki listened but showed no interest and asked no questions. It was frustrating and inefficient, but it was necessary to have patience if she was going to catch Jigsaw.

Three days on the streets and Aliki was feeling lean and hungry. She woke before dawn, cold and cramped, wet from a steady drizzle that was blanketing Toronto. She headed down to the train terminal and washed her hands and face in the public washroom, then brushed her teeth. Feeling almost human again, she checked that no street people were around, found the safe locker, and took out the phone.

Her call to Dr. Bates was short and to the point. "Morning."

"Good morning, Alberta. How are you doing out there?"

"It's raining, and I am sleeping under a goddamn bush. How do you think I'm doing? There is nothing new to report. I had a beer over at the Jarvis Tavern last night. The bartender had heard a woman laughing about the plane crash. Told him she'd heard it was an act of revenge and had nothing to do with terrorism. The description: five foot six, red shaggy hair, and a lazy eye that turns slightly in. Could very well be Jigsaw. I'm going back there tonight."

"Be careful. Do you need back up?"

Aliki snorted. "I thought I was on my own."

"You are. I am just protecting Dawn's interests," came the grumbled reply.

"I can manage." Aliki had her back against the grey, chipped lockers. The metal felt icy cold through her damp t-shirt. Her alert eyes restlessly scanned faces.

"I talked to Dawn last night. She is naturally worried about you. She and Mac have finished up all they can do here and are traveling up to Robbie and Janet's tomorrow morning. You will call her, I hope."

Aliki growled, anger surging through her and driving off the chill. "That's my business. I appreciate your concern, but butt out."

There was an audible sigh of frustration at the other end of the line. Bates was not happy with her attitude.

"Very well. I am here if you need me." He rang off without waiting for a response.

Aliki pulled a face at the cell phone, realizing that her part of the conversation had been rude and antagonistic, and she blushed. The continuing nightmares of the crash and the discomfort of her physical situation had left her short on both sleep and patience.

She punched in Dawn's number. "Hi, it's me."

"Hi. Are you okay?"

"Yeah, fine. I'm starting to pick up some leads. Nothing definite, but rumours that she is about."

"Be careful."

"Yes, I will." Aliki's words fell into silence. What more was there to say? An abyss of disagreement separated their actions and their hearts. Aliki hated the gulf between them. It made her feel lonely and depressed.

Dawn swallowed her hurt and pride and made an attempt to reach out. When she spoke, her voice was calm and neutral. "Robbie will be picking us up tomorrow as soon as she has finished at her office. We're going up to the lodge for a month."

Aliki felt the tightness in her heart. "Good, good. Aah, everything else work out okay?"

There was an angry snort at the other end of the phone. "What do you think, Aliki? It has been pretty difficult and embarrassing. Look, I don't want to leave town without seeing and talking to you. Can we meet somewhere?"

Aliki frowned. She didn't need this. She was deep into her character now and didn't want to risk blowing her cover. Yet she yearned with all her heart to see Dawn again, to somehow make amends for walking out on the woman she loved.

"I'll come by the house. Can you make sure Mac isn't there? We need...some time together."

There was thoughtful silence at the other end, then Dawn's voice came on the line again, sounding hesitant and cautious. "Mac will be out this afternoon at a swim party for one of her friends. Can you be here about one? I'll have a lunch ready."

Relief flooded through Aliki. Dawn might be really angry and disappointed with her, but she hadn't closed the door on their love. "Thanks. Yeah, I'll be there. Dawn...I...I'll be there."

"Okay. Bye then. Be careful."

"Bye."

For a long time, Dawn stood at the bedroom window, her arms crossed against the chill that seemed to have invaded her insides. She loved Aliki, but she couldn't let herself be so badly used. She wanted to support her lover because she knew the horror of those deaths weighed heavily on her conscience, yet she did not agree with what Aliki was doing. Tears slowly rolled down her face. *Be safe where ever you are, Aliki,* she prayed.

Aliki risked slipping into the forensics building after doubling back several times to make sure she was not being followed. She had a long shower and changed her clothes. She didn't look much better, but at least she didn't smell. She sat at her desk afterwards, using the rest of the morning to review Jigsaw's profile. Around eight, Bates came in and sat down opposite her. "I heard you were in the building."

Aliki turned from her computer to look at her boss. "Dawn wants to see me so I came in to clean up. I thought I might as well catch up on things here before I head over there. I'm sorry I was such a pain in the butt this morning," she finished with a self-conscious blush.

Bates leaned back, a twinkle in his eye. "You are intelligent, talented, and difficult, Dr. Pateas, and I don't suppose that is going to change." He considered for a minute, looking at Aliki with some interest. "I would hardly have recognized you. You do look...tough."

A deep flush crept up Aliki's neck. "I'm going to need to be a lot tougher before this is over, I suspect. You heard anything new?"

Bates shook his head. "There is an investigation underway into the misidentification of Higgins' remains. They are starting to collect and assemble pieces of the downed aircraft. Our early assumptions seem to be holding true. An explosive fire started near the port wing fuel tank and ripped through the fuselage. The cause has yet to be determined. Sabotage, terrorism, and mechanical failure are all still possibilities. We have talked about how Jigsaw might have just used this event to draw you out and that the plane crash might not have anything to do with her at all."

Aliki nodded and swallowed hard before responding. "I hope that proves to be the case, Dr. Bates. This is hell to live with."

Bates was deeply touched by Aliki's honesty and her allowing her vulnerability to show. "You go on with your research. I mean to have a walk over to The Coffee Guy and bring back bagels with cream cheese and some coffees for us."

She blinked back tears at her boss's kindness. "Thanks."

Dawn was deep in her thoughts, preoccupied with where her relationship with Aliki was going. On the one hand, she was so angry and hurt she could scream, but on the other she knew Aliki was risking her life to stop a killer. She didn't know how she could cope if anything happened to the woman she loved, especially at the moment, when there was such tension between them. Having closed the windows against a pending summer storm, she came out from the living room and found a stranger standing there. Her gasp of shock was almost drowned out by the drumming of her heart.

"Sorry, I didn't mean to startle you."

Dawn looked into grey eyes below shaggy, ill-kempt brown hair. The body was dressed in shabby black jeans and a t-shirt, and lean, hard muscle showed clearly through the thin material. A tanned wiry arm had a tattoo of barbed wire around it, and there was a death skull tattooed onto a strong, long throat. The overall effect was one of danger and strength. "Aliki? You look...different. You scared the hell out of me."

"I'm supposed to look different." She had gone over and over in her head the things she should say. Instead, so near to the woman that she loved that she could smell the heady scent of summer herbs that were so much a part of Dawn, Aliki impulsively took a step closer and leaned forward to capture Dawn's lips. "I hate being away from you," she growled.

Dawn's arms slid up her chest and wrapped around her neck. "I hate it, too. I want to be married to you and living as a family. I am so worried about you...about us."

"Don't be, babe. I know this is hell, but things are going to work out. I promise you that." Aliki held Dawn close, her hands moving seductively over her lover's back and bottom. Dawn responded by moving against Aliki, pressing hard against her sex.

Aliki nuzzled at the white underside of Dawn's throat. "I know we need to talk — to understand each other — but right now, lover, I need you real bad."

Dawn laughed nervously. This was a side of Aliki that she had rarely seen. Her lover prided herself on her responsibility and practical, controlled attitude. This Aliki was just a bit out of control — and very sexy. Dawn needed to say so many things while she had Aliki there, but she had missed having the woman in her bed and just at the moment all she wanted was the reassurance of Aliki on her, in her, and loving her. "You're kinda scary."

"I feel kind of scary," Aliki growled. She picked Dawn up in her arms and carried her up the stairs to their bedroom just as the first peal of thunder shook the house.

Aliki had felt rejected, that her life was tilting totally out of control. She needed to feel loved, needed to feel in charge. Rain drummed heavily against the window as she pulled the clothes from her willing lover. The kisses they shared were deep and demanding. Dawn was just as eager to get Aliki naked. Flesh touched flesh, and with a groan of need, Aliki pulled Dawn onto their bed, spreading her legs wide with her hips as she sucked and kissed nipples swollen with desire. "You excite me to the core of my being. I need to have you. Need to feel you come while I'm inside you," Aliki whispered, her voice rough with emotion.

Dawn groaned and let her fingertips rake down Aliki's broad shoulders. "Oh, God, you feel good."

Thunder rolled as Aliki's hands explored and caressed, finally demanding entrance into Dawn's being and rocking with the ancient rhythm of desire. Their coupling was hot and wild. The storm raged, and their bodies heaved to the tides of emotional hunger. When Dawn came, her cry of release was carried away on the wild wind. Aliki felt her own release, her eyes enjoying the naked form of her lover highlighted by the flash of lightning.

She rolled off and pulled Dawn to her, the two of them still breathless from the intensity of their coming. Dawn snuggled close, dropping gentle kisses on Aliki's hot flesh. The kisses intensified, and Dawn slipped lower to bring her kiss-swollen lips against Aliki's sex. The scent and silken feel was heady, and Aliki's moans of pleasure as Dawn licked the nectar of her lover's excitement drove Dawn wild with need again. She rubbed her own clit against Aliki's leg while she pleasured the woman she loved.

Aliki's eyes blazed with passion. Her lover's naked body moved against her, and she could see Dawn feasting at her sex. Waves of need flooded through Aliki, and she bucked violently as her climax rolled with the thunder outside.

They lay together in each other's arms listening to the moisture dripping now that the storm was spent, each contented and a bit dazed at the intensity and abandonment of their lovemaking. It had been indescribable.

"You okay?" Aliki whispered, kissing Dawn's head where it rested under her chin.

"Mmmm, yes. You?"

"Feeling better now. I hate us being apart."

Dawn's body pulled away slightly, and her response was dull, lifeless. "It was your choice."

Aliki sighed and sat up on the side of the bed. "I'm doing what I feel I must do. I know everyone thinks I have fucked with their lives pretty badly, and I'm sorry, but I feel pretty fucked over myself."

Dawn angrily wiped away tears. There was no point in getting into this. She didn't want to fight with Aliki, not now, while she was in such danger. "Look, just go. Phone me up north when you can. I really miss you and want you safe, but just at the moment, talking like nothing has happened is just too damned hard for me."

Aliki schooled her face into hard lines. She couldn't afford emotion. "I'll phone when I can." She got up and dressed while Dawn watched with sad eyes, and then she leaned down and kissed her lover goodbye. "Have a safe trip to Robbie's. I love you." Then she was gone, back on the streets, back to the world of darkness into which she had sunk.

Aliki once again rode the streetcar downtown. Dusk was settling as she prowled the back alleys looking for a place to keep warm until the bars opened. Depression had settled around her like a dense fog. She felt totally alone and miserable. Around six, she slipped into a lesbian working-class bar off Jarvis where she knew Jigsaw might have been seen. She settled at the far corner of the bar and ordered a beer.

"You've been here before," the young girl said, setting the beer in front of Aliki. "What's your name?"

"Alberta." Aliki sipped the beer through its bitter head and checked the girl out with bold eyes. She was tall and lean and at first glance looked a lot older than she actually was. Her hair was blond but darker at the roots, and her nose was a bit too narrow and her chin too sharp for her to be cute.

"Where're you from?" the girl asked, wiping the counter with a rag.

Alberta felt herself bristle with caution. Was the kid just hitting on her, or was she being pumped for information? "Out west. Been working at grounds maintenance for the Calgary Stampede Association. I got laid off so I thought I'd come out east and see what was doin'. Haven't been here in years. What's your name?"

"Alice." The girl wrung the rag out and started washing dishes in a small bar sink. "So, you glad you came?"

"I haven't...yet, but I'm working on it." Aliki gave her the look.

Alice laughed. It was a nice laugh that bubbled up and sparkled in her eyes. "Think you're hot stuff, eh?"

Aliki smiled. She hadn't played this game in years and found it fun. Not that she had any intention of taking it any further than bar talk, but for a while anyway it was companionship and understanding against a cold, wet night. "I learned to ride pretty good out west." She smirked and took another sip of her beer. "Can't say the East has improved any. I'll probably head back in the spring."

Alice was now drying and polishing the thick beer glasses and putting them back on the shelf. "I'd like to go west," she said, giving Aliki the once over. "I like riding...a lot."

"I'll keep that in mind," Aliki said with a wicked smile.

Alice returned the look. "I'm off in another half hour."

Aliki dropped a few bucks on the counter. Bartenders, especially ones hot to trot, noticed and heard a lot of things. She figured Alice could be of some use. Still, she'd have to be careful that Alice wasn't one of Jigsaw's fillies. "I'm going to play some pool. Join me later."

Alice watched Alberta out the corner of her eye. If this was the one that Jigsaw was interested in knowing about, she sure was a surprise. She didn't act like a cop. She was one tough, sexy woman. Alberta's strong, long back showed through her t-shirt as she stretched out to take a shot. Alice liked what she saw. Long fingers and capable hands, great buns, and runner's legs — Alberta would be a real mean machine in bed. She wondered if she was into anything kinky. You could never tell, not until you got 'em behind closed doors. Jigsaw liked it when she talked dirty about what Jigsaw was doing to her, but she didn't like Alice to move. That was freaky. Jigsaw liked to do the fucking, but she didn't like to be touched, not ever.

Gus, the owner, had told her that Jigsaw had killed a bunch of people and that she shouldn't have anything to do with the woman. Alice didn't care. In fact, it sort of turned her on. She liked rough sex. Not violent or anything, just on the edge, where it was kind of scary and real exciting all at once. She figured there was a fine line between pain and ecstasy. That's the way it had always been in her family anyway, and quite often that line got crossed.

She pulled a few beers, then made a phone call like Jigsaw had told her to. Bad things happen in life. That wasn't her fault.

Once Carla had replaced her at the counter, Alice drew two beers and took them over to where Alberta was playing pool with a couple of dykes that had come in. Alberta took the beer and kissed her neck. Alice felt herself getting hot and wet. She liked the way the other women looked on with hungry eyes. While Alberta waited her turn to shoot, Alice stood close at her side, her hand in Alberta's back pocket. Alberta didn't touch or look at her after the welcome kiss, but Alice knew she was turning Alberta on. She could feel the woman's heat.

They played three games, and Alberta took them to the cleaners. She was good, cool and calculating. Afterwards, she pulled Alice close, and they danced real slow in a corner. Alberta checked out what she had to offer with hands used to getting what they wanted.

"You coming back to my place?" Alice whispered as she sucked at Alberta's ear.

Alberta gritted her teeth. It had been a long night, and she was sick of this game. "Not tonight, babe. Got other arrangements."

"She can't do for you what I could," Alice purred.

Alberta laughed and took Alice's head between her hands, kissing her hard, "That remains to be seen. I'll see you around, hot stuff." It was a good exit line, and Aliki used it. She felt dirty and disgusting and hated herself for what she was doing. Her whole fucking life stunk.

In a foul mood, she walked through the empty streets back toward the park where she had been sleeping. She would need to find more shelter than the bush afforded. What was she doing out there anyway? Maybe Bates and her family were right, and she should leave the investigation to the police. She hadn't gotten very far. She winced with guilt and embarrassment. How did she explain to Dawn what she was doing?

The attack came suddenly and without warning. A meaty hand grabbed her by the hair and pulled her into an alleyway where her face was smashed against the rough side of a brick wall, once, twice, three times. Pain shot through her head and left her dizzy and disoriented. She could feel hard, callused hands under her shirt and her jeans being ripped open and pulled down. "Hey, bitch, we got somethin' for you," someone breathed into her face as she was pulled to the ground.

Panic seized her, and she thrashed wildly at her two attackers. The heavy weight of a man covered her, and a fist drove into the side of her head several times. She could taste blood and smell stale tobacco and beer and feel fingers groping at her body. "Stop your fightin', slut, and give us some tail!"

Aliki's hand slipped down her bent leg until the cool metal of a knife blade touched her hand. Rage at the violation of her body roared through her head. She lashed out with her knife and sunk it deep into the man's groin. With a howl of pain, he rolled off her, and she reached and stabbed at the hand that still pinned her shoulders to the ground.

"Fucking tart!" the second man yelped, letting her go and stumbling backwards.

Aliki willed her body to move and staggered to her feet, pulling at her torn jeans with a hand trembling with emotion while she kept her eye on the man she had wounded. Bikers, drunk and looking for trouble, she concluded. Well, they had found it. The one lay on the ground, holding his genitals as blood soaked his underwear. The other had backed up against the opposite wall and was holding a bloody hand under his arm. Aliki raised the knife. "Come at me and I'll rip your bowels out," she offered.

The man looked down at his comrade. No help there. He looked up at the knife in Aliki's hand. His decision showed in his eyes a split second before he pulled a knife from the sheath on his belt and lunged forward.

"*You can tell an amateur wound because the assailant will stab down.*" Aliki recalled hearing the words of her long-ago forensic instructor as if he was standing beside her. She ducked under the blade, letting it descend over her shoulder. Her knife plunged deep and ripped up, like a pro. There was no blood this time. Deep knife wounds bleed internally, not externally. The man gave a soft grunt and dropped to the alleyway. She knew he would not be getting up.

Sobbing and trembling with shock, Aliki leaned against the wall and tried to make sense of what had just happened. Her head pounded and muscles ached with strain. She had come very close to being raped. Her body stunk of male sweat, and her skin crawled from their bruising groping. She looked down at the man who lay on the ground whimpering. His jeans were wrapped around his boots and his big hairy ass mooned out of shorts soaked red with blood. She had stabbed deep into his groan. "Help me," he whispered between gasps. "I'm gonna bleed to death."

Aliki thought about what they had planned for her. They would have killed her after they had finished, that went without saying. By then she probably would have welcomed death. She wiped her knife clean on her jeans and slipped it into her pocket. Then she straightened her ripped clothes as best she could and walked away. A moan of despair followed her as she limped down the street.

The park was out of the question. She couldn't walk that far, and she didn't want to be alone. She staggered down a few streets and slipped down an alley that led behind a large department store. There, amongst trashcans, a pathetic group of street people huddled next to the exhaust fans of the building's heating system. She found a spot next to a drainpipe and slid to the urine-stained asphalt. A soft, crazy, female chuckle came from a heap of rags. "So was it good for you, too, sweetheart?"

"Fuck off," Aliki muttered, curling into a ball and crying herself into exhausted sleep.

Part 3

Aliki woke in the morning to the sound of garbage canisters being dumped. She tried to move, and pain shot through her body. The trauma of the night before exploded in her mind. She had killed one man and left another to die. What the hell had she been thinking? With a groan of pain that was more from her soul than the soreness of her muscles, she staggered to her feet and hobbled back down the streets to where she had left the man the night before. Perhaps it wasn't too late. Perhaps she could get him some help.

People stared at her in shock as she lurched by them — blood caked hard to her clothes and her face swollen, bruised and scraped. A block short of the alleyway, she stopped and stared with horror. Yellow police tape cordoned off the area. Fear dropped like an ice ball into her gut. She had murdered.

She turned quickly and pushed her way through the morning commuters. She'd need to change and clean up and then turn herself in at the police station. People moved aside, avoiding her as she limped into the bus station and made her way to the lockers in the back corner. Tears of despair rolling down her face, she searched for the key that should be in her pocket. It wasn't there.

A voice behind her observed softly, "It fell out of your pocket in the alley last night." Aliki turned to see Dr. Bates and Dawn standing behind her.

Dawn's face was stained with tears. She took Aliki by the arm and led her from the building. Bates followed, carrying Aliki's knapsack. His car, its certificate of police authority propped in the window, was parked by the curb in a No Parking zone. Stunned, Aliki meekly allowed herself to be led and deposited in the car. Dawn slipped in beside her, and Thomas Bates took the driver's seat.

He looked up into the mirror. "How badly is she hurt? Has she been..."

Dawn was trying to wipe dried blood from Aliki's face. "I can't tell. Aliki, hon, did they rape you?"

Aliki managed to shake her head. Her body shook with sobs. "No, they tried. Dr. Bates, I killed them."

Bates kept his eyes on the road, but the hands gripping the wheel were white with tension. "One lived. The police arrived shortly after the incident. Someone reported a woman being attacked in the alley."

Aliki nodded, eyes not quite focused as Bates drove them back to his house. Slowly, she started to become aware of the circumstances. "Where is Mac? Why aren't you on your way north?"

Dawn stopped her inspection of Aliki's wounds. "Thomas phoned me just as Robbie arrived. He suspected that you were in trouble. I insisted that he pick me up. Robbie stayed with Mac. Thomas reasoned that if you could, you would head for the lockers, so we went and waited there."

Dr. Bates' reasoning, as always, was sound. Aliki looked over at him. "How did you know it was me?"

"I was called in early this morning to examine the body. I found the key among his clothes. It must have fallen from your pocket as the two of you fought."

"I need to turn myself in," Aliki muttered.

Bates felt the muscles in his neck tighten. He was caught between a rock and a hard place. He believed in justice, and yet he recognized that politics, lawyers, and media hysteria often interfered with the judicial process. The system functioned on the letter of the law rather than the spirit of its intent, and that made its objectivity cruel and blind to human reaction. The system would not give Aliki a fair deal. The prison inmates would get her as soon as they knew she was a cop, and if she did escape incarceration, the bikers would mete out their own brand of justice.

"Unfortunately, the prints taken at the scene were inconclusive. The rain during the day, I imagine, made identification impossible. I saw no reason to report the key as part of the inventory of the victim's belongings."

Aliki looked up sharply; her eyes filled with shock, she met Bates' eyes looking back at her through the driver's rear view mirror. His face showed his resolve and determination. He had tampered with the evidence to protect Aliki.

"Dr. Bates—"

"Keep quiet, Dr. Pateas. That is an order," Bates snapped irritably.

"Yes, sir," Aliki whispered. Her head ached terribly, and she felt sick to her stomach. She must have a concussion. She lowered her head to Dawn's shoulder and let her partner hold her as the car made its way through the Toronto streets.

At Dr. Bates' home, he directed them to the guest bathroom. Dawn took Aliki inside, stripped her down, and got her under the shower. In the end, she had to take her own clothes off as well and get in and help her lover wash. Aliki leaned against the tiled wall and let the water run over her. Dawn was frantic. Aliki was not acting like herself. As evidenced by the bruising, she had come very close to being raped, and her head and neck showed signs of repeated blows.

Dawn helped her partner out of the shower and towelled the two of them down. She sat Aliki on the toilet seat while she dressed, then she gently took Aliki's face in her hands and kissed her forehead. "Aliki, I need to know the truth. Did either of those guys rape you? Do you need medical attention?"

Aliki looked up, her eyes still glassy. "No, I'm okay. They tried...beat me up good...but I reached my knife. I..." Sobs shook her.

"It's okay, Aliki. It's okay," she whispered, holding her lover close and rocking her like a child.

Dr. Bates was sitting in his den nervously puffing away on his pipe when Dawn finally came out. "How is she?"

"In shock, obviously, and I think she has a concussion. She wasn't raped, and most of the blood was not hers. Her face is a mess." Dawn shook her head.

"They must have really pounded her, and she's bruised where you'd expect her to be bruised."

Red, from embarrassment and from anger, crept up Bates' neck. That this ugliness could have happened to his friend and colleague appalled him.

Dawn flopped down in a chair. "She's sleeping, but I don't like her state of mind. This whole thing is tearing her apart. Now she has another death on her conscience." Bates nodded, looking miserable and not knowing what to say. Dawn looked at him with eyes filled with tears. "Thank you for protecting her."

Bates squirmed uncomfortably. "Nonsense. That is just the way things worked out."

A few hours later, Aliki lay in the spare bedroom, staring at the ceiling. She had always wanted to see where Dr. Bates lived. Now she was there, and she couldn't remember a thing about the place, not even the colour of the bathroom. She touched her head and winced in pain. She wasn't tracking very well, she knew. *Gather your thoughts, Aliki. Work through things from when you entered the bar last night and get everything straight in your mind.* Something didn't feel right. There was something important that she had overlooked, some key that would blast the whole mess open wide.

Slowly, methodically, Aliki went through the evening, forcing her aching brain to focus and function. Alice had a girlfriend who had been in prison. She had told her that while they danced. Jigsaw had probably been hanging around that bar. The bikers just happened to be waiting down the street from the bar for someone to rape. Jigsaw used to be a biker's girl. Gradually the pieces came together. Jigsaw had not been fooled by Aliki's disguise. Jigsaw knew she was out there and was setting traps for her. It hadn't been a coincidence that the two assholes had been in the alley; they had been waiting for her. Jigsaw knew she was there and had tipped them off to look out for a woman cop. It was Jigsaw's way of sending her a little present and welcoming Aliki to her world.

This changed everything. She had to get back out there. She had to show Jigsaw that her little game had failed and that she was okay and not intimidated. She needed to make Jigsaw angry so that she would get careless and make mistakes. She needed to protect Dawn and Dr. Bates. They had already put themselves at risk to help her, and that was just not right. So far she had been a real fuck-up; she was going to have to do much better to catch Jigsaw.

Slowly, with a groan of pain, she slipped from the bed. From her knapsack, she pulled her spare jeans and t shirt and slipped them on. Then on a sheet of paper that she took from the printer that sat beside a computer on a desk, she wrote a note.

Dearest One,

I need you to know that above all else I love you and want with all my heart to be your legal partner. Circumstance has pulled me from your side, and I know that has hurt you deeply. It is a painful ache in my heart, too.

Dawn, I know how to find Jigsaw, but the price is very high and so is the danger. I am going to use myself as bait by moving in with one of Jigsaw's girls, Alice. In case something goes wrong, I need you to know that I will not have slept with her. My heart, my body belong only to you.

Please take Mac to Robbie's place in the north. I love your loyalty and courage, but I need you safe. I can handle this. I am leaving now before you can stop me. Tell Dr. Bates that I will keep in touch.

I love you,
Always, Aliki

Some time later, Dawn read the note that lay on the bed. She had to read it twice before its meaning really impacted on her shocked mind. She turned and walked from the room, finding Thomas Bates in the kitchen making sandwiches.

"How is she?" he asked over his shoulder, then he put down the knife with which he was cutting tomatoes and hurried over to Dawn. "What is the matter?"

Dawn pushed the note into Bates' hand and sank down onto a kitchen chair. Tears rolled down her face. Bates read the note and swore.

"How could she do this to me?" Dawn sobbed.

Bates put his hand on the woman's shoulder. He didn't know how to answer. This was well out of his depth. He made Dawn some tea and then slipped down the hall to his study. He needed help. The phone number he dialled was answered on the second ring.

"Hello."

"Robbie?"

"Yes."

Bates sighed in relief and sank into his chair. "Robbie, this is Dr. Bates. I have quite a report to give you." He kept to the facts, giving a concise but complete summary of the events of that morning. When he finished and asked for assistance, Robbie swore.

"That goddamn sister of mine is more trouble than the plague. Next time I see her, I am going to beat her silly. Give me your address, and Mac and I will come over there and pick up Dawn. Honest to God, what the hell could Aliki be thinking?"

Bates gave his address and directions for getting there from Aliki and Dawn's home while he pondered Robbie's question more seriously than Robbie had meant him to. When he answered, it was with a warning. "Aliki is not acting like I would expect. I think the shock and guilt of the last two weeks is weighing very heavily on her mind. Her decision today to escape via the window was completely irrational. And to walk out on her wedding and then leave a note to say she was moving in with another woman...well, how insensitive and cruel. I am very worried about her state of mind." He could hear Robbie's pacing through the line.

"She won't need a mind once I've finished kicking her butt around the block," she answered, but Bates could hear the fear and strain for her sister and Dawn in her voice. "Stay with Dawn. I'm on my way."

Bates nodded, although there was no one to see it. "Yes, okay. See you in a few minutes."

Dawn had stopped sobbing and was sitting holding her teacup in her hands. Its warmth felt good. Shock had left her feeling cold to the bone. How much could she take before she gave up on love and walked away? She knew a lot of people would have given up on Aliki a lot sooner. Was she a fool to think Aliki was capable of making a real commitment to her and Mac? Tears threatened to overflow again at the thought of how hurt Mac was going to be. She wiped them away angrily. She'd be damned if she was going to cry over Aliki. She wouldn't let herself. She had to be brave for Mac's sake. This was going to be hard enough on her daughter.

Bates came in and sat down across the table from her. His pipe, unlit out of respect to her, was clamped between his teeth for security. With reluctance, he removed it to speak to Dawn. "I called Robbie. She and Mac are coming over."

Dawn nodded, then looked up into Bates' gentle eyes. "You have risked a lot to protect and help Aliki. I know if she was in a better state of mind, she would want me to thank you."

Bates looked down at his pipe as if seeking for guidance. "She is right, actually. Jigsaw has to be stopped, and the system might not be quick enough to do that before she strikes again. I just wish this was not such a personal issue for Aliki. It clouds her judgment. What are you going to do?"

Dawn took a sip of her tea to calm her nerves. "The first thing is to deal with the issues that I can do something about, then I'll deal with the harder issues. Mac and I will go up north with Robbie, and I'll deal with the fallout from the cancelled wedding and make sure that Mac is okay. Then I mean to come back here and do whatever I can to protect and help Aliki. I don't know if our relationship is going to survive this crisis, but I do know that I am not going to walk out on her because things got tough. I won't give her that out. Aliki is going to have to face me and explain herself to my satisfaction."

Bates smiled and clamped the pipe stem into his mouth, speaking around it. "Dawn, you are far too good a woman for that renegade assistant of mine, but you are just the sort of strong, compassionate woman that she needs."

The ringing of the doorbell made them both start. "I'll get it," Dawn said. "That, I am sure, is Robbie."

Dawn opened the door to find Robbie with her arm around Mac's shoulder. Robbie immediately stepped in and gave Dawn a comforting, sisterly hug. "Mac and I have talked it over, and we have decided to boil Aliki in oil first and then feed her to the seagulls."

Dawn laughed and hugged her daughter. "I'll agree only if the birds have dull beaks and ravenous appetites."

They all ended up down in the kitchen. Thomas Bates finished making sandwiches and coffee, and they sat around and discussed what a silly, stubborn ass Aliki was and what they could do for the idiot. An hour later, the three of them said goodbye to Bates and headed to the Toronto Island Airport, where a helicopter would fly them north.

Aliki sat on a park bench. She didn't feel good – sort of distant and queasy – and her head ached badly. She lay down on the bench. The sun felt hot and good. People passing by thought she was sleeping off a high. She slept for an hour or so. It took her a long time before she could make out where she was or why. When memory finally flooded back, a ball of fear exploded in her gut. What the hell was she doing? If Jigsaw had been following her, she would have been dead by now.

She sat up and tried to work the kinks out of her shoulders. Carefully, she reviewed her plan. It looked like Jigsaw wanted to play cat and mouse. It could be a long time before she got the chance to make an arrest. In the meantime, she couldn't continue to live on the streets. It sapped too much of her strength and was dangerous in itself. Alice would take her in, but she would also want money. Aliki needed a job. She headed down to the bar she had been at the night before.

Gus, the owner of the Jarvis Tavern, was behind the counter checking the inventory against the receipts. "We gotta sign out front. We ain't open yet."

"You got a sign saying you need help. That's me."

Gus looked at her swollen and bruised face and sneered. "Ya'd scare the customers away. What happened to ya?"

"Like your customers haven't seen bruises before. Let's just say I walked in front of a bus."

Gus grunted and smiled. "Seven bucks an hour and tips, if ya get any."

"That's below minimum wage."

Gus shrugged. "It's all I'm gonna pay. Take it or leave it."

"I'll take it."

The back room where the metal sink was located was small and hot. It smelt of stale beer, cigarettes, and cockroach spray. A pile of glasses and dishes remained from the night before. "Ya get these washed and then ya wipe down the tables and chairs and mop the floor. Ya got that?" Gus asked almost accusingly.

Gritting her teeth, Aliki smiled cockily at her new boss, "Yeah, I got it."

Later, Alice came in, looked at her in shock, and tried to make a quick retreat. Aliki had her hand around Alice's arm before she could. "Let's talk in the back, you."

Alice hid her fear behind aggressiveness as she tried to pull away from Aliki's hold. "I don't want to talk."

Aliki smiled and leaned in real close, trapping Alice between her body and the wall. She whispered into the woman's ear, softly but with a hint of a threat, "Then I guess I'll have to make you talk. Come on."

This time Alice let herself be dragged into the back room. Aliki pushed Alice onto a wooden chair and stood over her glowering. Alice tried to look defiant, swinging her hair out of her eyes. "You don't look so good. They must've done a real number on you."

Aliki yawned. "You ought to know. I'm sure Jigsaw's friends have docked in your harbour more than once. Sorry to disappoint you, but I had to kill the one 'cause he was getting fresh, and the other won't be using his plumbing for a long time 'cause he's got a catheter stuck up it. I had to make my point with my knife."

Alice paled. "Holy shit, Jigsaw will kill you."

With a snort, Aliki bent over Alice. "I don't think so. I need a place to stay, and I think your place will do nicely."

Alice laughed. She was a slow thinker, and the laugh came a few seconds too late. "You'd be throwing your life away. Jigsaw lives with me."

The police officer smiled. "You might be one of Jigsaw's fucks, but she doesn't live there. Jigsaw doesn't trust anyone that much, and she hates to be touched. She'll come and get what she wants and then leave. So I'll be sticking to you like glue."

The waitress looked both sulky and intrigued. Aliki knew the type. They came through the morgue all the time. In life, they were hooked on the rush of danger and pain in a relationship. In death, they wore the scars of brutality. They were moths attracted to an evil flame of passion. Alice's fate had been decided the moment she got involved with Jigsaw. Aliki would do her best to protect the woman, but she knew that there would always be a Jigsaw in Alice's life and sooner or later, the rough sex would be deadly. It was a fool who thought there could be boundaries in an S & M relationship. The envelope was always being pushed that bit further until the recipient ended up in an emergency ward or the morgue.

Alice looked up at Aliki. "What if I don't want you...there."

Aliki forced a smile. "You want me...there." She leaned in and kissed Alice long and hard. Alice clung to her, rubbing her body against her like a cat. Aliki tolerated it for as long as she could and then pulled away. "You have work to do, so do I. Get out of here." Alice straightened her clothes and did as she was told. Aliki washed her face and hands in disgust and forced her mind back to her work.

Her head ached, and her soul felt crushed. She wasn't sleeping well. The voices of the dead still cried out to her. Her family didn't understand. Her boss was angry with her and had taken great risks to protect her. She could still vividly feel the violation of her body and her anger and panic when she stabbed a man to death and wounded another. Now she felt like she was cheating on her partner. She couldn't sink much lower. Nothing mattered anymore except getting Jigsaw.

Aliki worked past closing time and then got on the bus with Alice and rode north along Yonge Street to the area where Alice lived in a room on the second floor of an old red brick that had been divided into small utility apartments of dubious quality. Alice's clothes seemed to be the principal decoration in the room, piled wherever she had discarded them. Dirty dishes sat in a yellowing porcelain sink, and the tap dripped. The bathroom was at the end of the hall and was shared by the four apartments on that floor. The only furniture in the room was a sagging mattress on the floor. Aliki flopped down on the mattress. "When I wake up, your clothes had better be folded neatly somewhere and the fucking dishes done, or I'm going to kick your butt around this shit hole." Her voice sounded tough and her body language was aggressive, but her heart ached. She felt so alone.

Alice had piled all her clothes in one corner and rinsed the dirty dishes under the tap before crawling on the mattress and trying to get under Aliki's clothing. Aliki rolled over, pinning the woman beneath her body, and kissed her hard while she held the woman's hands firmly over her head. Alice squirmed with delight.

"That's all you get," Aliki growled. "That's all you get for a long time yet until I decide that I want to give you more. You got that?"

Alice nodded, a look of sheer adoration in her eyes. Aliki rolled off the waitress and turned her back to her. Tears rolled down Aliki's cheeks. She hated herself. It was late when sleep finally came to her rigidly tense body. With sleep, came the nightmares. Hundreds of voices were calling to her to stop the plane from crashing. Their panicky hands clawing at her morphed into rough hands feeling up her body, tearing at her clothes, and violating her sense of being. Then Dawn and Mac were there, looking down at her. They turned in disgust and walked away. Aliki tried to call to them, but her voice became just one of the many screaming for help. She woke with a start. A pale grey dawn light was weakly trying to force its way through a grimy window. Aliki disentangled herself from the sleeping form beside her and went to wash the sweat and dirt off her body in the washroom down the hall.

Once dressed, she walked down to a corner variety and bought a package of honey doughnuts and two coffees. She ate breakfast sitting on the floor with Alice, who was obviously not a morning person, then she headed into work. Alice would be going on duty around the time that Aliki was going off. That suited the cop fine. She wanted the place to stay and she wanted a link to Jigsaw, but she didn't want Alice.

At the bar, she started clearing tables and washing floors before she tackled the mess of glasses filled with stale beer and plates caked with nacho cheese. She tried not to think while she worked. She didn't want to think about anything, thinking made her crazy; she just wanted to focus on getting Jigsaw. Getting Jigsaw was all that mattered.

At eleven, the bar opened. Sandy and Gus were on duty. Sandy looked like Alice, thought like Alice, and was destroying herself like Alice. She lived with some guy who had been between jobs ever since he'd moved in with her, drank her paycheque away, and bounced her off the walls when she complained. There were a lot of Alices in the world, taught by abusive parents and attracted to abusive partners. Aliki wished she could do something for them, but there was little that could be done if they refused to see that they had a problem that went deeper than the immediate issue. She would do what she could for Alice, but she didn't believe in happy ever afters anymore.

Dawn sat on the front deck of Robbie and Janet's home. It was huge and made of massive log supports and thick, wide cedar decking. The view was wonderful. The lake was calm and reflected the fall colours of the surrounding northern forest like a mirror. This should have been the happiest day of her life, the day that she and Aliki acknowledged their love and commitment before their family and friends. Instead, she hurt so deeply inside that she just wanted to curl up in a ball and whimper. A lump formed in her throat, and big tears ran unchecked down her cheeks. It had been a hell of a few days. She felt tired and worn and ever so fragile in body and spirit.

Damn Aliki anyway. She should have realized that Aliki would find an excuse to avoid going through with the ceremony. She didn't doubt Aliki's love, just her ability to once again take on the responsibilities of a family. Dawn dug out an already damp tissue from her pocket and wiped away tears with a shaky hand. She knew that Aliki had felt trapped and overwhelmed after her mother had died and Aliki had been called on to help her father raise her brothers, particularly her high-spirited younger brothers who were twins. Dawn also knew that Aliki had had a stormy relationship with her older brother before his death. Yet the Pateas family seemed to love each other and get along now. There was something else, Dawn was sure, something deep inside Aliki that made her mistrust commitment. Something that went far beyond the loss of freedom and childhood that came pursuant to her mother's death.

Then there was Jigsaw. Had Jigsaw sabotaged that airliner just to get back at Aliki for putting her behind bars? Nothing could have hurt her partner more. Dawn had lain awake those nights after Aliki returned from the crash site, listening to the nightmare that tore at her lover's sleep and shredded her soul. She had heard her pacing back and forth in the dark after she woke, afraid to go back to sleep. Dawn had tried to help, tried to comfort her, but Aliki had withdrawn behind her wall of silence. And that, that was what hurt the most – not the delayed wedding, not the embarrassment, not the confusion and pain in Mac's eyes, but the realization that Aliki didn't trust her, didn't need her. Dawn lowered her head and let the sobs come again, her small body shaking with emotion and pain. She felt so alone.

Janet watched Dawn from the window, wondering if she should go to her or leave her some space to come to terms with what had happened. Robbie moved restlessly from room to room, sulking. Janet had had to speak pretty firmly to her about not bad mouthing her sister in front of the girls or Dawn and had strictly forbidden Robbie from going after her sister and marching her to the altar at the business end of a shotgun. Despite her concern, a small smile hovered at the corner of Janet's mouth. Olive Oyl, as she often called her partner because, like olives, she took some getting used to, tended to use a bomb when a peashooter would do.

She sighed. It was time for some planning and feather smoothing. She turned from the window and followed the sound of pacing to the back hall. "Want some tea?"

"No thanks," Robbie responded sulkily, looking at her feet as if they had suddenly done something fascinating.

Janet rolled her eyes. Williamses could be so difficult. "Come help me make tea anyway. We need to talk."

Robbie opened her mouth to refuse until Janet raised an eyebrow. Robbie's mouth closed, and she obediently followed her wife to the kitchen. Robbie might rule a film empire and several other spin-off companies, but Janet ruled her heart.

Robbie swung her long, lean leg over a stool and leaned on the bar, watching Janet fill the kettle and get out teabags. They had been married almost four years now, and she still could not look at Janet without feeling a rush of love and desire. Janet had made all the difference in her life. She had turned a scary, dark world into one filled with colour and happiness. There was nothing Robbie wouldn't have done for her.

Janet leaned over the counter and planted a soft kiss on Robbie's lips. It was a peace offering. "Dawn's out on the deck, crying."

Robbie nodded sadly, looking miserable.

Janet gave her partner's hand a gentle squeeze. "She is going to want to go back to Toronto and help Aliki in any way she can. I need you to go with her, Robbie." Startled, big blue eyes, world famous on the movie screen, came up and met Janet's. "And I need you to be subtle in your support. You know how proud they both are. Dawn will need bodyguards, and she will also need information. I know her uncle left her financially very secure and she has made money from her writing, but she doesn't have the experience you have in protecting herself. You have the connections to get some good people on the case without getting in Aliki's way."

Robbie nodded, feeling a little overwhelmed by what Janet was asking. Being given permission from her true love to go hunt down bad guys was great, but supporting Dawn emotionally and being subtle were things she was having trouble wrapping her mind around.

"Aaah, I'm not much good at that supportive stuff," Robbie admitted with a blush as she played nervously with a teaspoon on the counter, spinning it around and around in a circle with her finger.

Janet took it away from her and reached over to plant another kiss on her lover's lips. "You have your moments," she reassured her famous wife.

"Why can't you come too and sorta hold Dawn's hand while I track down Aliki?" Robbie suggested, watching Janet pour the tea.

Janet shook her head. "If you have to be Dawn's big sister, then you can't go off on some mad, wild goose chase after Aliki, and that is just the way I want it. I don't want you to get hurt, Robbie."

A soft, knowing look passed between the two. They had gone through a lot together, and their love had gotten stronger through the years. Janet gave herself a mental shake and went on with her thought. "Besides, I'm needed here. Mac has really been undermined by Aliki's actions. You know that poor kid still has some real issues about rejection. If her mom leaves to go help Aliki, Mac is going to need all the support and understanding that she can get."

"I could do that," Robbie argued, trying to find a way out of having to be with Dawn in her present emotional state.

Janet raised an eyebrow. "You coward. No, it has to be you. Besides, if I left you with Ryan, Reb, and Mac, you'd probably decide to take their mind off the crisis by taking them all hiking in Tibet or something, and then I'd have to go and rescue you all from some mountain terrorist group."

Robbie looked indignant. "Hey, I can handle things just fine!"

Janet smiled. *Checkmate*, she thought. "I know, that is why you have to go with Dawn. Here, take these two mugs of tea and go discuss it with her."

"I was had," Robbie grumbled, taking a mug carefully in each hand and standing up.

Janet came around the counter and gave her lover a big hug while Robbie stood there arms outstretched so as not to spill hot tea on her. "You are the best woman for the job and my hero." They shared a kiss, and Robbie headed off to face the task that Janet had assigned her.

At four, Alice showed up to start dealing with the afternoon and evening crowd. Aliki gave her a spank and a kiss and left as quickly as she could. She didn't return to their room, wanting to avoid it for as long as she could. She went first to the variety down the street and ate a bagel and cream cheese with a small carton of milk, sitting on a bar stool at the milk bar. Then she walked over to a salvage store and picked up a few things she needed.

Back at the room, she started to work. With a roller, she put two coats of beige paint on the walls using a gallon of paint that was on sale because it had been mixed wrong. Then, using the broom and mop she had bought, she cleaned the floors. A few cleaners and a good scrub got the sink and counter back to some state resembling cleanliness. Then she tacked up the movie posters that she had gotten for free at the video store and placed a plastic plumbing tube across a corner of the room, holding it in place with a few brackets. Next, she untwisted the tie on a stack of coat hangers and hung Alice's clothes on the plastic rod. There were two new sheets for the bed and a colourful striped blanket. It wasn't much, but it helped.

She cleaned the small window as best she could from the inside. Would Alice appreciate her efforts? Maybe, if it was approached with enough rudeness. Aliki sighed. That was Alice. She wasn't really a bad person, just not very bright, and conditioned by a dysfunctional family and abusive lovers to believe she deserved to be treated like shit. Some day someone would go too far, and Alice would become another number in the police statistic files.

Aliki set two cheap plastic chairs by the grimy window, along with an old card table that she had gotten at the pawnshop. She opened a can of soup and buttered some bread for when Alice came in. As she buttered, she reflected on why she was wasting her day doing all that. *Probably just selfish*, she decided.

She couldn't live like a damn street person any longer, and Alice's place had been only one step above a flophouse. Maybe she had done it to make Alice happy. She wasn't sure anymore if she felt anything for anyone. All she felt was her own personal hatred for those that were hurting her and ruining her life. She was tired of the screaming ghosts of her dreams, tired of the groping hands that left her feeling unclean, and tired of caring. She was putting Alice in danger by being there, she knew that. But she also knew that Alice was on her way to hell in this life and the hereafter. Why not use her? It wasn't going to matter.

A stab of guilt, almost a pain in her heart, made her cringe with shame. Who was she? What had she become? When did life become so cheap to her? *When four hundred people went screaming to their deaths because of you*, came the answer from her sick soul. What was one more death?

Robbie hipped the screen door open and carried the two mugs of tea outside. "Here," she said, bending forward to hand one to Dawn. The tea steamed in the cool air. They were Robbie's favourite mugs, the ones that she had gotten from the Bartlett Volunteer Fire Department, of which she was a member. Janet was like that, thoughtful and attentive to details. The message to Robbie was clear: be brave and do your duty.

Robbie set her jaw and sat down on the step beside Dawn. She reached into her pocket to hand Dawn the handful of tissues that she had picked up before coming outside. "Here."

Dawn put her mug of tea down on the porch and took the tissues. "Thanks. Sorry, I'm an emotional mess."

Robbie waved off the apology. "Aah, Janet thinks it would be a good idea if I tagged along with you. She figures I have a better grasp of security matters on account of always having had to have bodyguards around. I think she's got a point."

Dawn wiped her eyes and swallowed hard. "I'd like that, Robbie. I know it sounds cowardly, but I don't want to be alone."

Robbie wrapped an arm around the petite frame. "You're not alone. Hell, we're family. We'll help each other and Aliki. You just wait and see."

Dawn relaxed in Robbie's arms. "I'm so worried about her, Robbie. I'm so angry with her, and yet I am so worried about her."

"I know, love. I feel the same way, but we're going to find her and help her through this. That's what family does. It took Janet to teach me that lesson, and I guess we have to teach Aliki now. Janet will help Mac through this while we're away. She is super with kids. You don't have to worry, Dawn. We'll get through this rough time just fine."

They drank their tea, watching the night close in and quietly planning what they should do. Dawn had herself under control now. She could feel the quiet and determined support of her family and felt like she was back in control of her life. They had a plan, and they would help Aliki and bring her home safely.

At three in the morning, Alice came in smelling of beer, cheap perfume, and stale cigarette smoke. She stopped dead three steps in and looked around with eyes like those of a deer frozen before the headlights of a car. "Fucking shit!"

"I don't like to live like a pig," Aliki stated bluntly. "You make sure you hang your clothes up, or I'll knock your block off."

"Sure, Alberta," Alice agreed quickly, coming over to rub her body against Aliki's. "Thanks." They kissed, Alice letting it be known that she wanted more.

Aliki pulled away. "When I say, not before," she growled. "You gotta table now, so serve up the soup, I'm hungry."

Looking pouty and frustrated, Alice turned to do as she was told. Aliki wiped her mouth with the back of her hand, then picked up the plate of bread and slammed it down on the table with more force than she had intended.

They ate their soup without talking, Aliki silently gritting her teeth as Alice slurped and chewed with her mouth open. Irritation overcame reason. "Why do you fuck shit like Jigsaw?" Alice shrugged but said nothing.

Overtired and emotionally strung-out, Aliki couldn't let it lie. "You're an idiot. You think she is going to let you dump her? You think she's going to take any chance of you talking. You're just asking to get hurt."

Alice looked up. "Jigsaw doesn't like to be touched when she makes love to me. It's freaky, scary, it really turns me on. You're a lot like her."

The impact of that statement shot to the centre of Aliki's being. The truth of Alice's words exploded in her mind. Aliki smiled bitterly, accepting what she had become. "Nah, I'm responsible for the deaths of a lot more people than Jigsaw. You didn't answer my question. Why do you fuck people like us? You could do better."

Alice shrugged again, and her attention returned to her meal. "Every moth has its flame. It's the same with people."

Aliki said nothing. Alice was right. Her flame was Jigsaw, and there was not going to be room for anything else in her life until the flame was extinguished or she was incinerated trying to put it out.

Robbie and Dawn left early in the morning, taking a helicopter to the Toronto airport and then a car to Robbie's condo. By the time they arrived, they were already under the protective aegis of Robbie's security personnel. While Robbie talked to the security officer in charge, outlining the situation for him, Dawn was on the phone to Dr. Bates, inviting him to Robbie's penthouse for a council of war. The three ordered pizza and opened a few beers, then settled down on the open terrace overlooking Lake Ontario to have a briefing.

"She contacted me yesterday. She is off the streets, I am glad to say, and has a job cleaning and washing up at the Jarvis Tavern."

Robbie snorted as she took a slug of beer from the bottle. "That's my sister, always moving up in the world."

Dawn, however, had caught the dodge in Thomas's report. "Where is she staying?"

Bates looked into intelligent, knowing eyes. "I am not sure exactly. She has moved in with one of the waitresses from the bar." The bottle lowered from Robbie's lips, and her eyes were cold and weary as she looked back and forth between Bates and Dawn.

Dawn appeared pale but calm. Her voice, when she spoke, was controlled and strained. "Jigsaw's girlfriend."

Bates nodded unhappily. Dawn became suddenly interested in scraping the label off her beer bottle. Robbie squirmed uncomfortably and tried to think of something to say.

It was Bates who broke the awkward silence.

"I think we need to work on this issue from two separate directions. I mean to pursue the forensic and engineering investigation of the crash. I do not believe that Jigsaw would have the expertise to manufacture an explosive or have access to an airliner flying from Canada to Europe. I think her letter was a way to get back at Aliki. If I can prove that, then this investigation won't be so personal for Aliki." Bates took his beloved pipe from his pocket.

Dawn looked at Robbie, a small plea in her eye. Robbie took the hint. "I don't mind if you smoke out here," she stated.

Bates beamed and immediately dug for his tobacco pouch. They all waited while he went through the ritual of packing, lighting, tamping, and drawing on his briar. Once settled and surrounded by an aromatic blue cloud, he continued. "I think you two should find out everything you can about Jigsaw's past, looking for patterns that she might have fallen back into. People like Jigsaw only feel safe and comfortable on their own turf. She needs to be in the know, have the power."

Robbie nodded her acknowledgment, but Dawn protested, "I want to find Aliki."

Bates looked at her with a fatherly but firm look. "No, Dawn. In doing so you might compromise her safety or endanger your own. No, we need to support Aliki in this, not try to stop her. She would never forgive us if Jigsaw killed again because we stopped Aliki from tracking her down. I am as worried as you are, but there is nothing to be accomplished by finding Aliki and trying to bring her back."

Dawn nodded sadly and went back to picking at the beer label, deep in thought. It was Robbie who voiced their greatest concern. "Dr. Bates, is Aliki making rational decisions?"

The old man sighed and reluctantly took his pipe from his mouth. "I don't know. I suspect that she might be on the edge of a breakdown. She has endured a lot in a very short time. I know she wasn't sleeping well, and she complained to me of headaches. She took a hell of a bashing to her head the night she was attacked. Aliki is a very strong woman, but...well...she is, in my opinion, obsessed about Jigsaw."

The two women exchanged a look. The message between them was clear. Neither of them believed that Aliki was either physically or emotionally up to the challenge of the investigation she had taken on. Robbie could see the pain, worry, and confusion in her future sister-in-law's eyes. What must she be feeling? One day she was making the final plans for her wedding, and now, only a short time later, Aliki was living with another woman, physically and emotionally battered, not thinking straight, and all the while a psychopathic killer out there was waiting for an opportunity to take Aliki out.

After Bates left, Robbie set the security alarm and made Dawn as comfortable as she could before going to her own room. Tomorrow they would start at the media library and trace Jigsaw's history back through the press, looking for patterns and names of people they could contact to learn more about the killer. Right now, though, she needed to talk to Janet.

She pulled out her phone and pressed one.

"Hello," came a tired voice from the other end of the line.

"Hi, love, how are you doing? You sound like you've had a tough time." Robbie sat down on the edge of the bed, desperately wishing she could hold her partner.

"It's been rough. At first, Mac wouldn't speak to anyone. Reb got pissed off with her favourite cousin refusing to speak to her, so she called Mac a very rude name, which she could have only picked up from a certain olive who is going to be in so much trouble when she gets home."

Robbie squirmed with guilt. "She learned it in grade one. It's an urban jungle in there. You wouldn't believe what sort of things they are discussing over their Harry Potter lunch pails."

Janet laughed, relaxing a bit. "You are so full of it! Anyway, I had to discipline Reb, who started to cry. In the meantime, *your* daughter couldn't leave anything lie and told Mac that it was her fault that Reb was in trouble because she was acting like a snotty, fucking bitch."

Robbie cringed. "We gotta talk to that school!"

Janet snorted. "We have to wash your mouth out with soap as soon as you get home. Anyway, *that* started such a yelling match as only two teenage girls can have when they are overstressed."

Robbie could hear the strain back in Janet's voice. She nibbled her lip in frustration, trying to think of something to make Janet feel better. "Well, at least Mac is talking again." That was always a worry. As a small child, Mac had lost her mother and then watched as her father stepped in front of a train. The trauma had been so overwhelming that she had been unable to speak for many years. No one wanted Mac to withdraw into silence again.

"Not anymore. I have sent them all to their rooms. Mac is in our bed because I wouldn't dare put her in with Ryan-the-mouth, and I didn't want her sleeping alone in the guest room and fretting. I gave her your albums of press clippings to keep her occupied, and she will undoubtedly have some interesting questions to ask you when you get back."

Robbie groaned. "It's all lies! I was the victim of a sensationalist media."

"Sure you were, Olive Oyl," snorted Janet, who was well aware of Robbie's wild past. "How is it going there?"

Robbie filled Janet in, using her amazing memory and her ability to mimic voices as an almost instant replay. Janet listened with only the occasional remark. When Robbie finished, Janet sighed. "I don't at all like the sound of your sister's emotional state. I'm worried, Robbie."

"Me, too, love. We'll do everything we can to help her. You can count on that."

"You just make sure you get back to me in one piece. You know what you're like – trouble just follows you around."

Robbie heard the catch in Janet's voice. It was hard for her being up there unable to help and having to deal with three very strong-minded girls. All of a sudden Robbie was glad she had been elected to be Dawn's support. She leaned back on her bed and turned on the charm, her voice softening to a deep purr. "I will be careful, my special one. You are my soul, my reason, and my deepest love. I am missing you terribly already, and I want nothing more than to hold you, love you, and chase away all your fears."

Janet smiled and leaned against the kitchen counter, feeling Robbie's voice like a soothing balm on her troubled soul. "You are something else, Williams," she said with a chuckle.

Robbie laughed. "You must have been reading my press clippings, too."

Janet whispered into the phone, "No, I have firsthand experience about how wonderful it is to feel your hard muscles tighten under hot, silken skin as you get ready to come for me. I can feel your heat and wetness, and the scent of your excitement haunts my mind."

Robbie made a noise that sounded a lot like a pressure cooker about to explode. "Not fair!"

"Good night, my sexy Oscar winner," Janet growled sensually. "Keep in touch."

"I won't be able to sleep!" Robbie protested, but it was too late. Janet had hung up. Robbie slammed back on her bed and snapped the phone shut, laughing at how Janet had turned the tables on her.

The next day, Robbie and Dawn were up early. Armed with file cards and a laptop, they went to the media library to start ferreting out data on Jigsaw's history. It was a long and tedious process, and it became clear that they would be at it for days. At the same time, Dr. Bates was calling in a number of favours to do whatever he could. Using his position as head of the forensic labs and with a good deal of talking, he managed to get access to Jigsaw's files. Although photocopying them was out of the question, he did spend several hours jotting down what he could of the police record of this troubled woman. It was a start. The next step would be to interview people who had known her and lived to recount the experience. Those individuals seemed to be few and far between.

Aliki woke with Alice snuggled close beside her. A bolt of guilt and self-loathing fired through Aliki's soul. If she lived, how was she ever going to explain this to Dawn? It was not that she had made love to Alice – she would never betray Dawn like that – but just being there, leading Alice on, she felt dirty in her mind and soul.

She got up quickly, dressed, and went down the hall to wash the smell of Alice off her as best she could. Life stunk. She looked at her troubled eyes in the cracked mirror. A hard, lean face looked back. Her hair was shaggy, and her tattoo was threatening rather than artistic. It didn't seem like her face anymore. The woman she had been was gone. This was a stranger, the embodiment of the darkest regions of her soul. She didn't like this person, nor did she particularly care if she lived or died, just as long as she took Jigsaw with her.

Aliki went back to their room to eat some breakfast before heading to the bar. She stood with her back against the counter eating stale bread and peanut butter, lost in her dark thoughts.

"Al?" Alice mumbled from where she lay only partly covered by sheets.

"I'm heading off to the bar. Go back to sleep," Aliki ordered, her eyes averted from the near naked form.

"Yeah, okay, Al. I just wanted to say...thanks. I like the place. Waste of time 'cause I don't figure I'll be here long, but thanks. No one's ever done nothin' like this for me before."

Aliki's eyes snapped to the scrawny form that seemed so suddenly vulnerable. "They should have. You're okay, Alice."

The waitress sat up, bare breasts exposed. She had a tattooed butterfly on the left. Or was it a moth, Aliki wondered, hardening her heart. What had Alice said? Every moth has its flame. "Shut up and go back to sleep. I gotta go to work," Aliki grumbled; she left as quickly as she could.

Alice sat for the longest time, looking at the home that Aliki had made from her cheap room. No one had ever done anything like that for her before. Never. It was weird. Maybe today would be a good day. She curled up on Aliki's side of the mattress and went back to sleep.

By four, Aliki had washed all the beer glasses in the sinks and was stacking the clean glasses back behind the bar. That was Alice's job, but Alice wasn't there. Aliki felt a growing dread.

Gus stopped counting the change on the counter and looked over at Aliki. "So, where is your girlfriend? Wear her out last night, did you? You tell her that she better not do this again or she's fired. What you need is a man's dick to give you some real action." He leered, rearranging his package as he spoke.

Aliki shot him a look. "I'm done. What you need is some manners screwed up your asshole." She was anxious to get to the room and find out what had happened. She could hear Gus' soft, laugh and feel his eyes on her as she left.

She knew before she even opened the door. The smell of blood was as familiar to her as any perfume. The first thing she noticed was the spray of blood drops across the wall she had painted only yesterday. The second thing was Alice propped naked on a chair. Her arms were hooked over the back of the chair, her head bent forward. Her legs were wide apart, and a kitchen knife handle protruded from her vagina. There was blood everywhere.

It was the last image of Alice that Aliki had. The blow came suddenly and from behind, hitting her hard on the back of the head. She fell forward into a streak of blood where earlier Alice had tried to crawl to the door to escape.

The call woke Dr. Bates at three in the morning. He was at the morgue by four. The detective on duty was Brad Chauhan, a second-generation immigrant who had been posted to the position because more visible minorities were needed on the force. He knew that and worked twice as hard to prove that he was up to the job to which he had been appointed. Bates found him moody but good at his job, and that was what counted.

At the moment, Chauhan sat on a stainless steel lab stool looking pale and sipping on a coffee. He looked up as Bates walked over. "If someone did that to my wife or daughter, I'd go crazy," he muttered. "All those people gaping at her and photographing...and now this. Shit."

Bates put his hand on the young officer's shoulder. He knew all too well what the cop had experienced. Lab people would have measured, marked, photographed, and dusted for fingerprints. The body would have sat there like some macabre exhibit at some oceanside house of horrors while each specialized division did their job. Shock and disgust would be hidden behind a facade of crude jokes and comments.

Bates went to the small changing room that he shared with Aliki and the others. He missed Aliki very much. Not just her professional expertise but also her companionship, he realized. Aliki was his friend and he missed her presence.

He slipped into surgical greens and shoe covers, tied on a plastic apron, and went out into the main autopsy room. There he slipped a recorder into his pocket and clipped the mic to his collar. He put on a safety shield and a double layer of plastic gloves and walked over to the table.

The victim was a woman in her early thirties. She had been tortured. There was evidence not only of knife wounds, but also cigarette burns and beating. Her upper arms and shoulders were particularly bad – defence wounds as she had tried to turn away from the blows. But her hands were relatively untouched, except for deep rope burns at the wrists. The assailant had tied her hands behind her back but had left her free to move about so that the killer could enjoy the chase.

Bates leaned forward. There was a particularly badly burned area on the woman's breast. It appeared that the killer had tried to burn off a tattoo. He would need to cut that area out and see if the layers of epidermis could be separated so that an imprint of the tattoo could be lifted. It might be a significant lead. While he made his observations, his lab assistant, Chen, was carefully slipping metal shish kebab sticks into each of the knife wounds. They were checking for the direction of the blows and calculating the force of penetration. The victim now looked like some giant-sized voodoo doll.

"Looks like a right-handed assassin," Chen murmured, picking up the camera that lay on a table nearby.

Bates stepped back and let him take his pictures, then stepped forward to examine the woman's vaginal area, from which the knife handle still protruded. "This wasn't placed in here after. By the looks of things, she was raped with it while she was still alive and then bled to death," he stated quietly. "Do we know who she is?"

Chen looked over at the chart. "Alice Bondy. Thirty-two. Worked as a waitress at the Jarvis Tavern. She probably picked herself up a real sick loser there and paid a hell of a price for it."

Bates looked up, horror in his eyes. "Get me Chauhan and Young. I need them in my office as soon as possible."

Part 4

Jason Young sat in the conference room with an expression on his face that could have melted glass. "Would have been nice to know what the hell was going on in our backyard," he complained. "How long has Aliki been working undercover, and how come I didn't know?"

Bates played with his unlit pipe. Smoking was strictly forbidden in public buildings, but mostly he wanted time to think. This had to be handled just right. "Dr. Pateas is not working undercover for either the forensic department or the RCMP. She took a personal leave to do her own investigation."

Young rapped the end of his pen on the desk in agitation. "So she's playing candy store cop. Jesus, Bates!" The forensic scientist just shrugged and sucked with dissatisfaction on his cold pipe. Young was not to be put off. He was a pretty smart cop, and once he was pointed in the right direction, he could follow a lead as well as the best of them. The wheels were turning now, and he was coming up cherries. His eyes narrowed. "There was a biker killed down that way and another stabbed in a nasty spot. I hear tell Pateas is pretty good with those fancy blades you see the ninja use. She wouldn't have had anything to do with that, now would she? The neighbours said it sounded like two guys had a woman down there."

Bates took his pipe from his mouth and looked at the stem with some interest. "Knives are the weapon of choice in Canada. Our labs get a lot of customers from that area of town. I doubt very much if a connection could be made. What does the surviving biker say?" His gaze came up sharply, and the eyes that looked at Young from under thick white eyebrow were challenging. The message was unstated but clear: you don't rat on your own; cops protect cops.

A red tide flushed up Young's neck, and he quickly changed the subject. "Bikers don't say shit to cops; they handle their own problems. Well, we're stuck with this mess now. Suppose you bring us up to speed."

Again Bates picked his words carefully. "There is really little I can tell you. I know that Aliki had established a friendship with one of the waitresses in the bar and was sharing a room with her. Her name was Alice Bondy; she was known to be one of Jigsaw's girlfriends. Alice showed up in the morgue in the early hours of this morning. She had been tortured, raped, and murdered. I'm sure Brad will fill you in on the details.

"Aliki has been in the habit of reporting in to me each morning. She has a locker at the train station and keeps a few clothes, her service revolver, and a cell phone in there. She didn't phone this morning. I sent someone over with the spare key that I had. Everything is still there. Jason, I know Aliki has stuck her nose into your turf, but she feels responsible for the deaths of hundreds of people. Wouldn't you do the same? Let's not waste time arguing over proper procedure. What's done is done, and I fear we must act quickly."

Brad Chauhan had been sitting quietly, now he spoke up. "Jason, what that bitch did to Alice Bondy while she was still alive was really sick. Aliki is one of our own."

Young looked at Bates with deep, penetrating eyes. "Do you think Jigsaw has her?"

Bates swallowed hard. It had been a hard meeting to sit through and conduct himself with calm objectivity. He was feeling anything but. He knew what Aliki might be going through right now, as they talked, and his thoughts turned his stomach. "I very much fear that Dr. Pateas is in grave danger of meeting the same fate as Alice Bondy, if she hasn't already."

Young saw the tears in the old man's eyes before he blinked them back. He had never worked with Pateas, but he had heard that she was a beautiful woman and damn good to work with professionally. She was a cop and knew what they had to face each day on the street. She did her job well and was known as a team player. He threw down his pen and stood.

"I'll go see the inspector and get him to put every officer we have out in the area to try and get a lead. A lot of men off duty will come in and help, too, once the word gets out. Brad, you start making phone calls. I'll get the inspector to agree to this if I have to sit on him and squeeze the consent out of him like toothpaste from a tube."

Bates stood and offered each man his hand. "Thank you." His voice was rough. The other two, embarrassed by the old man's display of emotion, made a quick escape.

Bates wiped a hand over his face. He was not going to tell Dawn or Robbie until later in the day. He would prefer not to worry them at all until he had something concrete. It could be that Aliki was fine but was simply unable, for one reason or another, to go to the train station that morning. He would have to tell them before evening, though, because it would be only a matter of hours before the media heard rumours of an officer in trouble. News like that sold papers.

Knowing he had done as much as he could to help Aliki, although it seemed very little considering the peril she was in, he tucked his pipe back into his pocket and headed back to the morgue. He wanted to finish his autopsy of Alice Bondy. When Jigsaw was brought to justice again, he meant to make sure that the evidence was there to keep her behind bars forever.

While Bates had been at his meeting, his assistant, Chen, had taken swab samples of the vagina, rectum, navel, ears, and any areas where the skin creased, hoping for DNA samples that would establish the identity of the assailant. He had taken scrapings from under the fingernails and then clipped the nails into an envelope for later analysis. Chen was just finishing looking for hair or fibre samples, using a huge magnifying lens on a spring extension arm. These, too, were bagged and labelled.

Bates nodded his approval as he slipped his protective face shield down. From the instruments on the stainless steel table, he selected a scalpel and made the large Y incision that was used to open up the chest. Once the sternum and ribs were exposed, his assistant used a tool to break the ribs back, and Bates carefully examined, weighed, and took samples from the interior organs, noting the extent of the damage done by the knife. Lastly, he took the Stryker saw and cut through the skull to expose the brain for examination.

Death by violence or causes unknown stripped away more than a life; it stripped away privacy and dignity. Alice Bondy's naked body would have been seen by over a hundred people – gawkers, police, EMTs, detectives, and forensic personnel. She had been photographed, examined, and dissected. In the end, a courtroom of people would look at her photographs and the evidence her body had revealed, then her photographs would be filed. Bits of her would remain in evidence bags and on sample slides for years to come. Bates worked quietly and methodically, speaking softly into the tape recorder. Later, he would type up a detailed report. Alice had been tortured by beating, jabs of a knife, and cigarette burns. She had been raped, her assailant using a knife for penetration. She had slowly bled to death at the hands of her killer.

On the other side of town, Robbie and Dawn gathered data right until closing time. Tired and frustrated by the slow progress they seemed to be making, they drove back to Robbie's place through the rush hour traffic. Dawn was at the wheel of Robbie's Jaguar at Robbie's request. Dawn accepted, knowing that the request came out of the respect that Robbie held for her wife, Janet. Janet didn't like Robbie driving in rush hour because, as she was known to observe, Robbie was capable of giving an Academy Award performance when it came to road rage. The woman simply had no patience.

She sat now beside Dawn, her leg bouncing with pent-up energy and a need to be doing something. Robbie had the same traits as Aliki, but they were expressed in such different ways. Aliki was all about control. She would have sat beside Dawn, still and silent while her mind raced a mile a minute.

Robbie's cell phone rang and, much to Dawn's relief, Robbie's leg stopped jiggling as she shifted her weight to reach for the phone on her belt. "Robbie," she stated with the confidence that there was only one person that the single name would identify, Robbie Williams.

Bates wasted no time getting to the point. "Tom Bates. Where are you, Robbie? Is Dawn with you?"

"In traffic, heading toward my condo. Yes, Dawn is here. Why?"

Bates sighed. "Robbie, I am going to have to ask you for the performance of your life. I have to tell you now because the media have the information, and I would rather you hear the truth from me. I think it would be best if Dawn is not told until you are safely back at your penthouse."

Robbie felt her guts constrict with fear, but her facial features remained calm. She was surprised when her voice came out relaxed and casual. "Sure, so tell me how your day went."

Bates gave the facts with as few upsetting details as possible. "I was called into the lab early this morning. The victim was Alice Bondy. She was tortured, raped, and murdered. The MO is not unlike that of Jigsaw's past victims. Aliki has not made contact today. I am concerned enough to have requested that the police take immediate action. They have started an extensive hunt for Aliki and Jigsaw."

It took Robbie several beats before she could answer, but she did so with her usual amazing talent for acting. "Okay. Got that. Can we meet to discuss what we have learned in more detail?"

Bates was amazed at Robbie's voice control. "I am just leaving the lab now. I will be at your place in half an hour."

"Thanks," Robbie managed and then snapped off quickly before the plethora of questions she desperately wanted to ask came pouring out without control. Robbie swallowed bile, but her voice sounded natural when she reported the conversation to Dawn. "Bates has been in the lab all day. He said he'd meet us at the condo in a half hour."

Dawn saw the light change and inched forward. "You want the news on or anything, Robbie? We're going to be another twenty minutes stuck in this mess, I should think."

Robbie jerked out of her thoughts in a panic. "No! Aah...a bit of a headache, actually, Dawn. I...I think I'll just close my eyes for a bit. I'm not used to wearing my glasses for so long."

Unaware of the anguish that lay ahead, Dawn smiled. She knew that Robbie was rather vain about wearing her glasses in public.

They parked the car in the underground parking lot and took Robbie's private elevator to the penthouse in the exclusive condominium complex that overlooked Lake Ontario. The entire upper floor had once been Robbie's only home. Now it was simply the family residence when they were in town. The small town of Bartlett in northern Ontario had become the Williams family's principal home and the centre of their film school.

Robbie was being uncharacteristically quiet and looked pale. Dawn wondered if her future sister-in-law suffered from migraines. As they stepped out of the elevator into the foyer of Robbie's home, she took Robbie's arm. "Can I make you some tea or get you anything? You're not looking well, Robbie."

To Dawn's surprise, Robbie pulled her into her arms and held her tight.

"Dawn, Alice Bondy was found dead early this morning. It was bad. No one has heard from Aliki. I guess the media have hold of the story now. Bates is on the way here to tell us the truth of what is going on." Robbie felt the small body stiffen.

Dawn held on tight so she would not fall over. Her legs felt wobbly and her head light. Robbie's voice seemed to come from far away.

"Come and sit down. I think what we both need is a drink. I'll need to phone Janet, too."

"Mac!" Dawn exclaimed, suddenly realizing what it was going to do to her already distraught daughter when she found out that Aliki was missing.

"Don't you worry about Mac. Janet has handled these sorts of emergencies in our family before. Mac will be fine. Janet will see to that," Robbie reassured, having total confidence in the woman she loved.

Dawn curled into a ball in the corner of the couch and stared at the empty fireplace. It was like living a nightmare only she couldn't wake up and each minute became more and more terrifying. If Alice Bondy was dead, it meant Aliki could be dead also. That thought went way beyond pain; it exploded her senses apart and left nothing in its wake but cold, raw emptiness.

Robbie brought her a brandy and then disappeared into the kitchen to phone Janet. Dawn could hear her strained, worried voice, but the words refused to make sense in her head. Nothing made sense anymore. Nothing.

She closed her eyes and immediately envisioned an image of Aliki smiling at her. She could see Aliki washing the car with Mac and hear their laughter as they sudsed each other more than the car.

Dawn sighed as images of her and Aliki's private times at night rushed back. She could see the love in Aliki's eyes and feel Aliki's fingers slipping into her. She could feel her lover's lips on her clit, bringing her to ecstasy as only she could. Tears welled and ran down her face. She didn't sob, she just died a little, as slowly she realized what she might have lost.

"Why, Aliki?" she moaned. "Why did you have to do this?"

Robbie leaned on the kitchen counter, keeping an eye on Dawn in the living room while she waited for someone at the lodge to pick up the phone. She could feel the sweat on her upper lip and smell her own fear.

"Hello, Ryan here," came the confident voice of her daughter.

"Hi, Ryan. I miss you, kid," Robbie said honestly, smiling despite her fear. Ryan was a handful but a really neat daughter, and Robbie was proud of her. "Look, I need to speak to your other mom; we've got a media situation here."

She heard Ryan sigh. Now seventeen and the daughter of a famous mother and a member of an equally famous family, she was used to the intrusion of the media in their lives. She knew that sensationalism always came before truth.

"I'll get her."

Robbie waited impatiently, listening to her daughter talking to Janet, then Janet's calm, quiet voice came on the line. "Hi, my olive, what's up?"

"It's not good, Janet, and the media have got hold of it. The woman that Aliki was living with has been found dead. She's been murdered. We don't know where Aliki is. She hasn't reported in."

Robbie heard Janet's sharp intake of breath.

"Aliki was living with another woman! She's missing?"

"She might be okay, you know, on Jigsaw's trail and too busy to report in," Robbie said in an attempt at reassurance.

"Do you think that?"

Robbie sighed raggedly, feeling suddenly exhausted. "No."

"How is Dawn?"

Robbie looked around the corner. Dawn was curled into the corner of the couch, rocking back and forth, tears rolling down her face. "Bad."

"I'm on my way. There is no protecting the girls from this. We might as well all be together and try to help as best we can."

Robbie felt relief flood through her. She always felt better when Janet was at her side. "Thanks. I'll send the helicopter first thing in the morning."

"Okay. And Robbie?"

"Yeah?"

Janet gripped the phone in tension, feeling at a loss for a way to help immediately. "You just hold Dawn, okay. That is what she needs. She is far too intelligent a person not to realize the danger. Don't try to bullshit her, just offer her quiet support. Let her know her family is behind her."

"Okay," Robbie answered miserably. "I'll phone you back as soon as we get the details from Dr. Bates. He should be here soon."

"Okay. I love you, Robbie."

"I love you too, hon." Robbie reluctantly hung up and walked back into the living room. She sat down close beside Dawn and pulled her into her arms. Dawn clung to her like a lost child.

"I don't know what I would do if anything has happened to Aliki. She is so damn maddening, Robbie, but I love her so much."

Robbie smiled weakly, rubbing Dawn's back comfortingly. "Yeah, I've kinda gotten used to having her as a sister, even if she is a cop. Aliki is a pretty tough customer. I mean, she is streetwise, and she is a damn good fighter. We gotta believe that if she has walked into something, she is using her head and will either get herself out of it or hold on until we can find her."

Dawn nodded against Robbie's shoulder but said nothing. They sat there quietly sharing warmth and comfort until the chimes indicated that Dr. Bates was in the lobby waiting to be admitted to Robbie's private elevator.

Robbie untangled herself and went to the security panel. She turned on the camera and verified that it was Bates downstairs and then clicked on the speaker as she opened the elevator doors for him. "Come right up, Thomas." She frowned as she watched the doctor step inside the elevator. He looked worried.

The last thing Aliki needed was another blow to her head. Her world had tunnelled and turned black as she fought to stay conscious. The next thing she was aware of was that her arms were being roughly pulled behind her. She vomited and struggled to regain full consciousness — it might be her only chance at survival — but her wrists were held fast in handcuffs, and Jigsaw was straddling her back still.

With a cry of pain and exertion, Aliki arched her back and rolled, sending Jigsaw flying. Then she stumbled to her feet and tried to make it to the door, even though her world was out of focus and swirling dizzily. Jigsaw was there before her, standing ready in the doorway with a gun in her hand, giggling excitedly. Aliki staggered back and leaned one shoulder on the wall for support.

"Gotcha," Jigsaw squealed.

Aliki didn't answer. Her heart was still racing from having found Alice's body, and it was taking all of her self-control to stay on her feet. She smelt of vomit and sweat, and her bowels were roiling. She forced herself to stay totally focussed on Jigsaw. One wrong move now and she would end up like Alice.

Carefully, Jigsaw sidled forward. She reached down and picked up the end of a chain that was attached to Aliki's handcuffs. Aliki would have liked to have made her move then, running forward and kicking Jigsaw in the head, but the gun was trained right at her and Aliki wasn't sure if she could complete a flying kick without falling over.

Jigsaw stood again and tugged on the chain. "Come on, bitch, I'm taking you for a walk." Dazed and disorientated, Aliki went with her, certain that the next hours would be a living hell.

Bates sat in a leather chair opposite where Robbie and Dawn sat on the couch, Robbie holding Dawn's hand. He knew these were both strong, intelligent women; there was no point in hiding facts from them. Methodically, he explained what had been done to Alice Bondy and the steps that were being taken to find Aliki.

When he finished, Dawn asked in a low voice, "Do you know if Aliki had returned to the apartment last night?"

Bates frowned. "We think so. We found traces of hair and clothes fibres in a smear of Alice's blood, as if Aliki might have been on the floor at one time. The fibres were certainly left after the blood. It is not conclusive evidence because it could be contamination debris deposited there before the police arrived. The killer left the apartment door open and a number of people from the building had entered the room to have a look while they waited for the police. Aliki had been liv— staying there. Such debris could have been transmitted on air currents."

Dawn was persistent. "But you don't think so."

Bates reached into his pocket for his pipe. "My instinct tells me we need to take this situation very seriously."

For a minute the three of them sat in total silence, each dealing with the enormity of the crisis. Robbie squeezed Dawn's hand. "If we're going to find Aliki, we need to get working. There's no time to lose." She stood. "Dawn, we need to start entering our database onto the computers I have here. Could you get some coffee on while I boot up the lab? Dr. Bates, is there anything else we need to know?"

Bates took the cold pipe from his mouth and stared at it intently before he looked up at the women. "Just something rather ironic. Just before I came over here, I had a call from the Bureau of International Aviation. They have every reason to believe that a cracked coupling on the hydraulic jack that controls the positioning of the forward landing gear broke off as the gear was raised. It flew back and pierced the port side wing, puncturing the fuel tank. Fully fuelled, the plane would have had about 10,000 litres of fuel in the tank. It sprayed out over the hot engine and exploded."

Dawn looked up with eyes wet with tears. "The crash was an accident? It had nothing to do with Aliki?"

Bates swallowed hard. "It would appear at this early date that it was a horrible accident. Jigsaw used the incident to set a trap for Aliki."

"Shit." Robbie sank back on the couch and wrapped an arm around Dawn. Dawn buried her head in her hands and let Robbie hold her.

They sat in shock for only a few minutes, then Dawn drew on her inner strength and determination and rose. She was pale, and her voice was a bit shaky, but she had herself together again emotionally. "I'll get the coffee on."

Bates and Robbie looked immensely relieved, neither of them knowing what they would have done if Dawn had gone to pieces. "I'd like to see what you have gathered, Robbie."

"Sure, this way."

A little while later, Dawn came in with the coffee. "Robbie, I was going to make some sandwiches or something, but there isn't a thing to eat here. We're going to need food."

Robbie nodded. "Here, you take over. I'll phone the restaurant downstairs and have them cater. That's what I always did before I met Janet."

Bates looked up from one of Robbie's computers in surprise. Dawn shrugged. "She can't cook. Janet says she burns the toast regularly."

He smiled. "Robbie was entering data on a spreadsheet for easy comparisons. I'm going through the list of old friends and family members that Jigsaw was associated with and highlighting those I feel might be worth talking to tomorrow." Dawn nodded and set to work.

The three worked steadily until a lemon soup and Greek salad were delivered with freshly baked bread. The three hardly noticed the quality of the food as they sat around the table talking in low voices about the patterns they saw in Jigsaw's mode of operation and how they could use the information to find Aliki. The meal completed, they went back to work, stopping only when they could not stay awake any longer.

Janet and the girls found them, tired and worn, in the process of eating breakfast as they reviewed what they needed to do on the second day of Aliki's disappearance. Robbie was up like a shot and hugging her family, while Mac flew into her mom's arms and held on tight.

They all ended up in the living room, discussing what should be done and by whom. In the end it was Bates who had the final say. "Robbie, I appreciate that you want to help find your sister and action suits your nature, but Dawn and Janet will have much better luck quietly getting information from people than you would. If you start dropping in on people, they will talk to neighbours about how the famous Robbie Williams talked to them, and it will only be a matter of time before the press are following at your heels. No, it will have to be Dawn and Janet who go."

Robbie slouched down on the couch, arms folded and looking murderous. "I hate being famous." Janet reached over and touched her lover's arm and immediately some of the tension left Robbie's face.

"I want to go with Mom and Aunt Janet," Mac declared.

Again Bates wisely handled the situation before a family squabble ensued. "Two is enough, Mac. A crowd might intimidate those being interviewed. Besides, I have work for all three of you young ladies.

"What about me?" Robbie demanded, sitting up suddenly.

"You are to continue following up on the list of leads that we made last night," Bates stated firmly.

"No!" Robbie groaned in protest.

"It needs to be done," he insisted. Robbie sighed but did not protest further. What was important was finding Aliki.

Across the room, Dawn sat in the corner of the couch with Mac curled close beside her. They both looked pale and worried. Dawn stroked her daughter's arm reassuringly. "What about you, Dr. Bates? What are you going to be doing?"

"I'm going to meet with Detective Young and Chauhan at ten a.m. at the forensic lab for a debriefing. We need to know what the police have done. There is no point in us covering the same ground. Time is of the essence."

The group quickly broke up and went their separate ways. Before Bates left, he showed Mac and Reb the information that he and their mothers had compiled during the night and explained that he wanted them to sort and resort the data, recording any patterns they might find. Ryan he placed on another computer to go through pictures of Jigsaw and try to build a good sketch of her, using the police artist software package. He looked over at Robbie and found she was already deep into her work, locating relatives and friends and recording addresses to pass on to Dawn and Janet by cell phone. He nodded his approval and hurried off to his meeting.

Aliki had been led at gunpoint to a room down the hall. Jigsaw had her open a closet door and move aside the old coats hanging there. A door was barely visible beyond. Jigsaw ordered her to open it, and they entered a room with no other doors and no windows. The walls were worn and of two styles of brick. At one time it must have been part of an alleyway between two buildings that had been bricked up later.

Aliki looked around, willing her eyes to focus. Her head throbbed painfully, and her heart still raced from the shock of seeing Alice's body. She felt nauseous. She turned on legs that felt like rubber. Jigsaw was quiet, but she was breathing hard, obviously excited. Aliki was pleased that her voice sounded calm when she spoke. "Why did you kill her? You didn't have to. She did everything you wanted her to."

Jigsaw just laughed.

"That's not any kind of an answer. Tell me; I want to know."

Jigsaw's answer was to lash out. Aliki ducked but not quickly enough. The barrel of the gun clipped the bridge of her nose; she felt the cartilage snap, and pain shot through her face. Blood dripped from her nostrils. She went down on one knee, and Jigsaw was on her immediately, beating her with the butt of her gun.

"The bitch wanted me to leave you alone!" Jigsaw howled in rage as she swung at Aliki over and over again. "But I showed her! I showed her! People don't tell Jigsaw nothin'. Stupid cunt! Fucking pig. I hate you!"

Aliki tried to protect her head as much as she could, but down on her knees with her hands cuffed, there was little she could do. When she passed out, it was a relief.

It was a beautiful day. The fall sun shone through the coloured leaves of the tree-lined street, and there was a crisp, fresh edge to the air. The brightness of the day was a sharp contrast to the weight of worry and strain that Janet and Dawn felt as they walked down the gentrified street to Number 139 Barlow Street. Dawn looked around, eyes puzzled. "It doesn't look like the sort of neighbourhood that any friend of Jigsaw's would live in."

Janet nodded her agreement and unfolded the slip of paper to check the address again. "This is the place. Jigsaw's sister, Krystle Neals." They rang the bell and waited.

A thin woman, prematurely grey and stooped, answered the door hesitantly. "Yes?"

"Mrs. Neals?" Janet asked after a moment's hesitation.

"Yes." The voice, already timid, was cautious now as well.

Janet took the lead, knowing Dawn might find it awkward to explain their visit. "Mrs. Neals, my sister-in-law is a police officer, and we have reason to believe that your sister might be holding her prisoner. We need to talk to you."

Krystle Neals gave a small gasp and put her hand to her mouth, as if to pull back the sound that had already escaped. "I don't know anything. I don't know what you are talking about. Please, I need to go."

Dawn gently but firmly put her shoulder to the door, and they were inside. "Mrs. Neals, we know that you are not involved. We're looking for leads, the slightest thing that might help us find Aliki. Anything!"

Janet thought that Krystle Neals looked like a frightened mouse that had been cornered by a hungry cat. The woman nodded nervously and wrung her hands. When she realized the two women were not going away, she led them into a living room overcrowded with furniture and sat stiffly on a straight chair in the corner. "I got everything," she stated defensively, "because Marsha killed them. That's the law. You can't kill for gain."

Janet indicated to Dawn to sit down. "Yes, we know. Did Jigsaw...Marsha bother you about that?"

Krystle wrung her hands. "She used to send me letters from prison, asking me how I was doing and how the property was, and was I managing the money well. They sounded like nice, concerned letters, but I knew better," she said with uncharacteristic confidence. "They were evil letters, threatening letters. I could read between the lines. I knew what she really meant."

"Has she sent you any letters recently?" Dawn asked.

"No! I don't care what the police say, she didn't escape from that fire. She's dead, I tell you! Dead!" Krystle buried her face in her hands and cried hysterically. "Oh God, please believe me! She's dead!"

Janet looked at Dawn, their eyes meeting in silent understanding. Krystle was terrified. And that could only mean one thing — Jigsaw had visited her since her escape. It was Janet who spoke. "Mrs. Neals, Krystle, we have to stop Jigsaw. You have to help us."

The hysterical woman leapt to her feet. "I won't! I won't! Stop bothering me. Jigsaw is dead! Get out of my house! Get out!"

Dawn and Janet left. There was little else they could do. Once they had moved out of sight of the house, Janet pulled out her phone. "Robbie, we just left Krystle Neals' house. ... She denies knowing anything, but she is clearly terrified. She inherited everything after Jigsaw was convicted of her parents' murder. We think Jigsaw has been in touch with her. Can you arrange a watch on the house? ... Good. Thanks. We're going to see if we can find Kyle Wyatt now. ... Yes, we'll be careful."

"Maybe we should go back and try again," Dawn said, the desperation showing in her face.

Janet shook her head and flagged the plainclothes detective who had been waiting in his car while Janet and Dawn talked to Mrs. Neals. "If we force the issue, she'll call the police, and they'll do everything they can to stop our investigation. No, we'll try to get information from other sources. She's terrified, Dawn, and not very stable. Even if she does know Jigsaw's whereabouts, and I doubt it, she is not going to talk."

The two women rode in silence as their bodyguard drove them downtown and dropped them off at the Salvation Army soup kitchen. They made their way through the rows of tables. Only a few bag ladies and a handful of men, worn and haggard, sat hunched over a late afternoon bowl of stew. They went up to the counter. Again it was Janet who did the talking.

"Hello, we're looking for Kyle Wyatt. My associate, Mrs. Williams, phoned you earlier this morning about us coming."

A beanpole of a man, with a face lined and weathered well beyond his years, stepped forward. "That's me. You two might as well sit at one of the tables. I'll come around and talk to you."

Janet noted the heavy tattoos on his arms that did not cover the marks of countless needles and collapsed veins. Wyatt had been mainlining for a long time.

He came around the serving counter and sat down on one of the metal folding chairs, lit a flattened cigarette, and inhaled deeply. His fingers were stained from smoking. "I haven't seen Jigsaw since they put her away."

Janet nodded. "We're not with the police. We have reason to believe that my sister-in-law is with her, and we are trying to locate her. We were hoping you might know where Jigsaw might hang out."

The man shrugged. "Jigsaw and I hung around the same biker gang. Neither one of us made it into the ranks. You do drugs and the bikers don't want you. They push the shit, they don't take it. And Jigsaw got sick of being traded from one guy to another for a quick fuck, least that's what she said. Truth of the matter was, she liked the women better. Jigsaw always had a screw loose. Now the good Lord reached me, so I gotta believe He can save her soul, too, but I'm not holding out much hope that when the opportunity to see the Light comes her way, she is going to see it."

Janet controlled her frustration. Wyatt seemed willing enough to help them, but the truth of the matter seemed to be that he'd fried his brain on drugs and was having a hard time staying on track. "Do you know where we could find her?"

"Well, she's not with the bikers anymore, that's for sure, although I think she still knows a lot of them. That's why she killed them, you know."

Dawn looked up sharply. "Killed who?"

Wyatt looked surprised that she had to ask. "Her parents. She wanted their property. It was handy like, you know."

"But she didn't get it, did she?" Janet asked.

"Not as far as I know. Went to the sister, I heard. A bit of a basket case, that one. Used to pee herself even when she was grown."

Janet interrupted before he could go off again. "So you haven't seen Jigsaw?"

"Nope, and the good Lord willing, it's going to stay that way. You seem like nice folks. You shouldn't be messing with the likes of Jigsaw. She don't care a shit for nobody. She's just crazy. Scary crazy."

The women tried for another half hour to get any sort of lead from Wyatt. He was talkative enough, but he never seemed to get to the point. They left feeling discouraged, depressed, and hungry, having missed lunch. They shared a power bar that Janet had in her pocket and moved on.

With their bodyguard parked nearby, they tried the few neighbours who still lived on the same working class street that the Higgins family had in the years Krystal and Marsha were growing up. If they knew anything, they weren't talking. As the last door closed in their faces, Dawn looked at Janet in despair. "Everyone is afraid. No one wants Jigsaw coming after them."

Janet gave Dawn's shoulder a squeeze. "We'll just keep trying. Sooner or later someone will slip, or the little pieces will come together to make a whole picture."

"We might not have a later," Dawn muttered as the two women headed down the street once more.

Two more days slipped past. They all grew haggard, their nerves ragged. Around the children, they tried to maintain a positive attitude, but in their hearts they knew that each hour that passed reduced the chances of Aliki being alive. They had searched, questioned, and checked, and no lead had gotten them anywhere. The police had questioned everyone in Alice's building and searched both the building and the neighbourhood. Officers were giving up their off days to help with the search, but Jigsaw and Aliki had fallen off the map.

The next attack, when it came, was more deadly than the first. While she had been unconscious, Jigsaw had used a combination lock to secure her chain to an iron ring in the wall. This reduced Aliki's mobility to a radius of about ten feet. Badly hurt from her first beating and unable to use her arms, she couldn't risk any high kicks. Once she was down, she knew what her fate would be. But she was able to kick Jigsaw's hand away, block a blow, or dodge out of the way, waiting for an opportunity that never came. Jigsaw was taking no chances. When her captor finally left her alone, Aliki was bleeding steadily from a number of deep cuts. Jigsaw was just toying with her, enjoying the power trip; she meant Aliki to die slowly.

Aliki forced herself to stay on her feet. She might not survive another sustained attack. She had lost a good deal of blood and was low on fluids. She wasn't sure how long she had been held prisoner. She was hungry and very thirsty. She had used the corner of the room to relieve herself several times, no easy task with her hands cuffed. She staggered over to the ring embedded in the brick wall and once again started heaving at it, trying to work it loose. Her flesh chafed painfully against the cuffs and scraped against the brick. Blood dripped from any number of wounds, forming a slippery puddle on the floor. She gritted her teeth and worked on compulsively. Her head hurt like hell.

By the time she heard Jigsaw returning, she had managed to scrape only a few brick fragments free. Now there was no thought, no planning. The reptilian brain deep within every person reacted. Aliki lay down on her side, still and quiet, and waited.

Jigsaw had wanted to stay away longer, to make the torment last, but she was drawn back to Aliki by her excitement. Torturing the pig who had put her away was even better than she'd thought it was going to be. She tightened her grip on the knife. The kill was going to be so good.

Aliki lay motionless in a pool of blood. Jigsaw frowned. She wanted Aliki conscious to know what she was doing to her. "Get up, you fucking bitch!" she snarled, kicking at Aliki's back. When there was no response, Jigsaw bent over her to roll her over. An instant later, Aliki's tethering chain was looped around Jigsaw's neck.

Jigsaw panicked, squirming frantically to escape Aliki's hold. Then, as black spots formed before her eyes, she lashed out with her knife, sinking it deeply into Aliki's side. There was a grunt of pain, and the chain around Jigsaw's throat loosened a bit.

With a superhuman effort born of her martial arts training, Aliki calmed herself and put the pain behind her. All her focus and strength, she willed to her hands. The chain tightened again, then tightened some more, and Aliki felt the flopping body suddenly go limp. She didn't stop. She pulled until the chain cut into Jigsaw's neck and crushed her larynx.

Weak and barely conscious, Aliki lay there with Jigsaw's cooling body on top of her. Finally, she wriggled out from underneath and, sobbing hysterically, crawled to sit with her back against the wall as far away from the body as she could. Her trembling hands kept trying to wipe Jigsaw's scent off her. She tried to focus on something — anything — but couldn't. She couldn't remember where she was or why she was there. "My flame," she kept muttering. "My flame."

It was a quiet, gloomy group that sat around the breakfast table on the fifth day after Aliki's disappearance. Dawn played with her food but ate very little. She was gaunt and pale.

Robbie gritted her teeth in frustration. They had questioned and re-questioned people, looked everywhere they could think to look, and had come up with nothing. The police, too, had come up empty-handed. "We'll stay here this morning, go through the data the girls have collected. There has to be something we have overlooked." No one said anything.

Reb asked to be excused and slipped off her chair. Janet, looking exhausted, rose to follow her. "We'll go, Aunt Janet," Ryan said, needing action of any sort. She and Mac got up and went to look for Rebecca.

They found her sitting in front of one of the computers with one of the sketches Ryan had made of Jigsaw on the screen. She sat there very still, a little child with the worries of an adult world on her shoulders.

"You okay, kid?" Ryan asked, rubbing her little sister's shoulders.

Reb said nothing. She clicked on her mouse and brought up a grainy black and white photo of a row of tenement houses that had been downloaded from the newspaper, then she clicked back to her sketch. This she darkened until it was almost black.

Ryan looked at Mac, worry plain in her eyes. Mac knelt down beside Reb, who stared at the screen as if the others were not there. "Reb, why don't you come out on the balcony with us for a bit and get some fresh air? We all need to take a little break."

Reb ignored her and clicked back to the poor quality photo. She isolated one window and expanded it, then she leapt from her chair and almost knocked Ryan over as she bumped into her on her way to the kitchen at a dead run. Ryan and Mac followed.

"Mommy! Mommy! I know where she is!" Reb yelled, grabbing Janet's arm and pulling her out of her melancholy musings

She smiled weakly at her daughter's excitement and pulled her into her lap. "Tell us then."

"She's in the brick building," Reb stated proudly.

Janet smiled. "The police checked that building very carefully, Reb. Your Aunt Aliki and Jigsaw were there, but they have gone now."

Reb slipped from her mother's arms and stamped her foot in frustration. "No! Not that building, the one next door. I just saw her!"

The adults in the room blinked and looked at the small child in amazement. It was Robbie who managed to squeak out the question that was on everyone's mind. "You saw her where, Reb?"

Reb was not a child to be intimidated, even by a room full of adults looking at her in baffled amazement. "On your computer, Obbie. Come on. I'll show you."

Janet stood up quickly, thinking to spare Dawn and Robbie from potentially false hope. "Ryan, Mac, and I will go have a look at what Reb has found. Why don't you two clear the breakfast things, and then we'll decide what to do next."

Reb had run ahead, and by the time the two teens and Janet entered Robbie's editing lab, Reb had already placed her darkened sketch next to the magnified window. When Janet arrived, Reb pointed to the dark window. Janet leaned forward and looked. Barely visible in the darkness was a face looking out at the street. It was not so much that the features could be seen as that the expression of madness was clear. Janet gasped in surprise.

"Christ, kid! I think you're on to something," Ryan muttered, leaning forward to peer at the screen.

Mac took off on a run to the kitchen. "Mom! Mom! Aunt Robbie! Come quickly. Reb might have found something!"

The women stood in a tight circle at the end of the street, which had been blockaded by the police. Dr. Bates stood beside them, for once without his pipe, looking grim and exhausted. The police had verified that both the tenement buildings had belonged to the Higginses and that Krystle Neals had inherited them. It did not take long for Mrs. Neals to verify that Jigsaw was using rooms in both buildings. A police SWAT team had entered the suspected building about ten minutes earlier. The occupants were being led from the building, apartment by apartment, and questioned. Everything seemed orderly and quiet, and the women fidgeted nervously, hoping this was not yet another dead end.

Another fifteen minutes went by, and then a police officer wearing a bullet-proof vest and a SWAT team jacket came out of the building and approached them. "Dr. Bates, we are going to need you, sir."

Bates nodded, his eyes filled with sorrow and grief. Dawn gave a little gasp, and Janet wrapped her tightly in her arms. Ryan stepped forward and put her arms around Mac. "I'm here for you," she whispered. Robbie picked Reb up and wiped away her tears, talking to her softly about what a good job she had done. Her voice was strained.

The officer led him not into the second building, but into the first, where Alice Bondy had been found. "It's the smell, sir. We probably wouldn't have found the door if it hadn't been for the stink. It smells like decay, so we thought we'd better get you before we opened up the door."

Bates nodded. He was a little winded from climbing the three flights, but he had nothing to say anyway. The worst experience for someone in forensics was having to identify and autopsy someone they knew. Yet he knew that was the way Aliki would want it; if she was dead, she would want him to handle it.

The smell was gagging when they opened the door, and several of the officers felt their stomachs heaving. The sound of flies buzzing seemed strangely loud and eerie in the room. Jigsaw lay on her back. Her eyes were open and her tongue hung out of her mouth, swollen and black. Flies ate at the edges of her eyes and at the rotting bloody mess of torn tissue around her neck. The body was swollen and discoloured, the blood having settled and leaving blue and purple stains on the lower regions of her body. The upper tissue was grey-white and turning green.

Bates took it all in with a practiced glance. "Get the EMTs up here," he called as he hurried over to Aliki's body. She was against the wall on her side, her body bloodied and battered, a knife hilt protruding from her side. Her eyes were closed and crusted, and one graceful hand was outstretched. In her own blood she had written, *Dawn, I love you.* Bates reached out a hand and gently stroked his assistant's temple. The skin was warm.

Bates spun on his heels where he squatted. "God damn it! Get those EMTs here now! She's still alive!"

Ryan at her side, Robbie paced up and down the hall of the hospital. In the waiting area, Dawn, Mac, and Janet sat in shocked silence. Reb had fallen asleep in Janet's lap. When Aliki had been brought out on a stretcher, IVs running fluids into her arm, Robbie had to physically hold Dawn back. As the ambulance left, lights flashing and siren blaring, the family was transported to the hospital in a squad car. Aliki had been in surgery for three hours.

Finally, the doctor appeared in the hallway and spoke to Robbie and Ryan. Dawn and Mac stood as Robbie pointed in their direction. The surgeon nodded and moved toward the waiting room, Robbie and Ryan on his heels. "Ms. Freeman?"

Dawn stood pale and trembling, holding Mac close to her side. "Yes."

"Inspector Pateas has survived the surgery. She is in serious condition in our recovery room. In an hour or so, we will move her into our intensive care unit. Fortunately, the knife slipped between the pancreas and the large intestine, and the other wounds did not penetrate deeply. She was incredibly lucky."

Dawn slumped against Janet, who had put a supportive arm around her. "She's going to be all right?"

The doctor frowned. "She is very ill, Ms. Freeman. Her body is badly dehydrated and in shock from loss of blood. There are broken bones, and she has a cracked skull and a bad concussion. She's running a low-grade fever as the result of an infection. We are doing all we can, but the situation is still critical."

"C...can I see her?"

The doctor nodded sympathetically. "Just you, and only for a minute or two. Come with me."

Dawn held Mac close as tears streamed down the teen's face. She followed the doctor, glancing back to see Mac looking lost and upset.

There was only blackness, and then a voice, soft and loving, reached her. "Aliki? It's Dawn, lover. I'm here. We all are. You fight, okay. We love you. I love you."

Aliki forced her eyes open and looked into worried eyes above a white surgical mask. "I love you," she tried to say, but all that came out was an unintelligible mumble.

It was several weeks before Dawn was able to take Aliki up to the lodge. They walked down to the lake and sat on the dock, looking at the last of the fall leaves. Aliki was drawn and quiet and had been eating very little. She was suffering from night terrors and still wore a sling to support her damaged shoulder. Her hands shook; she was on heavy medication and receiving therapy once a week.

They had not talked much or made love. Dawn was trying to be patient, letting Aliki find her own footing before they tried to deal with the issues between them. Aliki shivered, despite the heavy jacket that she wore.

Dawn looked over at her in concern. "Do you need to go in?"

Aliki shook her head. "No, not yet. I...I like it in the open."

"Okay." Dawn blinked back tears.

Aliki looked into the water moodily. "She was my flame," she finally said to the water. "I had to go – like a moth to the flame. It seemed like the right thing to do. I...I did things I'm not proud of, things I shouldn't have. All I could see was the flame."

Dawn felt her heart contract with pain, but she forced herself to remain calm. "What things, love?"

Aliki reluctantly looked up into Dawn's eyes. "I came on to Alice, kissed her, shared a bed with her. I used her, and now she is dead because of me."

"Did you make love to her?" Dawn asked quietly, feeling sick to her stomach.

"No! Of course not. B...but I still feel dirty, and I'm responsible for the actions that caused her death."

Dawn couldn't hold back the tears. They trickled slowly down her face, and she looked away. "Are you telling me so I can forgive you for what happened?"

Aliki considered that. "No, although I hope someday you can. I just needed to be honest with you."

Dawn nodded, her back still to Aliki. "Anything else?"

"You know that I killed one man, and I tried to kill another."

Dawn turned and looked into Aliki's eyes. They were hard to read now, cautious and hooded. "The person I knew would have tried everything to avoid that."

Aliki stared at her hands as she wrung them. "I know."

Dawn looked at her in worry. "Are you still getting the headaches?"

"Sometimes."

She considered her words carefully. "You've been sick, Aliki. It's going to take time. You need time, and I need time."

Aliki nodded. "I do love you."

Dawn wrapped an arm around her lover, and they sat in silence, watching the reflection in the water shift and change. "I love you, too."

Robbie wrapped her arm around the woman that she loved. From the window they could see Dawn and Aliki down on the dock. "Do you think they can work it out?"

Janet nodded. "Someday, but not soon. Aliki has a long way to go before she is healthy again, both physically and mentally, and when she is better she's going to have to work on rebuilding some trust."

Robbie frowned. "But they will be all right, won't they?"

Janet looked up into the worried eyes of her lover. “If their love is as strong as ours, yes, they will work through this.”

She felt Robbie relax in her arms.

“That’s okay, then.”

At the airplane crash site, nothing remained of the carnage of that terrible accident. The first snow fell, covering the ground with white. It was a time of rest. A time of healing.

Dead Ringer

A year after Aliki had been found alive after her kidnapping by Jigsaw, Robbie found herself sitting beside her sister on the small, well-traveled chartered plane that was taking them from Santiago, the capital city of Chile, to the small town of Atacoma in the north. Atacoma sat close to the Peruvian border and according to Aliki was one of the nerve centres of forensic anthropology.

Wisely, Robbie had done her own research. Atacoma was the ends of the earth. Sitting in a desert region with the dubious distinction of having had less than three inches of rain in the past forty years, Atacoma did command a wonderful view of the Andes Mountains across kilometres of pristine desert landscape dotted with fertile oases. Unfortunately, the high elevation could make the noon sun glaring and the nights cold.

"Aliki needs you," Janet had explained to Robbie when she'd grumbled, and so Robbie had gone along. She watched out of the corner of her eye as Aliki reached into her pocket and pulled out a bottle of medication. Her hands were bony and almost translucent, and they trembled as Aliki tried to shake out a pill. Robbie took the bottle and dropped one of the small pills onto her sister's palm. "You okay?"

Aliki popped the pill in her mouth and took a slug from her water bottle. She nodded but said nothing as she wedged the bottle into the seat pocket in front of her and took the pill bottle from Robbie to put back in her pocket. Robbie looked at her sister with worry in her eyes. Aliki had lost a lot of weight. She was skinny; no, more than that, Robbie decided, she was gaunt. Aliki's breakdown had taken its toll both physically and mentally. It had also put Aliki's relationship with her partner, Dawn, in jeopardy.

Robbie shuddered. She couldn't imagine life without her wife, Janet. She placed a hand over Aliki's and squeezed gently. To her surprise, Aliki's hand wrapped around her own and held on tightly. "It won't be long now," Robbie said with reassurance.

Aliki swallowed, and tears welled in her eyes; she bravely blinked them back. "I didn't think the flights would bother me," she croaked out in a hoarse whisper.

Robbie felt her own gut contract suddenly, understanding that Aliki had been suffering in silence through four flights and twenty hours of flight time, reliving the horrific events of the jetliner crash she had worked the year before. Robbie couldn't think of anything to say. She squeezed her sister's hand in understanding and held on, glad that Janet had made her come. Aliki did need her.

The Atacoma Hotel was a pleasant surprise. It was not the Ritz, by any means, but it was situated on a rustic side street and, as advertised, afforded a lovely view of the adobe mission church built in the 1500s. Better still, the world's largest open pit copper mine in Calama was kilometres away and downwind of Atacoma.

Robbie, her Tilley hat pulled low and sporting her "I'm not a famous actress" sunglasses, booked them into their room while Aliki stood silently beside her. Then, steering her sister by the elbow, Robbie headed across the small lobby to the rhythm of Indian panpipe music drifting in from the dusty village street.

They had almost made their way along open air corridors to their room when a large, loud man loomed up in front of them and scooped Aliki into his arms. "Alberta! Damn it's good to see you!" His voice boomed out, drowning out even the persistent panpipes. "Hell, look at you. Have you been sick? You look half dead. Hey, you'd better be careful. Victor's here, and you know how he loves to cut up cadavers."

Robbie put the cases down with a decisive thud and was just about to wade in and pull her sister free from the insensitive loudmouth when she was stopped by the sound of Aliki's laugh. She hadn't heard her sister laugh in a long time. "Put me down, Jed. I'm breakable. Jed, this is my sister, Robbie Williams. Robbie, this is Dr. Jed Philby, head of the palaenotology department at Kings."

A big meaty hand shot forward and lifted Robbie's sunglasses up off her nose, and Robbie found herself nose to nose with the massive doctor. "Damned if you are not right, Alberta. It is the actress Robbie Williams!" The glasses dropped down on Robbie's nose again and, much to her surprise, she found herself airborne in one of the doctor's hugs. "Nice to meet you, Robbie. I had no idea that you were interested in ancient Peruvian burial methods. Not that I don't understand an interest in mummies. It is hard not to get wrapped up in this work." Jed laughed, enjoying his joke as he set her down remarkably gently.

Extricating herself from Jed's iron-band arms, Robbie muttered sarcastically, "Actually, I came for the mountain air."

Rather than discouraging the doctor, this remark seemed to tickle his funny bone. Another powerful laugh exploded into the lobby, and Jed slapped Robbie on the back so hard she almost ended up in a side table arrangement of cactus. "Mountain air! That was a good one! You'd freeze your tits off up there this time of year, woman. We're all meeting at the Graveyard Restaurant at six, Alberta. See you there." With another laugh, the mountain of a man moved off.

"Please tell me they are not all like him," Robbie asked, watching the large form disappearing out onto the terrace.

"No. Most of them are not that retiring," Aliki said seriously and turned left into a river stone hallway without another word.

Robbie grabbed the remainder of the bags and followed, a smile on her face. Aliki had made a joke. Things were looking up.

They stood shoulder to shoulder outside their room while Robbie fished around in her pocket for their room key. "Did he say we were meeting at six at the Graveyard Restaurant?" Robbie asked, affecting nonchalance.

"He did." Aliki took the key, its copper tag engraved with an Indian motif like the one decorating their door. Unlocking their room, she picked up her bags and entered a basic but clean and comfortable room.

Robbie followed. "Please let it just be a silly name," she muttered with a sigh.

Sometime later, after Aliki had slept for several hours, the two sisters made their way down the street to the restaurant. Robbie looked at the large graveyard across the street and then back at the restaurant. "I'm not having any ice cubes in my drinks until I find out if they use well water," she said drolly.

Aliki shrugged. "It will put hairs on your chest."

"Hey, great. That will really help my career."

The room was dark and rustic. An open fire burned on the stone floor, the smoke curling up and out through a hole in the roof. To one side, in an alcove, an Indian band played local music, and to the other, six tables had been carelessly drawn together. There sat some of the greatest names in archaeology and forensic anthropology.

The mountain rose like Vesuvius erupting. "Alberta, over here. Didn't I tell you she looked half dead? Honest to God, I hardly recognized her. Victor, stop drooling. Gentlemen, and lady, this is Robbie Williams, the actress. She's interested in burial methods, too, and she's going to read Tidwell Jennings' paper tomorrow so we can get the damn thing over with."

"I'm what?" Robbie asked over a round of applause and "Hear! Hear!"

"Two pineapple margaritas over ice," Philby ordered from a passing waitress.

"Does this place get its water from a well?" Robbie asked as she collapsed into the seat that had been rammed into the back of her knees by a man who looked old enough to be her great, great grandfather.

"Don't think so, cutie," he said. "I think it's runoff."

"Oh, shit," Robbie muttered, and the table broke into gales of laughter.

The old man resumed his seat several places over, and Robbie leaned over to whisper in Aliki's ear, "Who is he?"

"That's Dr. Gerald Flex. He's a pathologist. His area is the analysis of keratin." Seeing the blank look on Robbie's face, she added, "The stuff hair and nails are made of."

"You're scaring me, Aliki."

"Philby is a palaeontologist with an interest in mummification methods. And Dr. Hilda Katz," Aliki pointed to a quiet woman with lean, well-toned features and heavy framed glasses, "is a palaeopathologist."

"Boy, what a fun group," Robbie muttered.

"The village gardens are just down the hill from the graveyard," Aliki countered and watched Robbie choke on the gulp of margarita she had just taken.

Aliki smiled innocently, and Robbie pulled a face at her.

"Okay, so who is Tidwell Jennings, who volunteered me to read a paper, and why can't Jennings read the damn thing?"

The tall, distinguished looking man to her right put his beer neatly on its paper coaster. "That would have been me, Dr. Archie Fenwick, Davenport University." He offered his hand. The handshake was brief and firm. Robbie returned it in kind, liking the man immediately.

"Tiddy was a colleague, a doctor of internal medicine at Dormer University. I don't think I would be wrong in saying that she was a considerable authority on intestinal enzymes."

"Bloody authority on near everything," someone murmured sarcastically into the sudden silence that had descended on the crowd around the tables.

Fenwick shot a look down the table and continued. "She was to present a rather interesting paper on the suppression of post-mortem actions of body enzymes in the mummification process. Awkwardly, she has disappeared. We thought, seeing as you are here, you wouldn't mind reading her paper."

"Awkwardly? What does that mean? When did she disappear?" Robbie probed, feeling that she was not being told all the facts.

"During our last gathering, actually, three years ago. It was...er...awkward. Anyway, during all the...aah...awkwardness, her paper was overlooked, and we felt it only fitting to come back this year to Atacoma and see that her paper is read."

"She disappeared from *here*?" Robbie queried, pointing to the table.

It was Philby who answered. "Excused herself to have a pee and never came back. Just like her to disappear when it was her turn to buy a round."

Fenwick frowned. "Yes, well, that hardly matters now. The important thing is we really need to see what she had to say about the suppression of the enzyme activity in mummification."

"Isn't anyone the least bit interested in what happened to her?" Robbie asked. There was an awkward silence filled by polite coughs and the embarrassed shuffling of feet.

"Did anyone read Samir's paper on ancient Mesopotamian pollen samples found in pieces of clay pots?" Katz asked politely, and people quickly jumped in to use the opportunity to change the subject.

Robbie's jaw worked in frustration, and she was just about to demand more information when Aliki kicked her under the table. "Let it drop. We'll talk about it later," she whispered.

Robbie sighed and kept her mouth shut as conversations about the art of mummification, the causes of death, and the latest development techniques in autopsies bubbled around her like some witch's chant from *Macbeth*.

Fortunately, Aliki was not drinking because of her medication, sticking to soda water instead. Robbie, who hardly ever drank, finished both margaritas and bought another and so managed to convince herself that sitting with a bunch of ghouls discussing the dissection of human bodies in the Graveyard Restaurant at the ends of the earth was all perfectly normal.

She had, in fact, mellowed to the extent that she felt quite comfortable about the discussion on the various preferred tools for the removal of fingernails when Aliki leaned over and whispered into her ear, "I need to get out of here." The strain in Aliki's voice was enough to convince Robbie that it was time to leave.

"Well, nice meeting you, folks, but we gotta get some sleep," Robbie announced, standing up a little too quickly and feeling her head spin. She held on to the back of her wooden chair until the floor stopped heaving. "We'll see you tomorrow at breakfast."

Negotiating her way to the door and dealing with the darkness outside after the lights of the restaurant took Robbie's full concentration, so it was only as they stood outside their room that she noticed that Aliki was sweating and rubbing her hands together as if she was washing them. Robbie felt her gut clench; she wrapped her arm around her sister and steered her into their room. Once the door was closed, she held Aliki close in her arms, feeling tears staining her shoulder.

After a few minutes, Aliki pulled away and disappeared into the bathroom. Robbie heard the sound of a pill bottle being opened. Aliki reappeared; kicking off her shoes and falling face down on the bed, she buried her face in the pillow to hide her tears. Robbie stood at the door, not knowing what to do. She licked her lips and resisted the urge to make a run for it. Instead, she sat gingerly on the edge of Aliki's bed and placed a hesitant hand on her sister's back. Only when she was sure that Aliki was asleep did Robbie go out onto the terrace to use her cell phone.

"Janet?"

"Hi, Robbie. I miss you."

Robbie heard the sound of a kiss coming her way across the kilometres between them and the tension inside of her eased a bit.

"I miss you too, love of my life. How are our girls?"

"Your sister Elizabeth has Ryan listening to Holst's *The Planets,* and the two of them have been lying on the dock staring at the stars all night. Reb has decided she wants to play the drums, and there is a good chance I'll have to put her up for adoption to maintain my sanity. How is it going there?"

"Aliki is acting really freaky. She seems okay for a while, and then she just sort of cracks and falls apart. She was rubbing her hands together this evening, and then she got all teary."

"Uh, oh, this is not good. What brought it on?" Janet asked, her voice conveying her worry.

"She said the flights really bothered her. Mind you, we did have drinks at the Graveyard Restaurant with a bunch of Aliki's ghoul friends and talked about dead people we know and love from the inside out."

"Charming."

"Aliki hangs with some very strange people. I suspect Victor Van Vogt is a vampire disguised as a parasitologist. He's got buck teeth and has a knife sheath on his belt."

"I can see this trip is going to be a source of stories all winter long." Janet laughed. "Dawn and Mac should be arriving any minute to spend a few weeks here. Ryan really wants some time with her cousin, and Dawn, well, she needs some support. She literally gets left at the altar, and yet she is still there to nurse Aliki through her breakdown. Then, as soon as your sister is on her feet, she decides to take off to South America alone."

Robbie sighed. "Yeah. I can't see why Dawn and Aliki just can't seem to get it together. I don't know what's the matter with them. They're clearly very much in love."

Janet snorted angrily. "Your sister is what is the matter!"

"Hey, Aliki went through hell! She's just really mixed up and confused at the moment," Robbie said hotly, automatically defending her half-sister.

"Yeah, I know," Janet was quick to agree with a sigh. "It must have been horrible for Aliki to believe that she had been responsible for all those people being killed. She is such a moral, upright person."

"She doesn't talk about it, but I can tell the rift between her and Dawn is really eating at her. I think she's lonely. Well, you know," Robbie finished awkwardly.

"Are you lonely?" Janet asked softly.

"I miss you like hell," Robbie admitted sheepishly. "I don't sleep well when you're not naked and cuddling into my side after we've made love."

Janet laughed. "Robbie, are you on your cell phone telling the world about our sex life?"

"Nah, I haven't got to that yet, but give me time."

"You are so bad, and I love you for it. I miss snuggling with you, too."

"You don't miss the sex?" Robbie wailed dramatically.

"That, too," Janet assured her.

"That's a relief. Okay, I'd better go. I just wanted to report in again so I could hear your voice. I love you, Janet. I am so proud and happy that you are my wife," Robbie admitted with a blush.

"If you were here, I'd be hugging the daylights out of you, my 'olive'. No one could be more lucky than me to have you and the family we have become."

"I miss you all. Give the girls a hug, and say hi to Elizabeth and David. Tell Dawn to forgive my stupid sister, and make sure Ryan doesn't corrupt Mac."

"I'll do my best. Bye, lover."

"Bye, darling." Robbie clicked the cell phone shut with a sigh. Talking to Janet always helped, but now it was just her and Aliki again.

Aliki was lying on her back staring at the ceiling when Robbie walked in. "Have you been talking to Janet?"

"Yeah. It doesn't matter how many times I go away, I miss her like hell every time."

There was a moment of silence, then Aliki asked, "D...did she mention how Dawn and Mac are?"

"Cut up about everything. Janet invited them to the lodge for a few weeks. They should be arriving there any time now," Robbie sat on the edge of Aliki's bed. "Sis, you gotta build some bridges. That's what Janet always says to me when I don't want to talk about something that has upset me. Why don't you phone Dawn?"

Aliki swallowed and blinked back tears from eyes already red from crying. "I'm no good at these things. I'd just make it worse."

"Yeah, I understand the emotional talks are tough." For a minute, the two sisters were quiet, each recalling times when their inability to talk about stressful issues had led to real tensions with the people they loved. Then Robbie got a smile of pure devilment. "I've got it!"

"Got what?"

"Prompt cards."

"What?"

"I'm no good at conversations in real life, but I sure as hell can write dialogue. I'll write down some phrases on the hotel stationery and then prompt you so you don't get tongue-tied."

Aliki snorted. "Boy, that's romantic."

"Hey, it's a start. Even Kennedy had his speeches written for him, and he did all right with the opposite sex." As good as her word, Robbie went over to the desk to find pen and paper.

"In case you hadn't noticed, I am not interested in a member of the opposite sex," Aliki grumbled. Robbie ignored her as she wrote furiously on pieces of stationery. "Are you listening to me? I think this is a really bad idea, and I'm not going to do it."

Robbie turned around and gave her a pointed look. "Look at you. You are a mess. Jed is right. All through the meal, Victor was sizing up your bones as he fingered his knife. Death warmed over looks healthier than you."

"I had a fucking breakdown, God damn it!" Aliki snapped, getting up off the bed in one clean movement and pacing about the room.

"Yeah, that was then; this is now. You need to build some bridges before you lose Dawn and Mac altogether. Do you want that?"

Leaning against the doorframe, Aliki stared out into the Spanish-style courtyard. "No, I don't want that."

"Then phone. Hey, this couldn't get much worse; what have you got to lose?" Aliki turned and looked at Robbie. "Trust me," Robbie encouraged.

Aliki smiled shakily. "As if!"

Robbie grinned with relief. "I'll phone Janet, and then she can put Dawn on, okay?"

Aliki looked like she was going to pass out, but she did come over and sit on the end of her bed, rubbing her suddenly sweaty palms on her jeans. Robbie had the cell phone out in a second and was punching in the numbers before Aliki could back out.

"Hey, it's me, lover."

"Oh, hi, Sally. Come on over; Robbie is away."

"Funny! And why did the name Sally come to your mind?" Robbie asked suspiciously, only partially in jest.

"Because she is here in my arms. Her name is Sally-slurp. It's a tabby kitten that Mac found and adopted."

Robbie smiled. "Sally-slurp, huh? Sounds like a porno movie. Hey, Aliki, your kid has a cat. Look, Janet, the reason I called back — other than to tell you again that I love you — is that Aliki wants to talk to Dawn. Could you put her on?

"This is good news. I'll get her."

Robbie could feel the smile cross the kilometres. It made her feel puffed up with pride. Making Janet happy was the most important thing in Robbie's life. She handed the phone to Aliki, who was as white as a ghost and could barely hold the phone for her shaking.

"Aliki?" a nervous voice asked.

"Aaah, hi. I was just...I mean..." Aliki looked at Robbie in panic. Robbie held up a sign. "I just needed to talk to you. I miss you," she read.

"I miss you, too. Mac and I have been worried. Thanks for phoning." The soft voice was filled with love and concern.

Robbie held up a new sign. "I want you to know that I need you in my life. I haven't shown you that very well, but I..." Aliki hesitated as Robbie flipped the sheet of paper over, "...really do. Look, maybe when I get back, we could talk."

"Okay. I need that. There seems to be so much misunderstanding and hurt that we need to work through. When you were so sick, nothing else mattered but being there for you, but after, I guess I needed some healing, too. Do you understand what I'm trying to say?"

Aliki looked at Robbie. The sign read: *I don't care about anything but our love*. Aliki shook her head frantically. Robbie grabbed another sign and held it up. It read: *Dawn, I just phoned to tell you I love you and for no other reason*. Aliki's eyes got big with panic, and she shook her head again. Robbie frowned and dug about once more.

"Aliki? Are you still there?"

"Aaah yeah, just...err..." Robbie grabbed a sign out of the pile and held it up. "I err, Dawn. I just want to say that I know I caused you and Mac a lot of stress by my actions. I thought I was protecting you, but I should have..." Robbie flipped the card. "I should have known that you would need to be at my side."

There was silence at the other end, and Aliki frantically signalled to Robbie to give her another line. Robbie scribbled madly and held up the last piece of stationery. "I love you. I need you. I miss you, Dawn."

"Aliki, I saw the movie," came a voice that was verging on laughter.

"What?"

"Your dialogue is from one of Robbie's movies. Is she there?"

Aliki flushed scarlet and glared daggers at her sister. Robbie shrugged, and with a sigh of disappointment threw the last card over her shoulder.

"Yeah, she's here. She was trying to help me get through this, you know."

"Yeah, I know," Dawn said reassuringly.

"Look, I don't want you to leave me. I hate this!" Aliki snapped in frustration. Robbie rolled her eyes and hit her forehead in disbelief.

"That's more like my pragmatic lover. I miss you, too, and I want to try and sort out the problem of trust between us," Dawn choked out, her laughter quickly replaced by the tears of pent-up emotion.

"I trust you," Aliki growled impatiently. Robbie buried her face in her hands in mock horror.

"Not enough to believe that I would stand by you in a crisis, but it's a start. I don't want to argue about it. What I want is to be with you. I love you very much."

"Would you take some money out of our savings account and fly down here?" Aliki heard herself asking.

There was a moment of surprised silence. "In a heartbeat."

Aliki grinned like a child. "Hey, that's great. You know I love you, don't you?"

"I know, Aliki. I never doubted that or my love for you."

Tears were rolling down Aliki's face. "Well, aah...okay then. I'll see you soon. Bye...I love you."

"Bye, I love you," Dawn responded as they hung up.

"That was pathetic!" Robbie snorted.

"No, pathetic is feeding me lines from one of your movies, damn it!" Aliki laughed in relief, throwing a pillow at her sister.

Robbie ducked. "Hey, for original lines, you have to talk to my agent first. Is she coming?"

Aliki nodded, a big grin softening her tired features.

"Hey, that's great! Is Janet?"

"I don't know. I only invited Dawn."

"Idiot! Give me that phone!"

Janet's arms encircled Dawn's shoulders. Her friend was leaning on the phone table, dry sobs wracking her body. "Hey, you want to talk?"

Dawn turned and hugged Janet close. "She asked me to come down there. She was so clueless, Janet. Robbie must have put her up to saying some of the lines from her last movie so she wouldn't be tongue-tied. You know how hopeless she is at that sort of thing." Dawn was laughing through her tears. "When I told her I recognized the lines, she went back to being the blunt, short-tempered woman that I love."

"You have to go, Dawn. I can arrange it through—" The phone rang. Janet smiled and picked it up. "Hi, Robbie."

"How did you know it wasn't Sally?"

Janet retorted, "*She's* curled up on my bed waiting for me."

"I hate that cat! You're coming, too, right?" Robbie asked, her voice laden with pathetic tones.

"Suck! What about the kids?" Janet asked, winking at Dawn.

"Oh, yeah, them. I thought you were considering putting them up for adoption," Robbie joked. "Would Elizabeth and David babysit for a week or so?"

"I'll have to ask, but I'm pretty sure they would. They're very fond of the children, and David is simply in his element caring and cooking for a big family."

"Great. I already called Brian, and he's making all the arrangements through the company. I told him to hire a Lear jet and to have it ready to leave tomorrow morning out of Toronto. Does that give you enough time?"

"You've hired a jet for tomorrow! Robbie, Dawn has just driven up here. You can't expect her to turn around and go back to the city tonight to catch a plane tomorrow morning."

"Yes, I can," Robbie stated selfishly.

"Let's do it, Janet. If Elizabeth and David don't mind. We can sleep on the plane," Dawn interjected.

Janet sighed. Robbie had a way of just steamrolling through life and sometimes she needed to be stood up to, but this was not one of those times. Janet had to admit that she was missing Robbie, too. Her partner had been away a lot the last few months, promoting her new movie. "If Elizabeth and David agree, we'll be on our way in an hour," she answered.

"Yes! Do you want me to lean on Lizzy for you?"

"No, I do not! I'll phone you later. Love you, Robbie."

"I love you, too. You're going to love this place. It's a pretty little town with a spectacular view of the mountains. They call it 'The Oasis of Time'."

"I thought you told me it was a dusty place, sandwiched between the ends of the earth and the hottest, driest goddamn desert in the world," Janet teased. "Not to mention the line about it having more dead life than night life."

"Hey, I might have overemphasized the negatives. The government office and mission were built in Spanish colonial times, and some of the stray village dogs look like the originals. And they make very full-bodied ice cubes here," Robbie said, finishing her sales pitch. Aliki sat on the bed shaking her head and trying not to laugh.

"I don't even want to know what that is about. We'll see you ladies in a day or so. Love you. Bye."

"Love you, sweetheart. Bye."

Robbie snapped the phone shut and gave Aliki a cocky grin. "I hope you were taking lessons, kid sister. You just saw the master at work."

Aliki raised an eyebrow. "What I saw at work was three margaritas."

The next morning, Robbie found that a thickish brown envelope had been wedged under their door. It turned out to be Dr. Tidwell Jennings' paper. Over breakfast in the hotel restaurant, Robbie gave Aliki the third degree.

"Actually, I hated her," Aliki admitted. "We all did. You can't imagine what a relief it was when she disappeared."

"Aliki, I am shocked. You of all people, speaking ill of the dead," Robbie teased.

"Not dead, missing," Aliki corrected. "And may she stay so."

Robbie looked at Aliki with sharp, penetrating blue eyes. "You think someone at the gathering three years ago bumped her off, don't you?"

"Probably," Aliki said calmly and took another mouthful of her coffee.

"And you don't want to find out because it would have to be one of your ghoulish friends."

Aliki shrugged. "There was no body. We looked, and yes, it was a detailed search. I wouldn't cover up evidence. There was none to be found. Tiddy just disappeared on the way back from the bathroom. And good riddance to her."

Robbie finished her slice of melon, then sat back and looked at her sister thoughtfully. "This is a side of you that I've never seen."

"You didn't know Tiddy."

"So, who had a reason to help her disappear?" Robbie asked, signing the bill.

"Just about every one of us. And there must have been fifty, maybe seventy-five people there."

"Oh, well, then, solving this mystery should be easy. Come on. Thanks to you, I have to give a free performance. If my agent finds out, he'll have a coronary."

An hour later, Dr. Fenwick politely manoeuvred his way into the crowd of admirers that was seeking Robbie's autograph and led her up to the stage. Robbie looked out over the crowd of people hastily finding their seats in the hotel's conference room, which doubled as a party room in the evenings. The floor was stone and the roof heavily beamed and covered with a thick layer of branches. A huge fireplace at one end was the only source of heat at night. Aliki sat beside Victor Van Vogt, who was talking to her with great animation and a good show of teeth. Aliki looked worried and kept glancing over to where Robbie stood patiently behind Fenwick as he tried to quiet the rowdy group and make his opening address.

Robbie's mouth tightened in determination. These people might be off the wall in their interests and lifestyles, but they were Aliki's friends and this forensic conference was important to them. All thoughts of making witty asides while reading Jennings' paper vanished. She would play her role as a dedicated academic and make Aliki proud.

"Now I would like to call on Dr. Alberta Pateas' sister, the actress and producer, Roberta Williams, who has kindly consented to deliver Dr. Tidwell Jennings' paper in her absence. Ms. Williams."

"Thank you, Dr. Fenwick. It is a pleasure to be here. Dr. Tidwell Jennings paper is entitled: 'The Post Mortem Suppression of Enzyme Action and the Relative Effectiveness in Various Mummification Processes.'

"A brief explanation about the function of enzymes in the human body is probably necessary for those of you who do not have a medical background. Enzymes are mostly found in the nuclei of our cells. They play an important role in our body's defence system by devouring foreign bacteria that enter our systems. However, in death, these enzymes eat their way out from the cell and begin to feed off the host body. For example, enzymes located in the intestines will eat away the intestinal walls fairly rapidly after death and travel through the blood system to feed on organs, muscle, and other body tissues. We are all sadly familiar with the stench of decay, which is the waste gas release by these active enzymes. This is the putrefaction process that will cause the deceased's epidermis to turn green and eventually to a purple-black and cause the body to swell until the skin bursts and the orifices leak with a watery blood." Robbie swallowed hard, gritted her teeth, and forced herself to continue.

When the group broke for a morning coffee break, Aliki found Robbie in the bar. "Starting a bit early, aren't you?" she said, as she slid onto a stool beside her visibly shaken sister.

"Now I understand why no one is particularly upset that Tidwell Jennings disappeared. I thought I was going to throw up before I got to the end of her paper."

Aliki shrugged. "Better reading about it than working on it," she observed practically. "It was an excellent paper. I think we all got a lot out of it. I had no idea that nicotine suppressed enzyme action. Not to mention—"

"Then let's not," Robbie cut in, holding up her hand.

Aliki smiled. "So what do you want to talk about?"

"Something pleasant, like who and why someone would want to kill Tidwell."

Again Aliki shrugged. "It's a small field of research. Although forensics fascinates the general public, there isn't much grant money to be had to fund work in this area. The people here work in other fields of research and add to this research when they can. Coming here to study the pot burials and mummies will help us understand the processes that can take place in burial rituals and in the natural drying process. We're a closely knit group that shares a common passion, so you hear a lot of gossip. It's hard to know how much is truth and how much is just jealousy and spite between competitive factions."

"You guys are competitive?"

"Ruthless at times. You gotta eat, and that means you have to get grant money or a position in a good university facility, and that means you have to publish first. It can get pretty ugly."

"Hmmm, I take it that Tiddy was inclined to play dirty." Robbie waved away the bartender's offer for a refill of her drink and joined her sister in a morning coffee.

"She worked with Victor Van Vogt for a few years on the tanned Iron Age bodies found in the Cornish bogs, then she published six months ahead of him, not only reporting her own findings on decay but also his research on parasites found in the intestines. It cost him a chance at becoming the head of the department at his university."

"Nasty. Anyone else got a grudge?" Robbie asked, stirring sugar into her coffee.

"Just about everyone. She ran away with Philby's wife, then dumped her. She squashed Samir Tagore's chances of a job in the same department by insisting that they needed to hire an American, even though he is the best in the field. She wrote a vicious review of Hilda Katz's work on the Tollund Man of Danmark; she was openly lobbying for Archie Fenwick's job; and she charged old Gerald Flex with sexual harassment."

Robbie snorted. "That was probably true."

"He couldn't get it up if his life depended on it. He's just the original dirty old man who also happens to be brilliant in his field. It was very embarrassing for him."

"Shit, the woman sure knew how to make enemies. Anything else?"

Aliki fiddled with her coffee cup for a few seconds, looking uncomfortable. "Well, there's me."

Robbie rolled her eyes. "You have a motive, too?"

"She came on to me pretty aggressively, and when I told her I wasn't interested, she was pretty pissed." Aliki blushed. "This was right after I met Dawn, but before we had a chance to really commit. It wouldn't have mattered, I wouldn't have wanted her even if we were the last two people alive. After that, she'd put me down and ride me every chance she got. A few times we had words at forensic conferences. It is pretty well known that I hated her."

"Enough to kill her?" Robbie asked uncertainly, well aware that Aliki had the skills to do it and had killed before.

"Sure," Aliki answered honestly. "But I didn't. Come on, Flex is going to deliver his paper on drug use amongst ancient Peruvians, and then we're all going down the street to check out the museum. It has a wonderful display of burial methods from this area and an extensive collection of grave goods."

"Gee, I can hardly wait," Robbie responded sardonically as she paid the bill and followed her sister out.

The various examples of pot burials, tombs, and mummies of Atacoma, as Robbie learned, were kept in a small but modern museum amongst a clutter of worn-looking buildings not far down the road from the Graveyard Restaurant. Although there was an excellent display of various burial forms in the public area of the museum, the bulk of the museum's collection was housed in cardboard boxes in the back room of a storage shed tucked back behind the museum under the shade of some ancient olive trees.

It was there, watching the delegates to the conference reverently studying each of the small bodies lying on their protective mattresses of sand, that Robbie started to understand her sister's ghoulish profession and her colleagues. The boisterousness and wisecracking were gone as they quietly observed the dead with gentle care and compassion.

These people lived in a shadowy world that few wanted to know about. They dealt with the sorrow and horror of society and were committed to learn from history how to make a safer, healthy world for the living or to find justice for the dead and peace for those that must go on. They were not ghouls after all, but scientists totally committed to life. Death to them was the consequence of having been born, and they wished to understand that passage.

Some amongst them used that interest to be guardians of life, searching within the grisly remains for clues to the origins and development of disease that still inflicted pain on society. Some sought to extend understanding of the past and enrich lives with the awareness of cultural roots. Others, such as Aliki, struggled to understand the animal within and the violence that one person could unleash on others. They helped the dead speak of injustices and gave peace to them and their families.

After the group had observed the mummies and skeletons, Robbie and Aliki slowly walked back to the hotel. Off in the distance, the sands of the Atacoma Desert threatened the edges of the town. Aliki seemed distant and brooding. "Those remains, they were children," Robbie muttered sadly, trying to get Aliki to talk.

Aliki nodded. "The Chinchorro culture, we believe, saw death as an extension of life, just in a different form. Parasites, bacteria, and diseases often claim the young in marginal societies. In Third World countries, half of the children die between conception and the age of five. To the people who lived here, that grief was too painful. They started to preserve the dead children. The bodies were carefully skinned and the meat removed from the bones. Then sticks and a mixture of substances were used to make a mold that served as the foundation to rebuild the body form. The skin was replaced and sewn closed. The face was covered with a mask, and the body and mask were painted with a blue-grey clay made with a magnesium base. The bodies weren't buried; they were decorated with feathers and placed lovingly on the hillsides."

Aliki pointed to the sand dunes in the distance. "The families would go year after year and repaint the bodies and decorate them again. Their children were not dead, but part of their lives. As time went by, the mummification process was extended to include all members of the family. About three thousand years ago, the Chinchorro fishing villages disappeared, and their dead were slowly buried in the shifting sand. Other burial types are found in this area, too. Pot burials and later, with the Spanish influence, coffins. In most cases, though, the dry climate caused a natural mummification process, and that is why we are here."

"For all our civilization, life is very tenuous."

Aliki shrugged. "Culture never really dies. It's part of us; it simply morphs and reappears in different ways. The Inca who moved into this area absorbed that reverence for the dead. They, too, mummified their dead and saw them as living links to another world. They honoured them with food and beer and even provided them with washroom breaks. They would come to their dead and seek answers to problems or help in making decisions. To the Inca, just as to the Chinchorro, the dead were still members of the society."

For a few moments they walked on through the dusty streets of Atacoma in silence, then suddenly Aliki sighed. "If anything were to happen to Dawn or Mac, I don't think I could handle it. I wanted to protect them. I didn't want them to have to deal with the horror of the violent death that a lunatic said she had committed in my name. I just wanted to track down the killer and bring her to justice so my family, everyone's family, could be safe. I...well...you understand," Aliki finished in a strangled voice.

"Yeah, I understand," Robbie whispered sympathetically; they walked on again in silence. Before entering the hotel, they stood for a while looking out at the sun-drenched mountains. Finally, Robbie found the words to express what she had been struggling to share with her sister.

"I have done what you did – kept Janet and my daughters in the dark while I dealt with issues in my past in order to protect them. That was wrong of me, and it almost destroyed my marriage. What I've learned from Janet is that one of the greatest gifts you can give the one you love is the right to stand at your side in times of danger and crisis. It is not a gift that is easy to give when you love and want to protect someone, but it is an important gift because it doesn't just show love, it shows respect and trust."

Aliki nodded. "I'll get it right this time," she said with quiet determination.

Robbie smiled. Maybe things between her sister and partner would work out after all.

"There is something else," Aliki said with a sigh.

Robbie frowned. She thought she had just sorted her kid sister out. "What?"

"I think I know where Tiddy is."

"Cool. Where?"

"The one place that the police would not look for a body – in a storage room full of them."

"Holy shit! One of the ghouls made Tiddy a 'mummy'?"

Aliki snorted. "Never would have happened, but I think someone might have mummified her."

"Isn't that a slow process? How would they have time?"

"They wouldn't. But you could slap a coat of blue clay on her and bury her in a sand dune and hope no one found her until nature did its thing. Then you could wrap her in some sheeting like the Inca did and stick her in a storage room where chances are her existence would never be questioned."

"Wouldn't you run the risk of someone unwrapping her and getting a hell of a surprise?"

Aliki shrugged. "Probably not. Particularly here, where the reverence for the dead goes so deep culturally. It's a big issue amongst archaeologists. During the Victorian Age, mummy unwrappings were box office events. The remains were often ground up and used as medicines and even in artists' paints. Even when that fad passed, early archaeologists were pretty cavalier about digging up and carting away other people's dead to study."

"Creepy."

"The research generated concerning those bones became the discipline of forensic anthropology, so I'm not pointing any fingers. That attitude all changed, however, when the US government passed the National American Graves Protection and Repatriation Act to protect and see to the returning of literally thousands of First Nation bodies. Many countries have followed suit. Now no one wants to deal with the dead. It's just too political."

"Ha! What about Victor-the-Vampire Van Vogt? I thought cadaver slicing was what he lived for."

Aliki raised an eyebrow. "You're talking about a true professional. Van Vogt, like others in such fields, is trying to trace the causes and sources of diseases that have plagued the world for centuries. They're looking for patterns and trends that might help us control these outbreaks in the future. It's really hard for them now because they have to beg for samples to study."

"Yeah, well, I'm not turning my back on him," Robbie retorted stubbornly.

Aliki smiled wickedly.

"What?"

"You know the old saying: 'pick your enemies well, lest you become like them'? Well, you and I are going to unwrap some mummies."

Robbie's eyes got big, and then she visibly relaxed. "You had me going there for a second. The government will never give you permission to tamper with their dead."

"Yeah, I know. That's why we're going to break in tonight," Aliki said nonchalantly as she turned and walked into the hotel.

For a second, Robbie stood there blinking in disbelief, then she turned and hurried after her sister. "Hey, wait! What did you say?"

Part 2

Restless, Robbie paced around their hotel room. "Now if it had been my idea, I could understand; breaking rules for me comes naturally. But you're about as conservative and uptight as mayonnaise. Saints have gone further astray than you have."

Aliki, in the process of pulling on a black t-shirt, raised an eyebrow but said nothing. The white lettering on the t-shirt announced: "Forensics: Bone Up on Body Language".

Robbie stopped her rant and read the t-shirt. "Okay, so under that deep layer of respected scientist there exists a truly twisted sense of humour. I concede that, but Aliki, this is not funny. We are going to end up murdered or worse — thrown into some medieval prison until we mould over and go mad."

Aliki smiled as she pulled a Shinto knife out of its sheath and checked its edge. Satisfied, she slipped it back into its sharkskin casing and strapped it to her leg. "That is a possibility," she admitted.

"A possibility? The potential for disaster is definitely in the red zone. Hey, haven't you seen 'The Night of the Living Dead'?"

Aliki smiled sheepishly. "No, actually, I haven't. Horror movies scare me."

That stopped Robbie in her tracks. "You make your living feeling up the bones of the dead, and you're afraid of a horror movie?"

"You asked." Aliki shrugged. "You ready to go?"

"No!"

"Afraid of being in a room of dead people at night?"

"No. Okay, yes. This is nuts," Robbie said with a nervous laugh.

"Are you coming?"

"Of course I am. Someone has to talk some sense into you." Robbie grabbed up her knapsack and followed her sister out.

They had dinner at the Graveyard Restaurant, making sure they were seen and then slipping out quietly when they got the chance. Walking down the street toward the museum, they did their best to stay in the lengthening shadows. By the time they got to the olive trees, it was dark. Without hesitation, Aliki headed through the orchard toward the buildings that housed the museum's burial collection.

As they went, Robbie kept up a running monologue in a whisper, her voice a little too tight to hide the nervousness behind her humour. Robbie was quite fearless in some ways, but her father's death had haunted her early life like a wraith, casting dark shadows over everything she did. Death was not something she was comfortable with. The wounds of her past were too recently healed.

"So how do you tell which is a good mummy and which is a rotten copy? Squeeze them like melons? What if there's a curse? There could be a curse.

There's always one of those for added tension in a mummy movie. Hey, maybe I could make a movie about this. Try to trash a dozen or so Undeads with a few good karate moves, okay? That would be cool. They could chase us through the olive grove. The play of light under the branches with a full moon would be terrific on film. Didn't the Inca rip out hearts that were still beating? You might have to die, but don't worry, I'll bring you back with some magical mummy dust."

"There it is," Aliki whispered, ignoring Robbie's patter.

"Oh, shit. Now would be a really good time to change our minds," Robbie suggested.

"Can't."

"Why?"

"I want the movie royalties," Aliki responded dryly. "Are you ready?"

Robbie raised an eyebrow. "I am learning a lot about your darker side on this trip, sister of mine. I'm as ready as I'm ever going to be. Somehow it's hard to get into character for breaking into a room of dead people in the middle of the night."

"Be a professional," Aliki snickered as she took a lock pick from her pocket and started working on the mechanism.

Robbie watched impatiently, literally jumping at shadows. "What's taking so long?"

"Nothing. It takes longer in real life than it does in the movies." After a few more minutes of nervous silence, Aliki smiled with satisfaction at the click that indicated the padlock had released. She slipped it out of the hasp and pushed open one of the double doors just wide enough for them to slip in, then she carefully closed the door behind them.

"I can't see a thing," Robbie grumbled. Aliki's flashlight snapped on, the beam focused on a table where human bones, bleached white by the desert sun, were in the process of being arranged in anatomical order on a workbench. "Oh, shit! Now I'm sorry I can see."

"Get out your flashlight. There are no windows so we should be okay. That room over there," Aliki waved her flashlight, "is the room where we viewed the Chinchorro mummies. I suspect the Inca mummies will be in the storage room over there."

"Why do you suppose we weren't shown those, too?" Robbie asked as she fished in her knapsack for her flashlight.

Aliki shrugged. "Probably didn't think it was worth it. Most of us will stop in the capital on the way back, and the Inca mummies at the museum there are vastly superior in preservation. Atacoma is known for its pot burials and mummies from local tribes, not so much for Inca."

"I can't believe it. You talk about body preservation like the difference between cheap screech and a vintage wine. You bunch are nuts; you know that, don't you?"

"So who's with me, breaking into museum property and assisting in an illegal mummy unwrapping?"

"Assisting! No way. I'm just here to protect my sister's soul from zombies."

Aliki chuckled and opened the door to the storage room to the left. Flashing her light inside, she saw the wall shelves lined with brown, emaciated figures distorted by pressure and time into creatures not far removed from those found in Robbie's monster movies. They lay in rows like soldiers asleep in a barracks. A stale, dusty smell of decay and mould sat heavily in the air. It was a sweet, unpleasant scent that left an acidic feeling in the back of their sinuses.

"She's not here," Robbie observed, looking over Aliki's shoulder. "Let's go."

"Over there are the mummies that haven't been unwrapped." Aliki pointed the beam of her light on a line of blankets, their brilliant colours faded by time and dirt.

"They don't look like mummies."

"No, they don't look like Egyptian mummies, which is what everyone thinks of when they hear the word. Inca bodies were wrapped in ceremonial clothes and then wrapped in fine, beautiful blankets or linen. Come on. You'll have to help me lift each mummy and set it aside."

"Oh, God. You know my other sister, Elizabeth, never gave me this sort of trouble. What is that smell?"

"You probably don't want to know. Here, grab an end and be careful. These are valuable archaeological finds."

Carefully the women lifted each body, one at a time, and laid it down on the sand that had been shoveled in to cover the floor. "We're leaving footprints."

"Ours and a lot of other people's. If we don't find her, we'll stack everything back the way it was, and no one will know we were here. If we do find her, we'll have to bring the police in."

"The police? Why do the police always have to be involved?" sulked Robbie, who was not fond of the police.

"Oh, I don't know, maybe because this is a murder investigation and I'm a cop," Aliki responded dryly.

"I try to forget that," Robbie muttered.

"This one," Aliki announced as they lifted the fifth mummy.

Robbie almost fumbled her end. "How do you know?"

"I don't. That's why we have to unwrap it. I am assuming by the slightly different scent, texture of the material, and small difference in weight, that this might be a more modern item in the collection. Let's carry it out to the workbench and see what we've got here."

Together the two half-sisters manoeuvred the blanketed and stiff body out to an empty bench and carefully laid it on top.

Aliki pulled latex gloves from her pocket and put them on, then she bent down and reappeared with her knife in her hand. She carefully cut away at the knotted cord that tied the blanket together and unfolded the stiff undersheeting. Beneath that was a thick ceremonial robe.

"Well?" Robbie held a flashlight over the operation with shaking hands.

"Hard to say. I'm not an expert on materials, but I don't think these are as old as they look. The layering is right, though. If it is Tiddy, whoever did this did a really superb job."

"Aliki, this is not the work of an artist; it was done by a murderer."

"Yes, but one with a beautiful eye for detail and a vast knowledge of Inca mummification," Aliki muttered wistfully as she carefully pried the cloth from around the withered face. Robbie rolled her eyes.

The wrinkled, tanned face of a woman looked up at them, her face flattened on the left as she had lain on her side in the sand. She looked asleep, her eyes closed and her lashes softly touching her skin. "It's her."

"Not good."

"No, not good at all. What we'll—"

"Hands up!" someone yelled from behind Robbie. The actress gasped in shock and dropped the flashlight, leaving them in darkness.

Archie Fenwick cleared his throat nervously and looked at the two newly arrived women. "It's a bit awkward," he explained. "They were here yesterday, but they seem to have disappeared."

A gigantic man behind Fenwick snorted. "We ought to be notifying the police. I saw the ladies last night across the room at the Graveyard Restaurant. I thought they'd join us later in the bar for drinks, but they disappeared, just like Tiddy. Went to take a leak and never came back, Tiddy did, and now Alberta and her sister have vanished."

"Granted, it's unusual, but we needn't rush to conclusions. It could be that they are pursuing some other interest or have gone sightseeing or something. They could walk in at anytime. I think it would be premature to go to the police. You said yourself, Philby, that Ms. Williams was here for the mountain air."

"She was joking, you idiot!" Philby roared in frustration. "Look, Fenwick, what do you think the chances are of Dr. Pateas coming all this way and missing Victor Van Vogt's lecture on intestinal parasites this morning?"

"Oh, dear, that is a point. That is distressing when you consider. I can't imagine Aliki missing such a riveting presentation. Outstanding research. I thought particularly his material on *c.parvum.Cryptosporidium* and its association with barnyard runoff during the yearly flooding was most interesting and—"

"Am I understanding you right: neither Robbie nor Aliki have been seen since dinner last night?" Janet felt a growing anxiety.

"Just like Tiddy. I hammered on their door this morning; I didn't want Aliki missing Victor's lecture," Philby explained. "I thought maybe they'd gone bar crawling and slept in—"

"Robbie doesn't drink," Janet interrupted with impatience.

Philby laughed loud enough to be heard several districts away. "Ha! Saw her down three pineapple margaritas just the other day, crushed ice and all."

Dawn caught Janet's eye. Her message was clear. Their partners were undoubtedly in trouble. It was Dawn who spoke up. "First, we want to see their room, then we'll need to contact the police. Dr. Philby, perhaps you will vouch for our identity while we try to get a key from the desk. Then, Dr. Fenwick, if you speak Spanish, perhaps you could assist us in talking to the police."

"Yes, of course, of course. Probably nothing, but, well, it is awkward..."

The three left him still muttering reassurances as they headed for the hotel desk.

Once they were in Robbie and Aliki's room, Dawn checked through Aliki's neatly organized suitcase while Janet went through Robbie's chaotic disorder. "Aliki has her knife with her," Dawn reported.

Janet nodded. Nothing unusual in that. Aliki usually carried a knife.

"I recognize the empty case. It's not her usual one; it's a helmless, short-bladed Shinto knife that she wears on a leg strap."

That got Janet's attention. "She was expecting trouble?"

"Maybe. She was certainly taking no chances. You know Aliki."

They shared a smile. Where Robbie was spontaneous and unpredictable, Aliki was measured and conservative in her actions. Two sisters could not express so many similar genes in such dissimilar ways.

"Nothing informative in Robbie's luggage, no notes, and no messages on their cell phones. What do you think?"

Dawn felt the first fingers of fear spreading through her. "They knew we were arriving today. They would have been here if they could. We'd better call the police."

Pale and quiet, Aliki sat on a narrow bunk while Robbie paced back and forth on the verge of panic. Being in jail again was bringing back memories that opened deep emotional wounds. "I told you we'd end up in some mouldy old jail!"

"Actually, it's not a bad cell – good light, clean, interesting brick work. I wonder if this was designed by Eiffel. He did some work in northern Chile."

"I'm going to kill you," Robbie threatened her frustrating sister.

"As soon as the el miembro de una comision gets back from Peru, we'll get out of here. I told you, I know the man. He'll vouch for me."

Robbie sighed. "You do realize that Janet and Dawn will have arrived and will be worried sick about us."

To her shock, her normally controlled sister was in her face in one swift, fluid movement.

"I have not thought of anything else!" she growled and then backed off to stand by the window, looking moodily at the endless blue sky as time crawled by.

Aliki was exhausted. Her hands were shaky, and her head ached. Tears kept leaking from her eyes no matter how hard she tried to stop them. She was depressed; she needed her medication to help stabilize her mood. She was getting better, she knew, but when she got overtired and stressed, everything had a way of caving in on her.

Robbie, she noted, wasn't in much better shape. She stopped pacing and sat on a cot, her head buried in her hands. Being back in prison was hell on her. Aliki knew she felt trapped and near panic. The worst part was that there was nothing they could do but wait until someone found them.

"Captain, it is a pleasure to meet you and a delight to find that you can speak English so well," Janet stated. "As you know, we are very concerned about the whereabouts of Roberta Williams and her sister, Dr. Aliki Pateas." The two women, Fenwick in tow, had spent a frustrating two hours being led from one office to another until they had been finally brought to the office of the acting chief and were relieved to find that his English was excellent.

"On that point, I can ease your mind. The two you seek are safe and being held in our women's jail."

"Good grief! What has the olive done now?"

The captain looked confused. "I do not understand."

"It's a nickname." Janet suddenly felt a lump in her throat and had to swallow hard before she went on. "What have the women been charged with?"

"Ah! Breaking and entering, and damaging ancient relics with the intention to steal."

Dawn snorted in disgust. "Aliki? Damage an ancient relic? Hell would freeze over first."

"Captain, we have come all the way from Canada in order to join our par...friends. I wonder...I do not know how your system works, but in Canada it is possible to post a bail bond in order to get someone out of prison until their court case. I'm afraid all we have is American dollars..."

Janet and Dawn waited impatiently in the warden's office. The papers for release into custody had cost them ten thousand dollars American. They had handed it over to the warden, along with their passports, and been told to wait. They had now waited two hours and fourteen minutes.

"Do you think we should go ask what the delay is?"

Dawn shook her head. "No. Best just to wait it out for a bit longer. If we don't hear anything by two, then we'd better call the captain to intervene."

Some thirty minutes later, a clerk returned with their passports. "You wait. You wait. Outside."

And so they waited again, this time on the doorstep of the town jail.

At one thirty a guard arrived at Robbie and Aliki's cell. "Stand up. Move back," he ordered. When the two women obeyed, the door was unlocked and they were motioned out with the end of a machine gun barrel.

"Remember, we only have to give them our name, rank, and serial number," Robbie whispered.

"If that works for you," her sister responded. "Personally, I'm going to tell them anything they want to know."

They were ushered down the hallway past the two cells that were used for male prisoners. At the moment there were none. They waited for the guard to unlock the door with an old skeleton key, then they were led down yet another hall to an office. There, they were told to sit in two straight back wooden chairs that were much scarred and dented. The guard posted himself at the door, his weapon cradled against his chest with crossed arms.

Robbie looked around the bare room. "You're right. Let's tell them everything they want to know and then some."

A woman entered the room and sat down behind the desk. She was thin, angular, and stern, yet when she spoke it was in quiet, well constructed English. "I am Senorita Isabella de Lome. I wish to know why you were found destroying a rare and sacred part of our history."

Robbie looked at Aliki. "I am Inspector Aliki Pateas of the Royal Canadian Mounted Police. I am also a forensic scientist here with some other scholars to study the museum's collection. As I am sure you are aware, three years ago one of our colleagues disappeared. The police suspected foul play, and I assisted them in the investigation. Sadly, we were not able to find a body, and so the case remained open. This year, I had the pleasure of once again returning to see the fine collection at the museum. It was during the tour that the idea came to me that the best way to keep a body hidden was to hide it away amongst the Inca mummies.

"My sister and I were not eager to discuss the idea with the authorities, lest we tip our hand to the murderer. So we came back at night to go through the mummies and see if one did not fit the age and pattern of an Inca burial. The mummy we were caught opening, Senorita Isabelle de Lome, is not the ancient remains of an Inca, but the partially mummified remains of Dr. Tidwell Jennings. We were just on our way to the police with our findings when we were caught by the security guard."

The warden nodded slowly, considering Aliki's explanation against the evidence she had in the report in front of her. "You have acted very highhandedly, Inspector Pateas. The Chilean police are very capable and do not need foreigners meddling in their affairs. Bond has been set for you. You will not leave this town until such time as the police have finished their investigation and you have written consent from the police to do so. Do you understand?"

"Yes, senorita," both sisters said obediently.

"You will follow me."

For the next hour, the two women filled out forms and had them stamped. Finally they were led down a hall to an exit door. Outside, they found their partners, looking tired and somewhat the worse for wear.

Janet immediately wrapped Robbie in her arms. "You okay, olive?"

Robbie shuddered with relief. "I am now."

"Hey, what's this I hear about you downing three pineapple margaritas? I've never seen you drink like that, Robbie."

"That's because you have never seen me sitting in the Graveyard Restaurant surrounded by ghouls discussing the best tools for removing fingernails from Undeads. Come on, let's get back to the hotel so I can give you a proper hello."

Aliki gave Dawn a hesitant hug and only relaxed and held on tight when she felt Dawn respond to her touch. Neither woman spoke; they just held on to each other and didn't let go.

"Hey," Robbie said softly, touching her sister's elbow, "the taxi is waiting. Come on."

The four piled into a cab, Robbie and Janet in the back and Dawn and Aliki jammed in the front. No one talked. Robbie held Janet's hand, and Dawn and Aliki sat close, yet stiff, side-by-side. They were all relieved to reach the hotel.

Robbie and Janet went off to book another room, and Aliki and Dawn stood by nervously, Dawn biting her lip.

"You okay, Aliki? You look shaky."

Aliki swallowed. "I'm okay. Better now. Look, why don't we find some place to talk? Aah, we could sit in the courtyard. I...If you want. I mean, I'd like that. I guess we need time for Janet and Robbie to move out. I mean, can we share a room? Is that okay? I don't want to pressure you or—"

Dawn stopped Aliki's anxious monologue with a hug. "You go get your medication, and I'll wait for you here. Some fresh air would be good."

In actual fact, she was exhausted. She had been traveling by car and plane for a day and a half and then had been looking for her partner since she had arrived. She was feeling really rough. But she knew that Aliki had been locked up for most of that time and was very stressed. Aliki needed to feel free, then maybe they could talk.

After Aliki returned from taking her medication, they walked across the courtyard and made their way to a quiet area that contained a moon pool. On nights of a full moon, the pond became a pearly surface lighting the small stone alcove with its glow. Now, during the daylight, it reflected the blue of the sky. They sat on a carved wooden bench and for a time watched birds circling high above reflected in the pool. Dawn slipped her hand into Aliki's and was surprised at how desperately her partner clung to it.

They sat silently for a while until Aliki suddenly snapped, startling Dawn with her sudden outburst. "I hate not sleeping with you. I hated living in my own house as a stranger. Damn it, we are supposed to be married. Why the hell did that murderous bitch have to come out of my past and...and..."

Tears rolled down Aliki's face, and she rocked forward, resting her face in her thin hands, her shoulders shaking with the sobs that wracked her body.

Dawn knelt down beside her, and Aliki buried her face against her shoulder. "I never cry. Damn, what is the matter with me?"

"Maybe it's just time you cried," Dawn soothed, rubbing Aliki's back gently.

"I'm supposed to be making a home for you and Mac and instead I walk out on you, and now I...I can't stop crying. Look at me, I'm a mess."

"You have made a wonderful home for Mac and me. We love you very much, and we need you. Do you know what Mac said when I told her I was coming here? She said, 'You bring Aunt Aliki home, Mom. She ought to be here with us.'"

Dawn held Aliki until the tears stopped, and then they sat close in the shade of the river stone wall, looking into the small bit of the cosmos that was trapped within the stone pool. Eventually, Aliki spoke.

"I can't live there with us living like...like friends. I know I messed up by not trusting you with what I was facing and just disappearing undercover. It was stupid. I was so upset. I thought...well, you know what I thought. I wasn't thinking very clearly. I was so afraid that she would kill again. And then I got to thinking of the danger my career can put you in. I felt like I'd been made into a dirty, nasty bomb that was going to go off and hurt everyone around me."

"Your work does sometimes put you in danger, and that means your family can be in danger, too. It's rare, but it can happen. We know that, and we take all the precautions we can. But most of all, we worry about you. We want to be your family, and family sticks together and is there for each other. You have to trust us, Aliki."

"My mom died."

"What?" Dawn asked in surprise.

"She told me she wouldn't and she did."

The wind rustled the leaves on the trees in the courtyard nearby. A dove cooed from the top of the mission steeple. Dawn tried to wrap her mind around what Aliki had said.

"Is that why you find it hard to trust, why you've always been such a loner?"

Aliki swallowed. Where had that come from, that pain that had welled up so intensely and bitterly? Why had she told Dawn? "I guess. I was so angry at her for lying to me, and I felt so rotten because I loved her and I shouldn't have been angry. And then I had to take care of the house and help Baba raise the twins." She took a deep, shuddering breath. "If you don't get close to people, you can't get hurt."

Dawn's stomach was churning. She was way out of her depth. "Do you regret getting close to me and Mac?"

Aliki looked at her in shock. "Of course not! I love the two of you more than anything else in this world."

Intense blue eyes, filled with confusion and pain, darkened as Aliki bent close. Their lips touched, and a rush of desire bolted through them like lightning. Dawn was gathered in Aliki's arms and lifted up onto the bench beside her.

Robbie settled Janet into their new room and then raced down the hall to get her belongings out of the one she'd shared with Aliki. Jamming things into her bags, she was back to the new room in short order. She heard the shower running, and her eye was captured by a note propped on the pillow. It was in Janet's neat, even handwriting. "Hey, sexy. It sure would be great to have my back washed." Robbie was out of her clothes and heading for the bathroom before the note hit the floor.

"Hey, lover, got your note," Robbie growled, stepping into the small, hot, steamy world. She wrapped Janet in her arms and gathered her wife in for a kiss. It was the kiss of lovers — no inhibitions and no doubts. The kiss was deep, probing, and demanding. Hands roamed and the body reactions were needy. Janet ran her soapy leg up along Robbie's thigh as she let the hot water rain down on them and mix with their own heat.

"I missed you," Robbie groaned. "I want you."

"Show me how much," Janet challenged.

Robbie turned off the taps, took her wife's hand, and stepped from the stall. Quickly, she dried their bodies, using her silky skin and the coarse towel in turns to tease and stimulate her lover's need to intolerable heights.

Janet got her back, capturing a nipple between her lips and teasing it with the tip of her tongue. Her hands moulded around her lover's sculpted backside and rhythmically pushed their sexes against one another.

With a growl of desire, Robbie discarded the towel, wrapped a strong arm under her lover, and carried Janet to their bed. Their lovemaking was hard and greedy, and when it was finished, they lay in each other's arms exhausted and sated. The scent of their lovemaking was Janet's last conscious impression as she drifted into a deep sleep.

With a shudder of effort, Aliki forced herself to end the kisses and pull away. "W...we'd better head back to our room," she croaked.

"Sure." Dawn refastened her shirt. They walked in silence, close but not touching. Their need was great. Feeling embarrassed and not sure why, they crossed the courtyard and followed the open-air hallway to their room. The door had barely closed before Aliki and Dawn were once again in each other's arms. The kiss they shared was that of lovers who had come to know each other with a deep and passionate intimacy.

Finally pulling away, Aliki was relieved to see that room service had made up their room and that Robbie's stuff was gone. Taking no chances, she turned the deadbolt and slipped the chain in place.

Then she and her lover helped each other out of their clothes.

"Are you sure?" Aliki asked as she trailed kisses across Dawn's throat.

"From the first moment I saw you. No more running away from our love, okay, Aliki?"

Aliki knew down deep that she had found some closure for a very old wound and that at last she might be able commit to a lasting, truly deep relationship. "No. No more."

Their love was tender, all the more powerful in its intensity because they held in the passion that threatened to explode them apart and worked to express their love as well as their desire. When each came in turn, it was with a cry of relief and wonder that started from deep, deep inside. They held each other close, the aftershocks of their lovemaking almost as intense as the coming. They made love again and then slept, curled close.

It was in the wee hours of the morning when Dawn woke and lay quietly looking at her lover. Aliki was skin and bones and so very pale. "I love you," she whispered softly and snuggled closer so that she could enjoy the comfort of the slow, steady beat of Aliki's heart.

Aliki reached out and drew her lover closer still. Her eyes blinked open. "I was afraid to wake up in case I had dreamed it all."

"No, I'm here," Dawn whispered gently against Aliki's breast.

"Dawn, I want you as my wife." Aliki gently stroked Dawn's bare shoulder. "I want to know that we are committed to a life together. I want to help you raise Mac as our daughter. Please forgive me for not accepting your right, as my love, to be at my side in a time of danger. I will never insult you like that again. I wouldn't be the mess I am now if I had turned to you for support instead of feeling I had to shoulder all the responsibility. I love you."

"I love you, too, my gentle one. I was very angry at you and hurt that you would run out on me. Now I have a little better understanding why you did what you did, and I think we have bridged that gap so we will never find ourselves in this same situation again. Yes, I want to marry you. I need that commitment from you, too. But we have a ways to go yet.

"Mac is quite confused. You're her hero, and you left. She was devastated. She desperately wants you back in our lives, but she is also angry and feels betrayed. You have a lot of groundwork to do there, sweetheart."

That hurt. It hurt to the bottom of her soul, but Aliki knew she had it coming. She was going to do everything she could to work it out with MacKenzie, the niece she loved as her own.

Several hours later, it was Philby hammering at their door that got Aliki out of bed with a curse.

"Well, about time. You keep that up, girl, and you'll go blind. I heard you were in jail," Philby bellowed joyfully. "Ah! One of those cops that have gone bad, huh? You okay? I was worried." He wrapped her in a hug.

Aliki sighed. "Yeah, I'm okay now."

He was looking over her shoulder. "Well, I'll be damned. Who is this cutie? And what have you done with that drop-dead good-looking sister of yours?" He reached over Aliki and offered his hand to Dawn. "Hi, I'm Dr. Jed Philby."

Despite the fact that she was feeling a little more than embarrassed by the circumstances, Dawn smiled.

"Hi. I'm Dawn Freeman."

"The author?" Philby demanded, pumping her hand.

Aliki pulled Dawn free. "Yes, the author. Jed, this is my future wife."

Philby blinked, and his mouth snapped shut. He blinked again, and the silence that he created seemed to overwhelm the space. Then all hell broke loose.

"Hell shit! Hey, everyone, Alberta's getting married!" he yelled down the hall. "And wait until you see who it is! Drinks are on me tonight at the Graveyard Restaurant!"

"Jed! For God's sakes, shut up!" Aliki hissed.

"No way. Hell, you don't think you can marry a cute little thing like this and stay in the closet, do you? Okay, okay, we'll all promise not to say anything back in North America. Mum's the word for all of us. But hey, we gotta have a stag! Come on, Dawn. I'll introduce you to the rest of us."

"Uh, thanks, ah Jed, but I thought I would get dressed first. I don't think this hotel housecoat is quite the thing."

"Oh. Too bad. I kinda liked the Inca funerary motif on the pocket. Hurry up, Alberta. You are going to miss Samir's talk on pollen spores. It promises to be a humdinger."

Philby caught sight of Robbie and Janet coming out of their room. "Hey, there's Robbie! Morning, Robbie. Did you know your sister is getting married to Dawn Freeman? Hey, who's that? Is that the schoolteacher you married? Runs in the family, eh? Hi, I'm Dr. Jed Philby. I read all about you in the tabloids while standing in line at the grocery store."

She laughed at his directness. "Hi, I'm Janet Williams."

Robbie shot a wicked smile at Aliki, who was a brilliant shade of scarlet. "I thought the tabloids would do; never even thought of getting a town crier to spread the word. Subtle move, sister of mine."

"Town crier; good one." Philby's laughter boomed down the hallway. "Hurry up, Alberta! See you all downstairs. Stag at the Graveyard Restaurant. Hey, Fenwick, wait. Hold the door. Did you hear? Alberta is getting married to a woman." The door slammed shut, and the hall fell silent once again.

"I'm wearing a housecoat with a funerary motif?" Dawn asked, nervously trying to fill the silence. The four women broke into gales of laughter, and Aliki and Dawn hurried to get dressed and join the others.

El miembro de una comision arrived at the hotel in the late morning and sent a messenger into the lecture hall to fetch Dr. Alberta Pateas from a talk on body preservation methods in the twenty-first century. He waited for her, as befitted his status, in the hotel manager's office.

Carlos Don Reinaldos liked Alberta. He found her beautiful and intelligent. She was one of the few North American women he had met who knew the power of only talking when it was necessary. She was, too, excellent at her profession, although he found such work unsuitable for a woman.

He stood when she entered, lifting slightly off his heels and then bouncing down again.

"Inspector Pateas. A pleasure."

"Commissioner Don Reinaldos. I am so glad to see you. I hope I find you and your family in good health and that God has been kind to you."

"Indeed. We prosper." Her clothes hung on her tall frame, and she was pale and shaky. Rank and position forgotten, he immediately came around the desk and held her chair for her. "You are ill?"

"Thank you. I have been ill, but I am on the road to recovery now," Alberta answered politely but vaguely. "Once again, Don Reinaldos, I find myself needing the help of the police department."

Carlos Don Reinaldos returned to his seat and gave a grimace of a smile. "You, my friend, are in a lot of trouble." He picked up a report from the desk. "Trespassing on museum property, breaking and entering, and damage of a national treasure with the intent to steal."

"I was continuing the investigation we started three years ago when Tidwell Jennings disappeared."

Don Reinaldos grunted, knowing that her simple explanation hardly did justice to the charges. "I have had a look at this mummy. It looks Inca to me."

"Yes, it does. But I can assure you it is not. That body is the remains of Tidwell Jennings. And, this was not the work of some random killer. Whoever committed this crime had to be well versed in the arts of mummification."

Carlos Don Reinaldos sighed, leaned back in the office chair, and steepled his fingers, his elbows propped on the arms. "The face is flattened on one side, the skin tanned brown, and the hair an Indian style. How can you be sure?"

"Tiddy wore her hair in just such a bowl cut. I have known this woman for years. Believe me, it is her."

Thoughtful grey eyes met Aliki's. "You might know this because you were the murderer. Following up on her disappearance, finding the body, it would deflect suspicion from you. Perhaps you killed her and have been drawn back to the scene of your crime."

"Commissioner Don Reinaldos, you did a thorough investigation of Jennings' disappearance. I am sure you are well aware that I disliked the woman intensely, many of us did, but I am one of the few people who would not have had time to mummify Jennings. As you recall, I left within a week of her disappearance. With the surrounding desert, this is not an area that is easy to enter illegally, and if you check with Customs you will see I have not been back before now."

The commissioner gave a brief smile. "I have checked. I think, however, a brief glimpse of the face by flashlight late at night is not a reliable identification. Our pathologist is currently doing an autopsy on the mummy. If you are well enough, I would ask you to assist in this matter and to make a proper identification."

"Certainly, Don Reinaldos, anything to assist the police in this investigation," Aliki deadpanned, knowing that she'd better toe the line despite the fact her stomach had tied in a knot at the thought of witnessing an autopsy for the first time since her illness.

"Good. If you are free, we will go now."

An autopsy is a clinical procedure. It is detached, invasive, and efficient. The victim, once alive and dynamic, is reduced to a database from which the pathologist will extract the evidence he or she needs to identify cause of death and to bring about a legal resolution.

After detailed photography and an external examination, the body is stripped naked, and the clothes sealed in plastic bags for further study. Hair, dirt, blood, insect samples, and a plethora of other trace evidence is collected and analyzed. The body is treated to a similar procedure. Using a spotlight and large magnifying glass, every inch of the body is checked and samples taken. Hair and fingernail clippings are saved, and the residue scraped from under the fingernails will be collected for testing. If the victim fought off the attack, the DNA of the attacker might be collected from skin or blood residue.

Wounds are examined for the telltale signs of the weapon used and the order in which the wounds might have been inflicted. Then long, thin probes are pushed into the wounds to estimate angle and direction of the attack. Skin samples, swabs of orifices, and fingerprints are saved, and the body is x-rayed, measured, and exposed to any number of specialized tests deemed necessary for the gathering of additional evidence.

It is only after all this that a Y cut is made from each clavicle and down the centre of the chest. The skin and muscle are peeled back, and the internal organs exposed. Again wounds are examined, this time from the inside, to establish order and the actual cause of death. Samples are taken from all organs, and they are examined for disease, drug and alcohol abuse, injuries, and evidence of decay by enzyme action, invasive bacteria and insects to help establish time of death. Any foreign objects — knives, bullets, shrapnel, insects — are collected and sealed in labelled bags for further study. Organs are removed, weighed, examined, and photographed.

Lastly, the skull cap is sawn off and the facial skin pulled down off the skull. The brain is removed for examination for disease and foreign substances and the remaining bones and tissue examined. What is left on the stainless steel table is a bloody, empty husk, far more terrifying than any horror movie could possibly convey. When the pathologist is satisfied that no further evidence can be gathered, organs will be packed back into the chest cavity, the skull cap put in place and the facial skin flopped back over bone. The body is sutured, the toe tag dated and signed by the pathologist, and the body is lifted onto a cart and wheeled away in its body bag for storage until such time as the family is allowed to claim the remains. The bloody examination table is hosed down, and life goes on.

Aliki watched all this from behind her safety glasses and surgical mask with the clinical detachment that was necessary in her profession. At least in the case of Tiddy, the natural mummification of the desert had made the remains far less grisly and foul smelling than most. Aliki hated it when the stench of decay was overpowering and maggots wiggled everywhere and crunched under foot as she worked.

Carlos Don Reinaldos stood on the other side of the room, not wishing his impeccable suit to be crushed under a lab gown. "It is her, Dr. Pateas?"

"Yes, no doubt."

"Cause of death?"

The presiding pathologist met Aliki's eyes and shrugged, so Aliki replied, "None evident. No wounds, no sign of strangulation, no broken bones. Nothing. Naturally, the lab will need to check for drugs and poisons."

"Anything of note?" sighed Don Reinaldos in frustration.

"No. The body shows no signs of physical violence. The mummification process is virtually complete, and there is little evidence of decay. The victim was buried in the desert sand very shortly after death, if not before. Sand certainly has been inhaled into the lungs. To what extent cannot be determined until the lab reports come back."

"You are saying she was buried alive?"

"Possibly. But I doubt very much that she was conscious. She was not tied, and there is no sign of a struggle."

"A most interesting case. When you are finished, Dr. Pateas, perhaps you will join me for a late lunch, and then I will return you to the hotel."

"I would be honoured, Don Reinaldos. I will join you shortly."

Once the commissioner had left, Aliki and the pathologist discussed their findings. It seemed likely that Tiddy had been rendered unconscious by some means and driven out into the desert for burial almost immediately. It was both a daring and hideous crime. Aliki hoped that Tiddy had been unaware of what was happening to her. Whoever killed Tiddy was filled with all-consuming hatred. Sadly, that narrowed the field very little.

It was late afternoon by the time Aliki got back to the hotel. Dawn met her at the door of their room and gave her a long hug and a kiss. "You look beat. I'll run you a bath while you get undressed, and then I'll order room service. Do you want me to cancel the plans for tonight? We would have to be there," Dawn paused to check her watch, "in three hours."

"No, let's get it over with." Aliki sighed, bending her head for another kiss.

"You okay?" Dawn asked softly, realizing this was probably Aliki's first autopsy since her breakdown.

"Yeah, I came through it okay. Once I got in there, it was business as usual." She hugged her lover close. "Thanks for asking. I...I was worried if I'd ever be able to do it again."

"You don't have to, you know. If it's going to bother you, you could go into another field."

"No, forensic anthropology is what I do, and I'm good at it. I'm going to be just fine as long as you're at my side," Aliki stated with more bravado than she felt. Although she had gotten through the procedure, she had to admit it had left her shaken and drained. Her job was bones, and she rarely had to watch the detailed proceedings of a regular autopsy, although they were often going on in the lab around her.

Dawn gave Aliki another quick hug, the worry plain on her face. "Go get changed, then, while I get the water running. Once I order us a light meal, I'll come help wash your back.

Aliki smiled, one eyebrow raised in challenge. "Promise?"

"You are so bad. I promise." Dawn stretched up to drop a kiss on luscious lips.

Her tasks completed a short time later, Dawn checked the lock on the room door, stripped down, and entered the bathroom. Aliki was asleep in the tub. Smiling softly as her eyes traced the beautiful form, Dawn went over and knelt by the tub. "Come on, lover, let's get you to bed," she whispered, kissing Aliki softly.

"Mmmm, what? Oh, fell asleep. Come here," Aliki murmured, reaching for her naked partner's alluring body.

"No. Come on, a quick dry and into bed with you. I promise to snuggle close, and once we get back from the party tonight, I'll take you up on that offer, okay?"

"Okay." Aliki sleepily allowed her partner to pull her from the cooling water and towel her down with care. She even let herself be led to the bed. After that, she made up her own rules.

They arrived at the Graveyard Restaurant a bit late, being teased unmercifully by Robbie all the way over until Aliki was about ready to punch her. Not surprisingly, the celebration was long underway by the time they got there. Someone had managed to hang ribbons in the colours of rainbows over the doorways, and a large purple heart emblazoned with "A. P. Loves D. F." was suspended over the bar.

"Hey, there they are! Belly up, the drinks are on me," called Philby. "All together, guys: For she's a jolly good fellow, for she's a jolly good femme. For they're a jolly good couple, and so say all of us!" The singing was terrible and the cheers and clapping deafening. Even those uncomfortable with the relationship had seen fit to make a token appearance because of their respect for Aliki as a scientist. Drinks in hand, they crowded around, laughing and talking.

"Two pineapple margaritas," Robbie yelled at the bartender over the racket, watching with amusement while colleagues tendered their congratulations by clapping Aliki on the back and shaking her hand and kissing Dawn.

"I'm not sure I want a margarita," Janet protested.

"They're both for me. What would you like?"

Janet frowned. "Robbie! You never drink."

"Wait until you've been with this group for ten minutes. You'll be ordering drinks by the half dozen," her spouse responded as she dropped some money on the damp bar counter and organized her drinks in front of her.

"Hey, guys, Alberta has to do the mummy toe!" someone called from the back of the crowd.

Aliki groaned, pulling a face. "No!"

"Hey, we make all bachelors do it to prove that they've got what it takes," Philby insisted.

"I don't have what it takes! I improvise," Aliki protested, her arms outspread.

Dawn buried her face in her hands and shook her head in disbelief. Janet's eyes were wide with surprise. She had never seen Aliki among her colleagues, and she was certainly a different person.

"Two whiskey sours," Robbie ordered after checking out the look on her wife's face.

There were gales of laughter and jeers. “Come on, Alberta, don’t let the rainbow team down.”

“How come Dawn doesn’t have to do it?” Aliki argued as she let herself be pushed toward a table.

There was a long wolf whistle from the back of the room. “Hell, we already noticed that she has the right stuff!”

“Hey, watch it back there!” Aliki growled with a fabricated scowl. She was pushed down onto a chair and a yard of beer was set in front of her in a glass bulb with a long thin neck and wide mouth.

“This I have to see.” Robbie slipped off her stool and moved over to the table where the assortment of very mellow scientists was standing. Janet and Dawn followed close behind.

Fenwick cleared his throat and spoke in his usual dignified, reserved manner. “As the current chair of the Sacred Society of the Toe, I am charged with the enormous responsibility of being the keeper of the mummy toe, which has been passed down from chair to chair for some years now. Occasionally at stags, weddings, funerals, and other happy gatherings...” at this point he had to wait for the laughter to stop, “it has been the responsibility of the chair to produce the toe and test the fibre of those colleagues about to take the plunge into a new life. Ladies, gentlemen, and others, the toe!”

To the cheers and applause of all those around, Fenwick pulled a rather grotty looking brown lump from his pocket. With reverence, he reached over and dropped it into the yard glass. A silence fell on the gathering as all watched the disgusting object float about in the suds until it became saturated and slowly nosedived to the bottom. A cheer went up.

Fenwick called for silence. “I now call on our distinguished colleague, Dr. Alberta Pateas, to show her worth. Doctor?”

“That isn’t a real mummy’s toe, is it?” Robbie asked Samir Tagore, who stood beside her.

“First tarsal off the right foot of a court scribe of the late Egyptian empire. I was sick for days after. It’s against my religion to drink, and I am not sure where my faith stands on the matter of human flesh. They do rather frown on beef.”

“Oh, dear God! Where is my margarita!”

“The story about how the tradition got going is really rather fascinating.”

Robbie held up a hand. “Too much information. Say no more.”

Aliki looked at Dawn to see how she was reacting to the ceremony. Dawn smiled and winked at her. Aliki stood, and the crowd went quiet. Aliki composed herself, drawing on her martial arts training to calm her. Then she picked up the yard and started drinking.

“Half way!” someone yelled.

“Three quarters. She’s slowing, I don’t think she is going to make it to the toe.”

“Go, Alberta! Don’t stop. You’re nearly there!”

“Come on, I’ve got five pounds on this!”

“She did it!”

Cheers filled the room. The yard glass was empty, and a soggy-looking brown toe lay in the froth at the bottom. Aliki wiped her mouth and smiled stupidly.

"Glad I don't have to sleep with her tonight," Janet whispered into Dawn's ear.

Dawn snorted. "The things one has to do for love."

The party was a merry affair, and Dawn found herself in her lover's arms out on the dance floor amongst other couples. "You are very drunk. You know that, don't you?"

"Damn," Aliki slurred with a goofy smile. "I was hoping there were three of you and I was in for a really kinky night."

Recognizing that Aliki was unlikely to make it back to the hotel under her own steam, Janet called a taxi. The three of them managed to negotiate Aliki into the back seat, where she promptly passed out.

She might have had to remain there until morning if Robbie hadn't been just about as drunk. With an amazing heave, she pulled her sister from the cab and threw her over her shoulder in a firefighter's hold and then staggered into the hotel singing the Volga Boat Song, loudly and off key.

Janet and Dawn followed behind, laughing so hard they could barely stand.

"They'll probably ask us to leave in the morning," Janet observed as Robbie deposited her unconscious sister on the bed in Dawn and Aliki's room.

"I think it is a given." Dawn sighed. "Do you think she'll be okay?"

Swaying dangerously on her feet, Robbie looked at her sister with a critical eye. "In a few days," she concluded. "Come on, Janet. Bedtime. Night, Dawn. Congratulations."

"Watch she doesn't choke," advised Janet as she was pulled from the room.

"Great. Just great," Dawn sighed, left alone to see to her lover.

Part 3

Janet met Dawn in the hotel's café for breakfast. Butter croissants, wine jelly, and coffee made by mixing a combination of water and rich, syrupy Colombian coffee were served to them by the fireplace, as the morning air was still cold. "How is she doing?" Janet asked.

"Slept like the dead until three o'clock and then threw up until nearly six. I think she lost a fair number of brain cells because so far her only communication has been grunts and moans." Dawn smiled, reaching for the preserves. "What about Robbie?"

"She's sitting in the sun in the courtyard, wrapped in a blanket and staring blankly out into space. She told me that as soon as her body had absorbed enough energy to get her blood moving again, she would try getting properly dressed. She wasn't sure she could manage it, though, what with the earth pitching about so badly this morning."

The two women laughed. "It was nice to see Aliki relaxed and smiling," Janet went on more seriously, as she buttered a roll.

Dawn nodded. "I think we have buried a ghost that has been haunting Aliki for a very long time. Maybe now she can finally commit to a relationship."

Janet put down her coffee cup. "Can I ask what ghost?"

"Her mother. Her mother told Aliki that she wasn't to worry because she wasn't going to die and then, of course, she did. I think deep inside, Aliki couldn't trust love after that. She wanted to, but she had never resolved the anger she had toward her mother for leaving her." Dawn played fretfully with her napkin.

"How did you find out?"

Dawn looked into the flames of the fire. "We went for a walk and sat by the moon pool. Suddenly it came out, and she just leaned forward, crying. I just held her for a long time until she was able to talk."

Janet put down her cup. "Poor Aliki. She's like Robbie in that way. They both feel they have to be so strong, and yet they are such softies inside."

Dawn nodded. "Aliki did her best by Baba and her brothers, trying to fill her mother's shoes, but it is not the life she wanted and she felt trapped and betrayed and that, in turn, made her feel guilty, because she loved her mom and her family."

"And on top of that," Janet observed, "there was the guilt she had to deal with about the suicide of that girl you told me about, the young woman who told Aliki that her brother had gotten her pregnant and Aliki didn't believe her."

"Aliki went through so much emotional pain then, and no one noticed. She kept it all inside and took care of the family like her father wanted. It's no wonder she made some pretty surprising decisions at that time of her life. She must have been weighed down with guilt and responsibility."

Janet nodded in understanding as the pieces fell together in her mind. "So as soon as she could, she left, and she has been avoiding emotional commitment ever since." She signed her room number to the bill.

"Seems that way," Dawn agreed, getting up. "I just hope that this time she is really ready to make a commitment to Mac and me. Mac was really shook up about Aliki's breakdown and her walking out on us." The two headed out to the hotel's small lobby.

"Aliki thought she was doing the right thing. She was following her old pattern of taking all the responsibility on her own shoulders and not showing her own pain. Old habits die hard," Janet suggested.

"Is Robbie like that?"

Janet snorted. "Robbie I-have-a-half-dozen-Oscars Williams? Not likely! Oh, she is brave and very protective of us, but believe me, if she is upset we *all* know about it!"

They laughed, and the tension was broken. They went on to lighter conversation as they had a morning walk along the rustic streets of Atacoma.

Answering the insistent knocking on the door, Aliki managed to get to the door on shaky legs and fumble it open it to find a near mirror image of herself staring back. "What was all the pounding about?" she groaned.

"You lived, too, eh?" Robbie muttered.

"I'm not sure yet," Aliki croaked through a sandpaper-dry throat.

"Come on. You need sunlight, it helps." Robbie crossed through the room to the doors that led outside, then stopped and turned around with some difficulty. "Bring water. Lots of it."

Aliki tried to nod, decided it was a bad idea, and went and got several bottles of spring water from the counter where the maid left them each day. The bathroom glasses rounded out the supplies, and she joined her sister in the courtyard where Robbie was having great difficulty arranging two plastic chairs. "There. Sit."

"Around three o'clock I thought I was going to puke up my guts." Aliki groaned, settling down and closing her eyes against the glare of the sun. The cool morning air and the weak heat of the early sun did feel good.

"At least they didn't make you swallow that disgusting toe."

Aliki moaned. "Don't even go there. I have nothing left to heave."

Robbie risked turning her head to look at her sister. Aliki looked like hell; zombies had more colour and more meat on their bones. Yet somehow, Aliki looked happier, calmer than she had in a very long time. "Well, look on the bright side, whatever happens in your marriage to Dawn, it can't be any worse than last night."

"My marriage to Dawn is going to be perfect," Aliki bragged confidently.

"Ahh! That's what I thought when I married Janet. Believe me, it has been a rollercoaster ride. I've been shot at, jailed, knocked out God knows how many times, roasted in a firestorm, and nearly drowned. And that was only the first year. Our love is perfect, but believe me, married life is a real grab bag of surprises."

"You have regrets?" Aliki asked in surprise, risking opening her eyes to look at her sister.

"Hell no! It's been great. I'm in for another hundred years or so."

Aliki smiled. "Yeah, that's the way I see my life with Dawn and Mac, too."

After that they sat quietly, cautiously sipping water and letting the sun restore some energy to their fragile bodies. Hangovers were hell.

"Hey, Janet, they're both out here," Dawn called down the hall some time later, having spied the two sisters through the sliding door across the room as she entered.

Janet came trotting back. "How are they doing?"

"Looks to me like they have regained the ability to walk on two legs, but there's no sign of language development yet," Dawn stated matter-of-factly.

Janet laughed. "Isn't evolution a wonderful thing?"

The two women joined their partners out in the courtyard. "We brought coffee and dry toast. Do you think you're up to it yet?" Dawn asked.

Aliki sighed. "I need to put something in my stomach, even if it is only so I have something to throw up again."

By afternoon, the two sisters had recovered sufficiently from the night before to join their mates downstairs. The others at the gathering were enjoying an off day for touring the area. A few had hit the tourist sites, but most had either nursed their hangovers or taken the organized field trip up into the Andes to see the field of geysers on the side of one of the local volcanoes.

The exterior courtyard was otherwise deserted and the day warm with a pleasant breeze scented by desert flowers. The four women stretched out on lawn chairs and enjoyed some quiet family talk and reading. Because she was far too vain to wear her reading glasses in public, Robbie had her nose deep in a new script. Janet was chuckling her way through the Harry Potter series. Aliki was deeply engrossed in a book on the Guanch mummies that had been recovered on the island of Tenerife, while Dawn was not reading at all but was jotting down ideas for a new book.

It was some time later, then, when the women became restless with their individual activities and conversation started up again. This time the topic was the mummification and possible murder of Tidwell Jennings.

"We've gotta solve this crime," Robbie said decisively, putting her script down and blinking like an owl.

Aliki looked up from her book. "It has yet to be established whether a crime took place."

"Come on, Aliki. She didn't finish dinner and decide to pop off and get herself mummified. Someone dried and tanned her and then wrapped her up for storage."

"I think it was Hilda Katz," Dawn offered. "It's always the quiet, mousy ones that have the bloody corpses in their basements."

"I think the court would need more information than that." Aliki smiled good-naturedly.

"What about Gerald Flex? Jennings made him a laughingstock with her sexual harassment charge," observed Janet, reluctantly marking the place in her book. She had just reached an exciting part. "My money is on him. Older people are not given enough credit for the passion they feel."

"That guy's passion is located a lot lower than his heart," Robbie snorted. "Nah, my bet is on Victor Van Vogt. The guy likes cutting up bodies. He gives me the creeps."

"Victor is a good guy," Aliki protested.

"Ha! It's always the one you think you can trust." Robbie tossed her script on the table.

Dawn ripped a piece of paper from her writing pad and wrote the heading "suspects". "Okay, let's be systematic about this and go through the list. Aliki, who are the most likely suspects?"

Aliki frowned, but it was clear the others were not going to be put off. "I looked it up — there were 67 delegates at our last gathering here. Any number of those people might have wanted to get rid of Tiddy. She made enemies; she was just that sort. Don Reinaldos handled the investigation himself, and I was allowed to assist. Seven people had significant motive and also had the opportunity that night to have committed the murder."

"Well?" Robbie asked impatiently, moving over to sit on the end of Janet's lawn chair. Janet reached out and rubbed her lover's back.

"It's the seven we already mentioned: Fenwick, Philby, Flex, Katz, Tagore, Van Vogt, and myself."

Dawn looked up sharply; Janet was quick to step in. "Let's clear your name first; that should be simple."

"Tidwell Jennings was gay, and years ago, she came on to me pretty forcefully. I made it clear I was not interested and she was quite spiteful about it. She took every opportunity she could after that to put me down and twist the knife. Over the years, we'd had a number of rather public and hot arguments at forensic gatherings. Everyone knew that I disliked her intensely."

Robbie, being Robbie, had to ask. "So, did you two ever get it on? Is that why she was pissed?"

Janet could have throttled her. She looked over and saw that Dawn was staring intently at the blank page she held.

"No! Damn it, Robbie!"

Robbie looked at the other three annoyed women in surprise. "Well, it was long before she knew Dawn. She might have."

"Well, I didn't," Aliki reaffirmed.

Janet swatted Robbie. "Don't consider the diplomatic service, okay, olive? All right, Aliki, you had motive. What about opportunity?"

"I'm afraid so. I'd headed to the washroom first and Tiddy followed me. We had words in the Ladies. She said that she was going to make mincemeat of me in the question period after I presented my findings on some early Inuit sites. I told her she could stuff her fat head in a toilet and flush for all I cared. As far as I know, I was the last person to see Tiddy alive. She gave me the finger as I walked out. I returned to the table fuming and told the others what had happened. Tiddy never returned."

"And *I'm* not diplomatic?" Robbie asked, nodding toward her sister.

Janet pointedly ignored the jibe. "Since you were a viable suspect, weren't the police concerned about you working with them?"

Aliki shrugged. "They gave me the third degree like everyone else. No one figured I was gone long enough to have killed her and stashed the body."

Dawn was quietly scribing the information. Now she changed the subject with relief. "Let's look at Archie Fenwick."

Aliki was quick to facilitate the new direction. "Tiddy wanted his job as chair of the Forensic Association."

"Not to mention keeper of the toe," Robbie added in disgust.

Janet gave her a poke. "Good, let's not. Aliki?"

"Fenwick found her abrasive, and it was obvious that he avoided her. Of course, you know Fenwick; he was far too polite to say anything to her. I know he takes some pleasure in being the chair of these gathering. It was his brainchild in the first place. He does a good job of arranging meetings and keeping us informed. He's had the job a long time and Tiddy argued it should go to someone else, but frankly no one really wanted the headache and we're all pretty satisfied with Fenwick's efforts."

"Then why did Tiddy want the job?" Dawn asked, taking notes.

"Tiddy wanted anything she couldn't have. One thing's for sure – none of the rest of us wanted Tiddy to have the job. She was one of those individuals who abused power. She'd have wrecked the gatherings for everyone."

"Did Fenwick have opportunity?" Janet sipped on her fruit juice.

Aliki nodded. "Yeah, he got a headache and left to get some pills at the hotel. He was gone about a half hour, and it was during that time that Tiddy disappeared."

Dawn frowned. "If he was not feeling well, it seems strange that he came back to the restaurant. Why didn't he just lie down for the night?"

"That's Fenwick. He was in charge, and he felt he needed to be there to make sure everything went smoothly."

"Wouldn't things go more smoothly if he offed Jennings?" Robbie asked, stealing a sip of Janet's drink.

Aliki rolled her eyes and didn't answer.

"Next on the list is Gerald Flex," Dawn stated.

Dismissing him out of hand, Aliki shook her head. "He's harmless."

"He doesn't think so. He thinks he's still packing a loaded pistol." Robbie laughed.

"Doesn't he have a motive?"

"Oh, sure he does. Tiddy charged him with sexual harassment. It was quite embarrassing for him."

"Was there any truth to it?" Janet asked.

"In this politically correct world, sure there was, but not anything beyond flirting. He is of another generation; we let him get away with his nonsense because he is old and harmless. Besides, inside the dirty old man there is a first-rate pathologist."

"Did he have the opportunity?"

"Yeah. He didn't have dinner with the rest of us. He said he had a date with a local girl. He came in much later, after Tiddy had disappeared, all upset because he had been stood up. The rest of us figured that whoever the girl was she was just going along with his nonsense to be friendly and never had any intention of meeting him."

"Could he have overpowered Jennings?" Janet asked. "I mean, he must be in his late seventies or early eighties."

Aliki considered. "Hard to say. Tiddy was in pretty good shape, although I'm not sure how fit she actually was. Flex has always kept himself fit, and despite his age, he is still lecturing. He would also know about and have access to drugs...I don't know, maybe. I'm not sure he could have carried or pulled Tiddy's body very far. She would have had to go with him willingly and that seems out of character of her."

"Hilda Katz?" Dawn prompted.

"Hmmm, I don't know a lot about her. Her speciality is paleopathology. She's retired now but still occasionally puts in an appearance at a gathering. I haven't really talked to her about her field, but I have found her published work still very informative and relevant. She is overly polite, formal, and very, very private. I've seen her over the years at conferences, and yet I know virtually nothing about her, outside of her work. She keeps to herself."

"My point exactly. Still waters run deep," Dawn emphasized. "And didn't you tell me once that Jennings had crucified her work on some Iron Age site? She seems rather young to be retired, too."

"Maybe the dust-up over her research made her decide to take an early retirement. Tiddy sure made a stink over Katz's findings. She said some pretty ugly things about Katz's lab work in print. But the truth of the matter is, no one gave her criticism much credence. Everyone knew that Katz did fine work and that Tiddy was a flaming bitch."

"Why did she have it in for Katz?" Janet asked.

"Don't know. With Tiddy, there didn't necessarily have to be a reason."

"How about opportunity?" Dawn asked as she jotted down points.

"She had dinner and left to go back to her hotel. That is not unusual for Hilda. She usually stays and has a drink to be sociable and then leaves. She's just not a party animal."

Robbie pondered the timeline. "So she certainly had the time to come back and waylay Jennings then?"

"Yes."

Dawn put her pen down. "The trouble with Katz, Fenwick, and Flex is that although they all had opportunity, none of them would have known that Jennings had left to go to the washroom."

"That leaves Aliki," Robbie joked. "Come on, Sis, 'fess up. We'll help you escape and get you a new identity; we promise." Aliki flicked a paper coaster at her sister.

"There are still a few more to consider," Janet reminded them. "Who's next, Dawn?"

"Philby."

"That was a bad scene. It is still a pretty touchy topic." Aliki grimaced. "In his early forties, Jed married for the first time to a woman some twenty years younger. He was head over heels in love with Kris and basically told the world so. You know Philby. Anyway, after a few years with Jed, she ran off with Tidwell Jennings. They had a stormy and very public affair for about six months that scandalized pretty much everyone, then Jennings gave her the boot."

"What happened to Kris?" Dawn asked.

Aliki shook her head. "I don't know. She wasn't in the field. I think she was a nurse or something. If I remember rightly, it was Katz who introduced her to Philby."

"How did Philby take being rejected?" Janet asked with a frown.

"He was shattered, I think. He doesn't talk much about it. I don't know if he divorced Kris or not. It was just like it never happened. After that, he just avoided Tiddy at conferences. I don't think he ever spoke to her again."

"I feel sad for him." Janet sighed.

"Yeah, he's a great guy, once you get over the size and noise of him."

"What was his opportunity?"

"He was doing work in the area that summer and was out in the field. He didn't arrive until some time after dinner because his Jeep got a flat tire and he had to change it."

"So he knew the area and would know where to stash a body," Robbie suggested.

"We all knew the area. We'd spent a few days touring around, just like they are doing today."

Dawn wrote down the information and then looked at the top of the page to see who was next on their list. "What about Samir Tagore?"

"He's a palynologist, one of the best," Aliki acknowledged. The group looked at her blankly, and she went on to clarify. "He studies pollen. In particular, he is interested in ancient pollens and how plant communities have changed over time."

"Be still my beating heart!" Robbie dramatized, slumping back into Janet's lap with some enjoyment.

"Hey, it's important work."

"So what was his beef with Jennings?" Robbie stole a quick hug before she sat up again.

Aliki tried to recall what she had heard. "He had a chance to work in the States at the same university where Tiddy lectured. He would have had the job, too, but Tiddy insisted that it should go to an American and he was turned down for the position. It was a real blow to his career, as it was a few years later before he got an opportunity to lecture in England.

"He argued with Tiddy that night. She was riding him, maintaining that a degree from a developing nation wasn't the same as a 'real' degree from a university in the industrialized world. He took it for as long as he could and then told her that if she was the representative of the professional standard of the industrial world, the level of competency was not all that high."

Janet grimaced. "Ouch!"

"Tiddy had it coming. Anyway, he stormed off after that. I got up to go to the washroom shortly after, and Tiddy followed me out a few minutes later."

"Okay, our last one is Victor Van Vogt."

"The man's a ghoul among ghouls. He's guilty," Robbie said with confidence.

"We are not ghouls," Aliki stated indignantly.

"So who else thinks it is a great tradition to drink beer laced with ancient toes?"

Janet changed the subject before the two hotheaded sisters could get into it. "Van Vogt had a grudge against Jennings, too, Aliki?"

"Yeah, they worked together in England just after they graduated. All through Europe, over the years, there have been finds of well-preserved bodies in old peat bogs. The lack of oxygen in the bog water prevents decay, and the natural tannin often found in swamps basically tans the corpse like leather.

"Van Vogt did some real groundbreaking work on parasites, but Tiddy scooped him, publishing his findings along with hers almost six months ahead of his disclosure. It made it look like Tiddy was the brains in the partnership and Victor was just along for the ride. That couldn't have been further from the truth. As a result, Tiddy got picked up as a lecturer and Victor didn't. He worked as an assistant lecturer in The Netherlands for a number of years before he finally got a position in California."

Dawn rolled her eyes. "Is there anyone she hadn't offended?

"I don't think she had many friends."

"Did Victor have opportunity?" Janet asked.

"Yeah, he went to get a drink and was gone a long time. When he did come back, he said that he'd been talking to some local guy at the bar about burial sites, but he couldn't support his alibi. The man had left, I guess, and no one had seen them talking."

"That seems strange."

"Not really. It was quite a big gathering that year with a lot of new faces, because it was the tenth anniversary of the association. People were coming in for dinner at different times all evening. It was a pretty lively gathering with a lot of comings and goings. You know how these things are."

"That's the lot." Dawn sighed. "It doesn't look like we got very far with this summary."

Aliki smiled. "That was the problem the initial investigation had: too many suspects and not enough concrete evidence. The reality is it could have been almost anyone at the restaurant that night, or for that matter, just some stranger lurking about."

Janet looked Aliki straight in the eye with her calm, serious gaze. "Do you believe that?"

Aliki blushed. "No. This was a well-planned-out crime, not one of passion, and it was done by someone who knew about mummification." Aliki looked down at her glass. "I am very much afraid the murderer is one of us."

For a minute, the group of women was silent as they pondered her statement, then Robbie spoke up. "What we need is more data. I suggest we split up. There are six primary suspects, if we don't count Pateas here, and three of us, if we leave Pateas out again. That's two suspects each."

"First of all, you three are not going to investigate anything. Leave it to the police. Second, why do I get left out?"

"As a suspect or as an investigator?" Dawn teased.

"I think we're willing to trust you didn't do it," Janet answered. "We would not really be investigating, just being good listeners and seeing if we can pick up any information that we can pass on to you. These people are your friends, Aliki. We know that is awkward for you, and besides, you're a cop and no matter how friendly these people feel toward you, they are going to be on their guard knowing that."

"It's just for fun." Robbie smiled. "It's gotta be better than sitting through another lecture on petrified intestinal worms."

Aliki was about to protest when Philby stuck his head outside. "There you are. Come on, Aliki, we need you to settle an argument about the effects of rickets on bones."

Aliki looked at the group. "I'll be back. Don't even think about this madness while I'm gone."

The three women watched her go, then Robbie raise an eyebrow in question. "Well?"

Dawn looked at her list. "I'm in."

"Me, too," Janet chuckled. "But what if Aliki comes back?"

"She's talking bones here, Janet. I'll be lucky if she remembers to join me for dinner."

Glasses were set down, and the women stood. Robbie issued a challenge. "Since this gathering of information might take us some time, we can meet for breakfast at eight to discuss our findings. The person with the least information has to pay the bill."

"I'll take Tagore and Fenwick," said Dawn.

"Flex and Katz are mine," Janet put in.

"Oh, great. That leaves me with Van Vogt and Philby. Mutt and Jeff," Robbie groaned. She wrapped her arm around Janet. "You be careful around Flex, darling. He's the grabby-feely type, and if he touches my girl, I'll have to kill him."

Janet gave her wife a reassuring pat. "I'm used to the type," she teased. "I'll be on my guard."

"Hey," Robbie protested, hands on hips as Dawn and Janet walked away laughing.

Robbie found Van Vogt clicking through pictures in preparation for his presentation. "Hey, I didn't think anyone was lecturing today."

Van Vogt frowned at the intrusion. "I'm presenting first thing tomorrow morning. I thought I'd take the opportunity to run through my material and make sure everything is ready."

"Aliki says you are one of the best."

"Aliki?" asked Van Vogt in puzzlement, looking up at Robbie with small grey eyes.

Robbie sat on the edge of a table, unconsciously looking both relaxed and sexy at the same time. "Alberta. Her real name is Aliki. It's Greek."

"Really? I have known her for years and never knew that. That she would admire my research is indeed flattering. I have been impressed by the detail and extent of her work." He clicked to the next slide.

A photo of bacteria attacking the intestinal lining popped up on the screen.

Robbie grimaced and carried on bravely. "She's a pretty private person. Finding Jennings' body has really opened up a can of worms, huh? I know my sister is pretty upset about it."

"It is sometimes best to let sleeping dogs lie," came the bitter, muttered response.

"I'm beginning to think so. Were you there the night she disappeared?" Robbie watched him closely for his reaction.

Van Vogt showed no emotion. "Yes, but as far away from her as I could get. As soon as she arrived, I went and joined some others in the bar. I talked to some local who claimed he knew where to find more ancient burials." Victor shrugged. "I think it was the beer talking, but it filled in an hour or so. Philby thought so too when I told him about it. After *she* left, I rejoined the group."

"You know, no one seems to have liked that woman."

"She could be charming," Victor conceded reluctantly as he slipped the disc from his computer. "But it was barely skin deep. She had a truly poisonous personality."

"Do you have any idea how she ended up mummified?"

"Don't know. Don't care," Van Vogt stated bluntly, dropping his disc of photos into his briefcase and snapping it shut. "But my hat is off to whomever it was. You'll excuse me, I am meeting Fenwick at five."

Robbie watched him go with interest, pleased with herself. A bit of the puzzle might just have fallen into place.

She hopped off the table and followed a big booming voice to Jed Philby.

"Victor, there you are! We were afraid you were off carving up the recently dead! Tagore is looking for you, something about wanting to swap slide samples, and Alberta's leading a hot debate on rickets with a young group of my students in the morning room."

Robbie smiled as she walked across the lobby. "Hi, Jed."

The big man spun and almost knocked over a potted rubber tree. Just in time, he grabbed it around its thick stem as if he was throttling it and set it back in place, knocking off several branches in the process. "Hi, Robbie. How is the head? You and your sister were the life of the party last night. If it hadn't been for your lovely partners keeping an eye on you, I think the two of you would have ended up in jail again." Philby laughed heartily, wrapped an enormous arm around Robbie, and gave her a one-armed hug.

"Aah, yes, well, I'm just on my way for a coffee now. I think the stomach can handle it. Would you like to join me?"

"Never turn down a coffee or a job offer; that's my philosophy. Where's that gorgeous girlfriend of yours?" Philby asked, as they headed over to the coffee shop.

"Wife. She's my wife," Robbie reminded him firmly.

"Oh, yeah. I keep forgetting. Waiter, two coffees. Thanks."

"Janet wanted to talk to a few people. She's always looking for documentary ideas for her students. She is president of the Bartlett College of Film and Animation."

Jed looked up from picking up the sugar jar that he had knocked over in sitting down. "No kidding? More than a pretty face, huh?"

"A whole lot more. Are you married, Jed?" Robbie asked, helping him pick up little paper packets of sugar and place them back in the jar.

The buoyant personality sank instantaneously. "I was once. Turned out she was gay. It sure as hell shot me out of the goddamn tree. Felt like a damn fool."

Robbie squirmed a bit, feeling bad about bringing Jed down. "Sorry. It happens. Sadly, a lot of gay women marry, thinking that it is what they need in their lives, and then realize that it is just not them, no matter what society and their families say. It was not a reflection on you, Jed. It was the action of a confused woman. I'm sorry you got hurt."

Jed looked over Robbie's shoulder, his eyes pained as he recalled the past. "She ran off with Tidwell. That's what really jerked my strings. Then the bitch dropped Kris like you would a dirty shirt. Now even her dead body is causing trouble. Shit."

"Was Kris in your field of interest? How did you meet her?"

"She was a mortician. A good one, too. I met her at a conference in Rome. Said she was there with her sister. I thought we had a lot in common, but I guess not. It's funny, you know, I still care about her. She had a little problem with gambling," Philby admitted with a blush, playing with his spoon nervously. "I sure hope she stayed out of trouble."

Robbie stirred the sugar into her coffee, letting Philby unload. When he stopped, she said, "I heard you and Victor hid out in the bar until Jennings disappeared that night."

"Victor? He said that? I was late getting there. Flat tire," Philby explained awkwardly. "Maybe I talked to Victor when I came in. I don't remember. So, tell me what it's like to be a famous movie star."

Robbie took the hint and let the conversation drift to other topics.

In the conference room, Janet was having her own problems. "Dr. Flex, you don't seem to quite grasp the situation here. Robbie Williams is married to me, and there isn't a chance in hell of me helping you arrange a date with her."

"Shame, that. Soon as she's been with a real man," he stopped to hitch his pants up with his elbows, "well, then she'd see things differently. So if she isn't available, what about you taking a spin with me tonight?" Flex asked, as he wrote the next day's schedule up on a plastic bulletin board.

Janet leaned back against the wall and crossed her arms. "When hell freezes over," she stated firmly, but without any real anger. There was no use banging her head against a stone wall. "Now, would you please tell me what happened the night Jennings disappeared? Like I told you, I'm collecting data for a possible documentary about the mystery."

Flex snorted and rolled his eyes comically. "What mystery? Katz killed her."

"What!" Her eyes got big with surprise as she stood up straight.

"Sure. Crime of passion. It was a woman, and Katz is the most likely. No one notices the quiet ones, but still waters run deep. Katz told me once she had a sister that was bad to the core. Those sorts of things run in families, I figure. Just because she's ladylike, people trust her. I like my women with a bit more fire, I do."

"I thought passion was your thing," Janet said dryly, settling back against the wall again when she realized that the old man's pronouncement was not based on any real evidence. "Maybe you killed her. You were angry with her, weren't you?"

"Made me look like a fool, she did. All that nonsense just because I pinched her bum. Hell, she should have been pleased. Don't suppose it happened to her very often."

Janet closed her eyes and counted to ten. "You were out on a date that night, weren't you?"

"Got stood up. Now there is a damn good reason to go to the police! Led me along, she did, and then stood me up. That's much worse than a pinched bum any day. Pretty young thing she was, too. Her loss. I got back just about the time people started to wonder what had happened to Tiddy. Alberta, that's Dr. Pateas, went and checked and came back to say that no one was in the washroom."

"Aliki, I mean Alberta went back into the washroom?" Janet asked in surprise.

"Yup, not that I think it was her who done it. She's queer, you know. I don't think them kind go in for passion; they haven't got the parts. Them lot are more into body buildin' and mountain bikes and the like."

Janet shook her head in amazement. "Dr. Flex, you did hear me say I was married to Robbie Williams, didn't you?"

"Sure, sure. One of them Hollywood marriages of convenience to keep her name in the paper, I imagine. She's gettin' up in age to remain a heart-throb. Women don't age well like men. Not that I'd mind finding her high heels under my bed in the mornin'." He laughed, putting the top back on the felt pen.

Janet mentally declared defeat. "Nice talking with you, Dr. Flex. I know you have things to do, so I won't take up any more of your time."

"Sure. But if you really want to get that story," Flex said, his eyes suddenly bright with mischief, "ask Katz about the blue scarf she had in her pocket that night."

Surprised by his parting shot, Janet watched the old man walk away with his bandy-legged shuffle. Then she went in search of Hilda Katz and to see if she could pass on Flex's remark to the others.

It proved to be an easier task then she had anticipated. Dawn was sitting at the bar talking to Fenwick when Janet looked out the patio doors to the courtyard. She took a small notepad and pen from her pocket and wrote down the information she had obtained, then sauntered over in Dawn's direction. "Hi, Dawn. Aliki asked me to pass this note on to you. Hi, Dr. Fenwick. Lovely day, isn't it?"

"Why, yes, it certainly is."

"You haven't seen Hilda Katz, have you? I am very interested in her work. It sounds like a field that would make a very interesting documentary."

"Palaeopathology? Well, yes, I suppose so. Not Egyptology, of course, but interesting enough. I believe she mentioned going to her room to freshen up."

While Janet was exchanging niceties with Fenwick, Dawn used the opportunity to read the note.

> *I just talked to Flex. He suggested we ask Katz about the blue scarf she had in her pocket the night Jennings disappeared. I'm going to do that now.*
>
> *Janet*

After Janet had moved off, Dawn finished her drink with Fenwick and then took her leave. She had done well, she thought. The man was not a gossip, but subtly and carefully she had managed to extract a good deal of information from him. To start with, Philby had not had a flat as he had told everyone. Fenwick admitted that there had been a "complication" of a personal nature that neither he nor Philby felt had any bearing on the investigation.

Secondly, she had learned that Fenwick had not planned to come back to the party but that he had "regrettably" overheard a private conversation and felt it better that he return to the gathering in case an "unfortunate" incident arose. Whatever had happened that evening, Fenwick was not prepared to elaborate on it. In fact, he seemed rather surprised that he had told Dawn as much as he had and asked for her discretion. Dawn smiled. She felt that she might be on a hot trail. She'd have to pass the information on to the others as soon as she could.

Janet found Hilda Katz just getting off the elevator and asked if she might have a word with her. The palaeopathologist frowned but cautiously agreed to sit in the lobby for a few minutes and hear what Janet had to say.

They sat across from each other on two Spanish-style leather and wood chairs.

"As you know, Robbie and I have started a school for film. We are considering having our students work with us on a documentary on the disappearance of Tidwell Jennings at the gathering three years ago. I wonder if I might ask you about the night she disappeared."

Katz looked uncomfortable. She hesitated for some time and then answered stiffly, "There is really very little I can say. I had dinner and left while Dr. Jennings was still there."

Janet saw that Hilda was not going to be an easy nut to crack. She appeared to be an individual with a highly developed sense of what was proper. The best approach, Janet concluded, was to appeal to her sense of moral justice. "Dr. Katz, if you have read any of my books you will know that I don't sensationalize. I know Jennings was not a particularly nice human being and that a lot of people had good reason to hate her, but someone took her life, Dr. Katz. Someone crossed over that moral line. No one has that right, for any reason. A grievous wrong has been committed, and maybe this documentary might help to correct that wrong."

Hilda Katz's eyes grew dark blue with anger. She swallowed, looked at her clutched hands in her lap for some time, and then swallowed again. Janet waited. "I don't want to talk here. Can we go out to the courtyard?"

"Of course." Janet followed Hilda Katz out, and they sat in a quiet corner away from the few people who had ventured into the afternoon sun.

Katz stared for a long time out at the garden, considering, and when she spoke it was as if she was reading out loud, her voice barely a whisper above the cooing of the doves in the mission steeple next door. "Kris was like that," she started, giving a north European pronunciation to the name. "She always was. The family said she had bad blood. Maybe you have met someone in your life that was just naturally bad. If so, you'll understand what I mean. I loved Kristiana, but I always knew what she was like. I foolishly hoped... I don't think anyone realized, but we had gone together to the conference in Rome; that's where Jed met her. The next thing I knew, she'd left me."

For a while there was only the lone, sad meow of a cat lying in the shade of the tree and the soft talk of some guests on the other side of the courtyard marking the seconds. Katz seemed to struggle with the demons of her past while Janet slowly realized what Katz had just told her. Katz sighed and spoke again. "I would have liked to warn Jed. He is such a...nice man, really, but," she smiled at Janet for confirmation, "he wouldn't have believed me, would he?"

"No, I doubt very much if he would have," Janet said sympathetically.

Katz nodded. "I wasn't surprised, you see, when she ran off. The only thing that did surprise me was that it was Tiddy who walked out on Kristiana. Kris would have been furious. Kris hated losing, and to lose face to that woman—" Katz's voice choked with anger, and she looked out with hard eyes across the sun-daubed courtyard.

"Tell me about the blue scarf," Janet said gently.

Katz turned and looked at her, blinking in shock. "I wouldn't want any of this in a documentary," she warned. "I just want to be seen as being co-operative. I have nothing to hide. Nothing. I should have spoken up then about the scarf, but to the police...I just couldn't."

Janet nodded; such a reaction was common. "You have my word. I will not use any material you do not wish me to."

Katz had held a secret for too long, and it would be a relief to tell someone, then her conscience would be completely clear. "I bought Kristiana the scarf. It was a Hermes, pale blue to match her eyes. She loved it because it was expensive, and she thought it suited her very well."

"How did you get it back?"

"I found it here."

"At the hotel?" asked Janet in surprise.

"No, at the Graveyard Restaurant. It was lying on the floor in the hall," Katz answered tersely.

"Kris was at that conference, then?"

Katz shrugged. "If she was, no one saw her that I know of. I still have the scarf. You'd think I'd have the strength to throw it away, wouldn't you, but I keep it to remember. I'll tell you what I think. I think Kris is dead. I think she probably lost that scarf in a card game here and whoever won it must have lost it at the restaurant that night. Kris had developed some big gambling debts, and people wanted to collect, one way or another. That's why Tiddy dumped her. She told me so."

Janet gave Katz's arm a gentle squeeze. "I'm sorry. Maybe now you will be able to find some closure." She left Hilda Katz looking into the shadows of the garden, eyes now concealed behind sunglasses.

Dawn found Samir Tagore on a bench in the town square, his nose in a book and seemingly totally unaware of the natural beauty around him. "Hi, Dr. Tagore. I'm Dawn Freeman. I don't know if you know me."

Tagore stood up quickly, looking a bit flustered. "Of course. You are our Alberta's close friend. Please, won't you be seated?" Charmed by the young man's old-fashioned graciousness, Dawn sat on the edge of the bench while Tagore carefully placed his bookmark in his book and sat at the other end of the bench. "A very fine day, is it not? I have found it hard to stay focused on my reading with such quaint beauty all around me."

Dawn smiled. There was a good deal more to Samir Tagore than she had given him credit for.

"Yes, it is a very beautiful place. I don't wish to take you away from your reading for very long, Dr. Tagore, but I wonder if I might talk to you about the night Dr. Jennings disappeared. We are considering doing a documentary about the event to see if we can shed some light on the mystery."

"Please, call me Samir."

"I'm Dawn."

"Dawn. That is a very pretty name. Your father must have loved you very much."

"I think so. My parents died when I was very young."

"Ah, yes, that is right. I have read your book and found it most refreshing."

"Thank you. Samir, could you tell me what happened that night?"

Samir gathered his thoughts. "It was a night when there was a tension in the air. There was so much discord, you see. No one could remain still for long, and the conversation was disjointed and awkward. It was all very difficult. I must admit that I argued that night with Tiddy. I regret doing so."

"I understand that she was a very difficult woman."

Samir smiled. "I am a Hindu. We see polarities in everything. Creation is balanced by destruction, good by evil, light by dark, and so on. Dr. Jennings blocked my chances of acquiring a position in the United States, but in the end I obtained a position much more to my liking. I believe in the Law of Karma. People get what they deserve. I very much fear that Dr. Jennings did, at any rate."

"It is pretty clear that she must have been killed."

"Yes. It is likely that the autopsy will establish the cause of death to be an act of murder."

"Shouldn't the person who committed this crime be held accountable?"

Samir smiled again. "I believe he or she will, you see. If not in this life, then the next."

"Did you see anything that night that would shed light on who might have killed Jennings, Samir?"

"I saw many things that night that foreshadowed the emergence of the darker side of life, Dawn. Any one of those small details might be the clue that points to the killer, but so many more would be dead ends or, worse still, misinformation that might wrongly incriminate the innocent. Perception can make us see what we want. It is better, I think, to let life find its own balance."

It was not the answer that Dawn had wanted, but she had to respect the man for his discretion and calm belief in the balance of all things. They talked a while longer of his worldview and then, late in the afternoon, Dawn went to find Aliki so that they could get ready to go to dinner. She found Janet waiting for her in the lobby, and they exchanged information.

"So, Hilda was one of Kris' conquests." Dawn sighed.

"She certainly knew Kris well. She called her Kristiana, with a north European inflection, and she knew Kris had a bad gambling problem. Yes, they were close. But I don't know – she said she always loved Kristiania, but that the family came to believe she had bad blood."

Dawn shared what she had learned from Fenwick and then pondered, "In light of what you found out about the scarf, I wonder if Philby knew Kris was in town. Maybe that was the complication of a personal nature."

"Could be. I'm off to find Robbie and see what she knows. We'd better have a meeting tomorrow and compare notes."

"Okay, talk to you tomorrow if we don't see you at the restaurant tonight." Dawn chuckled. "I don't know if Aliki is going to be up to eating." Janet laughed, and the two women went their separate ways.

Dawn found Aliki where she had been most of the afternoon – leaning on a table in the bar with a group of others, going through a stack of black and white enlargements of bones. "You have to remember that rickets is caused by a lack of vitamin D resulting in the improper assimilation of calcium and the trace mineral phosphorus. This results in poor mineralization of the bone. Look at how this piece of femur has such a thin cortex and a narrow medullary cavity. Check the length against the charts; growth rate has clearly been slowed. Here's another indicator – the metaphyseal ends are cupped."

Dawn smiled at Aliki. To know her was to love her, no matter how weird her interests. "Hi, Aliki."

"What? Oh, hi, Dawn. One of the students has brought some very interesting photos of bones from a gravesite in Iceland."

"So I see. Are you going to be finished in time to go out to dinner with me?"

"Dinner? Is it that late? Oh, sure. We were just talking, really. I'll see you guys later at the Graveyard Restaurant."

Aliki followed Dawn out, feeling just a little bit sheepish for having been gone so long. "Sorry, lost track of time," she said once the bar doors had closed. Dawn laughed and gave her partner a big hug.

"Aliki, did you know Kris Philby?"

"Not personally. I saw her from a distance once or twice, but the opportunity to meet her never arose. She was only with Philby a very short time."

"Would you recognize her?" Dawn asked as they stepped out of the elevator at their floor.

"I'm not sure; maybe."

Dawn stood deep in thought for a minute, then mumbled. "Perception can make us see what we want."

"What?"

"We need to talk." Dawn wheeled on her heel, pulling a surprised Aliki after her.

It took some convincing, but Aliki finally started to see the pattern that Dawn presented to her. If it was accurate, the killer was far more scary than any of them had realized. Before they could take Dawn's theory to the police, however, they needed some concrete evidence. Once again, Aliki found herself walking through the olive grove to the shed that housed the museum's collection. This time she requested the key from the security office, using her credentials as a forensic advisor with the local police.

With Dawn at her side, she unlocked the padlock on the shed door and flipped on the lights. They walked past the bones that still lay on the workbench and moved to the back room where the mummies were stored. Aliki explained what they had to do, and they slipped on plastic gloves and started sorting through the mummies, lifting each in turn so that Aliki could feel and smell any differences.

"I really wish you hadn't worked it out, Miss Freeman," said a voice from the doorway. Aliki and Dawn slowly lowered the mummy remains. "It is not that I have any problem with killing; it is just that the effort to silence the two of you is such a bore."

"If more people go missing, the police will not stop until they find you." Aliki moved closer to Dawn, unconsciously shielding her partner.

"I'll take my chances. There is a door at the back. Head toward it slowly. Don't try anything. I am an excellent shot."

Aliki put her arm around Dawn. "Don't worry," she whispered. "I know my sister. As soon as Robbie realizes that we're not around the hotel tonight, she'll swing into action."

After a light meal with Janet at the hotel, Robbie met one of the Chilean professors from the university in Santiago. He and some of his film students were in Atacoma to record a local festival. She had been introduced to him by the hotel manager that afternoon and had agreed to meet with some of the students in the hotel bar so that they could ask her about filmmaking. Robbie would have preferred to have gone with the others to the Graveyard Restaurant to gather more information, but such goodwill gestures were important. Besides, she felt it was good for the future of film to encourage young people into the field and share her experience.

Janet begged off, saying that she wished to phone Elizabeth and see how the girls were doing. She, too, had some other ideas in mind. After a long talk with their daughters and with Elizabeth, Janet lit candles for Robbie's imminent return, and the room glowed in soft light. The music she put on her CD player was hard and throbbing.

When Robbie entered, she smiled appreciatively and locked and bolted the door. They hugged and kissed deeply, their hips already moving against each other to the rhythm of the music.

Robbie slowly unbuttoned Janet's blouse and stole nips of her sweet skin as they moved and ground in their own form of dirty dancing. Janet slipped Robbie's t-shirt over her head and unhooked her bra. Then she moved back, still swaying to the music, and slipped out of her own. Robbie got a roguish smile, the one that just curled the right side of her mouth as her eyes roved over her partner's naked body.

Now it was flesh on flesh, and the arrow of desire shot straight to Janet's clit, making it throb with need. Kisses became urgent and demanding. The music ended and another piece started, unnoticed. It was not long before jeans and panties were gone and their dance had become earnest foreplay.

Janet felt Robbie's mood change from romantic partner to the raw passion of her lover. "Where?" she whispered into her olive's ear.

"Shower."

Robbie took Janet's hand and led her there, holding her close as she got the water ready and placed the candle she had brought with her on the counter. *Fire and water, passion and strength, elements of my lover*, Janet thought as Robbie ran her hands with familiarity over Janet's body, covering her with peach sherbet bath wash. Janet groaned with delight and rubbed herself against her partner – sharing, teasing, demanding. The warm water beat down, rivulets of passion running hot from one body to another.

Robbie pushed her leg between her wife's and pinned her against the steam-covered tiles. Janet groaned with pleasure at her entry. The ride was wild, exciting, and when Janet came, calling Robbie's name, her lover wore a cocky smile of triumph.

Later, in bed, Janet would feast long on Robbie's excitement and make her cry out when she came, too. For now, though, her lover needed to hold her and to feel the aftershocks of Janet's climax course through her body. Candlelight, warm water, hot music, and two lovers – the women's senses, bodies, and hearts were filled with the joy of their lovemaking. All else was forgotten.

Part 4

Robbie rolled over and looked at the face of her wife. Even sleeping, Janet was beautiful all the way through. It sometimes brought a lump to Robbie's throat to remember her life before Janet. It was just too painful. Their marriage had brought her happiness, family, and stability. There were many things that made Robbie stop and realize just how lucky she was, but the best thing was just waking up and seeing Janet sleeping beside her.

"Hey, what are you thinking about so seriously, Blue Eyes?" Janet murmured, waking slowly to the spicy scent of her lover.

"When did you wake up?" Robbie leaned over to kiss the end of her partner's nose. "I was thinking just how wonderful it is to wake up and know that I am married to you."

Janet's eyes softened and she cuddled in close to her lover. "You old smooth talker."

"Last night was—" A loud hammering at the door brought Robbie out of the bed with a curse. She slipped into a housecoat and stormed over to open it, a murderous look on her face.

"They're gone!" Philby said, and Fenwick, who stood beside him dwarfed by his massive body, nodded in agreement. "Come on, get dressed. We have got to do something."

"Who's gone?" Robbie asked, grabbing Philby before he could run off.

"Aliki and Dawn. They're gone. We tried to rouse them over three hours ago and couldn't. I finally got a key from the desk and entered their room. They didn't stay there last night. The bed is made. Would you get dressed, it's nearly noon!"

"Shit!" Robbie snapped, closing the door and heading for the closet. Janet was already pulling on clothes.

The gathering in the lounge was getting nowhere fast, and faces had gone from worried to gloomy. "Okay, let's go over it again. Who was the last one to see Dawn?" Janet asked with a sigh.

Samir looked strained as he balanced on the edge of his chair. "I believe I might have been. She found me in the old town square around six o'clock and told me she was interested in doing a documentary on Dr. Jennings' disappearance. I told her that the evening of the disappearance had been very tense and that I had, as a result, observed stressful behaviour on the part of many people, including myself. I didn't know what was relevant or not, and I observed that sometimes our perceptions prevent us from seeing truth."

"I might have seen her after that," put in Philby, rubbing his face. "She came and got Alberta from the bar where some of my graduate students were having a discussion with her on the appearance and identification of rickets. I didn't check my watch, but I believe it would have been later than six. At any rate, Dawn came to get Alberta to get ready for dinner just as I came in. I would guess it was around six thirty."

Victor Van Vogt walked in at that point. "Is it true what I heard?" he asked with concern. "That Alberta has gone missing?"

"And her partner, Dawn," Janet answered.

"This is not good," Van Vogt said bluntly.

"Can you remember when you last saw them?" Fenwick asked, reaching out to refill Janet's cup of coffee from the carafe that sat on the table.

"I saw them leaving the hotel last night around eight. They went up the street toward the Graveyard Restaurant. But when I arrived there about a half hour later, they were not there. I assumed they had decided to go somewhere else for a change."

Robbie was pacing, a frown on her face. "We need to call the police," she finally announced. Fenwick nodded, and as the others stood about silently, he went to place the call.

Don Reinaldos arrived looking frustrated and worried. He spent a lot of time questioning first Robbie and then Janet and then Robbie again, wanting to know what they had found out and why they were interfering in a police matter. In the end, it was only Janet's calming influence that stopped Robbie from having a temper tantrum of gigantic proportions. They were finally dismissed by the police with a sharp warning to stay out of an on-going police investigation, and the others were called one by one to make their statements.

Janet sat in the courtyard with her pissed-off spouse, looking thoughtful and oblivious to Robbie's muttering. "They weren't going to the restaurant," Janet suddenly announced, grabbing Robbie by the arm.

"What?"

"They weren't going to the restaurant. They were going to the museum to look at the mummies again."

"How do you know?"

"Because a body is still missing, and Dawn realized that. Come on, Robbie." Janet sprang to her feet and hurried through the gardens toward the road.

"Hey, wait! What do you mean?" Robbie whispered urgently, as she trotted along beside her determined wife. "You're not planning to do what I think you're planning to do, are you?"

"Yes, I am."

Robbie sighed. "I was afraid of that."

Janet stopped and her eyes were worried. "We should tell the police."

"Yeah, we should," Robbie considered. "After. Let's go do our own investigating first. On the way you can fill me in on what you've worked out, then we'll tell the police if we find anything."

Just short of the museum, Robbie pulled Janet to a stop. She crossed the street to a small store and emerged a few minutes later with a baseball cap. "Come on, we need to find a washroom in one of the government buildings."

Janet smiled, realizing what her thespian partner was planning. Only Robbie would have the confidence to pull it off.

Once in the washroom, Robbie set to work tucking her hair under the baseball cap and feathering it along the sides and front using Janet's nail scissors. She widened and darkened her eyebrows and used a touch of lipstick colour to make her lips look a bit thinner. Then, while she looked intently into the mirror, her body posture changed, her face appeared to elongate, and her expression became serious and controlled. Robbie Williams ceased to exist and instead a remarkably convincing Inspector Aliki Pateas stood before the mirror. "Come on, Janet, we have to find Robbie and Dawn," Aliki's voice said as the actor winked at her partner.

Janet smiled and stood on her tiptoes to kiss her lover's cheek. "You are good, Williams. You are damn good."

Together the two went to let the security office know that they were doing some more investigating in the shed that stored the museum mummies.

"Si, Inspector Pateas. I saw in the book that you were here last night. I will get you one of the keys again. Just drop it through the mail slot if I am out on rounds." Robbie risked a look at Janet, and green, serious eyes met her own. They were on the right track.

The conspirators took the offered key and headed down to the storage shed in the olive grove. Robbie opened the door, and they hurried inside, closing the door behind them. They stood looking at the bones laid out on the table. The shed was a makeshift place divided into three rooms. "It seemed like a good idea until we got here," Janet observed with a shudder, her voice amplified and sounding strangely hollow in the empty space.

"I gotta tell you, Sis' occupation creeps me right out. The adult mummies are through here. Would you believe that she could sniff the fresh ones out from the decayed?" Robbie led the way to the sliding doors that separated the mummy storage area from the work area of the shed.

"Please tell me there is another way of deciding," Janet muttered.

"Yeah, she could tell by the weight, too."

"Thank God. Oh, my God! Look at them all!"

"More 'mummies' than a maternity ward." Robbie sighed dryly. Gingerly and with looks of disgust, the women started to lift and move each wrapped mummy. They had only gotten to the third one when they both looked up and their eyes met. "This one?"

"Think so. I guess we have to check, huh?" Janet asked with a grimace.

The two women looked down at the body that they held much like a board between them. There was a momentary silence while each imagined having to unwrap the remains. Janet cleared her throat. "How about we put it somewhere handy and poke around to see if we can find any more evidence. Maybe we won't have to unwind it."

"Sounds like a plan. We left Jennings on a work table out there."

"Okay." Janet's voice echoed the nervous stress that she could hear in Robbie's. The women shuffled around and awkwardly carried the mummy into the workroom and placed it carefully on a workbench. "First, I'm washing." Janet held her hands up like a doctor prepared for surgery and headed over to a sink.

Robbie joined her. "They're probably okay," she said, more to reassure herself than Janet, as she scrubbed her hands under the cold water. "I mean, Aliki has a black belt, and Dawn knows how to take care of herself. Right?"

"Sure." Janet smiled nervously, drying her hands on her jeans and turning to start poking around. Robbie struck off in the other direction.

It was only a few seconds later when Janet tried the back door and looked out onto a set of deep tire prints. Between each track, in the soft sand, were the clear imprints of two pairs of running shoes in sizes that were most likely women's. "Robbie, over here."

The two women stood in the doorway, looking at the prints. After a minute Robbie said, "I'm a city girl; this is more your area. You come from the back bush."

"Robbie, they are tire tracks a good three inches deep! A blind woman could understand this one. Someone recently backed a small truck or Land Rover up to the door, and two people came out of this shed and probably got into the back of it."

"You think they got in willingly?"

"No. Whoever took them must be one cool character. They locked the women inside and then took the key back to the security shed. They probably dropped it through the mail slot while the guard was doing his rounds, then cut around the back of the shed, and got into the cab of the truck."

"You read that in the tracks!" Robbie exclaimed with surprise.

Janet swatted her playfully. "You got a better scenario, Lone Ranger? I figure it has to be the murderer, and that person now has to get rid of Dawn and Aliki. Mummification worked last time. I think the killer will try the same method again."

Worry gnawed at Robbie. "They headed out into the desert last night."

"Probably," Janet answered grimly.

"We need a helicopter. I'll flag a taxi and head out to the airport and see what I can do. You find Don Reinaldos and fill him in on our suspicions. I'll meet you back at the hotel." Janet nodded, and the two women sped off. Time was running out. Already they might be hours too late to help Aliki and Dawn.

Janet thought Don Reinaldos was going to have a stroke. He went all red in the face and bobbed up and down on his heels in aggravation. His flawless English deteriorated into a series of splutters, the gist of which seemed to be a debate with himself on whether he should throw Janet and Robbie in jail or send them packing on the next plane out. In the end, he did neither but spun on his heels and stormed out. Janet gave a sigh of relief and went to look out for Robbie.

The actor-director was having her own set of problems and arrived outside the hotel some time later driving a very old and very orange school bus. "All set?" Robbie asked as Janet boarded the bus with a smirk. "Hey, it was all I could get."

Janet shrugged, taking a seat behind Robbie. "Well, it is only to the airport, so I guess it doesn't matter."

Robbie closed the door of the bus and got underway before she answered. *No use in taking any chances.* "Actually, I wasn't able to get a helicopter."

"Small plane?"

"Uh, no. Seems you have to have a government permit to charter an aircraft, and it takes weeks to apply."

"So what do we have?" Janet asked suspiciously.

"A school bus built in 1972 and a map printed about the same year."

"Robbie! We can't go out into one of the most desolate deserts in the world driving a school bus."

"I couldn't get a taxi driver to do it for love or money, and you can't buy a car without a permit. I only got this through bribes and lies," Robbie grumbled as she negotiated the narrow streets out of Atacoma.

"Who did you get it from?"

"The Catholic mission."

"Robbie! You lied to and bribed a priest?"

"We like to look on it as a donation to the orphanage fund. And it was one of those Jesuit lies for the greater good." Robbie smiled wickedly.

"I hope God buys into your convoluted reasoning." Janet snorted. "What have you got back here?"

"A few things I was able to pick up in case we need them: a first aid kit, oil, antifreeze, spare tires, two gallons of water, a large jar of Skippy peanut butter, and four loaves of bread."

"I'm sure glad you remembered the antifreeze," Janet said sarcastically as she rooted around in the boxes. "I hear it can drop as low as 100 degrees in the afternoons. What the hell is this?"

"What?" Robbie asked innocently, stalling for time as she bumped the bus off the road and onto a dirt trail leading into the Atacama Desert.

"This bit of Army surplus that looks a lot like a bazooka."

"Oh, that."

"Well?"

"It's a bazooka."

For a moment there was a noticeable silence while Janet closed her eyes and counted to ten. "I don't want to know what was going on in your mind or where you got this. I just want you to know that if we survive it is *not* coming back with us."

The bus was swinging wildly back and forth as it struggled over rocks and out of potholes. Janet held on for dear life and with difficulty managed to get back into her seat where she clutched tightly to the safety bar in front of her. Robbie smirked at her through the cracked driver's mirror. "You're no fun." Janet rolled her eyes.

The desert was a vast plain of rocky hills and loose stone. "These barren hills are called *hammada* and the rocky plains are *reg* desert," Janet explained. "Sand dune desert is called *erg*. Although you see it in films all the time, it is really not all that common. Most deserts are reg, including the greater part of the Sahara. You won't find desert much more dry or barren than this one, though."

They drove until the sun was nearly overhead and the road had narrowed into little more than a footpath. Finally, they came to a narrow ravine in the dry rocky hills. The bus could go no further.

Dawn and Aliki had been forced at gunpoint to the back of the shed where they found a truck parked, its rear gate pushed up.

They were told to get inside and pull the gate shut. In the darkness, they heard a padlock being snapped into place.

Dawn snuggled up to Aliki, and the taller woman wrapped her arms around her partner. "We'll just have to bide our time until I get an opening," Aliki explained. Dawn nodded but said nothing. They sat down and waited. It was a long wait. Finally, the truck rocked as someone opened the driver's door and got in. The sound of the door closing cracked like a gunshot in the silence. The engine caught, and they were jostled about as the vehicle made its way out of the olive grove and onto the road.

"I'm sorry," Aliki mumbled sadly, giving Dawn's temple a gentle kiss. "I always seem to be putting you in danger."

"We have been down this road before. I am your partner, and if I choose to get involved in one of your investigations, then I have to be prepared to take some chances and so does Mac. We know that your work can sometimes be dangerous. We accept that because we love you and want to be with you. You have to accept it, too."

Aliki looked miserable. "I do, every time a crisis is over, but then another one occurs, and I can't stand seeing the people I love in danger because of me."

Dawn hugged Aliki as tightly as she could in the bouncing truck. "You don't ever have to stand for it, my lover; just accept that it can happen and that your family is willing to deal with whatever danger comes along. Just like Reb and Ryan have to deal with the dangers that come with having famous parents."

Aliki smiled into the darkness around them, but Dawn felt the smile in the hug that her partner gave her and in the subtle relaxation of her body. "You okay?" Dawn asked softly, well aware that Aliki was a long way from recovered from the breakdown that she had suffered.

"Yeah, a little strung out, but I can hold it together. I took a pill just before we left the hotel."

"Good." Dawn carefully kept her voice neutral. She hated that her partner needed to take medication to help her deal with her nerves. She also worried about Aliki's physical endurance. She held on to her lover as best she could, using her body to shield the tall gaunt figure from the worst of the bumps. It was some time before the small truck bounced to a halt and the engine shut off. Silence seeped in like a cold vapour as they waited for whatever was about to happen.

"Get in the far corner and stay low," Aliki whispered. Dawn nodded. Aliki moved forward and crouched like a runner a few feet away from the gate.

They heard the opening and closing of the truck door and then the sound of pebbles shifting as the killer walked to the back. The padlock rattled as it was undone. "Move to the back," a voice commanded.

"Okay." Dawn shuffled around a bit on her hands and feet to make it sound as if there were two of them. Aliki smiled to herself. Dawn was quick and resourceful.

The gate raised. It was barely halfway up when Aliki dove forward and tackled the person on the other side. They went down in a tangle of arms and legs. A gun flashed in the darkness. Aliki snapped her opponent's wrist sharply, and there was a sickening crack and a groan of pain. The gun dropped heavily to the ground, and Aliki used the opportunity to move behind the person and apply a chokehold. A few seconds later, the body slumped.

"Aliki," called a concerned voice from inside the truck.

"I'm okay. Come out and give me a hand."

There was rustling from inside the truck, and Dawn jumped out into the night carrying a length of cord from the back. "Is it Kris?"

Aliki paused in her trussing of the woman to take a close look. "Yeah, it's her, I think, although she sure could pass for Hilda." Aliki sighed in disgust. "I don't know how I didn't realize."

"Sometimes our perceptions prevent us from seeing the truth," Dawn consoled. "From what you've told us, Hilda was so quiet no one really noticed her. Kris was deeply in debt and apparently consumed by a need for revenge against the woman who rejected her. Her own life held no appeal for her, so she showed up at the last convention to kill Jennings, and then she had to kill Katz because she had found the scarf. Seizing the unexpected opportunity, she became Katz. They were about the same size and build and had similar looks. It was just a matter of cutting and dyeing her hair and wearing Katz's clothing and glasses. Hilda always stayed in the background anyway. All Kris had to do was retire from Hilda's career and keep a low profile."

"Think you are so smart, don't you, you bitch?" snarled the captive.

"She's a hell of a lot smarter than you," Aliki observed. "You made three fatal mistakes: dropping that scarf, showing off your talents by mummifying your victims, and feeding your oversized ego by coming back to this conference to mock us. Lady, you are going down."

"You're a stupid, arrogant queer, Alberta. I should have killed you, too."

Aliki ignored her. "Help me lift her into the truck, Dawn." The two women pulled Kris to her feet and carefully placed her in the back of the truck so as not to further injure her broken wrist.

Dawn pulled the gate down. "You okay?" she asked, wrapping Aliki in her arms.

"A bit shaky, but it felt good to be able to exert that much energy again."

"You are going to be fine, sweetheart. Come on, let's get this cargo back to town. People will be worried if they find us missing." Arm in arm, they walked to the cab and climbed inside. Aliki slumped against the passenger door while Dawn slowly turned the truck around.

A hot red ball of fire, the sun rose and spread its rays across the desert in a flood of heat. Dawn's shirt was grimy with dust and sweat, and her head ached from lack of sleep and the cruel glare of the sun. Beside her, Aliki slipped in and out of exhausted sleep, feeling queasy and out of sorts. It was the sudden jerking of the truck to a stop that brought her fully awake. "What time is it?"

"Close to noon, I think. We have a flat."

"Shit." Aliki rubbed the grit and sleep from her eyes. "We'll have to get Kris out of the back. She'll cook in this heat, lying there while we change the tire."

"She'll need some water, too," Dawn murmured through dry lips, pulling one of the canteens from between the seats.

They got out stiffly and stretched, then walked to the back and hauled Kris from the truck bed. "Just give me some water and then leave me the hell alone," their prisoner snapped.

Dawn held the canteen for Kris while Aliki got out the spare and the jack. "You have to come out. You'll fry in there while we change the tire. We'll put you in some shade to wait."

After Kris had drunk her fill, they assisted her out of the back and placed her in the thin shade of a boulder, then started to work changing the truck tire in the gruelling heat. It was slow, hellish work, and when they had finished they were burnt and exhausted, their throats parched and their lips cracked. Wearily, they went over to drag Kris up and put her back in the truck.

Aliki had had just about all she could take. Her nerves were on a hair trigger. It was sheer willpower that was keeping her together. She needed her meds.

"This is a really bad idea," Janet whispered urgently.

"We need to get their attention, don't we, so they'll know we're here," Robbie argued, reading from a dog-eared manual. "This will get their attention, even if they're kilometres away."

Janet sighed. "You're just using this as an excuse to fire that thing."

"That, too." Robbie grinned. "Okay, I got this worked out," she said, kneeling down and hefting the old bazooka on to her shoulder. "Just drop the shell into the cylinder."

Licking her parched lips, Janet picked up the heavy shell. "I hope Elizabeth and David won't mind raising our kids.

"I told you, it's not a live shell. Trust me."

Janet rolled her eyes. "Here goes." She dropped the shell down the cylinder and turned away, her hands over her ears. There was an earsplitting roar and the shell whistled from the barrel of the bazooka on a plume of smoke, sending Robbie onto her backside.

"Wow, that thing has a kick!"

The projectile, rather than arcing into the air, hit the ground in a belly flop and roared up the hillside, blowing away the ridge in a cloud of debris and disappearing down the other side in a landslide of pebbles.

"I don't think they saw that," Janet said dryly as they heard the dull thud of the shell impacting into something. There was a moment of silence, and then a tremendous explosion that fireballed into the air.

"They'll see that," Robbie gasped from where the two of them had run for cover behind the school bus.

"You told me it wasn't a live shell!"

Robbie grinned as she brushed dust from Janet's hair. "I must have been misinformed."

At the sound of the bazooka firing, Dawn and Aliki had turned in surprise and watched with shock as a shell came bouncing over the top of the ridge in a cloud of dirt and roared down the other side. Aliki dropped Kris back behind the boulder and grabbed Dawn, pulling her down behind the rock, too.

The shell flew off the high bank and slammed into the side of the truck. A second or two later, the truck exploded in a massive fireball, lifting it right off the ground and dropping it down on its side.

"I wish that had happened before we changed the tire," Dawn muttered as the debris settled.

"You okay?" Aliki asked, helping Dawn to her knees.

"Christ!" Kris shouted. "I'm in pain here. I'm going to sue you. Do you hear? You'll pay for this!"

Ignoring the outburst, Dawn brushed herself off. "Yeah. I'm fine. Do you think this is an Army test range?"

"I sure as hell hope not. You stay here and I'll go to the top of the ridge and see if I can see anything."

"I'm coming, too," Dawn corrected.

Aliki smiled at the back of her stubborn partner who was already scrambling up the rocky hillside.

"We'll be back to get you," she said to Kris. "Do yourself a favour and stay in the shade." Marshalling her waning energy, she followed Dawn to the top of the ridge and looked down into the valley. There sat an old school bus with a smoking bazooka at its side. Standing near the rear of the bus were her sister and her partner.

"You damned idiot! I should have known it would be you!" Aliki roared from the top of the ridge, causing the two women on the other side to start.

Aliki and Dawn, burnt red by the sun, grimy with sweat and dirt, and their clothes still smoking from being singed in the explosion, plodded down the hill. Aliki strode over to her sister. "If Dawn would let me, I'd shoot you."

Robbie frowned. "What for? We're here to rescue you. You got our message, didn't you?"

"Yup, right into the side of our truck." Aliki scowled. "363,000 square kilometres of nothing and you manage to blow up my truck!"

"Oh, that was the fireball! See, Janet, I told you it wasn't a live shell."

"That's it, to hell with the gun; I'm going to rip you apart with my bare hands!"

"Are you okay?" Janet asked Dawn, leading her over to the bus to get her some water.

"Yeah. It's been a rough night. We have Kris Philby over on the other side of the ridge. She killed both Jennings and Hilda Katz." Dawn sat on the steps of the school bus and took a long drink from the bottle of water Janet gave her. "Nice wheels. Was the train not running today?" Dawn asked with a snort.

"I sent Robbie to get transportation. Need I say more?"

Dawn grinned, although the effort cracked her lips painfully. "The bazooka was a nice touch."

Robbie was taking the moment of privacy to check on her sister's condition. Aliki looked pale and exhausted. "Are you okay? You gave us a hell of a scare."

"Yeah, I'm okay," Aliki pushed her hair back with a shaky hand, "but I'm pretty close to my limit. Could you climb over the hill and bring Kris back over here?"

"Sure thing," Robbie said softly. "First, let's get you on the bus so you can lie down."

Aliki looked at their transport and joked, "What did you do with the kiddies?"

Despite her concern for her sister, Robbie smiled. "It's a mission bus. I had to throw the Christians to the lions."

"I believe you, too. You damn near burnt us at the stake with that blast. What the hell have you done to your hair? You've got a funny raggedy bang."

Robbie laughed. "I was pretending to be you. It was easy, I just gave myself a bad hair cut and acted grumpy."

Aliki blinked in surprise and shook her head as she slowly climbed up on the bus. "I am too tired to deal with this. Just tell me how much trouble you've caused for me."

"Hey, hardly any at all. We went to the museum and found the missing body. Then we knew you were in trouble and that probably you had been brought out here." As she explained, Robbie guided her sister into a front seat on the bus.

Janet and Robbie fussed over Dawn and Aliki, making sure they had lots of water and were as comfortable as they could be on the hard bus seats. Then together, they climbed over the ridge to find Kris.

Robbie beamed as she took in the smouldering skeletal remains of the burnt and twisted chassis from the top of the ridge. "Wow! Look at that! Bloody amazing, I call it. Look, Janet, I killed that truck!"

Janet surveyed the blackened area around. "Looks like you came damn close to doing some collateral damage. Aliki, Dawn, and Kris are lucky to be alive."

"Hey, how was I to know they had parked the truck here?" Robbie complained as the two of them slipped and slid down the hill. "Come on, Kris. We've come to rescue your sorry soul. Up you get."

"About time. Water," croaked the woman, as she was yanked to her feet. Janet held a plastic bottle to Kris' lips and poured water into her mouth a little at a time. When she'd had her fill, Kris whined, "I gotta broken wrist, thanks to your sister's brutality, so be careful getting me up that hill."

Robbie pulled a funny face at Janet behind Kris' back, and Janet laughed.

"What are you laughing at, bitch?"

"Watch your mouth, Kris," Robbie snapped. "One more word out of you and I'll leave you out here to dry in the sun. I'm getting into this mummification thing."

Janet and Robbie pulled Kris up the loose, dry gravel ridge and back down the other side to the school bus. At the sight of the vehicle that they were driving, Kris sneered, "You gotta be joking."

"Yeah," Janet agreed dryly. "These hummers come with amazing camouflage, don't they? In you get, and right to the back so we don't have to put up with you on the ride back."

Once everyone was settled, Robbie started the bus and carefully turned around for the slow, hot journey back to town. It was late in the afternoon when, exhausted, dehydrated, and dusty, they pulled up in front of their hotel.

To their surprise, police officers immediately surrounded their vehicle and Commissioner Don Reinaldos, robot-stiff with anger, stormed out to them. He was hopping with pent-up fury as he waited for Robbie to pull the door open. He was up the stairs in a second. "You were *not* to leave! You have been where? You have been where?" he demanded, saliva bubbles forming at the edges of his mouth.

Robbie was so hot and tired, she wasn't even capable of forming a coherent sentence. Janet was first to rouse herself from the stupor engendered by the heat inside the bus. "We found Aliki and Dawn and helped them bring in the person who murdered Dr. Tidwell Jennings and Hilda Katz. Kris Philby, the former Miss Kristiania Katz, if I am not mistaken, is tied up in the back of the bus."

Don Reinaldos made a noise deep in his throat that sounded much like a growl. Turning quickly, he stomped off the bus and yelled a series of orders in Spanish. In no time, Kris had been transferred to a police vehicle, the ladies had been helped from the bus and sent to their rooms, and the bus was on its way back to the mission, driven by a police officer.

Dawn wrapped an arm around her exhausted partner, and together they went to their room. They took turns showering and then sat down to big bowls of chilled melon, fresh rolls, and a pitcher of iced lemon tea.

Afterwards, Dawn slipped a disc into her Walkman and took Aliki by the hand. She stripped the hotel terrycloth robe from her lover's body and then took a tube of green pear body lotion and squirted some on her hands. Slowly, she started to rub the cooling cream across Aliki's face and lips and then worked down to her shoulders and breasts.

Aliki, who had been passive until then, reached to lower the robe from her partner. Dawn let the cloth slip to the floor and then stepped back out of Aliki's arms, very much aware of the smouldering blues eyes that took in every detail of her petite form.

"No," she said softly. "You are not allowed to move. Not until I am finished with you."

Aliki's eyebrow went up in surprise, but she stood still, her arms at her sides, and let Dawn move closer to continue her sensual treatment.

Dawn circled behind Aliki and rubbed cream into her broad shoulders and down her strong back. She let her fingers rake and caress and dropped kisses at the back of her partner's neck as her fingers slid to a tight, round butt. Aliki groaned and squirmed with need.

"No, not yet. Not yet, lover. Control," Dawn whispered into Aliki's ear as she ran her own nakedness along the long, lean length. Dawn moved around her tall, beautiful lover, squeezing more cream onto her hands. Then, looking into Aliki's eyes, she ran the warm, creamy lotion over her own breasts.

Aliki watched every move with hunger burning in her eyes, her lips parted, and her breath ragged with wanting. Dawn's hands, fingers spread wide, trailed down her own stomach and hips, covering her body with a fresh, heady scent.

"Don't move now," Dawn warned as she walked up to her lover and wrapped her arms around Aliki's neck, kissing her with passion as she moved her hips against Aliki's sex. Their bodies slipped gently on the lotion, teasing, tantalizing, and tormenting. Dawn slowly dropped to her knees, leaving a trail of kisses that led her to where she could use her tongue on the very centre of Aliki's need.

Dawn heard the soft groan of delight and felt her lover shudder. Strong arms lifted her into Aliki's embrace and warm lips begged entry. Aliki carried her to their bed, and the liquid heat of their lovemaking blended them into one.

The following day, the four women were at the police station, sometimes being questioned, but most of the time waiting on hard wooden chairs in a variety of stuffy rooms. It wasn't until the day after that that they had the opportunity to explain things to their curious colleagues.

"It was the information that Janet picked up in her discussion with the person we all thought was Hilda that made all the pieces fall together," explained Dawn, sitting on the terrace surrounded by an interested group of scientists. She took a sip from her iced tea. "Janet said that Hilda called her Kristiana, not Kris, and that Hilda had mentioned that the family had claimed that Kris had bad blood. Janet and I both thought at first that Hilda had been one of Kris' conquests, too, and that Kris had dumped Hilda for Jed Philby. But the wording just didn't seem right. Finally, we realized, independent of each other, that Kris and Hilda might be sisters. In which case, who had been murdered – Kris or Hilda?"

Setting down her glass of lemonade, Dawn took up the story. "I twigged to it first because I talked to Samir. He had a feeling that Hilda was not who she seemed to be, but he wasn't sure. Rather than lead me in what might be a false direction, he planted the seed of an idea that he hoped might allow me to find the truth. He said, 'Sometimes our perceptions prevent us from seeing truth.' You see, everyone was used to Hilda being on the fringe of the group. No one took any notice of her. All Kris had to do to maintain her new identity was to be seen every now and again. With her blond hair dyed brown and cut short and styled straight and those thick glasses, she resembled her sister quite a lot, and of course she knew enough about her sister to carry it off convincingly."

Janet leaned forward to take a chip from the bowl on the table. "Her joy of revenge in killing Jennings was dulled by Kris' realization that Hilda had found the lost scarf and would know that she, Kris, had been there. She was also afraid to return to the U.S. because of her mounting gambling debts. She decided to solve both problems by killing her sister and assuming her identity. Don't forget, Kris was a mortician. She not only knew about preserving bodies, but she also knew about make-up."

"It was almost the perfect crime," Robbie observed, snagging the chip from Janet's hand and popping it in her mouth. She reached for the bowl of chips and offered it to her partner before going on. "Kris buried them out in the desert and once she knew they would be well dried out, she came back here, wrapped them, and hid them in the one place no one would ever be likely to look — the mummy storage shed. If, by rare chance, one of the bodies was unwrapped and found to be a recent murder, the suspicion would not fall on Kris but on someone attending the forensic convention that year; that was exactly what happened."

Aliki nodded and took up the story. "Getting away with the perfect crime wasn't good enough for Kris. She needed the ego rush of walking amongst Hilda's old associates. She came back to the gathering this year disguised as her sister. And once again, she almost got away with it. But she was taken by surprise by someone else knowing about the scarf, and she overplayed her hand just a bit. Dawn and Janet picked up on it."

"Well, I must say that is an amazing story. I feel so bad for Dr. Philby and Dr. Katz. Dear me." Fenwick sighed. "I wish now that I had spoken up at the time, but I don't suppose it would have prevented the tragedy. You see, when I went back to the hotel that night, I found Philby in a quite agitated state. He said he'd gone to the Graveyard Restaurant for a pint or two before dinner because he'd had a flat out in the desert that day and was thirsty. As he was standing at the bar, he was sure he had caught glimpse of Kris. He chased after her, but when he got outside there was no sign of her."

Fenwick blushed and coughed gently before going on. "I overheard him in a rather heated discussion with the hotel manager about whether or not Kris Philby was staying at the hotel. Naturally, I did my best to calm him down. I tried to convince him that it would be extremely unlikely that Kris would come to a gathering where she was likely to meet the other two corners of a very unpleasant love triangle. At the time, I sincerely believed I was right. Poor Philby. I am afraid he had become quite obsessed with Kris. He hoped, poor fellow, that she would come back to him. I saw no reason to embarrass him by telling the police."

"How is Philby holding up?" Robbie asked, absentmindedly resting her hand on Janet's knee.

"He feels a bit of a fool, as we all do a little. He asked to see to having the bodies buried. Said it would allow him some closure. I think he has finally seen Kris for what she is."

Two days later the gathering broke up, and the four women flew back to Canada. After a night at Aliki's home in Toronto, they took a helicopter north to Robbie and Janet's lodge near Bartlett.

From the window of the 'copter they could see their children running out onto the porch overlooking Long Lake, Elizabeth and David not far behind. Ryan and Mac stood side by side, waving to them, and Reb was standing by the massive family dog, Rufus, trying to get him to wave a paw.

The helicopter lowered, and soon the women were reunited with their families over a huge breakfast that David happily prepared with Elizabeth's help. The story of their adventure came out in bits and pieces with a good deal of laughter and some serious questions. Aliki said little. She was very aware that Mac, sitting by Ryan at the other end of the table, was watching her with hurt and confusion.

When the group finally broke up, Aliki quietly asked Mac if they could go for a walk. The young teen was silent for a second and then hesitantly agreed. Dawn worried as she watched the two slip from the lodge and head down the forest path.

It was a beautiful day. The summer heat cooled as it passed through thick green leaves whispering on a gentle breeze. Mottled patches of sunlight danced across the trail and highlighted here the deep green of moss on an old log or there a circle of red-capped toadstools growing from a carpet of dried pine needles. Shafts of sunlight spotlit the thick forest, turning deep, rich greens to emerald brilliance.

The two walked in silence, Aliki trying to think of the words that would help patch the distrust between them. "Aah, nice day," she said awkwardly.

"Yes."

Again they walked in silence, each lost in her own thoughts. The trail curved close to the lake edge, and they stopped to look at a black and white loon diving for fish not far off shore.

"I need to talk to you, Mac. Could we sit here for a bit?"

"Sure," the teen answered briefly, being co-operative but noncommittal.

Mac sat on the rocky ridge that bordered the shoreline; Aliki sank down beside her. "I didn't handle my last case very well, Mac. It became very personal. Finding the person I thought had brought that plane down became more than a job; it was an obsession. I was afraid for you and your mom and for anyone else that might become another victim of the killer's madness."

Mac picked up a bit of stick and focused on stripping its bark off, not willing to look up at Aliki.

Aliki swallowed painfully and looked out over the water. "Seeing all those people dead...I was in shock. And then when I got the letter from the killer...a...and I thought those hundreds of people had died because of me, well, I just cracked, I guess. I felt I couldn't have anything to do with you until I had somehow righted the terrible wrong that had been done in my name. It's all a jumble in my head. I went undercover, living a really low life and trying to think like the killer. It drained a great deal out of me, emotionally and physically. I guess you know that, huh? I must have been a real mess when your mom found me."

"Yeah. You were. It was scary. I didn't like you like that. But you weren't sick when you walked out on the wedding. Not then," Mac spat, her eyes ice and startling blue against the tawny skin of her Salish Indian heritage.

"I think I was, Mac. Maybe not as sick as I was going to become, but even then I was not thinking too rationally. I was wrong, Mac. I hurt and embarrassed you and your mom very deeply. I wish I could change what I did then, but I can't. All I can say is that I am so very sorry and that I really want to make a life with you and your mom. I love you both very much."

A lump rose in Aliki's throat, choking off any further words. Tears welled in her eyes and her lip quivered. *Shit, I've cried more in the last year than I have in my whole lifetime.*

In the silence that followed, she reached into her pocket and pulled out her pills. Suddenly a hand was over the top of hers. Aliki looked up into eyes filled with worry and determination. Aliki let the pill bottle drop into Mac's hand. With a cry of anguish, the teen threw herself into Aliki's arms.

"You scared me! Don't ever do that again, Aliki!" the teen wailed.

Aliki held on to her adopted daughter, and the two of them cried openly, each trusting the other with her pain.

Sometime later, after they'd let all the sorrow and anger out and had washed their hot, tear-swollen faces in the cool lake water, they lay in the noon sun and talked out a lot of things. Then, a lot happier than they had been in a long time, they walked back to the lodge to try and pick up on a future that had nearly been lost.

Epilogue

Three months later, Aliki stood on the balcony of Robbie and Janet's northern home, enjoying the fall weather and the trees that were a blaze of colour. The brilliant red of the soft maple, the crimson of the hard maples, and the gold of the beech and aspen blended against a rich background of oak rust and the deep greens of the evergreens. And on that special day, the lake was mirror calm, reflecting the clear blue sky. It was perfect, and it filled Aliki with happiness, despite her nervousness. She was about to get married. Turning, she rested a hand briefly on Mac's shoulder. Mac smiled. They were ready. Robbie and Janet's lodge overlooking Long Lake had never looked more beautiful. The railing and coachlights had been decorated with boughs of wild roses and white pine, and inside the lodge, a banquet of food catered by the Bartlett Women's Auxiliary awaited the guests.

Aliki, Dawn, and Mac had decided that they would all wear blue jeans and the lovely sweaters that Elizabeth had knitted for them. It was Aliki's father, Georgeos Pateas, who walked arm in arm with Dawn onto the balcony and placed Dawn's hand in Aliki's before kissing all three of them on the cheek and taking his seat beside his sons. Aliki couldn't help smiling like a fool. She had never been happier, and Dawn looked so very beautiful. They turned to face the minister, hand in hand. When the time came, Mac handed her mom's ring to Aliki with pride. In a quiet, confident voice, Aliki said her vows.

"I, Aliki Alberta Pateas, take you, Dawn Freeman, to be my wife. I will stand beside you in your successes and in your failures, care for you in sickness and rejoice in your health. I look forward to growing with you through the seasons of our life and helping to raise our daughter." Aliki slipped the ring on her Dawn's finger.

Mac gave her mom the ring for Aliki, and a lump formed in Aliki's throat as the woman she loved slipped the ring on her finger and said her vows.

"I, Dawn Freeman, choose you, Aliki Alberta Pateas, to be my lover and friend and a mother to our daughter. I will be there for you in the good times and in the bad, in sickness and in health, and in danger and in safety. I promise to respect, cherish, and support you always, to the end of our days."

When the minister pronounced them married, Aliki kissed Dawn softly and then hugged her daughter and wife close to her. As a family, they greeted the family and friends who gathered around to wish them well. Beaming with pride and happiness, Aliki held Dawn and Mac's hands, very much aware of the gold band that now encircled her finger, a symbol of her lasting commitment to Dawn and Mac.

She was delighted that all of the Pateas family had come out to see her exchange vows with Dawn. She felt at peace with her past, at last. She had never been happier.

The night before, Ari, as the only married man in the Pateas family, had taken it upon himself to have a talk with Aliki about her responsibilities to

Dawn. He had been married for over a year now, and he and his wife had just found out they were going to have their first child in the spring. Aliki had to listen while her kid brother, who she had helped raise, explained her responsibilities now that she was marrying. At the end of "the talk", Aliki had hugged her brother close and told him that she would do her very best to be the partner he would want her to be.

Much to Aliki and Dawn's delight, Fenwick and Philby had flown in for the occasion, and Dawn had several of her publishing associates there as well. A number of Aliki's colleagues had shown up from the city to see their friend married, including Dr. Bates; Dr. Becky Wilson, the lab's entomologist; Carl Ling, the lab assistant; and Phil Koo and his girlfriend, Alice Niles, from the Toronto Police Department. Much to Aliki's surprise, Detective Joe Volenni, who was not known for his liberal stand on any issues, had come, too.

After the buffet, Aliki led Dawn down to the beach, and they stood watching the sunset, red over the lake. "I never thought I would marry, never mind have a family," Aliki admitted.

Dawn snuggled closer to her wife but said nothing. She had learned that her stoic partner needed time to speak what she felt.

"You and Mac coming into my life has been the most special gift that I have ever had. I know that I haven't done very well at this courtship thing, but I want you to know that I love you and Mac so very, very much, and now that you are my family, I am the happiest person alive."

"No regrets?" Dawn asked, smiling up at her newly minted spouse.

"Only that I did not meet you and Mac sooner." Aliki smiled. "I love you." *Life is good and to be in love is wonderful,* Aliki thought as they kissed. Behind them, the sun set in a blaze of autumn gold.

Anne Azel lives in Northern Ontario. Now retired, she loves travelling whenever she can. She enjoys canoeing, kayaking and walks with her dog when she isn't writing.

You can contact Anne at a_azelca@yahoo.ca.

~ * ~ * ~ * ~ * ~ * ~

Other works by Anne Azel:

Gold Mountain

ISBN: 978 - 1 - 933720 - 04 - 3 (1-933720-04-2)

(Winner of a 2007 Golden Crown Literary Society's Award for Lesbian Dramatic General Fiction)

Gold Mountain has a unique and distinctive Canadian flavour which embraces the cultural diversity found in Canada today. It is a story of two women, not only on opposite ends of our cultural scale but also on opposite ends of our justice scale. It is the story of Kelly, the daughter of the concubine of a Chinese immigrant to Canada, and her struggle to find her place in both the Caucasian and Chinese world, both of which prefer their women heterosexual. It is the story of Jane, a woman who appears to have found her place in the world, but in fact her place is waiting to be discovered. Discovering for Jane and a place for Kelly come as a result of the night that Kelly's half-brother, her father's only son, an indulged young man, is murdered.

Seasons

ISBN: 978 - 1 - 933720 - 23 - 4 (1-933720-23-9)

Seasons is the story of Robbie and Janet, their family, and their life together. But life is not that simple, especially for a lesbian coupld in northern Ontario.

Seasons is also the soty of the issues that face womenkind as well as the strenght and courage that all women show in dealing withthe challenges of illness, today's society, and the forces of nature.

Anne Azel, the award winning author, has created another masterpiece filled with romance, adventure, humour, and a murder mystery from a past wanting to be forgotten.

Printed in the United States
100248LV00004B/130/A

9 781933 720388